Karen Charlton

THE WILLOW MARSH MURDER

The Detective Lavender Mysteries

THE WILLOW MARSH MURDER

© Karen Charlton 2019

Visit Karen Charlton's website to learn more about her historical novels and sign up for her occasional newsletter for the latest news about her writing, competitions and events.

www.karencharlton.com

Published by Famelton Publishing.
Cover design and illustration by Lisa Horton.

Dedicated to my friends,

Jill Boulton & Caroline Willder

Thank you for all your love and support.

Karen

xxx

The Detective Lavender Mysteries

The Heiress of Linn Hagh

The Sans Pareil Mystery

The Sculthorpe Murder

Plague Pits & River Bones

Murder on Park Lane

The Willow Marsh Murder

The Mystery of the Skelton Diamonds (short story)

The Piccadilly Pickpocket (short story)

The Death of Irish Nell (short story)

Other Works

February 1809 (short story)

Catching the Eagle

Seeking our Eagle (non-fiction)

Prologue

Twenty years ago
Southwark, London
October, 1793

Sixteen-year-old Ginny Atkins hummed softly to herself while she dusted the windowsill in Captain Delamere's bedchamber. Her gaze lingered on the top of the wigs and bonnets of the pedestrians in Tooley Street below. A gang of gin-soaked sailors staggered out of one of the narrow alleyways that wound down towards the taverns by Sellinger's wharf. Dawdling schoolboys in the distinctive uniform of St Olave's Grammar School mingled with early-morning shoppers. Through the closed window she heard the muffled cries of the hawkers, the rattle of carriage wheels over cobbles and the raucous shouts of the bargees and ferrymen down at the riverside.

Despite the gloom of the autumnal weather, Tooley Street, a long and meandering thoroughfare, was boisterous and brilliant with colour. Two servants in vivid green and gold livery carried a gilded sedan chair past a fruit barrow stacked high with rosy apples and glistening purple plums. The painted sign outside the coaching inn swung in the breeze.

Ma Forster's lodging house was the largest building in the vicinity and in Ginny's eyes the house was the grandest too. When her friend Annie turned her nose up at the news of her new job and said, 'Ooh, I wouldn't want to work so close to them stinkin' wharves,' Ginny had bristled with indignation. 'Ma Forster's is a respectable 'ouse. 'Er lodgers are from the gentry; she only rents rooms to a better class of person.'

'But what about the stink?' Annie persisted.

Ginny tutted. 'I'll barely notice it wi' the windows closed.'

She hadn't exaggerated about Ma Forster's lodgers. Their cuffs may be a bit frayed and their gowns slightly faded, but some had servants.

Yes, Mr Brown, who'd lodged with Ma Forster for years, was a bit touched in the head and was forever sending her to the butchers to buy pig's trotters. But as Ma Forster explained, her guests paid a goodly amount for their board and lodging and were entitled to make a few strange demands.

Mrs Delamere, who'd lodged there with her husband, the Captain, for the past two months, was the most demanding guest, despite having her own maid at her beck and call.

Heavily pregnant, the dark-haired lady spent a lot of time sewing baby clothes in the small parlour the Delameres rented along with their bedchambers. When Ginny entered the room to clean or to add coal to the fire, Mrs Delamere and her maid fell silent and followed her with their eyes in a way that made her feel uncomfortable. They'd often send her on a small errand to fetch something for their needlework from the haberdashers.

But Ginny didn't mind. In fact, she felt sorry for Mrs Delamere, who always seemed so sad. She kept herself aloof from the other residents of the house and seemed to have no friends. She rarely went out and no one came to visit. Her eyes were often swollen and red-rimmed from crying. Ginny didn't know whether her melancholy came from her condition, her loneliness, or some other tragedy that had befallen her.

Mrs Delamere also slept in a separate bedchamber, apart from her husband, which Ginny found odd. But Ma Forster explained this was often the way with wealthy toffs: 'He needs his sleep. The baby makes her restless in the night.'

Captain Delamere went out a lot, which may have been some of the cause of his wife's unhappiness, but this suited Ginny because she didn't particularly like the military man. He had an ugly purple scar running up his chin. It cut through the corner of his lips and distorted the corner of his mouth. Ma Forster told her he'd got the scar while fighting the black heathens on the Indian subcontinent.

But it wasn't the disfiguring scar Ginny disliked about him. It was his nature. He had what her mother called an 'edge' to him. When he spoke, he used a mocking tone and always sounded irritated. He also had close-set, cold, dark eyes, which followed her around the room and down the stairs in a way that made her skin crawl.

She hoped he was kind to Mrs Delamere, but she doubted it. She suspected he had much to do with the poor lady's unhappiness.

Ginny's eyes lingered on the rainbow of silk ribbons fanned out in the window of the haberdasher's shop opposite. A bubble of excitement rose in her when she suddenly remembered she'd just enough money left to treat herself to a new hair ribbon.

She was proud of the glossy brown curls that cascaded down her back when her hair was loose. She loved tossing her head to make them ripple in the sunlight. Wherever she went she attracted admiring glances. When she tied it back with a red ribbon, she knew she was as smart as any lady from Mayfair.

Her older sisters, especially Betsy, teased her about her vanity but she didn't care. She liked pretty things: pretty silk ribbons, pretty hair.

Her glance fell on the silver snuff box left by Captain Delamere on the windowsill. This was a pretty thing. She picked it up, surprised at its weight. It felt old and valuable and smelled faintly of the nutty tobacco inside.

7

She fingered the delicate diamond pattern etched in glittering silver around its curved sides and admired the deep-blue enamel lid. It was painted with the Delamere family crest. She traced the outline of the rampant stags and the fortified house or castle in the background with the tip of her finger and wondered if this was a picture of their home back in Cambridgeshire.

'You can put aside any notion of stealing that, you little bitch.'

Ginny spun round in shock and dropped her feather duster. Its cane handle clattered on the floorboards.

Captain Delamere's large muscular figure in his scarlet and gold-braided uniform filled the doorway. He carried a high-plumed regimental hat beneath his arm and gripped his walking cane in his other huge, hairy hand. His dark eyes glowered with anger – and something else, something unfathomable.

'I weren't goin' to steal it, sir,' she stammered. 'I were just dustin' it.'

'So says every thieving whore from here to Newgate. Damn it, wench, you need teaching a lesson.' He slammed the door shut behind him, hurled his hat to one side and stomped across the room towards her.

Confused, Ginny shrieked and cowered, her hands fluttering over her mouth. 'Please don't beat me, sir!'

He grabbed her arm and slapped her hard across her face, cutting off the scream welling inside her.

'Say a word and I'll be back with the constable.' His breath was sour with tobacco.

Stunned into silence and paralysed with fear, she stared up into his ravaged face and the cold, black pools of his eyes. He licked his tattered lips in anticipation and the loose flesh of his mouth quivered.

Suddenly, he pulled the red ribbon in her hair loose and yanked it out. 'I'll take that,' he said with a malicious grin.

She stifled the squeal that rose in her throat as her hair tumbled around her shoulders. The next second, he yanked at her bodice, ripping the flimsy material away, and mauled her tender little breasts. She gave a strangled yelp.

'No screaming.' He squeezed harder, then dragged her towards the bed.

Tears of pain and shame sprang to her eyes and she closed them tight, desperately trying to pretend this wasn't happening, that she was somewhere else. Some place safe. Anywhere except on her back on the bed with her skirts hiked up around her narrow hips, the heavy weight of this foul, ugly man on top of her and his sweat dripping down on to her face.

She turned her head, opened her eyes and fixed her watery gaze on the oblong of sunlight pouring into the room through the window. Out there was the street with people laughing and chatting. Outside, the haberdasher's window display gleamed with its rainbow of ribbons. As the pain seared through her like a flame and the captain lunged and grunted, she squeezed her eyes tightly shut again and thought of those pretty hair ribbons.

Finally, he gave a guttural moan, rolled away and climbed off the bed. He strode across the room, buttoning the flap on his trousers, his face dark and unreadable.

Trembling, she remained on the bed, not daring to move. Then, gathering herself, she jumped up and made for the other side of the room.

He grabbed her arm. 'I haven't finished with you yet!'

Her eyes widened with renewed horror and her fingers tightened on the snuff box still clasped in her hand. Instinctively, she swung it at his head with a strength she never knew she possessed.

He yelled and fell back, clutching his bleeding face.

9

Ginny fled. She was through the door, down the stairs and out of the front door of the building before she had time to draw breath. Too scared to stop and look behind her, oblivious to her pain and the bitter cold wind, she pushed her way through the startled pedestrians towards St Olave's Church. Staggering through the arched doorway, she sank to the cold flagstone floor in the dark shadow of a towering stone pillar.

She peeped round the column, but he wasn't there. He hadn't followed her.

Only now, in the gloomy candlelit protection of the church, did she stop and try to catch her breath. Great gulping breaths. She clutched her defiled little body in her arms and sobbed.

Eventually, her sobbing turned to hiccoughs and she dabbed away the tears from her swollen and bruised face. Next, she examined the state of her torn clothing and groaned. She couldn't go home like this. Her mother mustn't know what had happened. She didn't want to see the disappointment in her eyes.

There was only one thing to do, only one person to turn to. She'd go to Betsy.

Her sister would know what to do. She'd understand. She always did. Betrothed to marry Ned Woods, a constable with the Bow Street horse patrol, Betsy might even get her fiancé to arrest Captain Delamere and throw him in gaol for what he'd done to her. This thought gave her strength. She staggered to her feet, lifted up a flap of her torn bodice and tried to make herself decent again.

It was only then she realised she was still clutching the silver and enamel snuff box in the palm of her left hand.

She uncurled her fingers and stared at it in horror.

Chapter One

Present day
Ely, Cambridgeshire
Early September, 1813

'Heaven and hell! I've never seen so much water!' Constable Ned Woods used the cuff of his blue greatcoat to wipe away a large circle of condensation on the glass of the carriage window. 'There's bloomin' lakes everywhere.'

As if to emphasise his comment, the coach rattled over another rickety wooden bridge, one of many that criss-crossed the waterlogged terrain of the Cambridgeshire fens.

On the opposite seat, Detective Stephen Lavender glanced up from his news-sheet and a thrilling account of Napoleon's latest defeat at the hands of a combined Russian and Prussian army in Katzbach, to follow his constable's gaze out of the window. His vision was partially obscured by the rivulets of rain streaming down the windowpane but Woods was right. A wide ditch, brimful with muddy water, ran alongside the road and beyond it vast stretches of the flat landscape glimmered silver beneath a huge, brooding sky. The flooded river and the isolated lakes seemed to merge without a break into the line of the horizon and the grey sky above.

'We've 'ad a lot o' rain,' said the elderly man sitting beside Lavender. 'The rivers are swollen and have swelled o'er their banks.' A whiskery old fellow, he spoke slowly and paused often to suck on his long clay pipe. Lavender liked the smell of tobacco smoke but the stiffly corseted matron who was travelling with them did not. Every time the old man lit up his pipe, she tutted and her face creased with disgust beneath the faded rim of her bonnet.

Beside her, her young daughter smiled cheekily at her discomfort, while the old man would wink at the girl and grin toothlessly at the mother. 'Ye ought to try some bacca, missus,' he said. 'It'll help ye fight the ague.'

'I don't have the ague,' she snapped.

'How many rivers do you have round here?' Woods asked. 'There's just one big river where we come from.'

'That'll be London, will it?'

Woods nodded.

'We've three big 'uns,' the old man continued. 'They all flow into the sea at the Wash. The land 'ereabouts is naught but one gigantic marsh. It's allus been prone to floodin'.'

'I've heard said this marshland is treacherous,' Lavender said. 'I understand the rivers are tidal and much of the ground is impassable except to those who know the region well.'

The old man's grey-whiskered cheeks disappeared into his face as he sucked hard on his pipe and exhaled another billowing cloud of white smoke. His voice took on an ominous tone. 'Yerse, these fens are silent killers, they are. There's bogs that'll suck down a whole cow in minutes – and 'ollows that fill with floodwater in seconds.'

The young girl, squashed between Woods and her mother shivered.

'And the young lasses around 'ere,' the old man added with a wink, 'have yellow spotted bellies like frogs and webbed feet.'

'I don't have webbed feet!' the indignant young girl announced. Her mother shushed her to silence.

Woods bit back his smile of amusement. 'Why don't they just drain it?' he asked.

The coach dipped and lurched as it entered a ford. At least, Lavender assumed it was a ford.

This section of the road may be flooded. The vehicle lunged to the left and Lavender grabbed the door handle to steady himself. Pebbles churned and grated beneath the carriage wheels and muddy water splashed up on to the glass window.

The old man shrugged his thin shoulders. 'They've tried to drain the fens for centuries. Even them Romans tried it.'

'The early drainage schemes only succeeded in drying out the peat and lowering the level of the land,' Lavender explained to Woods while their vehicle lurched and rejoined the road. 'There are hundreds of pumps powered by windmills scattered across the fens but they barely skim the surface of the problem.'

Lavender tried to return to his news-sheet but it wasn't long before Woods distracted him again with another exclamation.

'Ooh! Look at that! Looks like the masts of a gigantic ship.'

The pale stone towers of Ely Cathedral had risen up over the treetops in the distance and appeared to be floating above the watery landscape.

'Ely's built on an elevated rocky outcrop in the middle of the marshland,' Lavender explained. 'Centuries ago it was known as the Island of Ely.'

The old man turned to look at him. 'Yer a knowledgeable young chap for a furriner,' he observed. 'Are ye the bookish type?'

Lavender nodded and smiled back at him. 'I've been called bookish, yes.' He turned back to Woods.

'Humph,' Woods said. 'I never thought to fret about drownin' while takin' a coach trip but I'll wager a few travellers have ended up in these ditches before now.'

The old man gave his toothless grin. 'The local coachmen know these roads like the back of their 'ands.'

Woods didn't look reassured. 'It's a pity they don't take their gloves off now and then, look at the back of their hands and use them for guidance.' As if to emphasise his point, the coach found another rut in the road and lurched again.

Lavender hid his smile and returned to the military dispatch in his news-sheet. Woods must have an issue with the coach driver's handling of their vehicle and the horses. Few other horsemen or coach drivers came up to Woods' exacting equestrian standards. Until last year, he'd been one of the most experienced and respected members of the Bow Street horse patrol. But he'd been shot in the shoulder while pursuing Nidar, a fiend of a man whose criminal gang had caused chaos on the streets of London eighteen months before. Woods still found long periods in the saddle painful and exhausting. He was now permanently assigned to Lavender as his assistant, an arrangement that suited both men. They worked well together and there was no other man on the planet whom Lavender trusted like he trusted Ned Woods.

The failing daylight outside meant Lavender now saw the outline of his own reflection in the coach window. A pair of dark brown, slightly hooded eyes glowered back at him from beneath a fringe of wavy dark hair. He needed to visit his barber again as soon as he returned to London. He sighed and bit back his frustration.

He and Woods were fed up and homesick.

They'd been away from London for three weeks and missed their families. After two weeks spent in Birmingham, helping the city's magistrates solve a perplexing forgery case, they'd travelled on to Cambridge to appear as witnesses for the prosecution against a murderer in the assizes.

Then, just when they thought it was time to return to London, they'd received a hasty note from Magistrate Read at Bow Street instructing them to go to Willow Marsh Manor in Ely. The owner, Mrs Olivia Quinn, had requested urgent assistance from England's most famous police officer to solve a particularly nasty murder on her estate. But the details she'd sent to Magistrate Read about the crime were sketchy.

Lavender knew the remuneration she'd offered Read must have been significant to make him divert two of his best officers to Ely at such short notice, but he was frustrated with the delay. His stepson, Sebastián, had come home from his boarding school for the summer holidays but he'd barely seen him. In addition to this, Baby Alice, the latest addition to the Lavender household, was changing every day according to the two letters he'd received from his wife, Magdalena. Lavender had an irrational fear that during his lengthy absence his baby girl would forget who he was. In fact, if they didn't get home soon, there was a danger twelve-year-old Sebastián might forget who he was, never mind the baby.

The old man next to him sucked on his pipe stem and watched Woods closely, his eyes lingering on Woods' bright red waistcoat and blue greatcoat, the distinctive uniform of the Bow Street horse patrol. 'You're runners, ain't you?' the old man finally said.

The young girl turned her head expectantly in Woods' direction and even her mother looked up.

Lavender nodded. 'That's right.' Runners. Bow Street Runners. The nickname given to the constables and principal officers of Bow Street Police Office. A nickname known the length and breadth of the land and one that made them sound more like messenger boys than experienced investigators of crime. 'I'm Detective Stephen Lavender and this is my constable, Ned Woods.'

'I'm Jack Abbot.'

'Pleased to make your acquaintance, Mr Abbot,' Lavender said.

'Why ye goo-in' to Ely?'

'We've business at Willow Marsh Manor. Mrs Quinn has requested our help.'

'Quinn? Who's she?'

'I presume Mrs Quinn is the owner of the estate.'

Abbot shrugged his bony shoulders and shook his head. 'No, she ain't. It's Lawrence Delamere who owns Willow Marsh Manor, although I've heard he ain't long for this world.'

Delamere.

Lavender frowned. He'd heard this name before.

But where? And when?

After fourteen years with the Bow Street Police Office, each case merged and blended into the next one – and each villain seemed fouler than the last. But there was something about that name that made the hairs prickle on the back of his neck.

Where the devil had he come across the Delamere family before?

Chapter Two

Ten years ago

The George Inn,
Hampstead Road, London
June, 1803

'Gawd's teeth,' Constable Ned Woods muttered in horror.

Beside him, newly promoted Detective Stephen Lavender brushed his long, wavy hair out of his eyes and steeled himself as the grisly spectacle unfolded before them.

They were on a piece of overgrown waste ground beside a disused well at The George Inn on the edge of Hampstead Heath. Two men were hauling the blackened remains of a young woman out of the well on the end of a couple of butchers' meat hooks. The cheap, faded material of her gown was torn and the bodice rent, exposing a pair of pale-veined breasts that swayed gently as they lowered her to the ground.

Mrs Eddison, the tavern's landlady, hastily crossed herself. 'What demonic spirit, hot from hell, has been loosed upon this earth?'

Despite not being a great believer in demons, Lavender silently agreed with her. Whoever had killed this girl must have been a monster. In the four years he'd worked alongside Ned Woods, this was definitely the most disturbing murder the two of them had uncovered together.

The viciousness of the crime was made worse by the callous disposal of the body. The murdering hellhound had folded up his victim and shoved her head-first down the well, an act that Lavender suspected required the strength of two men, not one.

Bent double, the corpse had jammed halfway down and the blood had pooled in her face and her long slender legs, turning them dark purple with post-mortem lividity.

The red weal and the line of bruises circling her pale throat caught Lavender's attention next. A doctor would need to confirm it, but it looked like she'd been strangled to death.

Screened from the road by nettles and tall, purple-headed willow weeds, the woman in the well had remained undiscovered for days until the sharp sense of smell and curiosity of Ned Woods led him to her body. Plagued by highwaymen, the Hampstead Road was often patrolled by the Bow Street horse patrol from London. Woods recognised the sickly, cloying smell of death when he rode past the inn; he tracked it to its source and raised the alarm. The tavern landlord and his wife clearly had no sense of smell. They were irritated, rather than concerned, that Woods had found a dead body on their property and fetched a Bow Street principal officer to investigate the murder.

Lavender's eyes never left the dangling form of the corpse while it was gently lowered on to a patch of flattened nettles. Her long, thick hair fell in a dull, matted curtain over her blood-suffused face. Filthy and laced with twigs and dead leaves, it was difficult to tell how luxurious and glossy those curls had been in life.

The labourers who'd hauled her out removed the ropes, yanked the curved meat hooks out of her corpse and stepped back. One of them was cursing, visibly distressed.

'It's Irish Nell,' said Eddison, the tavern landlord. 'I recognise 'er 'air.'

'She needs coverin',' his wife said. ''Tain't decent to leave 'er like that – without a stockin'.'

Ah, the mystery of the missing stocking, Lavender thought sarcastically. A dreadful case where the victim showed a bit of leg. The ability of the general public to focus on the inconsequential at times like this, when the tragedy of mankind's brutality was splayed out on the ground before them, never ceased to amaze him. His eyes flicked to the crumbling brickwork of the well. 'Constable, please can you see if there's anything else down there.' Woods nodded and left his side to peer down the gloomy shaft.

A skylark's merry song filled the awkward silence, its cheerful, trilling sound at odds with the grim scene before them.

Lavender turned to the landlord and his wife. 'Who was Irish Nell?'

The landlord's mouth opened but no sound came out. With her husband struck dumb, it was up to Mrs Eddison, a narrow-faced, pinch-lipped woman with dyed brown hair, to answer Lavender's questions. 'She worked fer us as a barmaid sometimes. She were a friend of Lizzie, our regular gal. They lived together on Swan Street.'

'And what other work did she do for your tavern?' Lavender asked. Tavern barmaids were notorious for drifting in and out of prostitution with their customers to supplement their meagre wages, and the innkeepers often encouraged them.

She bristled and pulled her shawl tighter round her shoulders, even though it wasn't cold. 'I don't know what you mean.'

'You know exactly what I mean.'

'We run a respectable 'ouse, we do,' Mrs Eddison protested.

'Of course you do. That's why one of your barmaids has been murdered. What's her full name and how long did she work for you?'

Mrs Eddison shrugged, unmoved by his tone. 'Ye'll 'ave to ask Lizzie about 'er real name. We just knew 'er as Irish Nell.'

Her husband finally found his voice. 'She drifted into Hampstead about two months ago with a band of tinkers. They left and she stayed on with Lizzie. She weren't much more than a gypsy.' He gave Lavender a knowing wink. 'You know the type.'

'She 'ad a liltin' accent – that's why we called 'er Irish Nell. And she 'ad a pretty singin' voice, too,' Mrs Eddison conceded. 'Her singin' were popular with the customers.'

'Too popular, by the look of it,' Woods said dryly as he returned to Lavender's side. 'There's nothin' else down the well, as far as I can see.'

Lavender nodded and turned back to the Eddisons. 'When did you last see her?'

'It were last week. Friday, perhaps?'

His wife shook her head. 'No, it were Wednesday – the night those soldiers stayed. Which's why we asked 'er to work alongside Lizzie. We were burstin' at the seams wi' the officers.'

'Officers?'

'Aye.' Eddison nodded and colour returned to his cheeks. 'From the 1st Royal Dragoons.'

Lavender raised a sceptical eyebrow. 'You've done well to remember their regiment.'

Eddison pushed out his chest proudly. 'I were a soldier myself back in my youth. I fought for King George against those colonial upstarts in the Americas. I always take an interest in any military who pass through.'

'And we may be grateful for your interest yet,' Lavender said generously. This was useful information. He almost forgave them their lack of care for the victim. Almost. 'Constable Woods and I need to speak to young Lizzie.'

'She ain't 'ere today. You'll find 'er at 'ome.'

Lavender nodded his thanks. 'We'll visit her now if you'll furnish us with her address. In the meantime, please send for the local doctor.'

'It's a little late for poor Nell, don't you think?' Mrs Eddison said tartly. 'Surely it's a pauper's grave for her?' She eyed him coldly; he knew she was trying to assess his age. He'd faced a surprising amount of resistance from members of the public like her who felt he was too young, at twenty-four, to be a Bow Street principal officer.

'A doctor will be able to tell us how she died, madam,' Lavender replied patiently. 'If we're going to catch her killer, we need to know exactly what he did to her. And in the meantime, don't even think about trying to bury the body until after the inquest; the jurors may want to examine it.'

'Inquest!' shrieked Mrs Eddison. 'That's a lot of trouble to go to fer a...'

'A what?' Lavender challenged.

'Yer knows what I mean,' she snarled.

Lavender lowered his voice and glared at her. 'Even a gypsy whore deserves justice, Mrs Eddison.'

The two barmaids, Lizzie and Irish Nell, had shared a single, damp basement room in a dilapidated cottage at the edge of the village. Lizzie, a thin, plain young woman in her early twenties, collapsed into a rickety chair and sobbed when they told her how her friend had died. Woods stood beside her, occasionally patting her heaving shoulders with his huge hand.

Although he was bursting with questions, Lavender was happy to let Woods soothe her first. Woods had the common touch, something Lavender knew he lacked. His constable had a knack for putting the working folk and servant class at ease, often eliciting more information from them with his gruff kindness than Lavender's incisive and intelligent questioning.

21

They were a formidable team and working with the older constable had become one of the most pleasurable parts of Lavender's job, although he didn't let Woods know this. Occasionally, Woods still treated him as if he were an apprentice – and he never missed an opportunity to poke fun at Lavender. Never. A situation to which Lavender, who was quite serious by nature, had slowly become accustomed. They'd drifted into a pleasant, easy way of working together.

When she'd calmed down, Lizzie told them the dead girl's real name was Eleanor Keogh. Like the owners of the tavern, Lizzie hadn't seen her since the night the officers of the 1st Royal Dragoons had passed through the town.

'I thought she'd gone with 'em!' she wailed. 'I never thought she were dead!'

'Was she a camp follower?' Lavender asked.

Lizzie shrugged and sniffed. Woods handed her his handkerchief and she blew her nose. 'I dunno about her 'abits, I ain't known 'er long.' She glanced at the second small truckle bed, neatly made up with thin blankets, pushed up against the far wall of the room. 'I took 'er in a few months back when she came with the tinkers. She said she wanted a new life – and I wanted someone to 'elp me out wi' the rent here.'

'I figure you gals don't earn much workin' at the George Inn, do you, treacle,' Woods said gently. 'Did she do a bit of whorin' on the side to make ends meet? She wouldn't be the first – or the last – to take this path.'

Lizzie nodded and blinked her swollen eyes. The crying hadn't improved her appearance. 'Aye, she put 'erself about a bit with the fellas – and she weren't fussy either.'

'What do you mean?' Lavender asked sharply.

The girl hesitated and Woods stepped in. 'What the detective means, treacle, is do you think she were with a man when she disappeared? What happened that night?'

Lizzie's dry mouth and pale cheeks puckered when she tried to remember. 'It were busy, very busy. The tavern were burstin' at the seams with soldiers and officers in their red and gold uniforms and their fancy feathered hats. They were on their way somewhere and they'd set up their camp in a nearby field and the officers 'ad come to us for some good food, a change from their army slop, they said.'

'You must have been rushed off your feet,' Woods said.

She nodded. 'Aye, and we spent 'alf the night fendin' off their wanderin' 'ands. I weren't in the mood fer their nonsense.'

'When did you last see Nell?'

She hesitated for a moment then frowned. 'I can't remember but I know she spent a lot of time with Lieutenant Clarke – and 'is nasty scar-faced friend.'

Lavender was impressed. 'You know the names of these men?'

'Aye, they've been 'ere before on the way to their barracks. They're a pair of devils, especially scar-face. There ain't no mistakin' 'im', 'e's got a sabre slash runnin' up 'ere through 'is mouth.' She placed her hand over her chin and lower face.

'How do you know them so well, treacle?'

She flushed and glanced away.

'There ain't nothin' you can tell me that'll make me think bad of you. I know you're saddened right now – we just want to find out who did this to your friend.'

'I went with 'im once, that Lieutenant Clarke,' she blurted out, 'but 'e tricked me. We was in one of the old attics in the tavern. There's an old mattress up there for us girls to use. Eddison takes 'is cut – though 'is wife don't know nothin' about it.'

23

Lavender nodded; he'd guessed Eddison had been keeping something back.

''Alfway through, Clarke's scar-faced pal joins us, didn't 'e?' Her voice trailed away and she winced at the memory. 'They were rough wi' me – real rough. Scar-face were the worst.'

'Did you see Nell leave the bar with these men?'

She shook her head.

'But you think she may have taken them upstairs to this attic.'

She nodded miserably. 'I meant to warn 'er,' she said. 'But we were so busy…'

'Do you know scar-face's name?' Lavender asked.

She breathed in heavily and sat taller in her chair. 'Oh, I know 'im alright.'

'You do?' Lavender couldn't believe their luck.

'He were Delamere. Major Frederick Delamere. I'll never forget that devil,' she added with a shiver.

Chapter Three

The George Inn,
Hampstead Road, London
June, 1803

Lavender found the mattress mentioned by the barmaid, Lizzie, well hidden behind a large stack of old packing cases and wooden chests in the front attic of the tavern. The low roof of the small garret had a few missing tiles and the rain seeped through. This attic space was unsuitable for human habitation but the metal candleholder with its tallow stub on the floorboards beside the stained and sagging mattress suggested someone had been there recently.

Lavender dropped down to his haunches and the tight fabric of his breeches strained over his thigh muscles when he lifted the filthy blanket to examine the unpleasant collection of stains on the makeshift bed. He breathed through his mouth to avoid the stale metallic tang that hung heavy below the low beams. There were several dark patches on the mattress that were perhaps dried blood but it was impossible to tell how old they were. He glanced around but found no other clues about the tragic death of Irish Nell among the dust, cobwebs and splinters of this seedy garret. There was no sign here of the dead girl's missing stocking.

He heard the heavy tread of Woods' boots on the floor behind him. 'The magistrate, Sir Robert Brody, is here, sir. He wants to see us downstairs. The doctor has finished his examination of the body.'

Pushing back his hair, Lavender nodded and stood up. 'What manner of man is Sir Robert?'

'The usual,' Woods replied, sighing, 'and in a great hurry to wind up this case.'

Lavender gave a half smile. Woods had a poor opinion of most magistrates apart from those who ran Bow Street. This wasn't surprising when you considered that the only qualification a magistrate needed to be promoted to this public office was a private income of one hundred pounds a year.

Most magistrates were eminently unsuited to the grim job of overseeing justice and had a poor grasp of British law. Fifty years ago, the Fielding brothers had done their best to raise the profile of the magistracy and inject some much-needed professionalism into the constabulary at Bow Street. Their successors, mindful of the police office's excellent reputation, had done their best to carry on the tradition begun by the Fieldings. But English magistrates were a varied bunch and justice was a lottery, depending on the parish where you lived.

It quickly became obvious when Lavender met the elderly, white-wigged Brody that the man found the murder of Irish Nell a distasteful matter. He shuffled anxiously from one foot to the other and held a perfumed lawn handkerchief over his thin face and receding chin, which he sniffed every time the tobacco and ale atmosphere of the tavern offended him.

'Have you seen the victim, sir?' Lavender asked.

'I have – briefly. We'll open the inquest in here tomorrow morning at nine sharp,' Brody told Lavender. 'I'm sure it'll be wound up by lunch. There's no need to linger. Trollops like her deserve everything they get, if you ask me.'

Lavender struggled to keep his features neutral and Woods stiffened beside him.

But Brody was oblivious to their discomfort. 'There's not much we can do to prevent crimes like this,' he continued, 'especially if the female lower orders *persist* in putting themselves in danger by lying with strange men made vicious by drink. I wouldn't try too hard to find the killer if I were you, Lavender; no doubt the harlot had many lovers. A case like this often serves to deter other women from taking the same sinful path.'

'Actually, we already have a clue about the identity of the murderers.'

Brody's eyebrows rose in surprise towards the fringe of his wig.

'Two of the officers of the 1st Dragoons are under suspicion.'

The corners of Brody's thin mouth contorted into a cynical scowl. 'Officers? I doubt that, Lavender.'

'Why?'

'Don't be impertinent, man. You know darned well this is the work of a monster, not an educated man.'

'I've a reliable witness—'

'I don't think so. Your informant must be mistaken – no doubt they harbour a grudge against the men accused. I'm not sure why you Bow Street officers are here.' He paused and gave them an irritated glance. 'The local constables can handle this situation. Why don't you return to the capital and leave it with us, eh?'

Lavender gave Brody his most disarming smile. 'I like to finish what I start.'

Brody scowled. 'Admirable, I'm sure.'

Lavender and Woods met Doctor Rogers, a pale-faced, sandy-haired man with freckles, in the cramped back room of the tavern where Mrs Eddison had reluctantly allowed them to leave the girl's body until the inquest. The grate was empty and cold but the scent of coal smoke still lingered in the air, mingling with the sickly-sweet smell of Irish Nell.

'Strangulation was the cause of death.' Rogers brushed the back of one hand wearily across his high forehead while he snapped the clasp of his medical bag shut with the other. He seemed more affected than the magistrate by the young woman's death. 'The killer used some form of thin ligature.'

'He – or they?' Woods murmured, almost to himself. When the doctor looked at him quizzically, he added: 'We heard there may have been more than one man involved.'

Rogers nodded sadly. 'From the extent of the injuries, I suspected this.'

'But you can't be sure?' Lavender asked.

'No, I can't be sure.'

Lavender glanced down at the bare, lifeless foot poking out beneath the muddy hem of Irish Nell's gown. 'Was she strangled with her own stocking?'

Rogers followed his glance. 'Yes, that's possible.'

'When did she die?'

'It's difficult to determine the exact time of death,' Rogers replied, 'but from the decomposition of the soft tissue, I suspect it's at least a week ago.'

Lavender paused before his next question. Despite the death pallor and bruising, Irish Nell had regained some dignity now her gown had been pulled down and her hair smoothed off her discoloured face. 'Was she…?'

'Raped? Oh yes, I'd say so – brutally. The skin in both the vagina and the anus is torn and bruised.' Lavender and Woods winced. 'This goes well beyond the usual carnal contract a girl like her would expect to make with a customer in the tavern,' Rogers added.

'But why strangle the poor gal as well?' Woods asked. 'If the bastards had already taken what they wanted, why did they need to kill her?'

'It might have been a vicious act of deliberate cruelty,' Lavender suggested. 'An extension of the brutality they'd already inflicted on the poor girl.' He walked over to the window and pulled up the sash. The doctor picked up his hat, bade them farewell and left.

'Do you think they killed her just for the fun of it?' Woods asked sadly.

Lavender nodded. 'Probably. Her life was cheap. She was expendable.'

Woods rubbed his stubble and he glanced out of the window towards the well. 'So, we're dealin' with a pair of godless, evil villains?'

'Yes, and there's an element of arrogance here too,' Lavender added. 'He – or they – barely made any attempt to hide their crime.'

Woods nodded grimly. 'A right cocksure pair by the sound of it.'

'Let's go and meet them.'

'You get the horses, sir,' Woods said. 'I'll join you outside in a moment. I want another word with Landlord Eddison. There's somethin' I want to check – I've got a hunch.'

Lavender nodded and went out to retrieve their mounts from the tavern ostler.

Woods didn't keep him waiting long in the cobbled stable yard. But despite Lavender's obvious curiosity, Woods wasn't ready to speak yet. He shook his head in response to Lavender's quizzical glance, hauled himself up on to the back of his animal and trotted out of the yard.

Lavender followed him. It wasn't until they were in the dappled shadow of the trees lining the London Road that Woods drew up and explained.

'I got Eddison alone – away from his prissy wife – and told him we knew about the mattress in the attic and that he were pimpin' out the barmaids.'

'How did he react?'

'He blustered a bit at first but when I threatened to tell his missus and charge him with pimpin', he confessed it were true. I asked him who Irish Nell were with on the night she died.'

'What did he say?'

'Like young Lizzie, he confirmed Nell spent a lot of time that evenin' danglin' on Delamere's knee.'

'Good. That's a second witness who puts them together.'

'Unfortunately, it ain't goin' to help us, sir.'

'Why?'

'He said he ain't goin' to court and repeatin' any of this. He reckons there ain't any point in tryin' to finger a toff like Delamere – it'll only lead to trouble in the end and no one will believe him.'

Lavender scowled. 'A subpoena will loosen his tongue.'

'I mentioned that, sir – and threatened him with his wife again – but he says there ain't any point in a poor man like him standin' up in court and expectin' his word to be believed against the words of two gentlemen like Delamere and Clarke.'

There was a short silence while their horses picked their way past a wagon piled high with produce for the vegetable market in Covent Garden.

'Do you agree with him, Ned?' Lavender asked.

Woods sighed, leaned forward and gently stroked his mare's neck. 'I can see you've got the makin' of a great detective, sir – and I'd be the last one to put you down and dampen your enthusiasm. All the learnin' you've had at your fancy school is comin' in useful and in twenty years' time you'll be as famous throughout London as John Townsend.'

A flicker of amusement flitted across Lavender's face. Townsend was notorious throughout Bow Street for his eccentric habits and clothing. 'Ah, but famous for what? Not for my poor choice of hats, I hope?'

Woods frowned. 'I'm bein' serious, here, sir. You see, it seems to me that even you, with all your fancy learnin', can't push water uphill.'

Lavender regained his gravitas. 'No, Ned. You're right. No man can do that.'

'And takin' on the gentry with only circumstantial evidence is like pushin' water uphill.' Woods' voice rose as he warmed to his theme. 'It doesn't matter how many barmaids or innkeepers stand up in court against toffs like Delamere and Clarke, unless you've got clear evidence linkin' them to the crime, you're whistlin' against the flood. No jury or judge will ever believe the word of common folk against the likes of them. You might as well save your time and take a trip to the barbers instead.'

'Is this a subtle way of telling me I need another haircut?'

'It has been said in Bow Street, sir, that those floppy locks of yours make you look a tad rakish.'

Lavender smiled. 'I'll tell you what, Ned. Here's a wager for you. If I can't get Delamere and Clarke arrested for the murder of Irish Nell, I'll shave it off and wear a periwig. How would this suit you?'

Woods laughed. 'You young braggart! You'll look a real sight in one of them periwigs.'

'So how about it, Constable?'

The smile dropped from Woods' face as another thought struck him. 'What's the other half of the wager? Don't tell me I'm to shave *my* head if you succeed and get those coves taken up and locked beneath the hatches. It might not grow back at my age.'

'No, if I win the wager you must stop behaving like my father and telling me to get a haircut.'

Woods gave him a sideways glance and chortled. 'He's great man, your da. I've worked with him for years.'

'I know you have. But you don't have to turn into him, do you? Do we have a deal?'

'It's a deal, sir.'

Despite his jesting, Lavender was thoughtful as they rode back to Bow Street. Woods had a good point; they needed strong evidence in any case against the gentry. How the devil was he going to get it?

Chapter Four

Present day

Ely, Cambridgeshire

Early September, 1813

'So why ye goo-in' to Willow Marsh Manor?' the confused old man persisted as the coach continued on its journey.

Abbot was a nosy old beggar, Lavender decided. 'There's been a murder on the estate. Maybe you've heard about it? We've been asked to investigate.'

The old fellow's watery eyes widened with surprise below his bushy grey eyebrows and he seemed speechless for a moment.

But the matron beside him bristled angrily. 'This isn't suitable talk in front of a young lady!' Her daughter, however, looked far from shocked; she leaned forward, her eyes gleaming with interest.

Abbot laughed. 'Nay, I've 'eard of no murder up at Willow Marsh – although with that family I ain't surprised. It were only a matter of time before they started batterin' each other to death.'

'Really, gentlemen!' The woman sniffed haughtily and her face contorted into an indignant frown. 'I must insist you stop this distressing talk in the presence of my daughter.'

Lavender smiled warmly at her. It was his best smile, the one he reserved for calming and charming Magdalena when she was tetchy and exhausted with Baby Alice. 'Our apologies, ma'am.' He turned back to the elderly man. 'Sir, perhaps we can stand you a tankard of ale at The Lamb once we arrive in Ely? We can continue this conversation before we drive on to Willow Marsh Manor.'

Abbot took his pipe out of his mouth and grinned toothlessly. 'Thank ye, but no. I'll cut orf home to my missus, Martha. This weather plays 'avoc wi' 'er rheumatism.'

'Very well.' Lavender shrugged off his disappointment.

'I 'aven't much to tell ye anyway about the Delameres,' the old fellow added with a wink. 'It's just the same ol' story of Cain and Abel – two brothers who can't stand the sight of each other.'

'I did ask you gentlemen—'

Abbot turned to the irritated woman. 'Stop worryin', missus. The detective and I were just discussin' the Bible. It's a godly discussion – I'm sure your young lass has 'eard of Cain and Abel?'

The girl nodded. 'Yes, indeed – the sons of Adam and Eve. Cain murdered Abel.'

The glowering matron sat back in her seat with tight lips, outmanoeuvred for the moment by the wily old man.

'Well, it didn't come to murder wi' Lawrence and Tobias Delamere.'

'That's good to hear,' Woods said. The matron gave him an approving nod.

'But the brothers would sooner cross over to the other side of the road if they met in Ely than speak a civil word to each other,' the old man continued. 'They weren't a pious family but they'd even ignore each other if they met in church. Mind you, I've 'eard Lawrence is ailin' now and ain't long for this world.'

The woman crossed herself hastily. 'Let's hope Mr Delamere makes his peace with his brother before he goes to meet his maker.'

'What were the cause of their rift?' Woods asked.

Abbot's eyes twinkled and he winked. 'What is it allus?' he asked dramatically. 'Women! Lawrence stole the gal 'is brother wanted to wed. But Lawrence were the eldest and 'eir to Willow Marsh Manor and marriage with 'im would make 'er lady of the manor. What gal could resist that?'

'I couldn't,' the young girl said candidly.

'Esther!' spluttered her mother.

Lavender grinned. 'Ah, the curse of primogeniture.'

'What's that?' Abbot asked.

'It's where the second son is relegated to the shadows and is forced to beg for crumbs from the plate of his big brother.'

'When you put it as unpleasantly as that,' Woods said thoughtfully, 'I'm surprised there aren't more toffs in Mayfair slayin' their kith and kin.'

'What happened next?' Intrigued by the old man's story, the matron forgot to reprimand Woods for talk of murder.

'Tobias wed another woman and raised 'is own family but would you believe it?' The elderly man's voice cracked with excitement as he neared the climax of his story.

'What?' Woods demanded.

'The same thing only went and 'appened with Lawrence's two daughters twenty years later!'

'Never!' exclaimed the matron.

'Aye, they squabbled over the same man. The elder sister married the fella and the younger one were jilted – almost at the altar!'

'None of them sound like they've much moral fortitude,' the matron said.

'That's quite a coincidence,' Woods conceded. 'It seems strange two generations of siblings from the same family should end up arguin' over their lovers.'

'Maybe it's not that strange,' Lavender suggested thoughtfully. 'This is a rural backwater. There'll be a limited supply of suitable marriage partners for the gentry in a small town like Ely. There's bound to be competition for the eligible men and women.'

'Ely is *not* a backwater,' the offended matron exclaimed, 'nor is it a town. It's a city. A very nice little city with a proper cathedral.'

'The detective meant no offence, ma'am,' Woods intervened hastily.

Lavender lowered his head and twitched a cynical eyebrow. He couldn't help wondering what an *improper* cathedral was like. Abbot's description suggested the Delameres were an unnaturally close family, constantly at war among themselves and possibly incestuous. And if those millions of gallons of water trapped in the peaty marshes of this landscape didn't merit the application of the name *backwater* to this region, he didn't know what did. 'Can you remember the names of these daughters?' he asked.

The old man shook his head. 'I think Miss Miranda were one o' them. But it were allus Lawrence and his brother I knew best. Anyway, tha won't be drivin' down to Willow Marsh this weather. The road will be flooded.'

Lavender frowned. 'How shall we get there?'

'Ye'll need to go down to the quayside and take a boat to the manor. As for the Delameres,' he added with a wink, 'don't ye worry – I'm sure a smart young detective like ye will soon find out the rest.'

I'm sure I will. Lavender thanked him and sat back against the cracked leather cushions as the coach climbed gently up the incline to Ely.

The overcast sky darkened into a gloomier shade of grey when their coach finally rattled into the cobbled streets of the tiny city. The area around the double-towered cathedral and the beautifully preserved monastic buildings had a leafy tranquillity. The drizzle emphasised the coloured patterns in the brickwork and ornate chimney stacks of the gabled merchants' houses. The coach turned sharply under the arched entrance of The Lamb and drew to an abrupt halt.

Lavender and Woods clambered out of the vehicle and glanced around at the bustling courtyard and the tall walls of the tavern. Despite the rain, they both paused to stretch their stiff limbs and breathe in the fresh air – a welcome change after the tobacco-scented, stuffy fug of the coach. The smoked earthy tang of peat fires mingled with the smell of damp masonry. Over the cries of the ostlers and the snorting of the tired horses, Lavender heard Woods' stomach rumble and the clatter of crockery from the kitchen.

The landlord at The Lamb confirmed what their elderly travelling companion had suggested – the road to Willow Marsh Manor was already under water. The only way to complete their journey and reach their destination was by boat. The man assured them there were plenty to hire down the hill at the wharf.

'It'll be good to stretch our legs after our journey,' Lavender said, after they'd collected their luggage.

But Woods wasn't listening. He gazed longingly towards the warm yellow glow emanating from the open door of the tavern. His broad nostrils twitched as the wonderful aroma of roast beef wafted towards them.

Lavender grinned. 'I suppose it won't hurt for us to grab a bowl of food first.'

Their walk to the quayside took them through narrow streets crammed with dilapidated cottages, pawnbrokers and cheap lodging houses. The rickety wall lamps of crude fish-blubber oil cast flickering light on the wet road, animating and deepening the shadows and leaving pools of total darkness between the lamps. They picked their way carefully between one insubstantial puddle of light and the next, avoiding where possible the unidentifiable piles of refuse on the cobbles. Occasionally, the sharp angles of a dark and silent warehouse or a peat-drying shed with its peaked roof loomed out of the gloom.

'This is Britain's biggest inland port,' Lavender told Woods. 'We're about thirty miles from the coast and the maritime port of King's Lynn.'

Born and brought up in the shadow of the mighty London docks, Woods was unimpressed. He sniffed disdainfully. 'I thought I caught a whiff of Rotherhithe.'

He's right, Lavender thought. The rich summer stench of the Great Ouse guided their steps towards the riverside wharves, the noisiest and busiest part of town that night.

They heard drunken singing and tuneless dirges emanating from the alehouses. Shadowy figures materialised out of the night. Some lurked down dark alleys, between the brothels and the taverns. Others staggered out of the alehouses into their path and blowsy whores called out from the upper windows of the squalid buildings.

One of Lavender's hands rested lightly on the pistol he kept in his greatcoat pocket; the other guarded his pocketbook.

The river slapped heavily against the blackened wooden legs of the wharves and heaved with a scum of sludge and sewage. Lighters and barges, piled high with sedge and reeds for thatching, rocked gently on their moorings. The ropes tethering the vessels grew taut then slackened with the ebb and flow of the tidal river.

38

Several larger ships were moored mid-stream and beyond them lights glimmered in the tumbledown dwellings and taverns on the far bank. More bawdy singing drifted across the water on the breeze.

There was no sign of any boatmen.

'They'll all be in the taverns,' Woods said.

'I'm damned if I'll let a drunk row us out on a swollen tidal river in the dark.'

A hunched figure suddenly stepped in front of them, clutching a lantern with hands where arthritis had swollen the joints to almost double their normal size. A pair of sunken eyes in a brown, leathery face regarded Lavender suspiciously from beneath a thick thatch of matted white hair. 'Warrup, sir. Where be you goo-in'?'

'We need to get to Willow Marsh Manor,' Lavender said.

The strange fellow held out his lantern closer to Woods. He might be any age from forty to seventy. ''Im too?' he asked.

'Yes, him too.'

'It'll be sixpence – each.'

Lavender opened his mouth to protest at the price but the old man had already turned to untie the rope of a large rowing boat. When his stiff fingers struggled with the knot he bent down and used his blackened teeth to tug on the rope. He nodded towards the ladder that led down to the rocking vessel. 'Gerr-in,' he mumbled with a mouthful of rope.

'I hope he knows what he's doing,' Lavender muttered as they clambered down into the boat.

'At least he seems sober,' Woods said.

The old boatman soon joined them and took up his position at the rowlocks. They eased away from the wharf into the tidal stream and glided through the choppy water with ease; the receding tide took them with it towards the coast. Arthritic hands or not, the old fellow knew how to handle the vessel.

Woods offered to take an oar and share the rowing, but the boatman shook his head and leaned back into a strong, steady rhythm.

Only the slap of the heaving water against the side of the boat, the monotonous creak of the oarlocks and the occasional cry of a nocturnal creature on the riverbank disturbed their peace. They rowed in silence with their coat collars raised against the persistent drizzle and eyes strained against the poor visibility.

Suddenly, the clouds cleared and thousands of glistening diamond stars filled the vast velvet sky above. The moonlight turned the surface of the water into a glistening black mirror. It also rippled across the waterlogged fields, shadow chasing shadow.

Clumps of tall reeds swayed and rustled in the breeze but they were heard rather than seen. Beyond the riverbanks, the dark marshes stretched out in every direction with no break between land, water and sky. All was black shadow. Who'd have thought there were so many shades of black in the world?

'It looks like good smugglin' country to me.' Woods turned to the boatman. 'Say – you fella – do you have a problem with smugglers in these parts?'

A broad grin spread across the old man's weathered face. 'We don't have a *problem* wi' it, as such.'

'Of course they don't have a *problem* with it,' Lavender said sharply, 'they'll all be involved. Everyone round here will enjoy a sideline in stolen brandy.'

The old boatman grinned and said nothing, so Lavender continued. 'This fenland is awash with smuggled goods – especially brandy from France. The watery terrain makes it a devilish task for the local excise men to police the area properly.' The old man just lowered the brim of his hat over his eyes and kept his own counsel.

40

'The road's vanished.' Woods pointed to the bank. A dark ribbon had hugged the contours of the riverbank for the past few miles but now it had disappeared into the water. Here the river bulged inland into a shallow inlet. The boatman followed the bank and rounded the bend.

A towering wall of grey stone with a large arched entrance suddenly appeared at the neck of the inlet. Barely ten feet away from the river, it was as if the building had risen out of the water itself like some long-lost palace of Atlantis. Behind this defensive wall, two solid crenellated towers and several tall Elizabethan brick chimneys were silhouetted against the pearly moon. Lavender could smell coal fires.

''Ere's Willow Marsh Manor,' the boatman said.

The hairs on the nape of Lavender's neck prickled as an unpleasant memory jolted him. He'd seen this fortified manor house somewhere before.

But *where,* damn it*? Where?*

Chapter Five

Lavender had no time to dwell on the stubborn refusal of his memory to work. The boat grated across shingle and juddered to a halt. Woods leapt over the prow and held her steady while Lavender found a shilling for the boatman and climbed out himself. 'Call back here for us at noon tomorrow.'

The old fellow grunted and touched the brim of his cap in what Lavender hoped was a gesture of agreement.

'Do you reckon we'll have wound this case up by then?' Woods asked hopefully when the boat pulled away.

'No – but I don't relish the prospect of being cut off here without some form of escape. If we don't need him to return to Ely, I'll just pay him, send him home and add his exorbitant fee on to Mrs Quinn's bill.'

They strolled unchallenged through the arched entrance and a short tunnel into the inner courtyard of the manor house. They encountered a large mound of drying firewood but no servants.

Lavender paused and quietly whistled his appreciation. Willow Marsh Manor was a magnificent sight. Bathed in silver moonlight, its tall fourteenth-century arched windows glowed with candlelight. The medieval great hall was flanked at either end by two sturdy stone towers complete with crenellated parapets. On their own, either of the towers would have drawn the appreciation of scholars of medieval architecture but it was the rare and beautiful baronial hall in the centre with the intricate stone tracery of its windows and the sheer height and steep angle of the slate roof that made Lavender pause in admiration.

On the larger of the two sturdy towers, a covered stone porch rose above the main entrance to the house. Lavender reached for the metal doorbell pulley.

'Should we go around the back to the servants' entrance?' Woods asked.

'It's not the servants who've invited us here.'

A small, middle-aged woman with wild grey hair imperfectly contained by a mobcap answered the door. She seemed unalarmed by their sudden appearance after dark at a house cut off from civilisation but her frequent glances over her shoulder suggested she was busy within. Lavender introduced himself and Woods and asked to see Mrs Quinn.

The woman looked confused. She pushed back an errant tendril of grey hair, opened the door wider and let them into the flagstone hallway. 'I'm Mrs Mabberley, the housekeeper. I'll tell the mistress you're here.'

'We're expected,' Lavender reassured her.

A genial hum of conversation emanated through a large open door on their left, one of a pair leading into the great hall. On their right, another partially opened door led into a candlelit parlour with a small fire in the hearth. Beyond that, the warm air, delicious smells and clatter of pans indicated the location of the kitchen.

'You'll have to wait, though,' the servant woman added. 'They've only just finished their meal – and there's business to discuss yet wi' the guests. Mistress said to take the coffee pot in wi' the port. The ladies are stayin' at the table.'

Lavender frowned. 'There are guests here?' At the same moment, his eyes alighted on the black crêpe band wrapped round her upper arm.

'They're mourners,' she said. 'The mairster's just died. 'Tis his funeral supper.'

Lavender's tired brain leapt back to the letter Mrs Quinn had sent to Bow Street. 'Is this the funeral of the murdered man, the victim?'

The woman blinked and her cornflower-blue eyes stared up at him in surprise. She must be at least a foot shorter than him, he realised. 'No, this be Mr Delamere's funeral. He were the mairster here.'

Lavender grimaced and remembered the story the old man on the coach had told them about the ailing Lawrence Delamere A second death on the estate, even one by natural causes, would make their job more difficult.

'My condolences, madam. How did Mr Delamere die?'

'Why, bless you, dearie, he died peacefully in his sleep. He were seventy, after all.' She turned and headed towards the double doors, calling over her shoulder as she went: 'It were a blessin' in the end.'

'So, he's not our murder victim?' Woods asked when she disappeared into the hall.

Lavender shook his head, took off his hat and placed it on the seat of one of the hard-backed chairs pushed against the stone wall. 'It looks like the elderly master has also died. Mrs Quinn – whom I assume is his married daughter – will be very distressed. We need to proceed carefully.'

He glanced around at the attractive mellow oak staircase that wound round the exposed stone walls to the upper floor of the tower. There was a small wooden door beneath it, blocked by a large carved chest. Most of the walls were rough-hewn stone but one had been plastered. Here, a few gilt-framed paintings jostled for space with an arched window.

The hum of conversation inside the banqueting hall stopped suddenly. No doubt the servant's announcement that two officers from Bow Street waited outside had caught the interest of the mourners. Woods shuffled uncomfortably and Lavender gave him a quick, reassuring smile.

The tiny housekeeper reappeared and gestured for them to enter the hall. 'Mistress will see you now.'

The towering stone walls of the great hall were a dazzling display of ancient silk banners, colourful flags and glittering silver armour. Gleaming broadswords arranged in semicircular patterns swirled round medieval shields. Pikes pointed deadly blades towards the black-beamed rafters of the roof, drawing their eyes upwards. At the other end of the hall, an immense fourteenth-century stone-carved fireplace dominated the far wall. Beside it, a twisting dark-oak staircase led to the upper chambers of the north tower. All this baronial hall needed was a minstrel's gallery and it would be a perfect setting for a Plantagenet court.

In the centre of the room, a huge banqueting table groaned under the weight of three gleaming silver candelabra heavy with beeswax candles, white china and heavy silver cutlery. Twelve places had been set but only eight adults, whose ages ranged from about twenty to sixty, sat around the remnants of their meal. Swathed in the black crêpe and grey flannel of mourning clothes, they stared curiously at the two police officers, although one young fellow, with long black hair tied back with a velvet ribbon, ignored them and continued to peel an apple with a silver knife.

Lavender's eyes flitted over the four women present, seeking someone who might be Mrs Olivia Quinn.

There were two young girls, one fair and one dark, whom he suspected were too young to be Mrs Quinn, and a huge fat woman whose place halfway down the table suggested she was a guest rather than the chatelaine of Willow Marsh Manor. Swathed in a gown of black bombazine silk, she also wore a black silk turban topped with a swaying black ostrich feather. Beneath it, her hair was pure white.

Lavender's gaze finally settled on a thin, middle-aged woman seated at the head of the table in a wicker wheelchair. A walking cane rested beside her. She had fine dark eyes that sparkled with intelligence. Probably about forty years old, years of chronic pain had gouged deep lines of suffering into her face and her dark hair was streaked prematurely grey. Her shoulders were hunched forward as if her disability originated in her back rather than her legs.

'Good evening, Detective Lavender.' Her tone was cool, polite and gave no hint of any discomfort she may be experiencing. 'I'm Miss Miranda Delamere, mistress of Willow Marsh Manor.'

Lavender hesitated, confused. But before he could reply, an overweight, bald man of about sixty, seated further down the table, interrupted their conversation. 'Not for much longer, you aren't, madam,' he snapped. 'Don't presume such a thing.' The fellow's small eyes were almost lost in the fatty flesh of his face and his multiple chins were sunk deep in the elaborate folds of his white cravat.

Beside him, the fat woman nodded in agreement. The ostrich feather in her turban quivered. 'Quite so, husband dear,' she said, 'quite so.' She had a faint foreign accent, which Lavender couldn't place

Miranda Delamere ignored the obese couple's provocative comments and continued to address Lavender. 'We're mourning the passing of my father, Detective. Today was his funeral.'

'My condolences, ma'am,' Lavender said hastily. 'Would this be Mr Lawrence Delamere? I've heard of him. My informant spoke well of him.' His mind raced. Something was wrong. If Miranda Delamere was the chatelaine at Willow Marsh Manor, what role did Mrs Quinn play in this household? And which one was she? He glanced again at the fat woman but she was oblivious to his discomfort and had resumed her assault on her dessert.

'We buried my father in Ely this afternoon,' Miranda continued. 'Normally I would ask you to wait until the morning before stating your business, but my housekeeper tells me you've travelled here post-haste from Bow Street in London. I understand there's some urgency about your investigation?'

'There may be, ma'am. This is Constable Woods, my assistant. I'm sorry we've arrived so late at night and at such an inopportune moment, but Mrs Quinn was most insistent we came as quickly as possible to help solve the murder. Perhaps you could introduce us?'

'Murder?' exclaimed several of the guests at the same time. The pretty young brunette beside Miranda dropped her dessert spoon into her dish with a clatter. Her large dark eyes widened with shock.

'Did he mention Olivia Quinn?' The obese older woman spat out the name with disgust.

'There's been no murder here!' the fat, balding man insisted.

With a growing sense of foreboding, Lavender pulled a folded letter out of his pocket and handed it across to Miranda Delamere. 'Mrs Quinn wrote to Bow Street about a terrible murder committed on your estate and begged us for our assistance.'

Miranda Delamere pulled back her hunched shoulders, sat up straight and breathed heavily. 'I don't know how to tell you this, Detective, but I fear you've been the victim of a terrible hoax.'

'Oh? How so?'

'I don't know who penned this letter – but there's been no murder on this estate. The only death we've had to deal with this year has been my father's.'

The gentleman seated on her left, a florid fellow with gingery whiskers and a thick head of red hair that curled exuberantly and was fading to white, nodded and spoke quickly: 'I was Lawrence Delamere's doctor and I can assure you, Detective, his passing was long expected and perfectly natural. He wasn't murdered.'

'Thank you, Doctor—?'

'Bendall, sir. Doctor Bendall.'

Lavender nodded and turned back to Miranda. 'I'm pleased for your sake that there's been no murder on the estate but where's Mrs Olivia Quinn? May we speak with her?'

'You'll have to join the bloody queue, Lavender,' the elderly fat man snapped. 'There's a long line of people who want to speak to that hussy!'

His fat wife sniggered.

'Olivia Quinn – is – or was – my sister,' Miranda explained.

'She broke her mother's heart, she did,' the fat man continued.

'Who are you, sir?' Lavender asked, irritated by the fellow's constant interruptions. 'Your name, please?'

The man's features flushed with a fine sheen of sweat. 'I'm not sure it should matter to you, Lavender, but I'm Tobias Delamere – the next owner of Willow Marsh Manor. This is my wife, Mrs Birgitta Delamere, our son, Mr Adrian, and our eldest daughter, Miss Ursula.' His sausage-like fingers pointed towards the thin, blonde-haired girl and the silent young man with the long, dark hair and the apple who sat opposite.

Lawrence's fractious younger brother, Lavender thought.

Amusement flitted across Miranda Delamere's face but her watchful eyes remained cold. 'Let's see what father's will says about the future of Willow Marsh Manor before we jump to any conclusions, shall we, Uncle Toby?' She pointed towards the fourth and final man sitting with them, an elderly, bewigged fellow. 'This is Mr Symonds, our lawyer,' she explained for Lavender's benefit. 'He's waiting to enlighten us about the contents of my father's will.'

Mr Symonds avoided eye contact with everyone and looked like he would rather be anywhere in the world than sitting at this table.

'So, where is your sister, Mrs Quinn?' Lavender asked again.

'My sister isn't here,' Miranda replied sharply. 'She hasn't been in England for twenty years. She ran off to the Americas in 1793 and may be dead as far as I know.'

Chapter Six

Tobias and Birgitta Delamere sniggered and Lavender took a deep breath to steady his temper.

He didn't know what the devil was going on in this household or who'd written that damned letter, but someone would pay a heavy price for wasting the time of himself and his exhausted constable. 'Very well, Miss Delamere. I understand our services are not required to solve a murder. But perhaps you can help me identify the culprit behind this cruel joke. Do you recognise his – or her – handwriting?'

'Culprit?' Miranda's composure faltered for a second and the smirks of the rest of the guests faded away.

'Yes, ma'am, it's a crime to waste police time.' It wasn't, but she wouldn't know this. 'And I intend to prosecute.' Symonds, the lawyer, said nothing to contradict him and Lavender's statement had a sobering effect on the rest of the company. 'Pray tell me if the wax seal on the letter comes from Willow Marsh Manor?'

'I don't know,' she murmured.

'May I be of assistance, Miss Delamere?' Symonds took the crumpled letter from her hand then pulled a pair of pince-nez out of his coat pocket and balanced them on his large hooked nose.

'I don't think this is my sister's handwriting,' Miranda said, 'but then again it's been a long time since I last saw it.'

'The wax seal has melted and been squashed out of shape,' Mr Symonds announced. 'It's impossible to tell if the Delamere seal was used for this letter or not.'

'In that case, madam,' Lavender said wearily, 'if you can provide us with a bed for the night, Constable Woods and I will depart as soon as we can in the morning.'

'Of course.' Miranda beckoned to Mrs Mabberley, the housekeeper, who still hovered in the background. 'We've a full house tonight, as you can see, but there's a spare room at the top of the north tower. You can have that and your man can sleep in the gatehouse with the other servants. This should be possible, shouldn't it, Mrs Mabberley?' The housekeeper nodded in reply.

Lavender was too exhausted to correct her understanding of Woods' position. He gave her a short bow. 'Thank you, ma'am, we'll retire and leave you to your mourning.'

'Yes, bugger off, Lavender.' Tobias Delamere dabbed at his mouth with a white linen napkin. 'We've got business to conduct here and we've spent enough time on your sideshow. I've waited a long time for my inheritance and I'm damned if some silly practical joke is going to make me wait a moment longer.'

Lavender backed away with his eyes cast down to hide his anger at the man's unmitigated rudeness.

But Miranda's voice cut through the sniggers of her cousins and made him pause. 'Wait! I've forgotten my manners, Detective. Please stay a while longer. You and your constable must have some refreshments. Coffee, perhaps? Or a glass of port?'

'Goddamn it, Miranda!' Tobias Delamere exploded. 'We're about to read my brother's will – they can't stay here!'

'Why not?' The devil danced in her eyes and her lined faced relaxed into a gentle smile. 'They're officers of the law. Who better to oversee the proceedings and ensure fair play?'

The flabby jowls of Birgitta Delamere wobbled with indignation. 'Fair play? What rubbish you talk, Miranda! There will be nothing complicated about the transfer of the estate into our ownership. You've always had a wild imagination.'

Lavender would have preferred to leave these unpleasant people to their squabbles and take a quiet glass of refreshment in the kitchen before retiring to his bed. But he still harboured a hope he might find the culprit whose hoax had brought them here. He moved towards the vacant seat next to Adrian Delamere and sat down before Tobias could object further. 'That's kind of you, Miss Delamere. I'll take a cup of coffee, please, and my constable will have a glass of ale.'

Woods slid silently into the seat beside him. Woods would leave all the talking to him, but Lavender had no doubt his constable would have plenty to say about this strange turn of events later.

Mrs Mabberley hurried over with the coffee pot, while the rest of the company adjusted to their presence.

'Excellent,' Miranda Delamere said, 'and when you leave to fetch the ale, Mrs Mabberley, please fetch in your husband – and Pammenter – too. I'm sure my father will have left them both a handsome bequest in his will. They'll need to be here for the reading.'

The serving woman poured Lavender's coffee then hurried from the room.

'I can't believe she still employs that Pammenter woman.' Birgitta hissed to her husband.

Lavender sipped his drink, sat back and scrutinised the other guests. He now knew who they all were apart from the pretty, dark-haired young girl sitting next to Miranda. She hadn't spoken since they'd arrived.

As if reading his thoughts, Miranda waved a hand towards her. 'You've been introduced to everyone else here except my niece, Miss Susanna Delamere. She's the orphaned child of my late brother.'

'My condolences on your loss, Miss Delamere,' Lavender said instinctively.

The young woman smiled back nervously. 'It was many years ago, sir.' Long, dusky lashes framed her doe-brown eyes. Attractive, with a sweet smile, everything about her, from her voice to the way she tilted her head, suggested gentleness.

'To avoid confusion with myself, Lavender,' Miranda continued, 'Susanna and Ursula are usually referred to as *Miss Susanna* and *Miss Ursula*. Please do likewise.' Lavender nodded.

Ursula's voice was shriller than her cousin's. 'It's such a shame Hal can't be with us. He's missing all the fun.'

'Funerals are not fun, my dear,' her mother reminded her.

'No, but Uncle Lawrence may have left him a bequest,' the girl continued sulkily. 'Hal should be here, too.'

Tobias snorted in his port. 'Don't you think my brother has done enough for that bastard already?'

Lavender raised a silent eyebrow at the coarseness of the man's language, but Miranda's reproof was surprisingly mild. 'Now, now, Uncle, please restrain yourself.'

'Is the estate entailed to the male heirs only?' Lavender asked. This was the only explanation for Tobias Delamere's arrogant confidence. From what Lavender could see, the dead man's immediate family were all female and if the estate were entailed then Willow Marsh Manor would pass to Tobias as the estate's next legitimate male heir. However, the lack of an entailment put a different perspective on these proceedings. Without an entailment, Willow Marsh Manor could pass to any one of the family members, including the women.

The lawyer, Symonds, stopped fussing with his papers and turned to him. 'Do you know the law, Lavender?'

'A little,' Lavender confessed. 'I studied it for a year at Cambridge in my youth before I joined the Bow Street Police Office.'

Symonds nodded and started to clean his pince-nez with his pocket handkerchief.

'Then you may understand my trepidation when I tell you, sir, that the estate is *not* entailed. I've no idea what is contained in this will. It was drawn up two years ago by Mr Lawrence Delamere and my former partner, a man who has since retired from the practice and died.'

'My brother will have made sure the estate stays in the Delamere family,' Tobias snapped. 'Anything else is unthinkable.'

Miranda Delamere bit back a smile. Symonds might be ignorant of the document's contents, but Lavender felt Miranda knew what they contained.

Mrs Mabberley returned with her husband, a tall, stooped and greying man. Behind them walked a middle-aged woman with a dull complexion, whom Lavender assumed was the other servant, Pammenter. She carried a shawl up to Miranda and gently placed it round her mistress's tense shoulders. Neither woman spoke a word, secure in the routine familiarity of her action.

Pammenter's silver-grey hair was centrally parted and scraped back into a tight bun in the nape of her neck. She wore a dark, high-necked gown. When she stepped back, she seemed to disappear into the shadows cast by the candlelight against the stone walls of the medieval hall. Her submissive demeanour and downcast eyes suggested she was a shy woman who'd spent her life perfecting the art of being invisible. He wondered what she had done to attract the disapproval of Tobias and his wife.

Mr Symonds cleared his throat, opened his file of papers, lifted out a document and broke the seal. 'This is the last will and testament of Lawrence Delamere Esq., lately of Willow Marsh Manor, Ely,' he announced. Silence fell among the assembled mourners.

A few paragraphs of legal jargon, followed in which Lawrence Delamere proclaimed himself to be of sound mind.

The next section of the will left small bequests to the faithful family retainers, especially the Mabberleys, whom Lavender sensed ran the house and the estate between them. Lucy Pammenter and two other manservants, called Thrup and Hawkes, also received small amounts of money.

One hundred pounds each was bequeathed to Lawrence Delamere's nephew, Adrian, and his niece, Ursula. The youngsters looked pleased with themselves but their parents shuffled impatiently in their seats at the opposite side of the table, eagerly waiting to hear how the bulk of the estate had been bequeathed.

At this point, Miranda politely interrupted Mrs Symonds, thanked the Mabberleys and asked them to return to their duties. Lucy Pammenter remained by her chair.

The next bequest completely changed the mood of the room. Five hundred pounds per annum for life was to be given to Mr Henry Pammenter, whom Lavender assumed was the missing 'Hal'.

'That's a disgrace!' Tobias Delamere bellowed. 'I don't know why he just didn't come out and acknowledge him openly as his bastard!'

'Shocking!' screeched his wife.

Miranda was quiet, her face impassive. Young Miss Susanna looked upset and uncomfortable.

Lavender glanced at the female servant, Lucy Pammenter, and wondered if she was related in any way to the fortunate but much-maligned Henry Pammenter. The woman stood perfectly still, her eyes downcast. Only the faint flush of red creeping up above the high neck of her plain gown betrayed any emotion.

Mr Symonds glared at Tobias Delamere over the top of his pince-nez. 'Can we move on, Mr Delamere? There's still a lot to get through and as we're all trapped here tonight, there will be plenty of time later for point by point discussion.' The reading now took on a more personal tone.

'"To my dear and most loyal daughter, Miranda Delamere, I leave an income of one thousand pounds per year and the right to live in Willow Marsh Manor until the day when you draw your last breath. Never was a father more blessed in his child than I."'

'How lovely,' Miss Susanna said softly, gazing up at her aunt. 'What beautiful words to write about you.' Her tender response was in stark contrast to the reaction at the other end of the table. Birgitta gave an indignant 'Humph!' and followed up the unladylike noise with the words: 'We'll see about that!'

'What happens to the bulk of the estate and Willow Marsh Manor?' Tobias demanded.

Mr Symonds braced himself once more, then spoke rapidly and with the utmost formality: '"The remainder of my estate, all monies and incomes from my investments, rents, leases, shipping interests and mining ventures, plus the property known as Willow Marsh Manor, I leave in a trust, managed by my daughter Miranda, for my granddaughter, Susanna Maud Delamere, until she cometh of age."'

'No!' screamed Birgitta Delamere.

Tobias leapt to his feet and slammed his fat fist down on the table, knocking over a milk jug. The rest of the Meissen crockery shuddered and rattled. 'Damn him to hell and back! He scorned me! He scorned me again!' His domed pate gleamed with a fine sheen of sweat and his face reddened with fury. 'To overlook his own brother – his only male heir! For the sake of a chit of a girl!'

'Oh, for heaven's sake, Uncle,' Miranda Delamere said calmly. 'Did you really think he would leave his own family penniless?'

'Adrian and I are the last surviving Delameres!'

'Do not include me in this!' The young man with the long black hair flushed with embarrassment, rose hastily from his seat and strode out of the room. The doctor and the lawyer looked like they wanted to follow him.

'Last surviving Delameres?' Miranda scoffed. Now named as the future chatelaine of Willow Marsh and secure in her future, her patience with her uncle had finally snapped. 'What are Susanna and I, then? Are we not Delameres?'

Susanna looked like she wanted the ground to open up and swallow her whole. 'I never meant to cause—'

Her aunt reached out to stop her. 'Don't you dare apologise to them, Susanna!'

'Who knows what she is?' Birgitta screamed across the table, jabbing a podgy ringed finger in the direction of the young girl. 'Who knows what she is with a father like Freddie!'

Freddie? Frederick? Major Frederick Delamere? Lavender's breath caught in his throat as his memory lurched into action. He cursed silently as the final pieces of the puzzle fell into place.

Still on his feet, Tobias pointed a fat, accusing finger at Miranda and Symonds and suggested they had colluded to deny him his rightful inheritance. Miranda and the lawyer hotly denied the charge.

Lavender stopped listening. He stared in horror at the sweet young woman who sat two seats away from him. How could such an innocent be the daughter of that monster, Frederick Delamere? And why the devil had this family – and that dreadful case – come back to haunt him after all this time?

58

Chapter Seven

Horse Guards,
Whitehall, London
June, 1803

Lavender and Woods cantered across the dusty parade ground towards the creamy stone Palladian facade of Horse Guards. The barracks and stables of this military headquarters rippled with activity and a grim sense of urgency, suggesting a deployment was imminent.

Red-coated cavalrymen on powerful, snorting horses wound their way between rows of foot soldiers on parade. Wagons stacked high with provisions and equipment crunched slowly across the gravel, hauled by pairs of straining dray horses.

It's easy sometimes to forget we're at war again, Lavender thought.

After an uneasy truce, lasting barely a year, Britain had once more declared war against France. For most of the British, Napoleon Bonaparte was a distant, evil spectre; a nightmarish ghoul used by irritated mothers to frighten naughty children into behaving. But the brilliant French general and his vast professional armies were a real threat to the frenzied men here in Whitehall. Horse Guards was the beating heart of the British Army. Lavender could smell the excitement – and the fear – of the men, mingling with the stink of the stables and the faint tang of gunpowder.

They slowed to a trot as they passed beneath the main archway into the central courtyard. In the turret above their heads, the bells of the seven-foot clock rang out the quarter hour.

A sentry challenged their approach. Lavender pulled his bronze-topped tipstaff, his badge of office, out of his coat pocket and made enquiries about the 1st Royal Dragoons.

The sentry told them the regiment was preparing to disembark for the Peninsula and directed them to the office of Major Illingworth.

The major seemed a conscientious young officer but he was as hard-pressed as everyone else here with the pressure of the deployment. His pale eyes widened with alarm when they explained they needed to interview Lieutenant Clarke and Major Delamere about the death of a young woman in Hampstead.

'We only returned from India a month ago and we're leaving for Europe tomorrow evening,' he spluttered. 'We're as busy as the devil in a high wind.'

'I'm sure it won't take long,' Lavender lied. His stomach clenched in frustration at the thought that his main suspects were about to depart for the continent.

'I'll take you to see Colonel Grant.' Illingworth led the way out of the room but stopped in the doorway and turned back, his face shadowed with uncertainty. 'How did she die?'

'She was murdered – strangled.' Lavender said. He saw Illingworth flinch and added: 'The bastards who did it shoved her body down a well.'

The colour drained from Illingworth's face and left it ashen against the vivid red and gold-braided cloth of his uniform. He broke eye contact with Lavender and hesitated as if he wanted to say something. Then he drew back his shoulders and stood up straighter. 'Colonel Grant's office is this way.'

'Good grief, man, are you aware there's a war on!' the colonel boomed when Lavender explained the purpose of their visit. Spittle flew from his mouth as he yelled. He glared through narrowed piggy eyes at Lavender and Woods across his cluttered desk as if they were a pair of irritants and time-wasters sent by Bonaparte himself to distract him and his officers from their vital war work.

'It won't take long, sir,' Lavender said firmly.

60

'It had better not!' The colonel sent Illingworth to fetch Major Delamere and Lieutenant Clarke while he continued to sign and stamp the papers handed to him by his impassive aide. A blank-faced secretary sat at a lower table, quill in hand. His staff were obviously used to these outbursts.

They didn't have long to wait. Illingworth soon returned with the other two officers, both in uniform. They saluted Colonel Grant and stood to attention in front of his desk.

Lavender would have recognised Frederick Delamere anywhere from Lizzie's description of his face. An ugly purple scar ran up his chin and cut through the corner of his lips, distorting his mouth. His thick black moustache was partially stained yellow with the nicotine from his snuff.

Beside him, Lieutenant Clarke, a younger man with curly black hair, shuffled nervously from one boot to the other, occasionally glancing for reassurance at the senior officer beside him.

'This detective wants to ask you about a dead girl,' Colonel Grant said to his officers. 'He claims she died on the night we stayed at Hampstead last week.'

'How unfortunate,' Delamere murmured. His words sounded sarcastic and there was no compassion in his dark, scowling eyes. There was a hardness about his stance that went beyond battle-hardened. Lavender sensed cruelty.

'Her name was Nell, although she was known as Irish Nell on account of her accent,' Lavender said. 'She was a barmaid at The George and had long red hair.'

Colonel Grant leaned forward over his desk. 'Do either of you remember her?'

Delamere's face remained impassive. 'I'm afraid not, sir.'

'No, sir.' Clarke echoed after a quick glance at the man beside him.

'Yet we've two witnesses who saw you with the girl. They claim you spent a lot of time with her that evening,' Lavender said hastily. 'One said she sat on your knee for a while, Major Delamere.'

The major shrugged and continued to look straight ahead at his superior officer. He licked his ravaged lips and gave a half smile that was more of a leer. 'What can I say? I'm an attractive man.'

Clarke snorted with laughter. Colonel Grant shot them both a warning glance. 'We need to take this seriously, gentlemen – a young woman is dead. The detective is only doing his job.'

Delamere straightened his frame. 'My apologies, Detective, for not being more concerned about your tavern wench but I'm damned if I can see what this has to do with me. There were several women serving at the tavern that evening if I remember rightly – and several of them sat on my knee.'

Grant turned and spoke directly to Lavender. 'There you have it, Lavender. My officers remember nothing that will help you find your killer.'

Lavender ignored him. 'Did either of you take a woman upstairs to the garret in the tavern?'

'We did not,' Delamere said. 'We were together all night and we returned to camp at the same time.'

'How much had you had to drink?' Woods asked.

'The usual brandy or two,' Clarke said. 'We weren't in our cups if that's what you're thinking, Constable.'

'Did you return to your wives at the camp?' Lavender asked. 'Can anyone else verify when you returned to base?'

'I'm unmarried. Neither of us has a wife,' Delamere said casually.

Clarke grinned. 'Yes, we're bachelor boys – married to the British Army.'

Colonel Grant's eyes narrowed beneath his bushy brows. 'What are you implying, with this line of questioning, Lavender? Why do my officers need to verify their movements on that night?'

'Irish Nell was brutally raped then strangled. Later, her body was dumped down a disused well. As I said, two witnesses claimed the young woman was seen mostly in the company of Major Delamere and Lieutenant Clarke that evening.'

Colonel Grant's bushy eyebrows met in a frown across the bridge of his nose and his florid facial skin became a darker shade of claret. 'Are you suggesting my officers had something to do with this whore's death?' For a moment, Lavender thought Grant would explode. Then his jaw set and he fixed Lavender with a steely glare. 'My officers are gentlemen,' he growled in a voice that brooked no argument. 'The officers of the Ist Royal Dragoons *always* behave in a courteous and exemplary manner when wearing the regimental uniform. To suggest otherwise – for anyone else to suggest otherwise – is calumny.'

A small clock ticked on the mantelpiece. It was the only sound in the strained atmosphere of the office.

'Well, someone killed the poor girl,' Woods said.

Lavender didn't waver beneath Grant's glare. 'It's my job to follow where the evidence leads.'

'What evidence?' The loose flesh of Delamere's mouth quivered as he snarled. 'The testimony of a tap boy and some half-pissed local farmer? You'll have a hard time making claims based on hearsay and tittle-tattle stick against us, Lavender.'

'I think this interview is over,' Colonel Grant snapped. 'Major Delamere is right. Unless you've some hard evidence to support your preposterous suspicions, Lavender, it's time you left. Major Illingworth will show you out.'

Lavender bowed to hide his frustration. 'Thank you for your time, gentlemen – Colonel.' *Don't leave the country*, he wanted to add as he and Woods followed Illingworth out of the room. But there was no point. By midnight tomorrow, his chief suspects would be sailing for the continent on the evening tide.

He had one last chance to try and glean something useful from this visit. Once they were away from Colonel Grant's office, Lavender turned to Illingworth: 'Is there something you'd like to tell us?'

Illingworth stopped in his tracks. His pale, almost colourless eyes blinked rapidly. 'What? I don't understand...'

'I think you do,' Lavender pushed. 'Something's bothering you, Major. Ever since we first told you about the fate of that poor girl, I sensed you wanted to tell us something. I can see you're a decent man. I think you need to unburden yourself.'

Illingworth glanced down the corridor behind them and said quietly: 'Follow me.'

He led them outside and round the edge of the administrative block into the shadows of the stables. A few yards away, a young ensign rubbed down a sweating horse with a large handful of straw. Stripped to the waist, with his braces dangling behind him, he whistled while he worked and paid them no attention.

'Look, it's not much help to you – and this goes no further than us three – but this has happened before.'

'When?'

'In India, last winter. Two girls disappeared. One was later found dead – strangled. They were the nieces of one of the village elders and a deputation came to the fort and accused Delamere and Clarke of the atrocity.'

'What happened?'

Illingworth shrugged his shoulders. 'I'm not sure. It was covered up. The colonel wanted to keep the peace. Money exchanged hands in reparation and the village elders departed. The body of the second girl was never found.'

'Why weren't they court-marshalled?' Woods asked.

A large wagon piled high with crates and barrels rumbled towards them. Illingworth shook his head and waited until the noisy vehicle had passed before he spoke. 'Low-caste native girls in India are...' He paused and licked his lips while he searched for the right word. '...expendable. The regiment was about to march to put down an uprising. Colonel Grant lets nothing stand in the way of regimental honour and he needs Delamere. He's a brilliant tactician – brilliant but brutal. The men...' He hesitated again. 'Many men fear him – but all admire him. He has a well-deserved reputation for cruelty.'

Lavender and Woods winced.

'Well, there won't be any justice for Irish Nell in England either, unless you're prepared to stand up in court and tell a jury what you've just told us.' Lavender said.

Illingworth shook his head. 'No. I'm sorry for the girl – and I think someone needs to investigate those two further – but I can't get involved.'

'I'm not a miracle-worker.' The frustration made Lavender brittle. 'I can investigate Delamere and Clarke until I'm blue in the face, but I can't stop them leaving the country and get justice for these poor abused women unless witnesses like you help me.'

Illingworth looked guilty but he shook his head. 'I've said enough. I've got the regiment to think of.'

'You weren't thinking about the regiment two minutes ago when you told us about those poor Indian gals,' Woods said angrily. 'You're scared of Delamere as well, aren't you?'

65

Anger flashed across Illingworth's face. Woods had touched a nerve. 'In all conscience, I can do no more.' The major turned and marched off.

Lavender fell silent. Disappointment rose like bile in his throat.

But Woods hadn't finished with Illingworth yet. 'Delamere's the leader of that pair, isn't he?'

Illingworth nodded. 'Lieutenant Clarke is the weaker character, yes. He looks to Delamere in everything.'

'Aye,' Woods retorted. 'Even in murder.'

Lavender turned and stomped out of the barracks. Outside, he kicked the wall and swore. He felt sick with anger and frustration. 'I can't believe it! We have our murderers – but they're going to get away!'

'You never know,' Woods said stoically, his eyes on Lavender's scuffed boots. 'With luck, they'll end up on the receivin' end of a French musket ball.'

'I'll be damned if I'll wait for Napoleon Bonaparte to do my job for me!'

'Well, either way, sir, they're not worth the ruination of a good pair of boots – especially as you've got to find a shilling for a new periwig.'

Chapter Eight

Willow Marsh Manor, Cambridgeshire
Early September, 1813

'You and my father barely talked to each other for the last fifty years!' Miranda Delamere shouted at her uncle.

'Stop this now!'

Woods' voice jolted Lavender out of the shocked trance he'd sunk into the moment he'd realised the link between Susanna and Frederick Delamere. The family were still arguing. 'It's the man's funeral,' Woods pleaded. 'Show him some respect.'

'My uncle has no respect for my late father,' Miranda Delamere snapped. 'He only cares about his money.'

'Don't you insult my husband – you dried-up, twisted old jilt!' Birgitta Delamere screamed.

'Be careful, madam!' Miranda replied. 'Have a care for your allowance – remember who pays it now!'

Woods leaned forward to intervene again but Lavender grabbed his arm and pulled him back. 'It's time we retired for the night. I've had enough. Unless they murder each other, we've no jurisdiction here.'

But before they could stand, the double doors at the entrance to the great hall flew open. Two young men strode energetically towards them and the atmosphere in the room changed dramatically.

'Cousin Hal!' Ursula shrieked in delight. She flew out of her seat in a flurry of black muslin and ribbons and raced towards the first man, a handsome fellow in his late twenties who wore his golden-tawny hair fashionably disarranged and complemented it with an exquisitely cut coat and buckskin breeches.

'Ursula!' scolded her mother. But even Birgitta Delamere's forceful personality seemed muted by the sheer animal magnetism radiating from the handsome and grinning young man gallantly bent over her daughter's hand.

His companion, a darker-skinned chap with a prominent nose and nervous eyes, hung back. There was something slightly foreign about this fellow's clothing and appearance. He had a black stock tie wound round his neck instead of a cravat. His plain grey coat was looser, almost shapeless, and his black waistcoat unadorned with the embroidery or embellishment so fashionable in England. Lavender's sharp eyes also spotted a bracelet of tubular painted beads the young man wore around his left wrist. He trailed awkwardly in the wake of the blond Adonis.

Hal Pammenter offered his arm to his cousin and gallantly escorted her back to the table. 'Aunt Miranda, Little Susie.' He disentangled himself from Ursula and gave both women an affectionate kiss. They looked delighted to see him and ignored his companion for the moment.

Tobias and Birgitta glanced away coldly when Hal turned to greet them. He ignored their rebuffal and turned back to Miranda. 'I'm sorry I've missed Uncle Lawrence's funeral, truly I am.'

Uncle?

'He was a good man who treated me well,' Hal continued, 'far better than I probably deserved.' He sat down in one of the two remaining empty seats at the table and his friend slid down beside him. 'We've had a devilish difficult journey from London – and of course, the damned river has flooded the road again. It took us ages to find a sober boatman in Ely.'

'That's what we found too,' Woods muttered.

Mrs Mabberley hurried to the side of the new arrivals with the port decanter in one hand and a jug of ale in the other.

Hal glanced across the table at Lavender and Woods. 'Who are your guests, Aunt?'

'This is Detective Stephen Lavender and Constable Woods from Bow Street in London,' Miranda said. 'Lavender, this is our distant, but very dear cousin, Mr Henry Pammenter.'

Hal's light brown eyes were the same gold-tinted tawny shade as his hair and they twinkled with mischief. 'Police officers, eh? What on earth have you been up to now, Cousin Ursula?'

The young woman shrieked with laughter as if this was the wittiest thing she'd heard all year. 'Now, that *would* be telling!' She leaned across the table and patted his hand flirtatiously.

'Lavender and his constable were brought here as part of a mysterious hoax,' Miranda explained.

'A hoax?'

'Yes, someone claiming to be my sister, Olivia, invited them here to solve a murder.'

'Murder!' Hal exclaimed. 'This is indeed a cruel jest – especially as it comes so soon after Uncle Lawrence's death. It's also cruel to use Aunt Olivia's name.'

'Why so?' Lavender asked.

Hal turned his leonine eyes towards him and fixed him with a frank, unblinking stare. 'Because my Aunt Olivia is dead, sir. I saw her obituary earlier this year in an old copy of the *New York Post*, which had found its way into our London office.'

'And you didn't think to inform any of the family about this?' Tobias asked brusquely.

The young man shrugged. 'I wasn't sure anyone would be interested after all this time.' He turned back to Lavender. 'I work as a lawyer for a shipping company at the Port of London. Keeping up to date with the events in the Americas is useful for our business.'

Lavender sat back, sighing softly with disappointment. He'd harboured a lingering hope that Olivia Quinn would suddenly appear from behind one of the threadbare tapestries on the walls of the banqueting hall to explain why he and Woods had been summoned to this rural backwater. Miranda had been right all along; they'd been the victims of a cruel jest. He glanced around the table and wondered which one of them had penned that damned letter.

'She's dead? My sister is dead?' Miranda's dark eyes blinked furiously in her pale face. Lucy Pammenter stepped forward and placed a comforting hand on Miranda's shoulder.

Hal nodded sympathetically. 'Yes, I'm sorry, Aunt Miranda.' He reached for the port decanter and topped up his glass and that of his silent companion.

After a strained silence, she shrugged and gathered herself together. 'Don't be. She is – and was – nothing to me.'

Hal glanced round the table and gave a small frown. 'Why isn't Adrian here?'

'He stepped outside for some air,' Ursula said. 'They've been arguing again – Uncle Lawrence left Willow Marsh Manor and just about everything else to Susanna. But you've done well, Hal – five hundred a year! You could live comfortably on that – and marry.'

Hal laughed and he poured himself more port. 'I'd need a good deal more than that before I take a wife.'

Disappointment flashed across the young woman's face.

'I'll explain your inheritance to you later, Pammenter,' Mr Symonds said hastily.

But Hal wasn't listening to either of them. His wide-set eyes were fixed on the young heiress next to Miranda. His gaze was affectionate, tinged with a little sadness. 'So, Little Susie, you've inherited the lot, have you?'

'I never expected it,' she replied with a modest blush.

'Let's hope it's a blessing for you.'

'Well, some of us expected it,' Miranda said, glaring at her Uncle Toby. 'The Willow Marsh Estate now passes in its entirety to Susanna and her descendants.'

'Naturally, I shall challenge this in the courts of Chancery,' Tobias informed them pompously. 'Willow Marsh Manor has been in the Delamere family since the time of the Conqueror. It's inconceivable the estate should pass out of the family into the hands of that chit's future husband.'

'Tread carefully, Uncle,' Miranda replied through gritted teeth. 'Or you may find yourself without the means to pay for your tailor, never mind a Chancery lawyer.'

Tobias bristled again but some of the fire seemed to have gone out of him. 'You would threaten me and my allowance, madam?'

'I would.'

Hal raised his hand and intervened. 'Now, now. Let's not quarrel today. Today of all days – especially as we've a guest who's travelled halfway across the world to meet you.' He finally turned towards his silent companion. 'Besides which,' he added mysteriously, 'the situation with regard to Willow Marsh Manor may not be quite as clear cut as you think.'

'As a trained lawyer, yourself,' Mr Symonds intervened sharply, 'you'll be aware of the strength of a man's last will and testament.'

'Ah, but sometimes we have to do what's right – rather than just what's legal – don't we?'

'What the devil are you talking about, man?' Tobias asked.

Miranda's eyes flicked suspiciously over the quiet young man at his side. Lavender sensed her unease.

'Susanna isn't Lawrence's only legitimate grandchild. May I present my new friend and acquaintance, Robert.'

'Robert who?' Tobias demanded.

But the young foreigner was already speaking: 'Good evening, ma'am – sir – ladies. I'm delighted to meet y'all.' His accent was unmistakable: American. The older Delameres tensed. The War of the Rebellion had not been forgiven by the British ruling class. Most of them still assumed a disapproving stance whenever they encountered a rebellious colonial.

'So, what is he? This Robert?' Tobias asked sharply. His eyes lingered on the young man's beaded bracelet. 'One of your passing fancies from a Cheapside molly house, eh Hal?'

Lavender raised a shocked eyebrow and Woods stiffened beside him, but the rest of the family were either too fascinated by the foreigner to notice, or didn't understand the implications of Tobias's malicious comment.

'You're an American?' Miranda asked sharply.

'Yes, ma'am. I was born on Manhattan Island, New York but raised in the Carolinas, near Charleston.'

'What are you doing over here, Mr – what did you say his name was, Hal?' Ursula's thin face turned enquiringly towards her cousin.

'It's Quinn,' Hal said after a slight pause. 'Mr Robert Quinn.'

Behind Miranda, Lucy Pammenter stumbled and knocked over the walking cane resting against her mistress's wicker wheelchair. It fell to the flagstone floor with a clatter, making everyone jump. In the silence that followed, Lavender heard the ancient rafters above their heads shifting and creaking in the night wind. The human resentment washing across the table in waves towards the young man was nothing compared to that primeval creaking. Even the bones and sinews of Willow Marsh Manor seemed to object to Quinn's presence.

72

'Quinn?' Miranda Delamere's throat strangled the name as she uttered it. Birgitta's jaw dropped open, revealing the blackened teeth in the back of her mouth. Even Tobias looked like he'd just seen a ghost.

'Yes, ma'am,' the young man continued blithely, unaware of the dramatic effect he'd had on the older adults in the room. 'I'm the son of Peter and Olivia Quinn, both formerly of Ely, Cambridgeshire. I believe we're related.'

'And you thought to bring him here, Hal – today of all days?' Miranda's voice rose with anger.

Robert Quinn blushed beneath her scrutiny. 'I'm mightily pleased to meet you, ma'am,' he said awkwardly. 'I believe you're my aunt.' It was as much a question as a statement.

Lavender remembered his conversation with the old man in the coach, who claimed the two Delamere sisters had fallen out over the same man. Presumably the warring siblings had been Miranda and Olivia and the object of their mutual affections was Peter Quinn, father of this embarrassed young American.

'The timing of this is bad, I know,' Hal confessed hastily. 'I never meant to upset you, Aunt Miranda. Like I said, I read about Robert's existence in Cousin Olivia's obituary earlier this year. It said she'd left one son. I wrote and invited him over here to meet his grandfather. I thought Uncle Lawrence might like it. I knew he'd never forgive Olivia but I thought he'd be curious to meet her boy. It took many months to organise this – and Lawrence's death has rather overtaken events.'

'So, he's arrived just in time to claim an inheritance.' Miranda's voice was pure ice. 'How convenient.'

'That was never my intention, ma'am,' Quinn said hastily. 'I've just been excited to meet y'all. I'm an only child and never knew any family other than my mother and father.'

73

Miranda smoothed down the black silk of her gown in a desperate attempt to control her temper. 'It might not have been your intention to make a claim, Mr Quinn – but I see it was Hal's.'

Mr Symonds leaned forward towards Quinn and glared at him through his pince-nez. 'Do you have any proof of your identity, young man?'

'Yes, sir,' Quinn said hastily, 'I've several documents and testimonials in my trunk. I'll be mightily pleased to show them to you.'

Tobias let out a harsh laugh. 'So, for the second time tonight, the ghost of my niece, Olivia, has risen from her trollop's grave to haunt us.'

Robert Quinn reddened. 'Trollop, sir?'

'Yes, Mr Quinn. Trollop.'

'My mother was a decent woman, a virtuous woman.'

No one round the table looked convinced. 'Olivia was no better than she ought to be,' Birgitta added cryptically.

Sensing another family row was about to erupt, Lavender pushed back his chair and rose to his feet. 'If you'll excuse me, ma'am, Constable Woods and I will retire now.' He bowed stiffly before she could reply and the two of them left the great hall. He knew his own room was up at the top of the wooden staircase at the far end of the medieval hall, but he needed fresh air to clear his head and a quiet chat with Woods.

Chapter Nine

It was still dry and clear outside and the silvery moon rode high in the velvet sky through flimsy skittish clouds. 'Let's take a walk around the grounds,' Lavender said, relishing the breeze. 'The atmosphere in that hall was stifling.'

They followed a gravel path that hugged the stone walls of the south tower and led them to the formal terraced gardens on the far side of the building. Not that they could see much out here. The beeswax candles in the chandeliers of the great hall cast yellow pools of light out of the tall windows, illuminating the sharp angles of the raised beds, which gradually merged into the blackness of the night. Lavender was reminded again of the dark stillness of the country compared to the restless capital. Only the rustle of sedge and reeds and the deep-throated croak of a frog disturbed the peaceful night.

'This is a queer case,' Woods said, articulating Lavender's own thoughts exactly. 'Why would someone write to Bow Street and ask us to come here if there's no murder committed?'

'There's no crime to solve – yet,' Lavender agreed. 'But if this family continue to argue like this, I wouldn't be surprised if someone wasn't killed soon.'

Woods laughed. 'Yes, if looks could kill – young Robert Quinn is already dead. I've never seen a woman so unhappy to meet her new nephew.'

'That's if he *is* her nephew,' Lavender said dryly. 'Funerals – and the prospect of money and an inheritance – can bring all sorts of ghouls and fraudsters out of the woodpile.'

Lavender sensed rather than saw Woods nod his wise old head beside him. 'It reminds me of the time Betsy's rich Uncle Billy died back in Southwark. He weren't rich like Lawrence Delamere but he had a few nice pieces of furniture and a bit of cash put by. He were a widower and had fell out with his two daughters. They hadn't spoken for years. But this didn't stop the two of them hirin' handcarts and rushin' to his house as soon as they got wind of his passin'.

'They met up on the corner of Snowsfields and Crosby Row and realised with a shock they both had the same thing in mind. They hitched up their skirts and sped off in a frenzy, tryin' to elbow each other out of the way and ram each other's handcarts. Both were determined to get to their dead da's house first. It were quite a sight as they sped down the street.'

Lavender grinned at the image. 'Who got there first?'

Woods heaved his broad shoulders in a huge shrug. 'It didn't matter in the end. It turned out that old Uncle Billy had married again since his daughters last saw him. His widow met them on the doorstep and sent them packin' with a flea in their ears.'

Lavender laughed. 'Death brings out the worst in human greed.'

Woods' head turned sharply in his direction. 'You don't think that young fella, Quinn, is genuine?'

'I don't know – I suspect no one here is exactly what they seem to be. And heaven knows where Hal Pammenter fits into the family.'

'He's the old man's by-blow, isn't he?'

'If he is, they're the most tolerant family in Christendom. It's one thing for the gentry to educate their illegitimate offspring – many of them do. But it's quite another to welcome them into the bosom of the family like this.'

Woods nodded again. 'That does seem a bit easy, like.'

'But they're not easy people,' Lavender reminded him. 'And one of them is the trickster who wrote the false letter that drew us here '

'That's a disturbin' thought,' Woods growled. 'Why do it? Why write to Bow Street and ask for us by name if there's no crime to solve? It's a queer prank.'

'That's exactly what I thought. It was also convenient for the writer of the letter, whomever he or she may be, that we were already in the vicinity at the Cambridge assizes.'

Woods' voice lowered to a growl. 'What are you sayin'?'

'I don't think it's a coincidence we were so close, Ned. I think the letter-writer knew we were in Cambridge. Someone is following our movements.'

'So, this isn't a simple prank?'

'No, there's nothing simple about it at all. The whole thing has been carefully thought out and planned – but I don't know why. And there's something else not quite right.'

'What?'

Lavender hesitated a moment, but there was no escaping this revelation; Woods needed to know. 'Do you remember that tragic case we had about ten years ago, where a young tavern wench was murdered and her body was pushed down a well?'

Woods hesitated, then nodded. 'Yes, Irish Nell she were called, the poor lass. Hellish case that.'

'Well, we arrested and convicted the son of this house, Major Frederick Delamere, for the crime.'

'Gawd's teeth!'

'I've only just made the connection.'

'Are you sure it's the same family?'

'Yes, I believe so. They call him Freddie but we knew him as Frederick Delamere. He is – was – the father of that young heiress, Susanna.'

'Heaven and hell! Do you think they know it was us who arrested him? Is that why we're here? Is someone out for revenge, do you think?'

'Revenge might be their motive.'

'Delamere had some family at the trial – an old fella, if I remember rightly.'

'Yes.' Lavender's memory came back. 'And a veiled woman.'

'His father and his wife, do you think?'

Lavender shrugged. 'I don't know.' Something still niggled him. Something he'd forgotten. He lowered his voice further, grateful to be sharing his unease with Woods. 'I think we need to be on our guard, Ned. There's forces at work here I can't fathom.'

'Thank goodness we're leavin' tomorrow mornin'.'

Lavender didn't reply. His sharp ears caught the gentle crunch of gravel. Sound carried in the stillness of the night. Someone else was out there in the garden with them.

'We *are* leavin' first thing tomorrow mornin', aren't we?' Woods persisted desperately. 'At noon, when the boatman comes back for us.'

Lavender's ears strained against the quiet of the night, but he heard nothing more. 'Maybe,' he said slowly.

'What do you mean, "maybe"?'

'I don't think the writer of that mysterious letter has finished toying with us yet. Be on your guard, Ned.'

Most of the beeswax candles in the chandeliers and candelabra in the great hall had been snuffed out when Lavender returned. The impressive arsenal of medieval swords, shields and lances that towered up the walls took on a more sinister appearance in the half light, glimmering viciously above his head as he strode towards the wooden staircase leading up to his room in the north tower.

There were only three members of the household still left in the hall. Ursula Delamere, Hal Pammenter and Robert Quinn sat on the ancient oak settles around the huge smoke-blackened stone fireplace at the far end. A small fire still crackled in the grate. There was an air of relaxed familiarity about the group of young people. Ursula had pulled her legs up beneath her in a lewd and racy manner and leaned back against the cushions. Hal clutched the brandy decanter in one hand and a glass in the other.

Lavender wondered why the young woman was still up so late and – family or not – why she had been left unchaperoned with the two young men. His eyebrows rose higher in disapproval when he realised she also cradled a glass of the amber liquid in her slim hands. The normal rules of polite society clearly didn't apply to this godforsaken corner of England.

The group fell silent as he approached. Lavender sensed a faint, inexplicable undercurrent of resentment. He wished them goodnight and started to climb the twisting wooden staircase up to his chamber.

'May we see that letter in your possession, Detective?' Hal Pammenter called after him. 'The one supposedly written by Mrs Quinn.'

Lavender turned, pulled the crumpled note out of his pocket and passed it to him. Hal immediately handed it over to the young American.

Quinn shook his head the moment he laid eyes on the handwriting. 'My mother didn't write this – that's not her style of cursive. Besides which, she passed away nearly a year ago.'

'Then 'tis a strange mystery,' Hal said. 'Do you have a theory to explain this, Detective?'

'Not yet,' Lavender admitted.

'Well, if there's anything we can do to help solve this conundrum, please don't hesitate to ask. Quinn and I are as baffled as you – and we're annoyed someone is despoiling his mother's memory with such a prank.'

'To be fair, Cousin Hal – and no offence, Mr Quinn—' Ursula giggled, '— after eloping to America with her sister's fiancé, Aunt Olivia's memory is already rather tarnished in Cambridgeshire.'

Hal shot Ursula a warning glance but the girl didn't seem to care. The alcohol had flushed her cheeks and loosened her tongue. She continued to smile at the two men, oblivious to their discomfort. 'He's a detective,' she said, laughing. 'Don't you think he'll find out our history sooner or later?'

'It's not just that, Ursula,' Hal said softly, 'this is Quinn's mother you speak of with disrespect.'

She shrugged. 'No offence intended, Mr Quinn.'

'None taken, ma'am.'

'Is that what happened twenty years ago?' Lavender asked. 'Did Mrs Quinn really steal her sister's fiancé?'

Hal sighed. 'I suppose there's no point in trying to keep family secrets from you, Lavender. Yes, originally Aunt Miranda was betrothed to Quinn's father.'

'Their elopement must have been distressing for her,' Lavender said.

'I was only a small child at the time,' Hal continued, 'about six years old, I think, but I can still remember the upset – and the grief – in this household that summer. Uncle Lawrence's wife – my Aunt Gertrude – was already ill and very frail. The elopement upset her even more and she died soon after the couple departed. My uncle adored Aunt Gertrude and he felt – whether fairly or not, I don't know – that Olivia's wild actions had killed her mother.'

'I'm sorry to hear that, sir.' Quinn squirmed with discomfort.

Hal nodded. 'Soon after this, Aunt Miranda had to go away to London to help nurse an elderly relative of her mother who had taken ill. It was a miserable year, nothing but sickness, sadness and funerals '

'My condolences,' Lavender said glibly, 'but I'm confused – why on earth, after all that misery and distress, did you think your Uncle Lawrence would be pleased to meet Olivia's son?'

Hal shrugged. 'It was worth a try. Robert is, was, Uncle Lawrence's grandchild, after all.'

Lavender turned to Robert Quinn. 'Did you know anything about this scandal when Pammenter invited you over to England?'

In the glow from the fire, Lavender saw another flush of embarrassment creep up Quinn's neck above his shirt collar and stock tie. 'No, sir, I didn't. My parents were truly happy with each other and they rarely talked of their early lives here. I knew nothing about the circumstances of their departure for America. I'm an only child and they're both dead now, so when I received Hal's invitation to the family plantation—'

'It's an estate,' Hal corrected. 'Not a plantation.'

'I apologise, sir, yes, estate. I felt real curious about my English kith and kin and thought to come over here and meet them. I was mightily excited to have a family again, although it wasn't until I'd landed in England I learned the truth about my parents' elopement.'

'I thought Uncle Lawrence might appreciate a reconciliation with Olivia's son before he died,' Hal persisted. 'I underestimated Aunt Miranda's reaction. That was a mistake on my part.'

'Oh, she'll forgive you soon enough, Hal,' Ursula said, 'She always does.'

'Were you brought up here, sir?' Lavender enquired.

Hal nodded. 'Yes. I'm a poor relation of sorts, etcetera etcetera.'

'Etcetera etcetera?' Ursula teased softly with a half-smile and a raised eyebrow.

Hal ignored her. 'Uncle Lawrence and Aunt Miranda were always kind and generous to me.'

Ursula's burst out into laughter. 'Kind and generous? That's an understatement!' Her thin body shook with amusement and the brandy swirled in her glass. 'They spoilt you and treated you like a son!'

'Well, perhaps,' Hal said with a small smile.

'Oh, don't worry, Mr Quinn,' Ursula said. 'Aunt Miranda will mellow soon enough and accept you. She always does.'

'I sure hope so,' Robert Quinn drawled. 'I've come a long way and it would be good to feel more welcome around here.'

'You have my sympathies, Mr Quinn,' Lavender said dryly as another wave of weariness washed over him. 'It's a long way to travel if you're not wanted. I know exactly how you feel. Now, if you'll excuse me, gentlemen, Miss Ursula – I'll retire for the night.'

Chapter Ten

Lavender's chamber at the top of the north tower was a chilly room but richly furnished. A huge dark-oak Jacobean cupboard dominated one wall. It was a stately and beautiful object with fluted columns, architrave and a carved frieze along the top. Designed in two parts, it had a column of large drawers that reached almost to the ceiling on the left-hand side and a cupboard large enough to conceal a man on the right.

Lavender examined the carving closer. Even the drawer fronts with their small brass handles had been intricately worked with swans, coronets and floral emblems. The workmanship was exquisite; despite its age, the door clicked open and shut almost silently. A few old coats hung on hooks inside.

On the opposite wall was a single bed with clean bedlinen, a feather mattress and a tall headboard carved with the same emblems as the vast cupboard. Water for washing and shaving stood in a jug on a small table by the casement window. There were no drapes and the brilliant silver light of the moon poured through the leaded panes onto the soft rug covering the floorboards.

Lavender took off his shoes, coat and waistcoat, pulled out his book from his bag and, plumping up his pillows, he lay down on the eiderdown to read for a while. His mind was uneasy and he knew it would be a while before he would sleep. The flickering glow from the single candle, combined with the moonlight, gave the illumination he needed to pick out the words on the page but he struggled to concentrate.

He couldn't believe this damned case had come back to haunt him. Of all the mysteries he'd solved over the past thirteen years, his resolution of the murder of Irish Nell gave him the least satisfaction and his behaviour back then still filled him with guilt and left him with a bad taste in his mouth. It didn't matter how many times he told himself he'd done the right thing and he'd taken a vicious criminal off the streets – he'd compromised his own integrity, broken the law, and lied to his best friend and partner in the process.

Young, foolish and desperate to convict Delamere, he'd entered into a hurtful conspiracy and *chosen* to deceive his loyal constable. Even after all this time, he suspected that if Ned knew the truth, he wouldn't forgive him. *You're tired,* he told himself. *Sleep on it; the situation will look better in the morning.*

Sighing, he rubbed his eyes, blew out the candle and let his head fall back onto the pillow.

He found himself swaying in mid-air. It took him a moment to realise he was climbing down a rope ladder into the hot and sulphurous stinking depths of hell. His eyes and ears strained against the darkness. Water dripped ominously around him. Why was it so hot down here? The only light came from a circular pinprick high above. He was in a well. The old well outside The George tavern in Hampstead where they'd found Irish Nell.

A child's piteous cry echoed eerily. *Oh God, no.* It was Baby Alice. He'd brought his child into this godforsaken hellhole, strapped to his back. While his scrambled brain tried to make sense of this sick twist, his boots splashed into foul, brackish water. He'd reached the bottom of the well.

And he and Alice weren't alone.

84

A blast of cold air made him shiver. He turned his head, distracted, and glanced up. A figure loomed menacingly out of the shadows above him, oozing malevolence. It grabbed little Alice and yanked her away from him. Screaming, he lashed out – but the figure dodged his blows and disappeared with a soft click, taking his precious child with it.

Drenched in sweat, Lavender sat upright in the semi-darkness of dawn, yelling like a wounded animal. He threw back the covers and thrashed around, fumbling for his tinderbox.

Every fibre of his being, every instinct, was on fire.

This was no dream. Someone else, some menacing phantom, had been in the room with him.

The wick caught and the darkness receded. His room was empty, the apparition gone.

He strode to his coat, which hung on a hook on the back of the door, and pulled his loaded pistol out from the pocket. Cocking it, he lifted the latch and stepped out onto the wooden landing.

There was no obvious route up to the battlements at the top of the tower and when he descended the wooden staircase swiftly and silently in his stockinged feet to the cavernous gloom of the medieval hall below, no mysterious figure was pelting across the flagstone floor. Above him, the arsenal of deadly weapons decorating the stone walls glinted in the weak light from his candle. For a moment, he doubted himself. He'd been convinced the sound of the latch had been the soft click he'd heard and the cold blast of air had come through his open door. No. His instincts were right. The intruder had been real.

He climbed the staircase to the chamber directly below his own. Raising his candle, he threw open the door.

Hal Pammenter and Robert Quinn lay in the twin beds, either side of the room. Hal was sound asleep but Quinn woke up, alarmed. 'Lavender! What's the matter, sir?'

'I'm looking for an intruder. Don't worry. Go back to sleep.' He stepped back and softly closed the door. *Could his visitor have been one of them?*

He returned to the ground floor of the tower. The bottom room, directly below Hal and Quinn's chamber, was a library. The air was heavy with the rich smell of old leather bindings and dusty parchment. The towering bookcases and glass display cabinets were shrouded in dark shadows but none of them were deep enough to conceal a full-grown man – or woman. *Woman?* Was his mysterious visitor a woman?

Another disturbing thought suddenly entered his head. He raced swiftly back up the staircase to his bedchamber and threw open the carved door to the vast cabinet. Nothing. No one hid there.

Sighing, he slumped down into a hard-backed chair by the window. Damn it. Was his mind playing tricks? Had he imagined the whole thing?

Something glinted in the candlelight on the small bedside table and the hairs on the back of his neck rose in horror. It was a small silver box. A snuff box. A very familiar snuff box. His late-night visitor had left him a present, only inches away from where his sleeping head had lain on the pillow. He felt sick to his stomach at the thought of the intrusion and the warped significance of this unwanted gift.

Cursing, he picked it up and held it up to the light of his candle. The light bounced off the delicate diamond pattern etched in glittering silver and the deep cobalt-blue enamel on the lid.

The Delamere family crest was unmistakable.

Chapter Eleven

Ten years ago
Southwark, London
June, 1803

Lavender sat beside the fireplace in his mother's parlour, staring into the ashes in the empty grate.

Ostensibly, he'd come in here to read but his book remained unopened in his hands. In truth, he wanted somewhere quiet to think, away from the bustle of the kitchen and the chatter of his family. His eyes drifted across the mantelpiece and his mother's much-loved collection of porcelain shepherdesses. He heard voices out in the hallway but was too lost in his thoughts to pay them much attention either.

Time was running out. Tomorrow, the Hampstead magistrate, Sir Robert Brody, would open the inquest into the death of Irish Nell at The George tavern. And he didn't have enough evidence to link those scurrilous villains, Delamere and Clarke, to the murder of the poor girl. Without it, his suspects would sail away from England on the evening tide and the case would never be solved. Irish Nell would be buried in a pauper's grave and her murder forgotten.

The unfairness of it all ate away at him and threatened to set off his indigestion again. He'd always known there were huge inequalities in the British justice system. Several times, Woods had suggested he should lower his expectations. But Lavender had never felt this disparity so keenly as he did today.

He ran his hand through his thick, wavy hair and remembered his wager with Ned. Once Sir Robert had adjourned the inquest through lack of evidence, Ned would haul him down to the barbers to have his head shaved. Then there would be an embarrassing trip to a second-hand stall to purchase a moth-eaten periwig. No doubt Ned would force him to wear it until he'd learned his lesson – and quite rightly so. It had been sheer arrogance to think he could make a difference in a system steeped for centuries in corruption and inequality.

The door opened and his mother entered, wiping her hands on her apron. 'You've a visitor, Stephen.'

Betsy Woods followed Alice Lavender into the room, clutching a shawl over her plump shoulders. Lavender rose to his feet quickly. 'Is everything all right, Betsy? Where's Ned and the boys?'

'Everything's fine, Stephen,' she replied. 'I've left the boys with my sister, Ginny. Ned's gone fishin' while it's still light. I just need a quiet word with you, if that's all right?' She gave his mother a pleading glance.

Alice Lavender nodded her silver-grey head and took the hint. 'I'll make us a pot of tea in the kitchen, Mrs Woods. You have your talk with Stephen and come through when you're ready.'

Lavender was grateful for his mother's discretion, but not surprised.

Feared and distrusted by most of their neighbours, the families of the Bow Street police officers were a tight-knit and supportive community. His parents and Ned and Betsy Woods had known each other for years, although they still remained formal in their manner of addressing each other. Lavender's younger sister, Elizabeth, often helped Betsy with her young boys, Eddie and Dan.

Betsy sat down in the chair on the opposite side of the hearth and stared into the empty grate, frowning. He couldn't read the expression in her soft brown eyes, but the tightening of her lips told him her errand was serious.

She pushed some unruly brown curls back inside her white cap and pulled a small silver box out of her pocket. 'I'll come straight to the point, Stephen. Ned has told me all about this latest case of yours and explained how you suspect that monster, Delamere, murdered the poor gal.' She fiddled with the silver box in her lap while she spoke.

'Yes. That's right. Delamere – and Lieutenant Clarke – are our main suspects.'

'Well, I think he did it,' she said firmly.

Her words didn't make sense, of course. Lavender waited for her to explain. The passion of her outburst, when it came, surprised him.

'I don't know nothin' about this Clarke chap, but Frederick Delamere is a black-hearted devil who deserves to hang. In fact, he's worse than the devil.' Her eyes gleamed with anger.

'How do you... what has he done to you, Betsy?' He tensed, dreading her answer.

'There ain't no easy way to tell you how I know this, Stephen, so I'm just goin' to say it as it all happened. Ten years ago, that ugly cove Delamere attacked my baby sister, Ginny.' She gave Lavender a meaningful look.

He frowned, conscious of the flush of embarrassment creeping up his neck. 'You mean he forced himself on her?'

Betsy nodded and glanced away.

Lavender swore and sat back in his chair, horrified. He knew Ginny Atkins well. She was a kind, cheerful young woman of about his own age. She often helped Betsy out with the boys and would have been barely more than a child herself ten years ago. The thought that Delamere had violated Ginny sickened and angered him. 'I'm so sorry, Betsy,' he spluttered. 'Ned never told me anything about this.'

'Ned never said anything because Ned doesn't know.'

'He doesn't know?'

'No. We never told him.'

'Why?'

'It happened at Ginny's workplace about three months before Ned and I were wed. She were in service in a lodgin' house in Tooley Street and Delamere were a guest there. Once Ned described his ravaged face, I knew it were the same man who despoiled our Ginny.' She gave a short cynical laugh. 'The devil even stole her hair ribbon as a souvenir!'

Lavender winced again. 'I'm sure Ned would have helped you if you'd told him what happened.'

'Oh yes, he'd have helped all right,' Betsy said, with mock cheerfulness. 'He were always real fond of little Ginny. He'd have tracked down Delamere, lynched him and spat on his corpse.'

'I'm sure…'

She waved her hand to silence him. 'You didn't know Ned back then, Stephen. He were a lot more passionate about things – a hot-headed damn-boy at times. He would have beaten Delamere to a pulp for hurtin' her – and hang the consequences to himself and us.'

Lavender understood. Right at this moment he also had a burning desire to rip Delamere's head off his shoulders and trample it underfoot.

'Besides which,' Betsy continued, 'there were another problem with Ginny reportin' the attack.'

'What problem?'

90

She held up the small silver snuff box towards him. 'She accidentally picked this up when she ran away. She hit him with it to make her escape – but she were still holdin' it when she ran out of the house.'

Lavender took the pretty, oval-shaped box from her and ran his finger along the delicate diamond pattern etched in glittering silver on its curved sides. A painting of a family crest adorned the deep cobalt-blue enamel lid. *The Delamere family crest?*

'I knew it were expensive,' Betsy continued, 'and I knew if she reported Delamere, he'd counter the accusation by accusin' her of theft.' She swallowed hard. Her curls quivered with indignation beneath her cap. 'There isn't a jury in the land who would believe a slip of a girl like Ginny over the word of a toff like Delamere.'

Lavender grimaced. It was the same hard truth he'd had to swallow earlier about Irish Nell and her barmaid friend, Lizzie. 'What happened next?'

'I hid the box and sent word to Ginny's employer that she were too ill to work. We held our breath – I expected Delamere to send the constables around to arrest her for stealin' the box. As it turned out, Delamere and his wife left the lodgin' house pretty sharp after that.'

'Wife?'

'Yes. He were stayin' there with his wife. She were expectin' their first child.' She paused, sensing his confusion. 'Does that matter – about his wife?'

'No, not at all. It's just earlier today Delamere claimed he was a bachelor, wedded to the army. None of the other officers corrected him and I'm sure they'd have known if he was a family man – or a widower.' There was an awkward pause as he tried to make sense of this. Then he shook his head. 'It doesn't matter. Please go on, Betsy, tell me more. Did... did Ginny recover?'

Betsy frowned and humphed. 'Well, the physical damage is healed – but she's still too shy of men for my likin'. It's as if she's scared another one will attack her.'

'I can understand that,' Lavender said sadly. 'After an experience like that it would have been hard for her to trust anyone again.'

'I don't think she'll ever wed.' He heard the catch in Betsy's throat.

'That will be a shame. Ginny will make some lucky man a lovely wife – and she's a natural mother.'

Hope suddenly leapt into Betsy's round brown eyes and he realised he'd just made a mistake. All the women in his acquaintance, from his mother and sisters to family friends like Betsy, were keen to see him settle down and wed. Now Betsy would think he had feelings for Ginny. 'What do you want me to do?' he asked hastily.

'Ned tells me you need evidence to link this cove to this horrible murder.'

'Yes, we do.'

She leaned forward and took his hand in her own, curling his fingers round the snuff box. 'Well, you have it now.'

'What do you mean?'

'It's Delamere's snuff box. Ginny says this is the family crest on the top and a picture of their fancy manor in Cambridgeshire. Use it to get that sick cove off the streets of London.'

He sat back in shock. 'Are you suggesting I plant this snuff box at the scene of the crime to incriminate Delamere?'

She rolled her eyes to the ceiling. 'Ned also tells me you can be very dense at times, Stephen.' She leaned forward and tapped the enamelled lid. 'Of course I'm suggestin' you do that. A man like him will have several snuff boxes – he'll never keep track of them all.'

Lavender lowered his voice. 'That would be perverting the course of justice, Betsy.'

'Justice?' She spat out the word in disgust. 'What justice is there in this world for girls like my poor Ginny, Irish Nell or those other poor gals in India he defiled?'

'Ned told you about that, did he?'

'There'll be others besides the ones we know about,' she said quietly. 'A brute like Delamere won't be able to stop himself once he's tasted a woman's fear. London may be full of his victims, Stephen, most of them too scared to complain. You've got to stop him.'

She was sweeping him along with her logic and soothing his doubts with her pragmatism. If he did what Betsy suggested and planted the evidence somewhere to incriminate Delamere, there'd be an outcry tomorrow. Sir Robert wouldn't hesitate to issue arrest warrants. Hanging that bastard, Delamere, was now his priority. The snuff box alone wouldn't convict Delamere but Lieutenant Clarke was a weak man who may be persuaded to turn King's evidence against his superior officer.

Perverting the course of justice or not, Betsy's plan had merit. This snuff box gave him the power to destroy Frederick Delamere once and for all.

But what would be the cost to his own integrity, his own high ideals and self-respect? Perverting the course of justice was a serious crime. He'd be no better than the law-breakers he clapped in irons every day. And what about Ned? Did he involve Ned in this, or not?

Betsy stood up and pulled her shawl tight round her shoulders. 'I'll leave it with you, Stephen.'

'I need to think about this carefully, Betsy.' He rose to his feet to see her out.

'I know you do.' She reached up and kissed him on the cheek affectionately. 'I'll not blame you if you don't do it,' she whispered. 'It's your choice – but at least now you have a choice. You didn't before.'

He swallowed hard and gave her a short nod in reply.

'Don't forget,' she added, as she turned to go, 'Ned knows nothin' about any of this and I don't want him to.'

He nodded again, aware he was now bound for life into a clandestine pact with his constable's wife. 'It's our secret.'

She turned and left him alone to wrestle with the biggest moral dilemma of his life.

Chapter Twelve

Willow Marsh Manor, Cambridgeshire
Early September, 1813

The silver snuff box burned in Lavender's hand like an accusation.

Why had his mysterious nocturnal visitor left it in his chamber? And how had the intruder walked in and out of the room so easily? *Think, think!* he told himself. *There has to be a logical explanation for all this.*

As far as he knew, the snuff box Betsy Woods gave to him ten years ago to use as evidence against Delamere was still locked away in the archives at Bow Street Police Office in London. Oswald Grey, the magistrates' chief clerk, kept all the evidence used in court cases down in the damp cellars beneath the building. Unless the family had specifically asked for it back for some reason after Delamere's conviction, this couldn't be the same snuff box. It must be its twin.

His comment last night to Woods that the author of their mysterious summons was toying with them had been proved true. This was another message. Someone in this manor house wanted to remind him of the part he'd played in the arrest and conviction of the Delamere family's son and heir. It hadn't been forgotten and it wasn't forgiven either.

A new – more menacing – thought entered his head. The use of an identical snuff box might not have been a random choice. Maybe his darkest secret was also discovered. Perhaps his sinister visitor knew the truth and wanted to remind him he'd broken the law? If so, how far would this silent avenger go? Was his life in danger? And what about Ned? Did this phantom think Ned had also been part of the conspiracy to frame Frederick Delamere?

He rose to his feet and paced anxiously around the room. How the devil could he investigate this mystery without revealing the truth to Ned about his secret pact with Betsy?

His mind returned to that foggy morning ten years ago when he and Woods arrived at The George in Hampstead for the inquest of Irish Nell. Lavender had brought a rope ladder with him.

'I just want to check the bottom of the well,' he'd said to his surprised constable.

'I had a good look yesterday, sir. There's nothin' there.'

'You never know.' Lavender had persisted. 'Something may have fallen down when Delamere and Clarke pushed down Irish Nell's body.'

Woods gave him a quizzical glance and shrugged. He helped him secure the rope ladder. Lavender scrambled over the crumbling rim of the overgrown well and descended down its dank interior.

He still remembered Woods' surprise – and delight – when he re-emerged from the gloomy depths clutching Delamere's snuff box in his hand. He'd accepted it without comment.

Everyone else did too, including the magistrate, Sir Robert Brody. They were immediately dispatched to arrest Delamere and Clarke. Clarke soon turned King's evidence against his superior officer. Much to Lavender's delight, a search of Delamere's room in the barracks revealed a grubby stocking in a box with a grim collection of other unexplained items belonging to women. There were hairpins, bangles, a shoe buckle and a faded red hair ribbon.

The hair ribbon nearly unmanned him. He remembered Betsy telling him how Delamere had ripped it from Ginny's head as a souvenir. Gulping back the wave of emotion that threatened to overwhelm him, he pocketed the ribbon and focused on the single stocking.

It matched the one worn by Irish Nell and although Delamere's barrister later dismissed it, claiming it was too common a garment to have any significance as evidence, Lavender knew that it cast further doubt on the major's innocence in the minds of the jury.

Not once, in the intervening ten years, had Woods even hinted that he suspected Lavender had lied and perverted the course of justice during that case. He'd been as gratified as himself at Delamere's conviction. But how would he react now if Lavender told him the truth?

The darkness lifted outside and a watery landscape formed beneath the faint fingers of a chilly red dawn. Beyond the solid wall of the gatehouse, the meandering silver snake of the engorged river slid into view, its banks lined with a row of alders and ancient, drooping willow trees, which no doubt lent their name to the house. The early-morning light filtered down through their leafy canopy. It glinted on the slow-moving water in quick bright flashes.

Lavender sighed, reached for his shaving equipment and poured cold water into the bowl on the washstand. The house would wake soon but he was too impatient to wait for a servant to bring him hot water.

The first thing he needed to know was the fate of the murderer, Frederick Delamere. Delamere was condemned at the Old Bailey to hang but sentences were often commuted to transportation. Convicts had been known to escape from New South Wales and return home. The villainous wretch might be back in England and living here at this remote spot with his family for all Lavender knew.

Dressing quickly, he pocketed the snuff box and descended to the banqueting hall. A maidservant was on her knees in front of the great carved fireplace, sweeping out the cold ash. She glanced up as he reached the flagstone floor. She had a smut of ash on her snub nose and stared at him out of the same startling cornflower-blue eyes he'd seen last night in the housekeeper.

97

'I'm sorry, sir,' the girl said, 'but it'll be another ten minutes or so before breakfast is ready. My ma – Mrs Mabberley – is cooking the eggs and ham now.'

'Please don't worry yourself, miss, I intended to take a turn around the garden before breakfast anyway. I know I'm an early riser.'

Lavender hesitated. He wanted to question the girl about Frederick Delamere but suspected she was too young to remember him clearly. He was also acutely conscious that charming the staff was the area of their job where Woods excelled rather than himself. But there were things he was desperate to know, which only the servants could tell him.

'By the way,' he said awkwardly. 'I've been overwhelmed with your hospitality since we arrived. My room is extremely comfortable and clean.'

The young girl beamed up at him with pride. 'Why, thank you, sir. It's good of you to say so.'

'Did you get it ready especially for me?'

She paused, frowning with confusion.

'I was also impressed that there were already places set at the table last night for us,' he continued. 'Were you expecting us to arrive, despite the lateness of the hour?'

Her face relaxed. Dropping her brush and pan, she pushed a loose strand of fair hair back into her cap with a grubby hand. 'Oh, sir – you'll be accusin' us of fortune-tellin' next! No, it were the mistress, Miss Delamere. She told us what rooms to dust and which beds to make up. She told us to set the table for twelve. I think she thought more folks might come back from Ely after the funeral but the road were blocked by the river and no one else wanted to chance it.'

'Of course.' Lavender nodded and dismissed this line of questioning.

He pulled the snuff box out of his coat pocket. 'This lovely trinket box you left in my chamber particularly impressed me,' he said. 'But I can see it's valuable and I wondered if it had been left there by mistake?'

The girl's bright blue eyes widened with alarm. She scrambled to her feet, wiping her black hands on her apron and peered closer. 'Oh, my goodness! You're right, sir – that shouldn't be in your chamber. It's part of old Mr Delamere's collection from the case in the library.'

'Case?' Lavender's head turned instinctively towards the library, the location of which he knew from his midnight wanderings. 'Does it normally live in a case? Are there others?'

'Yes, sir. Mr Lawrence's father collected them. The old gentleman had some specially made with the family crest and others he brought back from his grand tour of the continent. They're all valuable.'

'I'd like to see them,' Lavender said. 'Please don't worry yourself – I'll take this back to its case myself.' He popped the silver box back in his coat pocket and turned towards the library.

The fusty old room with its strips of oak panelling and towering bookcases was less sinister now the mellow first light of dawn was seeping through the arched leaded window at the far end. Dusty tapestry cushions were scattered on the window seat built into the alcove. Dominating the far end of the room was an ancient wooden lectern with a battered black Bible.

Against one of the wood-panelled walls stood the glass cabinet mentioned by the maid, glittering with its gold and bejewelled treasures. About fifty snuff and patch boxes resting lightly on a faded blue velvet cushion in the case. They ranged in shape from simple rectangles and ovals to the porcelain containers resembling trunks.

Each snuff box was an exquisite example of the art form. The most antique among them were simply gold studded with diamonds, amethysts and sapphires. The later boxes were more ornate and often featured panels made of decorated ivory, agate or tortoiseshell. Several, like the one in his pocket, were hand-painted and depicted everything from miniature landscapes to tiny portraits and cameos of their owners. Among them, Lavender saw a portrait of the Sun King, King Louis XIV of France.

The snuff box in his pocket had been part of a set of four, presumably commissioned by old Mr Delamere as gifts for his family. Two of them remained, cushioned in the velvet. Beside them were a pair of telltale indentations in the cloth, indicating where their fellows once sat. Lavender lifted the glass lid and, ignoring the strong whiff of tobacco that wafted upwards, replaced the box in its place. The fourth empty slot would never be filled. That snuff box had taken an undulating journey through the hands of Frederick Delamere, Ginny Atkins, Betsy Woods and himself to end up as evidence in the gloomy archives of Bow Street Magistrates Court and Police Office.

He closed the glass lid and turned to the old Bible on its lectern. Lifting the battered leather cover, he scanned the four beautifully inscribed vellum pages at the front of the book. It was, as he'd hoped, a family Bible inscribed with the details of every member of the Delamere family since the English Civil War.

Some of the ink had faded through the centuries and some parts of the elaborate swirling handwriting were easier to read than others, but the latter names were legible enough. He skimmed down them until he came to the ones he recognised and was surprised to see that Lawrence and Tobias had had a sister, Diana, whom no one had mentioned the night before.

In 1766, Diana Delamere married *Graham Pammenter Esq. of Ely*. Among the recorded births of the three Delamere siblings at Willow Marsh Manor was a short entry about the birth of *Lucy Pammenter of Ely* in 1768. The insipid and silent maid-cum-companion was exactly the same age as Major Frederick and she was Miranda's first cousin.

He found a bleak entry for 1780:

November 6th, 1780, deaths of Diana Pammenter (née Delamere) aged thirty-three and Graham Pammenter Esq. of Ely aged forty-one

Lucy Pammenter was now an orphan, which probably explained how she ended up living with her uncle and cousins. A poor relative dependent on charity, she occupied that uneasy twilight world between the family and the servants.

The births of Adrian and Ursula Delamere were duly recorded in 1785 and 1790 but there was no sign of the birth of Henry 'Hal' Pammenter, whom he thought would be about the same age as Adrian. Last night, he and Woods had toyed with the notion that Hal Pammenter may be the illegitimate son of Lucy Pammenter and Lawrence Delamere. Now he knew that Lawrence was Lucy's uncle, and she his niece, he sincerely hoped not.

Considering the bad blood between the two old men, Lavender was surprised Lawrence had included Tobias's branch of the family in the Bible but continuing a two-hundred-year-old tradition was perhaps more important to the old man than the feud with his brother.

There was a flurry of entries for the year 1793, all written in Lawrence's swirling hand, which never faltered despite the tragedy underpinning several of the events:

January 4th 1793, Captain Frederick Delamere of Willow Marsh Manor married Susan Jane Pender of Calcutta, Bengal, India

August 13th 1793, death of Gertrude Delamere (née Barwell) of Willow Marsh Manor

December 2nd 1793, birth of Susanna Maud Delamere of Willow Marsh Manor

December 2nd 1793, death of Susan Jane Delamere (née Pender) aged twenty-two

During that single year, the family had welcomed Susanna into the world but lost her mother in childbirth. It was also the summer Olivia betrayed her sister and allegedly hastened her own mother, Gertrude's, death by eloping with Peter Quinn.

And unknown to any of them, it was also the year Frederick Delamere raped Ginny Atkins.

Lavender's heart hardened. Reading about the Delamere family tragedies had made him sympathetic for a few moments and the disconcerting events of the previous night had unmanned and disorientated him. But when he remembered what Delamere did to Ginny, the bile rose in his throat and his angry, professional detachment returned. This family didn't deserve his sympathy; they'd nursed a viper in their bosom. He would do well to remember that.

The final entry was written in a different hand. *Miranda's, perhaps?* It announced the death the previous week of Lawrence Delamere.

He slammed the Bible's cover shut harder than he'd intended. It was time to track down the warped individual who was toying with them.

Chapter Thirteen

It was the argument that woke Woods. That, and his stomach rumbling with hunger.

For a moment, he couldn't remember where the devil he was, then it all flooded back to him, along with the cheerful thought that today they would return to London. He'd been apart from Betsy and his little nippers for too long.

He swung his legs over the side of his bed, rubbed his stubble and listened to the muffled voices of the man and woman yelling at each other. The small room he'd been allocated in the servants' quarters in the gatehouse of Willow Marsh Manor had just enough room between the two low beds for a man to stand up.

The arguing couple were too distant for him to identify but he doubted it was Matthew Mabberley and his housekeeper wife, Connie. He'd got to know the elderly couple a bit better the night before and found them pleasant and contented in each other's company.

No, the arguing couple must be some of the other servants. That lady's maid, Pammenter, lived here, as did the two manservants, Thrup and Hawkes, and their families. That was a lot of people in a small space.

He dismissed the argument as unimportant, fetched himself some hot water from the communal kitchen area and concentrated on giving himself a good shave, using a small piece of mirrored glass balanced on his washstand. He didn't want Betsy complaining about the sharpness of his bristles when he pounced on her later that afternoon. The thought of his reunion with his feisty wife made him grin. He just hoped something else didn't crawl out of the woodwork of this old house to delay them further. Lavender was a devil when he scented a mystery and Woods had seen that 'look' in his dark eyes last night.

The grey-haired steward, Matthew Mabberley, was sitting quietly in a large faded armchair by the fireplace in the communal kitchen, reading a news-sheet through wire spectacles. 'My wife is over at the main house cookin' breakfast, Constable. We normally eat in the kitchen in the manor house after the family have been fed, if you'd like to join us.' He put down his newspaper and rose to his feet.

Woods beamed. 'Thank you, I don't mind if I do. Are you walkin' that way, yourself, sir?'

'Not yet. I have to visit one of our wind pumps which's stopped workin'. I were just on me way now. It shouldn't take me more than half an hour.'

Woods remembered the rows and rows of black wooden windmills with their white sails he'd seen from the coach window the previous day. They looked like insects standing upright on the horizon with their four latticed wings. His stomach complained again but it seemed only polite to stop and have a bit of a chat with the old steward. 'Are there a lot of them windmills hereabouts?'

Mabberley gave a small smile. 'About a thousand in the fens round Ely. They drain the turf and peat pits. You're welcome to join me if you'd like to see how they work.'

'Thank you, but no. That's very kind, but I might want to stretch my legs a bit later, before we leave for our coach,' Woods replied. 'It'll be a long journey back to London.'

'Well, take care you don't fall into one of the lodes.' Mabberley reached for his coat and hat from a hook on the wall and prepared to leave.

'Lodes?'

'Aye, they're the narrow waterways criss-crossing the fens. If you don't watch where you're steppin', you're in one before you know it.'

'Thank you for the warnin', sir.'

Woods left the building and stomped down the exterior stone steps into the courtyard, where chickens pecked hopefully among the cobbles. Nearby, the manservant, Thrup, was grooming an old chestnut horse by the stables on the lower levels of the gatehouse. Thrup was a burly fella with a bushy grey beard and big whiskers. Woods didn't bother greeting him because he'd found out last night that the man was very hard of hearing.

The main door to the hall opened and Lavender crunched his way across the gravel towards him, scattering a pair of indignant chickens in his wake. Woods glanced down at his own muddied boots and crumpled overcoat and wondered, not for the first time, how Lavender and his clothes always managed to look so clean and smart, as if both had just received the attention of a valet.

A huge, ice-blue sky unfurled above their heads. It would be a clear day but surprisingly cold for this time of the year, almost frosty

'Mornin', sir. How did you sleep?'

Without speaking, Lavender gestured for Woods to follow him under the short tunnel in the gatehouse wall that served as the entrance to the manor house. On the other side, they saw the swollen river and the marshland stretching out as far as they could see in every direction. Waterfowl called to each other in the reeds and the sky was filled with birds hurrying to their favourite feeding grounds.

They stopped next to the massive pile of drying wood.

Lavender glanced around furtively to check no one could overhear them, his eyes lingering on Thrup.

'Don't worry about him,' Woods said. 'He's deaf as a post – just like his elderly mother. They live here in this gatehouse together and when they talk to each other they have to shout to be heard. I overheard them last night shoutin' about the weather.'

105

Lavender nodded. 'I had an unknown visitor in the night. They left me a silver snuff box on the table beside my bed while I slept. It's identical to the one we found that incriminated Frederick Delamere in the murder of Irish Nell.'

'Heaven and hell!' Woods' broad forehead creased with frown lines.

'But why make a pantomime out of it all?' Woods asked when Lavender had finished explaining the events of the previous night. 'If someone's remembered us from that damned investigation, why don't they just say so? What point are they tryin' to make?'

'I assume they want to unnerve us. I assume they're after revenge.'

'But what for? For doin' our jobs? That cove Delamere were rightly convicted – everyone knew that. You'd found the snuff box – and his partner in crime, Lieutenant Clarke, turned King's evidence against him.'

'I know, I know,' Lavender sighed.

But Woods hadn't finished yet. 'Clarke told the jury how they'd tortured and raped the poor gal then strangled her when she threatened to report them. No one could ever argue with Delamere's arrest and his conviction. Even his counsel had no argument left for defence. He were duly tried for murder and rape and were sentenced to hang. This family should be grateful to us – and I'll tell that to anyone here who queries what we did.'

Lavender's Adam's apple bobbed up and down as he swallowed hard. 'Thank you, Ned. I needed to hear that. To be honest, I don't know what this prankster wants – and they don't seem prepared to reveal themselves just yet.'

'Well, they'd better hurry up,' Woods said, winking, 'because we're leavin' at noon.'

Lavender laughed and seemed to relax. 'Damn it, you're right, Ned – and the sooner we row away from this place, the better.' He broke eye contact and glanced over towards the river.

Woods frowned. He'd seen this evasion before. 'Wait a minute, sir – you're not gettin' us involved, are you? We *are* leavin' at noon, aren't we?'

'Of course, we are.'

'You promise? I know what you're like once you get a scent of a mystery. You're like a ruddy dog that won't leave its bone.'

'I'm not.'

'Yes, you are.'

'Look, Ned,' Lavender pleaded, 'we'll leave as soon as the boatman comes back for us at noon but in the meantime, let's see what more we can find out about these people, shall we?'

Woods narrowed his eyes sceptically and was about to protest, but Lavender's tone became brisker and more confident. 'Talk to the servants and see if anyone will tell you what actually happened to Delamere. In the meantime, I'm going to have another word with Miranda Let's use the time we've got left to get to the bottom of this mystery and catch this prankster.'

Woods sighed. There was no point arguing with Lavender when he was in this mood. 'What about Lieutenant Clarke?' he asked. 'Could he be part of this?'

Lavender shook his head. 'No, but that's good thinking. Ned. No, Clarke's dead. I know this for a fact. After he turned King's evidence against Delamere, they threw him out of his regiment for disreputable conduct. He died in debtors' gaol about a year later.'

'Well, that were good riddance,' Woods growled.

'This is definitely all about Frederick Delamere – not Clarke.'

'But if it were revenge they wanted, why didn't they just stab you to death while you slept last night?'

Lavender gave a half smile. 'Am I supposed to take comfort from that?'

107

Woods grinned. 'I'm just glad I weren't with you. I slept like a log, I did. There were no nasty creepers in my room – and there were a second empty bed in there too.'

'Was there?' Lavender looked thoughtful. 'Mm, I wonder why they gave us separate rooms?'

'Well, I don't think you need to be a detective to work that out. Someone were plannin' all along to pay you a visit in the night. You were set up.'

Lavender's dark eyes narrowed. 'It's time I asked Miranda Delamere some straight questions, I think. It is a mystery, though, how they got up and down that creaking wooden staircase so fast. They must be very light on their toes.'

Woods grinned. 'That rules out Mr Tobias Gundigutts and his wife – they're not light on their twinkle toes. And Miss Delamere needs a stick to walk. It must be one of the younger members of the family. My money's on that troublesome little cat, Ursula.'

Lavender frowned. 'But why? They would all have been children ten years ago when Delamere was convicted. His daughter, Susanna, probably has the biggest cause to resent us but she doesn't look like she'd say boo to a goose, never mind hatch an elaborate plan like this.'

Woods saw a familiar look descend on Lavender's face. This mystery had started to eat into his soul. 'That reminds me, sir – didn't Delamere claim – in front of his regimental colonel – that he were an unmarried bachelor when we arrested him ten years ago?'

'Yes, he did.'

'So, where's that little gal come from?'

Lavender shrugged. 'He must have been lying. Her birth is recorded in their family Bible – I've just read it. Go and see what you can uncover from the servants, Ned. Eat your breakfast in the kitchen with the staff.'

'What about you?' he asked.

'I've already had mine. Mrs Mabberley let me have a plate of fried ham. I'm going to speak to Miss Delamere as soon as I can. I'll meet you back out here in an hour.'

Chapter Fourteen

Woods enjoyed a long and pleasant breakfast at the kitchen table. Mrs Mabberley and her daughter bustled around him as he ate. Although they were busy, both women still found time to chat with him about the weather and this year's harvest. Woods had a second helping to prolong his stay in the kitchen and give them more time to relax in his company. Eventually he smacked his greasy lips together, pushed back his chair in the kitchen and let out a small but satisfied belch.

Mrs Mabberley was frying more eggs at the range while her daughter, the young housemaid, scooped porridge out of the pan into porcelain dishes.

'Would you like a third plate of ham and eggs, Constable?' the kindly housekeeper asked.

'No, thank you, ma'am. The ham were excellent but two helpin's is more than enough for me.'

She beamed with pride. 'We rear the hogs and cure them ourselves, you know.'

'And a good job you make of it, ma'am. No, I'm a man who has to watch himself these days – I'm prone to fat if I'm not careful. So, I always stop at two helpin's.'

'What, a fine figure of a man like you?' the housekeeper said with mock surprise and a wink.

'Ma! Behave yourself!' the young girl exclaimed. 'Da wouldn't like you talkin' like that!'

'Away with you, our Annie,' Mrs Mabberley laughed. 'You youngsters are too serious, you've forgot how to have a bit o' fun. Take these eggs in before they get cold and take the teapot round again.'

The young girl disappeared, muttering, and Woods saw his chance for a bit of subtle questioning with the jovial housekeeper.

'They keep you on your toes then, this Delamere family?'

She laughed and plonked her ample bottom down on the chair opposite his own. 'Normally it's too quiet here for me,' she confessed. 'With just the master, Miss Delamere and Miss Susanna. They rarely use the big hall or the rooms in the north tower. But I enjoy a bit o' company.'

'Were he sick a long time, your master?'

She shrugged. 'A few months at the end. He's been fadin' for years, mind you. But fadin' quietly, if you know what I mean.'

'You'll still miss him.' Woods lowered his voice sympathetically. 'And so will your mistresses. Who's to be in charge here now? I weren't too certain about that from what I heard last night.'

'Miss Susanna inherited everything, but she defers to her aunt in most matters. I don't think we'll notice much difference. Miss Delamere has run this house for the last twenty years since her mother died; I think she intends to carry on doing the same and Miss Susanna will let her.'

'She's a sweet young thing is Miss Susanna. What happened to her parents?'

Mrs Mabberley's cheeks, already enhanced with colour due to the heat of the range, now developed an additional flush. 'Her ma died when she were born,' she said softly. 'She and Mr Frederick were married out in India. He were a captain in the army back then. But they'd barely been married a year when she died. Miss Susanna came to Willow Marsh as a motherless sucklin' babe.'

'That's a tragic story,' Woods said.

'Miss Delamere sorted it all out, of course,' the housekeeper continued. 'She found a wet nurse and a night nurse and raised her niece as if she were her own while he went back to the army.'

112

Woods nodded his head gravely. 'What happened to Captain Delamere? Did he take comfort in his daughter after the death of his wife?'

Mrs Mabberley gave an unladylike snort. 'Did he heck. We barely saw him after she were born. I hate to speak ill of the dead, Constable, and he were abroad a lot with his regiment, but he never bothered with the child even when he were in England.'

Woods shook his head sadly and steered the conversation towards what he really wanted to know. 'Were Major Frederick fightin' with Wellington in the Peninsula campaign?' he asked. 'Did he die in battle?'

'No.' Her lips tightened with disapproval. 'There were no hero's death for him.'

She glanced at the door, lowered her voice and leaned across the table. 'I'll tell you this, Constable, because it's common knowledge round these parts – although rarely spoken of in this house. Master Frederick were a wrong 'un. A real wrong 'un. He died of gaol fever on a transport ship bound for Botany Bay. The scandal nearly broke Master Lawrence's heart, it did.'

'Gawd's teeth!' Woods muttered. 'What did he do?'

'Murder.' A dark shadow passed over her face and her voice dropped to almost a whisper. 'He killed a young gal up in London He were a bad 'un, all right. He left nothin' but upset and misery wherever he went.'

'That's shockin', that,' Woods said blithely, 'and he were gentry, too? It sounds like it were a blessin' he 'ad no part in the raisin' of Miss Susanna.'

The housekeeper nodded. 'Yes, it were a blessin' but the scandal were huge and it's been a heavy burden for the family to bear. It were particularly awful for the poor young gal, growin' up knowin' her da were a killer. Everyone in the neighbourhood knows it too and sendin' her away for school didn't help. Miss Delamere had to fetch her home from her last school because the other girls had uncovered the truth and were tormentin' her.'

Woods shook his head sympathetically. 'That's bad, that.'

'Well, thank goodness she's got her inheritance now,' Mrs Mabberley continued. 'It might help a young man overlook her da's badness and come forward to offer for her. I know Miss Delamere were worried Miss Susanna would never find a husband because of the scandal.'

'Yes, an estate like this will sweeten the pill.' Woods could barely keep the cynicism out of his voice but Mrs Mabberley didn't notice his struggle. She was too busy enjoying the gossip.

Woods often struggled with the mercenary way the upper classes dealt with the marriage of their offspring. And he didn't like how they punished youngsters for the behaviour of their parents either. For him and Betsy, their marriage had been about love and a strong, healthy physical attraction. No one had fussed that Betsy's da had been a hopeless gambler or that his own da had abandoned his family and run off when he was just a nipper. Woods reckoned that if everyone visited the sins of the fathers on their children, no one would get wed.

Mind you, there would be a new way of going about things when his own daughters came to marry. Any young fellas who wanted to wed either Miss Rachel or Miss Tabitha Woods would need to show evidence of their wages and savings and possess testimonials of good character from at least three vicars.

'Mr Adrian has always had a thing for Miss Susanna, of course,' Mrs Mabberley continued. 'He adores her sweet nature.'

'Does he now?'

'Aye, he's mooned around after her since they were children but Miss Delamere won't encourage his suit because she can't stand his father, Tobias.'

'No one minds that they're cousins?' Woods asked.

Mrs Mabberley raised one eyebrow and gave him a peculiar sideways glance. 'Not round here.'

The door opened and Lucy Pammenter glided into the room, dressed in the same simple black mourning gown she'd worn the night before. The jutting angles of her shoulder blades poked through the thin fabric. She was a plain woman with narrow features and painfully thin grey hair. She's no looker, Woods decided.

She carried a tray of used china crockery to the great pot sinks at one side of the kitchen.

Mrs Mabberley hastily rose to her feet and returned to her range. 'Morning, Miss Pammenter. Does Miss Delamere require anything else this mornin'?'

'Miss Delamere is now dressed and discussing business with Mr Symonds in the parlour,' Lucy said. 'They'll ring the bell if they require anything.'

'Yes, ma'am.'

'Is Detective Lavender still talkin' with them?' Woods asked. 'He said he'd call in and have a word with Miss Delamere.'

Lucy Pammenter gave Woods a hostile glance. 'Your Detective Lavender left them some time ago.'

'What about yourself, Miss Lucy?' Mrs Mabberley said hastily. 'Do you want some porridge or ham?'

115

The woman continued to glare at Woods. 'I'll take a small bowl of porridge with me to my room, if you don't mind.' Her voice hardened and rose slightly as she added: 'Miss Delamere might not mind these men, but I'm fussy whom I share a table with.'

'Miss Lucy!' Mrs Mabberley looked like she wanted the flagstones to part and the ground to swallow her up.

Woods wiped his mouth with the back of his sleeve. 'I apologise for any offence I may have caused you, ma'am, although I must say I'm at a loss to know what it is.'

Her eyes narrowed and her face contorted with spite. 'You would say that, wouldn't you? You *and* him? Neither of you would ever own up to your villainy.'

Woods pushed back his chair and stood up. 'Again ma'am, I can only apologise for any wrong you feel you've suffered at our hands. Will you not tell me where our fault lies?'

But she just curled her lips in distrust and continued to watch him through cold and narrowed eyes.

Woods wondered how she was related to Hal Pammenter – and to the Delameres in general. A 'distant cousin', Miranda had said the night before. He also wondered if she was quite right in the head; this outburst seemed odd, almost childish.

When it became obvious she had no intention of voicing her complaint, he gave her a short bow. 'I'll leave you to your meal in peace, ma'am – and again, on behalf of myself and Detective Lavender, I apologise for any wrong you feel you may have suffered.'

He left the room and shrugged. He didn't know or care why that woman was glaring at him. He'd got the information he needed about Frederick Delamere and he refused to be drawn any further into the affairs of this unpleasant and argumentative family. He would go home on the afternoon coach to London and with any luck he'd never see any of them again.

'Constable Woods!' Mrs Mabberley had followed him out of the kitchen into the hallway, wiping her hands on her apron. He heard the clatter of crockery and the low murmur of voices from the great hall, but they were alone at the moment in the chilly entrance to the south tower.

'I'm sorry for Miss Lucy's behaviour,' Mrs Mabberley said quickly.

Woods beamed. 'It's all right, ma'am. Not everyone likes police officers. I've known this for years.'

'No, it's not that.' She grabbed his arm, glanced round to check they were alone and whispered conspiratorially, 'She can be a bit strange, at times, can our Miss Lucy. She suffered a lot when she were younger. Miss Delamere had allus taken good care of her, of course, but sometimes it's hard to hide it from visitors.'

'Don't worry yourself, Mrs Mabberley – and thank you again for an excellent breakfast.'

The woman nodded and returned to her kitchen.

There was no sign of Lavender in the courtyard or beneath the arched entrance where he'd last seen him. Woods decided to check the rest of the grounds and get a bit of fresh air at the same time. This might be his last chance to stretch his legs before they climbed into a cramped coach to return to the smoky city.

His path took him round the rough stone walls of the south tower towards the formal terraced gardens at the rear of the hall.

117

The gardens were large rectangular beds of full-bodied pink and red roses, huge swathes of lavender and deep plum hollyhocks, all of which still smelled wonderful despite the lateness of the season. A small orchard of gnarled fruit trees spread out below and the swaying reeds of the marshland stretched as far as his eye could see.

A blustery wind had sprung up and a tumble of low grey clouds scuttled across the horizon. The breeze picked up the scent of the late roses and Woods paused for a moment to enjoy their perfume. Apart from when he crossed the great piazza of Covent Garden, he rarely got to enjoy the smell of flowers and even then it was usually tinged with the stench of the river and the heaving city.

Careful, fella, he warned himself. *Don't enjoy it too much. We're not staying...*

Chapter Fifteen

Lavender found Miranda Delamere with her lawyer in the cluttered but cosy parlour on the ground floor of the south tower. They sat on two plump upholstered chairs around the hearth of an intricately carved marble fireplace, diligently sifting through a pile of papers. Her wicker wheelchair was behind her by the latticed window. The cool marble of the fireplace with its golden flecks was tastefully echoed in the cream wood-panelled walls hung with dozens of gilt-framed family portraits and landscapes.

Lavender coughed discreetly at the half-open door and tapped on the door jamb.

Miranda glanced up and waved him over. 'I'm pleased to see you, Lavender. I hoped for a moment of your time. Please close the door and come in.'

He took in the comfortable wealth of the room as he walked across to them. A round, beautifully inlaid teak table dominated the centre of the room. Its glossy patina and elegance matched the sideboard, upon which a vast array of silverware, including two candelabra, a coffee pot, a punchbowl and a tea set, glittered in the sunlight streaming through the windows.

Miranda put down her papers and watched him approach. Dark circles underpinned her intelligent eyes. She looked tired and Lavender wondered if it was grief for her father or her painful disability that kept her awake at night. Her back and shoulders seemed less rigid this morning. Perhaps the pain was worse at night?

'I wanted the chance, before you left, to say how sorry I am you and your constable have been inconvenienced in this way, Detective. Mr Symonds and I knew my late father's will would be contentious for some members of the family. I was well aware how my father had settled his affairs – he had no time for anyone else except myself and Susanna. But I never expected one of them to go to such despicable, spiteful lengths to distress everyone at his funeral.' She stared at him calmly, her soft gaze never faltering.

'However,' she added, 'I think I may have found a way I can make amends for the inconvenience you've been put to – and pay you for your time.'

'Really?' He paused, vaguely aware that he was on the cusp of hearing something significant. He'd sought this audience in the hope of learning something new about the prankster who'd drawn them here and disturbed his sleep, but now the ground was shifting beneath his feet again.

'Yes.' She glanced at her solicitor for reassurance before she continued. They both looked serious. 'My niece, Susanna, was involved in a dangerous situation last week, and I would like you and your constable to stay on for a while and investigate the matter. Naturally, I'll pay you at the usual rate charged by Bow Street.'

'What happened?'

'Susanna was out in the marshes, walking along the bank of one of the lodes, when someone leapt out of the reeds and pushed her into the water and tried to drown her.'

'Good grief!'

'It was a deliberate and callous attempt to murder her.'

The lawyer cleared his throat, readjusted the pince-nez on his nose and nodded. 'It's true, Lavender.'

'What happened to Miss Susanna?'

'She does swim – albeit weakly. The killer didn't know this because he disappeared again quickly into the reeds. She managed to keep afloat and call out for help, but her gown and heavy boots dragged her down. Fortunately, Adrian was in the vicinity at the time of the assault. He heard her cries for help and rescued her.'

Lavender frowned. 'Did she get a good look at her attacker?'

'Unfortunately not. The coward pushed her from behind and left her to drown.'

'What did the local constables say?'

Miranda and Symonds exchanged another conspiratorial glance.

'My father was hours away from death, Lavender…'

Symonds cleared his throat again and gave a nervous cough. 'The constabulary in Ely are stretched and more concerned with helping the excise men track down a local smuggling gang. We didn't involve them.'

You sent for us instead. So that's why we've been summoned. To act as bodyguards for a young woman.

'Have you any notion who's behind this? Who wants Miss Susanna dead?' Lavender asked.

Miranda stared unblinking across the room into his eyes. She didn't need to answer.

Lavender spluttered. 'You can't suspect your Uncle Tobias, surely?'

The thought of Tobias Delamere sneaking around the marshes trying to drown his great-niece was preposterous. The man was all bluster and had the physique of a walrus rather than an assassin. An attempted murder like that required stealth.

'You heard him last night, Lavender,' Symonds piped up. 'He has the most to gain if anything happens to Miss Susanna.'

'How so?'

'He and Master Adrian would inherit Willow Marsh Manor if something should happen to Miss Susanna before she marries and bears an heir.'

Lavender frowned again. 'Yes, Symonds, but to resort to *murder...* and he'd have to kill both women to inherit the estate. Surely Miss Delamere would inherit the estate ahead of her uncle?'

There was a short silence, then Miranda said solemnly: 'I don't expect to outlive my uncle, Detective. If something should happen to Susanna, my Uncle Tobias will be master at Willow Marsh within a few years.'

Symonds gave a little groan and struggled to hide the distress that flashed across his face. Lavender wondered again about the nature of her illness. A tumour on the spine, perhaps? Her features remained inscrutable. There was no sign in those clear, intelligent eyes that this woman was staring death in the face – or that she was a habitual user of opiates, like most of those afflicted by tumours.

'I – we – need your help, Lavender,' she said. 'And Susanna needs your protection. I may be wrong about my uncle's devious intentions – but this doesn't detract from the fact someone tried to drown her.'

Lavender sighed. Provided he returned to Bow Street with the fee, he knew Magistrate Read wouldn't care if their role here had changed from investigating a murder to preventing one. But Ned would care. He'd be furious if they didn't set off back to London this afternoon and he felt a keen sense of disappointment himself. He wanted to see Magdalena again.

'I've followed your progress in the London news-sheets for years,' Miranda continued. 'You and Constable Woods are celebrated for your successful mystery-solving and your detection of murderers – and I can afford to pay you handsomely for your help.'

Disappointment made him reckless. 'But if you wanted our help, why perpetuate this elaborate charade with your sister's name, Miss Delamere?' His disappointment sharpened his tone. 'Why all this pretence?'

A flicker of alarm crossed her face. 'You've worked it out? You knew all along it was me?'

He hadn't, of course, but he wasn't prepared to admit that. 'The person who wrote to Bow Street knew we were in the area at the Cambridge assizes. Apart from the circuit judges and the criminals themselves, the assizes are crawling with lawyers.' He turned to Symonds and glared at him. 'And you, sir, are a lawyer.'

Symonds shuffled uncomfortably beside Miranda. He must have a strong sense of loyalty to this woman, Lavender thought, to waive his professionalism and allow himself to be drawn into this ridiculous charade. 'Were you in Cambridge at the assizes, sir?'

The lawyer nodded miserably. 'Yes, I had a conveyancing case at the start of the week.'

Miranda's narrowed eyes and impassive expression suggested that she wasn't convinced by Lavender's explanation. 'You worked out that I was the author of that letter because you suspected Mr Symonds attended the assizes?'

Lavender sighed silently. To outsmart this woman he needed to distract her. 'At one point, last night, I suspected that Mr Henry Pammenter had lured us here,' Lavender said. 'He's another lawyer, I understand? He also seems an exuberant and fun-loving young man who'd enjoy a good prank.'

Miranda smiled fondly at this description. 'Your assessment of Hal's character is astute for such a short acquaintance. Yes, he was a bit of a rogue in his youth but nowadays his legal work and his life in London keep him very busy. We barely see him.'

'Apart from this,' Lavender added pointedly, 'he's been busy organising another little surprise for you.'

'Ah, yes, Mr Robert Quinn – my alleged nephew.' Miranda glanced at the papers in the lap of her black silk gown and a frown flickered across her features.

Lavender wondered if they were the 'documentation' Quinn had promised to provide that validated his claim to be Olivia's son.

'So, in the end, I dismissed the idea that Mr Pammenter was involved in this affair,' Lavender continued, 'and decided you and Mr Symonds had come up with this plan to hide behind your sister's name.'

She nodded. 'You're right. It seemed like a good notion at the time but I feel like a foolish schoolgirl now.'

'Why did you do it?' He already knew the answer to his question but he needed to hear what she had to say. The spectre of Frederick Delamere remained between them, hovering in the dark corners of the room.

'I wondered, sir, if you'd come to our assistance if you saw the name *Delamere* on the letter requesting your presence.'

'You mean would I have been prejudiced against you because of my history with your brother, Major Frederick Delamere?'

There was an almost imperceptible pause, then she straightened up and sat taller in her chair, a movement that made her wince with pain. 'Yes, I did wonder about that.'

'Then you've more faith in my memory, ma'am, than it deserves. It wasn't until halfway through the proceedings last night that I made the connection between you and the major.'

She flashed him a winning smile. 'Then you don't mind? You'll take the assignment and investigate this attack on Susanna?'

Lavender breathed heavily. 'I didn't say I didn't mind about the deception – and I haven't decided yet about your request. This whole thing has been most irregular. And I'm still curious, ma'am, about why you asked for myself and Woods?'

'Your reputations precede you, Detective.'

'Maybe so, but aren't *you* prejudiced against *us* because of the part we played in the arrest and conviction of your brother?'

Her smile drained away. 'Freddie is dead. Susanna is the future of Willow Marsh Manor and she's precious to me. Very precious. It's as simple as that.' She paused, swallowed hard, and when he didn't respond she added, 'I went to the trial with my poor father. I realised then that Freddie was the devil incarnate. His crimes were intolerable. He had to be removed from society and… and punished for what he did.'

Lavender suddenly had a strong sense that he and Woods had barely skimmed the surface of Frederick Delamere's depravity. Something unspeakable lay behind Miranda's stilted choice of words and the shadow that passed over her face.

'His sentence was just,' Miranda continued, 'although it was commuted to transportation.'

'Transportation? Is he still alive in New South Wales? Are you in touch with him?'

She shook her head and lowered her eyes. 'He died on the voyage out. There was justice for his victim in the end.'

'I'm glad we agree on this, ma'am. However, someone in your household doesn't share our opinion of your brother. Someone is angry and determined to remind me of the part I played in your brother's conviction and perhaps wants to seek revenge.'

'What do you mean?' Both Miranda and Symonds looked genuinely startled.

Quickly, he explained about his mysterious nocturnal visitor and the unexpected arrival of the snuff box on his bedside table.

'This person did you no harm, sir?' the lawyer asked hastily.

'No. But I still struggle to understand what he – or she – wanted and how the devil they entered and left my room with such ease.'

Miranda gave a wan smile. 'If we've another prankster in the house, besides myself, then that's bad news.'

'Who else in the family knows about the connection between myself and the arrest and conviction of your brother?'

She shrugged her thin shoulders. 'Perhaps all of them. We never talk about the disgrace Freddie brought to the family but every one of us is keenly aware of his crimes. However, I may be able to help solve the other part of your mystery, Lavender. There's a secret passageway running through the thick walls of the north tower from the library up to the battlements. We loved exploring it when we were children. I believe one of the entrances is through the large cupboard in your room.'

So that was the answer! Damn these secretive old houses.

'Is that the legendary priest hole?' Symonds asked.

'No, the priest hole is just outside here in the hallway, below the staircase.' She turned back to Lavender with a faint smile. 'The two towers of Willow Marsh Manor were added to the medieval manor in the sixteenth century, although there's no secret tunnel in the south tower or access to the battlements. My ancestors were wealthy merchants but staunch Catholics for a long time after the Reformation. They hid many priests here who'd arrived from the continent via King's Lynn. They helped them slip in and out of the country.'

Lavender felt a mixture of relief tinged with frustration. One riddle was now solved but another one had been posed. 'I'd assumed my mysterious visitor and the author of the fake letter from Mrs Quinn were the same person.'

Miranda gave him another faint smile and pointed to the blanket covering her legs. 'I admit to penning the fake letter that drew you here, Lavender, but even you can't suspect an invalid like myself of running up and down the steps of the north tower?'

'No, ma'am, I don't. That prankster is still at large.'

'But despite this nonsense last night, Lavender, will you take the assignment? Will you investigate this attack on Susanna and lend us your support and protection for as long as it takes to track down the villain who tried to drown her?'

Lavender sighed and tried to picture Baby Alice in his mind. 'I'd need to discuss this with Constable Woods, but yes, ma'am. I'm sure there's some way we can help you. In the meantime, here is a letter from Bow Street that outlines our fees and expenses.'

Chapter Sixteen

Lavender was determined to take a stroll around to the back of the manor house before he met up with Woods. He wanted to try to get some idea of the lie of the land and understand how Miss Susanna nearly met her death in the marshes.

However, the first thing he wanted to see was that damned secret tunnel in the north tower. He strode back through the hall, nodding politely at Tobias and Birgitta Delamere, who were guzzling their breakfasts at the banqueting table. A vast black and grey striped silk waistcoat strained over Tobias's belly. Birgitta was again swathed in her generous gown of black bombazine.

When he reached his bedchamber, he threw open the door of the ornate Jacobean cupboard that dominated the room and pushed aside the old coats. The large closet now revealed its secret – in the daylight, he saw what he'd missed the night before. The tall column of five drawers on the left-hand side of the cabinet weren't drawers at all. They had beautifully carved false fronts and behind these was an empty space, tall enough for a man to step into. He entered and felt for a catch for the hidden door at the back that would take him into the secret tunnel, marvelling at the clever design of the cabinet. If he remembered rightly, there was an identical one in Hal Pammenter's chamber below. He'd only caught a brief glimpse of it last night, but that had been enough.

With a quiet click – the same gentle click he'd heard in his nightmare – the false door at the back of the cupboard swung open on to a narrow landing. He fetched his bedside candle, lit it and peered inside the gloomy passageway. The small landing was a stopping point in a flight of shallow stone stairs. He squeezed into the passageway and climbed up through the rough-hewn walls of the tower.

At the top, a heavy trap door blocked his way up onto the battlements but when he reached up it glided smoothly to one side on its runners. Someone kept these ancient mechanisms well greased.

He clambered out onto the battlements, blinking in the brilliant sunshine.

The cold wind whipped his hair back off his face as he walked to the parapet and took in the magnificent views of the surrounding landscape, especially the rear of the manor.

He rested his hand on a stone merlon to lean forward and get a better look, but pulled it back in alarm when the merlon rocked beneath his hand. Three hundred years of erosion had taken its toll on these battlements. He doubted this crumbling parapet would survive the next winter storm.

His eyes swept across the magnificent view. Surrounded by small clipped box hedges with a topiary ball at each corner, the formal terraced gardens at the rear of the hall dropped down towards a sprawling orchard. A flight of worn stone steps led towards the gnarled apple and pear trees, heavy with ripe fruit. Half a dozen fat pink pigs rooted for grubs and windfalls among the fallen bark and litter in the tree roots. On either side of the orchard, the irregular-shaped fields were full of grazing sheep and a few cattle.

Beyond this reclaimed and cultivated land, the wilderness of the marshes took over. The occasional tantalising glint of silver indicated the presence of water behind the swaying reeds. The melancholy cries of the waterfowl travelled for miles across the flat, soggy landscape.

Lavender wondered what it must be like to own a huge estate like this. Then he realised, with a jolt, that he did.

Between them, Magdalena and Sebastián owned two estates in Asturias, a rugged and mountainous region in northern Spain. An only child, Magdalena had inherited her late father's property and since her first husband's death at the battle of Talavera, their son, Sebastián, was sole heir to the de Aviles family estate near Oviedo. However, they had no idea if either of these properties had survived the French occupation of Spain.

It had been impossible to get accurate news out of the country since the invasion. Magdalena believed the de Aviles family had all been murdered and their family lawyer in Oviedo seemed to have fled; he didn't reply to Magdalena's letters. Her own distant relatives in Madrid had scattered along with the government and the royal family when Bonaparte had installed his own brother on the Spanish throne. It was time to go to Spain and see for themselves what had become of Sebastián's inheritance.

Meanwhile, his attention returned to the impressive inheritance of young Miss Susanna Delamere. There were a few scattered black-and-white wind pumps on the horizon but not another house or farmstead in sight.

The only person he saw was the tall figure of Adrian Delamere standing beneath one of the trees on the edge of the orchard with his distinctive long hair tied back in a ribbon. The young man was staring at something – or someone – in the shadows at the back of the orchard, with his coat collar turned up against the morning chill.

Lavender decided to make his way down to him. He'd ask Adrian to take him to the spot where he'd fished Susanna out of the water. Carefully, Lavender lowered himself back down the narrow passageway, replaced the trap door over his head and picked up his candle.

One thing was for sure, he decided as he descended, neither Tobias nor Birgitta Delamere would be able to squeeze their bulky forms down this flight of steps. This had probably been the original staircase up the tower. No doubt the twisting wooden structure was added at a later date.

He passed the shallow landing outside his room and was surprised to see a shaft of weak light falling across the landing down the next flight of steps. It came from the half-open door that led into the back of the cupboard in the room shared by Hal Pammenter and Robert Quinn.

The closet door into their room was also partially open, allowing the strong, masculine odour of young men to waft into the secret staircase. It brought with it the sound of heavy breathing, the creak of the bed frame and the unmistakable gentle suck of slow kissing.

'My darling, my gorgeous darling.' Hal Pammenter's voice was deep with desire.

Lavender froze, rooted to the spot with curiosity and a slight revulsion. He remembered Tobias's barbed comment the night before about how Hal may have met Quinn in a 'molly house'.

Then Hal let out a small sigh, groaned and rolled away from his lover. 'For God's sake, Ursula, stop teasing me, damn you.'

The girl gave a low, sensual laugh.

A few feet away, Lavender let out a quiet sigh of relief.

'I've told you before, Hal. If you want relish, you have to marry me.'

'Huh! A proud minx nowadays, eh? Or have you found yourself another fellow for a bit of tousling? Is that why you rebuff me?'

'What if I have?' she taunted. 'How hard will you fight for me, Hal?'

'You know damned well you're the only woman for me, Ursula.'

'So, marry me. You've got Lawrence's five hundred pounds a year now. I can easily persuade father to overlook your parentage if you ask for my hand.'

Hal must have hesitated too long – or revealed some doubt in his face – because the next second, the bed creaked and Lavender heard the sound of heeled leather shoes being dragged angrily across the floorboards towards the bed.

'Where are you going?' the young man complained. 'Put your shoes down. Come back here, wench, sit on my lap and finish what you started.'

'You ignored my comment about marriage.'

Hal groaned. 'Oh, Ursula, you know marriage is impossible at the moment. I've just set myself up in London. I need time to find my way forward in my new profession.'

'And no doubt you're busy losing your wages at the card tables and spending what's left on coats from the most fashionable tailors...'

He must have leaned back over her and stopped her mouth with his own because her complaints ceased.

'A man must make a good impression in London, Ursula,' he said when they broke apart again. 'It's an expensive town.'

'I'm sure Uncle Lawrence's five hundred a year will help.'

'It'll help, but I've another scheme in hand that should bring in some money. Be patient, my love.'

'Oh, you and your damned schemes! I'll be an old and dried-up jilt like Aunt Miranda by the time one of your precious schemes comes to fruition. I might as well find another beau, someone more local. And don't think I can't – I've had offers! There are men queueing up for my hand.'

'I'm sure there are, my darling.' There was amusement in Hal's voice. 'Although I doubt if any of them are as charming and handsome as me.'

'You're – you're insufferably arrogant!'

Hal laughed. 'Just have patience. This latest scheme of mine has potential – great potential.'

'Well, go on... tell me. Is it something to do with that stupid American you've dragged up here?'

'You'll know soon enough.'

'What is it?'

There was silence for a moment, then something was thrown across the room and hit the far wall.

Hal laughed softly. 'Temper, temper, miss.'

'Damn it, Hal – tell me!'

'When did you become such a gentry mort?' He must have reached for her because she gave a soft shriek and there was more rustling of muslin and linen clothing.

'Where do your parents think you are at the moment?' Hal asked eventually. 'Not that I'm complaining. I thought a goddess had appeared before me when you glided out of the old cabinet.'

'Why do you ask about them? Are you worried my father may suddenly appear from the same cupboard and thrash you within an inch of your life?'

Lavender tensed. If Ursula had used the closet to enter the room unobserved, no doubt she'd leave the same way.

'I probably deserve a good hiding – considering where my hand rests on his daughter at the moment.'

She giggled. 'They think I'm reading in the library to improve my mind. Father seems to have forgotten all about the secret staircase up to these rooms. He commends my studiousness.'

'You've taken a risk, my love – especially with those police officers snooping around.'

'How else am I ever to get time alone with you, Hal?' she complained. 'I see so little of you these days. Your letters are so, so irregular – and now you've burdened yourself with that clinging American. He's worse than a chaperone.'

'I apologise, my darling. I'll try to do better with the letter writing. And I wouldn't underestimate Quinn, if I were you.'

'You're not going to tell me, are you?'

'About what?'

'About your latest scheme.'

'It's probably best you don't know about it.'

'Damn you, Hal Pammenter.' The bed creaked again and Lavender sensed that Ursula had risen angrily to her feet.

She came into view through the small crack in the cabinet door. She was pinning up fallen strands of her fair hair. Her gown was creased and crumpled and its top buttons were undone. A strong pair of male arms, in billowing white cotton sleeves, suddenly encircled her. Pammenter was in his shirt with his waistcoat undone. His golden mane fell forward as he bent to kiss the nape of her neck gently. She arched her back like a cat and leaned into his caress. 'Just tell me this fanciful scheme of yours doesn't involve you marrying our dumb little heiress,' she murmured huskily.

'Never,' he murmured. 'You know I can't marry Susanna, Ursula – and you know why. Now stop sulking and come and sit on my knee again, wench. God only knows when we'll ever get another opportunity like this.'

Lavender stepped back carefully into the silent gloom of the narrow staircase. He'd seen and heard enough.

Slowly he descended to the library below. This door didn't swing inwards like the two above but slid sideways. It was a panel of bookshelves, part of a bigger bookcase. Smiling gently at the ingenuity of the designer, he strode back through the medieval hall and outside into the sunshine, where he breathed a sigh of relief.

Eavesdropping on suspects was an unavoidable part of his job, but it always made him feel dirty.

Chapter Seventeen

'Good morning, Mr Delamere.'

Irritation and anger flashed across Adrian's face when Lavender joined him in the terraced garden at the rear of Willow Marsh House.

'Morning, Lavender. I've just come out to check the river.'

Lavender nodded, suppressed a smile and resisted the urge to point out that the Great Ouse flowed on the other side of the building. He knew what Adrian was 'checking' and it had nothing to do with the river level.

In the shadows at the back of the orchard, Susanna Delamere strolled among the most distant trees with the American, Robert Quinn, at her side. She wore a warm brown cloak over her black gown and carried a flat wicker basket or her arm. Quinn wore the same shapeless grey coat he'd arrived in the previous night.

Quinn looked much more at ease this morning than the young man who'd sidled into the banqueting hall in Hal Pammenter's wake. His tanned face was creased with smiles, which softened the prominence of his nose. Unaware of Lavender and Adrian's presence, the young couple were laughing.

'I was worried the flooding might get worse after last night's rain,' Adrian continued, 'but it seems to have receded. With any luck, the boats should get here by ten o'clock and we'll be able to return to Ely as planned.'

'Do you live and work in Ely?' Lavender asked.

'Yes, my father has a house on St Mary's Street. At the moment, I live there but my business prospers and I hope—' – there was a slight inflection in his voice and another almost imperceptible glance in the direction of Miss Susanna – '—to move into my own home shortly.'

137

The young couple walked towards them. Quinn's brown leather boots were mud-splattered and the hem of Miss Susanna's cloak was damp with dew. She carried a large quantity of mushrooms in her basket.

'What line of work are you in, sir?' Lavender asked.

'Trade imports,' Adrian said. 'My mother's people are Swedish and have traded between here and the Baltic for generations. I'm an agent for the importation of timber. They've a lot of trees in Russia and Scandinavia.'

Lavender was impressed. 'Do you speak Swedish?'

Adrian nodded. 'I have a working knowledge of the language. Ely is Britain's biggest inland port and there's plenty of opportunity here for anyone prepared to put in some honest hard work.'

Adrian had a sensitive mouth and the dark complexion prevalent in the male line of his family. His blonde sister took after her mother. The resemblance between Adrian and his cousin Susanna was striking; they shared the same long-lashed dark brown eyes.

'My father was gifted a lifetime allowance from the Willow Marsh Estate,' Adrian continued with a hint of jealousy in his voice. 'But I'll always have to work.'

'There's no disgrace in working in commerce or the professions. Your cousin Hal also seems to have done well in his chosen career.'

Adrian snorted. 'Yes, but he had to move to London to find work. His laziness is legendary around here. Even old Symonds wouldn't give him a job in his Cambridge practice.'

Lavender raised a surprised eyebrow at his tone but there was no time to ask for clarification. Susanna and Quinn arrived by their side and greeted them warmly.

'Mr Quinn has told me all about the Carolinas.' Susanna's pretty brown eyes shone with excitement. 'Their trees are enormous there. They're older and far bigger than ours.' She waved a dismissive gloved hand at the gnarled fruit trees in the orchard. 'They're often draped with a white plant called Spanish moss, which floats down like gossamer and whispers in the wind. They've marshes too – but they're filled with alligators and poisonous snakes.'

'Swamps, ma'am,' Quinn corrected gently with a smile. 'Back home, a house like yours would be covered with trailing purple wisteria, which grows mighty fast and tears down the shutters from the windows.'

The young woman radiated happiness today and seemed far more at ease than she'd been the night before. Lavender wasn't surprised. Her last few months would have been marred by sadness because of the steady decline and death of her grandfather.

Today was the first day of a new phase in Susanna's life; she'd been notified of her inheritance and a bright future lay ahead. Her excitement was palpable and judging by the smile on his face, she'd ever charmed Adrian out of his bad mood.

'They've wild dogs called coyotes,' she continued 'and a troublesome cheeky creature called a raccoon with a ringed tail that's bigger than our squirrels.'

'Oh, we've squirrels too – thousands of them – but ours are grey, while yours are red.'

Lavender smiled at their enthusiasm. 'It sounds delightful, sir. I'm surprised you could tear yourself away from such beauty to come to England.'

'They've bears and wolves in their forests too!' Susanna interrupted. 'It must have been so *exciting* to grow up in such a place.'

A shadow crossed Quinn's face and his smile drooped. Once more he became a rather plain young man with a prominent nose. 'To be honest, ma'am,' he drawled softly, 'it was rather quiet. I'd have given anything to have had some siblings – or cousins like y'all. My childhood was kinda lonely.'

'Well, you've a whole new family now, Mr Quinn. Oh! And can you believe this, Adrian? Mr Quinn and I have just realised we almost share the same birthday! We were born a day apart! He was born in New York the day after I was born in England.'

While her cousin smiled and exclaimed at the coincidence, Lavender did a quick mental calculation. Based on the information he'd gleaned from the family Bible earlier, *if* Robert Quinn really was Olivia's son, then the woman must already have been pregnant when she eloped with his father to the Americas.

'Are you going in for breakfast now, Susanna?' Adrian asked. 'Shall I escort you? You've been out here for a while, you don't want to catch a chill.'

The young woman lifted her brilliant eyes to his and dazzled them all with her smile. 'Not yet, dearest Adrian. It's such a lovely morning after the dreary rain of the last few days, I'd like to stay out a little longer and make the most of it. The weather is so unpredictable at this time of year.'

'If you wish to return to eat, sir,' Quinn said. 'I'd be mighty happy to escort Miss Susanna on another turn around the grounds of her plantation.'

'Isn't that amusing!' Susanna exclaimed to Lavender and her cousin. 'Mr Quinn calls Willow Marsh a *plantation*.'

Yes, and he's doing it deliberately, Lavender thought, *despite being corrected last night by Hal Pammenter.*

Quinn offered Susanna his arm. 'Shall I escort you, ma'am?'

'Oh, *would* you, Mr Quinn? You're *so* kind.' She linked her arm through his and they walked away, their heads close together in conversation.

Adrian Delamere scowled.

Lavender bit back his smile. 'I understand the cause of your solicitude about Miss Susanna's safety.'

Adrian started. 'You do?'

'Yes, your Aunt Miranda has told me about the attack on her person last week. In fact, Miss Delamere has asked me to remain and investigate the assault.'

'She has? Good. To be honest, I thought this was why you *were* called here in the first place. I don't understand that nonsense about Aunt Olivia.'

'I'm sure everything will be explained later. Can you take me to where the attack took place before you go in for breakfast? I would have asked Miss Susanna herself, only she seems otherwise preoccupied today.'

'Yes, with Quinn – damn him! I hoped to spend some time with her alone. Very well, follow me, Lavender.'

Lavender fell into step beside the young man and hid his smile. Adrian's jealousy was blatant – but perhaps not surprising under the circumstances.

Quinn was clearly determined to inveigle himself with the young heiress and she was ripe for exploitation. This innocent young woman had lived her life in the shadow of scandal at this remote and lonely estate. Now she was a rich young woman with several adoring admirers who hung on her every word. Adrian. Quinn. And what about Hal Pammenter?

Lavender had just heard Pammenter deny any interest in Susanna but would he like to be one of Susanna's suitors as well? Lavender hadn't missed the rosy flush that rose from Susanna's breast to her face when the young Adonis walked into the hall last night. With all these young bucks around her, no wonder she was too excited to eat breakfast.

Adrian led him through the dappled shade of the orchard to a wide grassy track, scythed short, that wound slowly through the tall sedge and reeds of the marsh. As the familiar trees fell away, the ground became soft and they entered a tunnel of reeds. Six or seven feet tall, the vegetation rustled dryly in the wind.

A broad track suddenly dissected their own narrow one and Adrian took them left. Glancing back, Lavender realised they'd now lost sight of Willow Marsh Manor on its promontory. The only thing he had left to guide him back was this young man he barely knew and the position of the sun in the vast ice-blue sky arching above.

'These old paths are called droves,' Adrian told him. 'Some of them follow routes that are hundreds of years old.'

They turned again and startled a small bittern out of its roost in the reeds. Yellow silverweed and clumps of delicate late-flowering mauve orchids broke up the monotony of the feathery grasses and swaying reeds.

After a hundred yards, Hal stopped abruptly. 'It was further along here: Willow Marsh lode.'

Lavender nearly bumped into him and it took a second or two before he realised that they were on the low bank of a long, straight stretch of water, which mirrored the azure sky and skidding white clouds above. A dragonfly with gossamer fine wings skimmed the glassy surface. Nearby, a frog, oblivious to the feast around it, basked in the sunlight on a lily pad. A small muddy path, edged with purple-headed weeds, ran beside the lode. The amethyst flowers rippled like the froth on the crest of a wave.

'What happened?' Lavender asked as he carefully followed Adrian along the bank. 'And why were you here at the time of the assault?'

'It was about this time of day,' Adrian said. 'I was on my way to King's Lynn but I called in at Willow Marsh for half an hour to offer them my support – we all knew Uncle Lawrence hadn't long left to live. Aunt Miranda said Susanna had gone for a walk. When I couldn't find her in the orchard, I assumed she'd come out here for a longer stroll and took the same paths we've taken today.'

'Were you worried about her?' Lavender's sharp ears caught a plop as something large slid down the muddy bank into the water about ten feet away. A rat? Otter? Grass snake, perhaps?

'No, not about her safety. Like myself, Susanna knows this terrain as well as any fen man or woman. Anyway, suddenly I heard a large splash and a scream. I raced here and found her floundering in the water, dragged down by her heavy gown and boots.'

Lavender eyed the cold water with a frown. 'How deep is it?'

'It varies from stretch to stretch. Susanna said her feet never touched the bottom, so perhaps five, six feet here? The slippery banks made it difficult for her to haul herself out unaided because she couldn't get a foothold.'

'Did either of you see who pushed her into the water?'

'No.' His eyes narrowed and his sensuous mouth tightened into an angry line. 'The bastard pushed her from behind and had vanished without a trace by the time I arrived. I was too busy hauling her out of the water to chase him. Susanna was my priority.'

'I understand.'

'She was freezing cold, terrified and desperately shocked. I had to almost carry her back to the house.'

About a quarter of a mile away, the still, white sails of a wind pump loomed up ahead over the top of the reeds. Adrian glanced up at them, got his bearings and stopped. 'That's the Willow Marsh wind pump. I found Susanna in the water about here.'

'Wait here a moment, please,' Lavender said. 'I need to look around.'

He knew it was a forlorn hope that Susanna's silent attacker had left any clues here but he had to check. The cove would be familiar with this terrain. A pair of nervous moorhens bobbed briefly among the waterlilies then vanished into the tall reeds. Like them, Susanna's attacker had melted back into this watery world with barely a ripple or a rustle.

Lavender thrashed around in the reeds, disturbing a cloud of insects and butterflies, before he returned to Adrian, shaking his head. The stationary sails of the distant wind pump suddenly caught his attention and he frowned. The breeze snaking through the reeds was cold and fairly strong – why were those sails so still?

'Let's visit the old wind pump. There may be something there.'

Adrian's eyebrows gathered in a frown. *What was that glance? Annoyance? Alarm?* 'Don't you think we should return to the house and keep a watch over Susanna?'

'I'm sure Miss Susanna will be quite safe today surrounded by your family.' He cast Adrian a sharp sideways glance. 'Unless you think a member of your family is to blame for the attack?'

'No, no. That's a preposterous suggestion, Lavender. No one in my family would hurt Susanna.'

'Then humour me, please, Mr Delamere – take me to that wind pump.'

Still frowning, Adrian led the way. He reached up and ran a finger round the inside of his cravat as if he suddenly found its folds restrictive.

144

Darkened with pitch, the black conical body stood on a mound between the shimmering water of the lode and the flooded ditch it was supposed to drain. Battered by the elements for centuries, it looked forlorn and neglected. The white paint on its sails peeled badly.

But it wasn't the wind pump that riveted the men's attention. It was the body of a grey-haired old man in a brown coat who lay beside it. Face down in the mud, one arm dangled into the still water.

They both cursed and broke into a run at the same time. Squatting down beside the man, Lavender pulled him over on to his back and reached for a pulse.

Adrian fell to his knees in the mud beside him. 'For Christ's sake! It's Matthew Mabberley – Aunt Miranda's steward. Is he dead?'

'Yes.'

Chapter Eighteen

Mabberley's glassy eyes reflected the scudding clouds now lowering over the marshes as they stared lifelessly up at the sky.

A dark crimson stain had spread out around a series of vicious slashes in the steward's old coat. The cooling blood emitted a noxious ferrous tinge that Lavender loathed.

'He's been stabbed in the stomach.'

Breathing through his mouth, Lavender yanked open the coat to take a closer look at the lethal damage. 'He was stabbed four times, by the look of it. Whoever did this intended to kill, not maim.'

A fly suddenly crawled out of Mabberley's gaping mouth.

Adrian turned a greenish-tinged shade of white. He leapt to his feet, staggered over to the wall of the wind pump and retched. Lavender ignored him and continued his swift examination of the body, using the same procedure he'd seen used countless times by Sir Richard Allison, the surgeon attached to Bow Street Police Office.

There were defensive wounds on the dead man's ungloved hands, slashes from the same knife that killed him, no doubt. He checked Mabberley's eyelids and jaw and found both still flaccid. This lack of rigor mortis suggested the steward had been killed in the last hour or so. Mabberley's pocketbook contained coins to the value of nine shillings and sixpence halfpenny and his battered old pocket watch was still there on the end of its chain. This wasn't a robbery.

Lavender stood up and scanned the trampled ground around the body. Boot prints patterned the soft mud but they didn't seem to lead anywhere. He backed away from the corpse, trying to make sense of the freshly crushed vegetation and the compacted mud on the riverbank.

Then he had it. Two small wooden stakes protruded from the ground next to the lode and the silt on the bank between them was heavily churned with several sets of footprints. The murderer – or murderers, as it now seemed – had moored a boat here and rowed away after killing Mabberley.

Two of these sets of footprints had the distinctive hobnailed appearance of labourers' boots but one didn't. They were smooth-soled, like the prints from his own boots. He returned to the body and checked the size of Mabberley's own, rather large, hobnailed boots. None of those prints by the water's edge were large enough to be the steward's. They belonged to the murderers.

Adrian still leaned against the wind pump, retching. Lavender walked across and patted his shoulders. Tears streamed from the young man's eyes and an unattractive gob of spittle dangled from his mouth and swayed in the breeze. *It's a good job he hadn't already eaten his breakfast,* Lavender thought wryly. 'Is this the first time you've seen a dead body?'

Adrian nodded. He looked wretched.

'Get yourself back to Willow Marsh Manor and fetch help. Get my constable and Doctor Bendall – and some form of contraption to carry Mabberley back home. A stretcher or a door, perhaps?'

Adrian nodded and tried to straighten up. The treacherous heaving of his stomach had calmed.

'Before you go – tell me where this lode leads to?' Lavender pointed downstream in the northerly direction taken by the murderers.

Adrian's voice rasped through his inflamed throat. 'It joins up with the Great Ouse.'

'If you get back and I'm not here, tell Woods I've gone after the killers.'

'Killers?'

'Yes, there was more than one of them.'

Lavender watched him go then dropped down beside the corpse and closed Matthew Mabberley's eyes. Wincing, he allowed himself a moment of grief for the poor man and his family. Then he rose, pulled his pistol out of his coat pocket and started to jog down the riverbank. The Mabberley family wouldn't want his sympathy; it was justice for the murdered steward they needed from him.

He'd no idea how much distance lay between him and the fiends who'd stabbed Mabberley – or how long ago the attack had happened – but provided he kept his footing on this narrow bank and did not fall into the lode, he might just be in time to catch a glimpse of them.

But it wasn't that simple. Within fifteen minutes he'd already seen a smaller lode dissecting the waterway on the opposite bank and then found his own way barred by another intersection. The whole area was criss-crossed with drains and the reeds provided too much cover. The boat he sought may only be yards away, rocking silently among the reeds, while the murderers sniggered quietly among themselves. He'd no alternative but to turn back to the scene of the crime.

Mabberley still lay where he'd fallen. A yellowish-green butterfly had landed on his shoulder. It fluttered away quickly when Lavender approached. Above the steward, the white sails of the wind pump creaked loudly in the wind but remained still.

There was no sign of Woods, Adrian Delamere or the rest of the help he'd requested, so Lavender turned his attention to the wind pump. Judging by the extent of the large pool of brackish water spilling over from the flooded ditch, it had stopped working some time ago. He forced open the two large wooden flaps at the base of the structure and peered into the dim interior.

The component parts of the pump were a rusty collection of wheels, cogs and axles, which looked like they needed greasing, but that wasn't the reason they'd stopped moving. Two massive wooden stakes had been jammed at angles into the internal workings. He leaned over the large flat platform between the doors and the pump mechanism, grabbed the nearest stake with both hands and heaved. It wouldn't budge. Someone had used a lot of force to hammer this obstructive post into the machinery.

He felt a sharp stab on his wrist. Pushing back the cuff of his glove, he saw the red pin-prick of an insect bite rise on his skin. A small black object leapt off his hand and joined a cluster of others of its kind, jumping around on the flat platform inside the wind pump.

'Sir!'

Lavender turned with relief at the sound of Woods' voice. Adrian led Woods and a group of men towards him. They included the gingery-whiskered doctor and Thrup and Hawkes. These last two carried a makeshift stretcher between them.

Doctor Bendall knelt down beside the dead man. Adrian and the two servants peered grim-faced over his shoulder.

Woods joined Lavender beside the wind pump. 'What's happened here, sir?' he asked quietly.

'The footprints suggest there were three of them. Two of them wore hobnailed boots; the third didn't. His boots were smoothed-soled, like mine.'

Woods' grey eyebrows rose slightly. 'A gentleman killer, eh?'

'They arrived and left by boat. I tried to follow them down the lode but it was hopeless.'

Woods nodded and he glanced up to the creaking white sails above them. 'I saw Mabberley first thing this mornin'. He said he were comin' out here to see a broken wind pump.'

'It's broken because someone's jammed it.' Lavender turned and beckoned for Woods to follow him. He pointed inside the structure at the wooden staves wedged into the mechanics. 'Give me a hand, Ned. Let's get them out.'

The two men gripped the closest stave and heaved. With Woods' impressive strength now added to his own, the posts came away easily. The cogs ground, the axle lurched and the ancient wind pump screeched back into life. In the ditch to their right, water sucked as the pump began to work again.

'Well, that were a bit like openin' the jaws of hell.' Woods observed. His glance fell on the pile of watery vomit next to the pitch-blackened wall of the structure. 'What's this? Did young Mr Adrian cast up his accounts?'

Lavender nodded. He examined the two wooden posts for clues, some indication about why they'd been shoved into the pump – and why a man had been murdered when he'd set out to remove them.

Woods pointed to the flat platform just inside the doors. 'There's a lot of space in there and it doubles in size when the piston is jammed up. I reckon it's been used for storage.'

'Storage?' Lavender peered back inside the gloomy interior of the wind pump and scratched the flea bite on his wrist thoughtfully. Insects still jumped across the boards of the wooden platform. There were dozens of them.

'It'll be smugglers, sir. Brandy. Mabberley will have disturbed a smugglin' ring.'

'What, in broad daylight?'

Woods shrugged. 'It's a queer place, this – I've not seen anywhere so empty of folks since we had that case back in Northumberland. I reckon the smugglers here can afford to be more brazen like.'

Lavender scratched his wrist again and wondered. 'Can you smell any alcohol in here?' Often the brandy fumes seeped into the surrounding wood of its storage areas and left a strong and pleasant aroma lingering in the air. Many a hidden cache had been discovered by a customs man with a sensitive nose.

Woods' great nostrils flared as he sniffed. 'No. It smells more like a wet dog in here than a brandy casket.'

'That's what I thought.'

The other men had lifted Mabberley's body onto their makeshift stretcher. Adrian glanced nervously in their direction, unsure whether to follow the doctor and the servants or to stay with the police officers.

'Let's go back to the manor,' Lavender said, 'We've seen everything there is to see here.'

A reed warbler sang its plaintive song as the grim-faced men began their sad procession back to Willow Marsh Manor.

Chapter Nineteen

Lavender and Woods fell behind the others and quietly exchanged the information they'd gleaned earlier that morning.

'Frederick Delamere's been dead ten years. This case is nothing to do with him.'

Woods nodded. 'I know. Mrs Mabberley told me he'd escaped hangin'. She said he died of gaol fever on the transport ship to Botany Bay.'

'Gaol fever?' Satisfaction flooded through Lavender. 'A horrible death – but well deserved in his case. Miranda Delamere sent that letter to Bow Street under her sister's name. She thought we wouldn't come if she used the name Delamere because of our past history with her brother.'

'Well, she were right there,' Woods said with a chuckle.

'I've also learned,' Lavender continued, 'that there's a secret tunnel in the walls of the north tower which leads to my bedchamber and all the way up to the battlements. In addition to that, there's a priest hole beneath the staircase in the south tower. According to Miranda, everyone in the family is well aware of the existence of both of them.'

Woods' eyebrows twitched with amusement. 'So that's how the creeper managed to get in and out of your room so easily.'

'Yes. I suspect it was a prank – maybe one of the youngsters is behind it. They all know our history with Frederick Delamere and there's some resentment about our presence. Besides which, Hal Pammenter is up to something. He's got money problems. He also has some sort of scheme in hand that sounds unsavoury and is probably illegal.'

'You've been busy! How do you know all this?'

'The secret staircase has an entrance on each floor. I went exploring and overheard an intimate conversation between Ursula Delamere and Hal Pammenter.'

Woods gave a short laugh. 'I got an inklin' this lot like to keep it in the family, so to speak. Accordin' to the housekeeper, Master Adrian is sweet on Miss Susanna, too. It's all kissin' cousins around here. Anyway, what's this murder Miss Delamere wants us to investigate?'

'It's an *attempted* murder. Someone tried to drown Susanna in the lode, just here by the wind pump. They crept up behind her and shoved her into the water.'

'Well, that mystery's solved now, in't it?'

'Is it?'

Woods gave him the look that he preserved for when he thought Lavender was being particularly dim. 'It'll be the smugglers! Same ones who killed the steward. If they killed poor Mabberley to protect their secret cache of brandy in the wind pump, they'd think nothin' of drownin' the girl if she got too close.'

Lavender frowned. 'Symonds mentioned there was an active gang in the area but let's not jump to conclusions, Ned.'

'Smugglin' is the problem of the local customs men and constables; it's not our jurisdiction. This isn't your case anymore.'

'We have to go to Ely to alert the magistrate about Mabberley's murder and give him the details so he can open the inquest,' Lavender said.

'And then we'll get the coach to London?'

'We might. We may have to stay for the inquest. Don't forget: I was one of those who discovered the body.'

'*Might?*' Woods growled and glowered at him below his bushy grey eyebrows, a ferocious action that would turn half the criminals in London into a quaking blancmange. Lavender ignored it.

'You promised me we'd return to London today. You can always come back for the damned inquest.'

'One more day won't hurt, Ned. Let's make sure we've got to the bottom of this case before we rush off back to London.'

'You think you've got the sniff of another one of your complicated mysteries, don't you?'

'Possibly. Now don't get testy.'

'I'm not testy,' Woods snapped. He surged forwards in a petulant temper and took hold of the fourth corner of the stretcher, joining Hawkes, Thrup and Adrian as they carried Mabberley's body.

Lavender fell behind, sighing. He thoroughly understood Woods' disappointment; he wanted to go home as much as his constable did, but he'd a nagging suspicion the ghost of Frederick Delamere hadn't finished taunting him yet.

Susanna and Robert Quinn were still in the garden when they returned, standing beneath the walls of the north tower. By the stricken look on Susanna's face, they'd already heard about the death of the steward. Her gloved hands fluttered in distress to cover her face when they approached. 'Oh, no! Poor Mr Mabberley – poor Mrs Mabberley!'

'Susanna!' Adrian dropped his corner of the stretcher, leaving the other men to counteract the lurch, and raced to her side. 'You shouldn't be here!' He gathered Susanna up in his arms. She sobbed into his shoulder.

'I had to see for myself!' she wailed. 'It's awful! Mrs Mabberley has already been told She and her daughter are beside themselves with grief!'

The doctor took Adrian's place at a corner of the stretcher and they continued their sad journey to the servants' quarters in the gatehouse.

Lavender paused beside the young people.

'You poor, poor girl!' Adrian soothed. 'You shouldn't have to face another loss like this so soon after your grandfather's death.' Quinn shuffled nervously beside them.

Susanna's tears slowed and she took Adrian's handkerchief to blow her nose. 'It's not me who needs the sympathy – poor Mrs Mabberley! And poor Annie!'

'Where are your family, Miss Susanna?' Lavender asked gently. 'I need to speak to everyone. They need to gather in the great hall.'

'I, I don't know…'

Woods was still carrying the stretcher with the other men. They'd reached the corner of the house. Lavender called him: 'Ned – meet me in the great hall.'

Woods glanced back over his shoulder to nod but his chin lifted higher when something in the battlements above caught his eye. His moon-shaped face blanched. 'Gawd's teeth!' he bellowed. 'Move away, sir! Run!'

Lavender didn't hesitate. He grabbed the arms of the two young Delameres and leapt forward down the shallow flight of steps. Their sudden movement knocked Quinn out of the way. The next second, a merlon from the parapet crashed onto the ground behind them, shattering into a hundred pieces.

Woods was by his side before he'd even had time to catch his breath. 'There's some bastard up there! I saw him rockin' a large stone loose!'

Lavender thrust Susanna Delamere into her cousin's arms. 'Get Miss Susanna safely inside to her aunt!'

He raced past the startled doctor and manservants and turned down the side of the manor house with Woods thundering beside him. 'So much for your notion that smugglers tried to kill Susanna Delamere!'

'Who said it were her they was tryin' to kill?' Woods replied cryptically as they skidded to a halt in the gravel at the kitchen door.

'Did you get a good look at him?'

'He wore a dark coat with a black hat pulled low over his face.'

'If we don't get there in time – someone may see him leave the tower!'

The Delameres were sitting in the comfort of Miranda's parlour. Lavender heard their voices drifting through the open door as they clattered down the hallway.

'Someone's just tried to kill Miss Susanna!' Lavender yelled to her over his shoulder. 'Mr Adrian is with her.'

Shocked exclamations of alarm followed them as they tore down the cool interior of the massive banqueting hall.

'He may still be in the tower. You take the wooden staircase. I'll use the secret one in the walls. Leave the doors open and check every room as you go up. Don't hesitate to shoot!'

'Yes, sir!'

Lavender yanked his own pistol out of his pocket when he reached the library door.

He heard Woods thudding up the exterior staircase as he slid the bookcase to one side and started up the gloomy flight of steps. Without a candle, he'd probably stumble into the murdering fiend before he saw him, but he was armed and he had Woods' support. If the would-be killer was still in this tower, they'd catch him.

He heard raised voices when he reached the small landing outside Hal Pammenter's room. He threw open the door and burst into the chamber just as the main door to the room flew open and Woods' broad frame filled the entrance.

Lucy Pammenter and Hal stood opposite each other, both red in the face from arguing.

157

'What the devil do you think you're doing?' Hal asked angrily.

The woman glared silently at Lavender then gave a short scream at the sight of the pistols aiming in her direction.

'I could ask you the same question,' Lavender replied. 'What are you doing?'

Hal gave him a look of pure scorn. 'We're talking, Lavender. Is that against the law now?'

'Didn't you hear the crash?'

No, of course they didn't. Lavender realised his mistake the instant the words left his mouth. The window in this room faced out to the west and the river, not to the terraced gardens and orchard in the east.

'Someone just tried to kill Miss Susanna and your friend, Quinn.'

'What!' Hal looked genuinely alarmed. 'Are they all right?'

'Go down and join your family in the parlour. We'll discuss this later.'

Lavender jerked his head up to the ceiling. Woods nodded, backed out of the room and set off up the wooden staircase to the next floor.

Lavender stepped back into the cupboard and half ran, half stumbled up the next flight of steps to his own chamber. When he got there, he found no one in his room except Woods. He beckoned him over.

'He may still be up on the roof. Follow me.'

Cautiously, they moved up the last section of the stone staircase. Woods' broad shoulders scraped against the rough stone. The trap door was wide open. One of them would have to stick their head up there and risk being bashed to death by a desperate and insane murderer who'd already proved himself handy with the stonework.

'There's nowhere else to go!' Lavender shouted up at the sky through the trap door. 'I've got armed officers at the exits. You might as well give yourself up now.'

Nothing. The only reply came from the screeching gulls wheeling in the sky above.

Lavender swore with frustration. 'Cover me, Ned. If he kills me when I poke my head up, I want to know that will be the last thing he ever does before you shoot him dead.' Before Woods could respond to this, or try to stop him, he leapt up the last few steps.

There was no one there.

The only signs anyone else had been up there since Lavender were the open trap door and the gap where one of the merlons of the parapet used to stand. It had been rocked backwards and forwards until the mortar crumbled and the merlon toppled forwards in a shower of fine powder.

Had the would-be killer jumped? It was highly unlikely, but Lavender checked anyway, half hoping to see a smashed and bloodied body lying on the terrace.

There was no one in sight.

Chapter Twenty

'Where the devil is he?' Woods joined him at the edge of the battlements.

'He got away.'

'It must be Hal Pammenter,' Woods said. 'Let's get back down and arrest him – quick.'

'We need to find out what everyone saw – and who was accounted for and who wasn't – before we make any arrests. Ned…?'

'Yes.'

'When I was here earlier today, I noticed the parapet was unsafe and crumbling. It wouldn't have needed much help to fall. You definitely saw someone up here, didn't you?'

'I'm not in my rheumy-eyed dotage yet,' Woods growled. 'There ain't nothin' queer about my lamps. I saw a fella up here rockin' the wall. And it were a damned good thing I glanced back too or else you and those youngsters would be dead or maimed.'

'He wore a dark coat and a hat, you said?'

'Yes.'

Lavender thought of the old coats in the closet in his room. Were there hats down there too? He'd check them for clues on the way down. His mind turned to the motive for the attack. Tobias had the most to gain from Susanna's death, but his sheer bulk made him a poor suspect for any of these crimes. Of course, he may have hired someone to murder his niece. But would anyone working for Tobias risk injuring the man's only son in the attack? Did the killer even notice that he and Adrian had joined Susanna and Quinn by the wall of the tower?

'Come on,' he said. 'We need to question this family further.'

Woods nodded but his eyes were troubled. He held up his hand to stop Lavender in his tracks. 'Just before we go down, sir.'

'Yes, Ned?'

'Do you think Miss Susanna were the intended victim?' His eyebrows met in a frown across his forehead and his mouth tightened into a grim line.

'Yes. That makes sense, considering there's already been an attempt on her life. I don't think the family are pleased to see Quinn but I can't see why they'd want to kill him.'

The wind lifted Woods' coat collar, but the steady gaze of his unblinking brown eyes never wavered. 'What if she *weren't* the intended victim? What if it were *you* he wanted dead?'

Lavender opened his mouth to protest but Woods beat him to it. 'Hear me out, sir. Miranda Delamere has already played us false once. How much do you trust her? What if there never were any attack on Miss Susanna? What if it were just a ruse to get you out here into the backwaters of Ely – and the whole damned family's in on this conspiracy?'

Lavender froze. 'What the devil do you mean, Ned?'

'I'm suggestin' this killer might have his sights set on you. Last night he were tauntin' you – today he means business.'

Lavender shivered in the cold wind and he relived the jolt of fear he'd felt last night when he chased the prowler from his room. The wind had turned blustery now and sent a tumble of angry black clouds across the huge sky towards them. A shifting pattern of light and shadow flitted across the surface of the river below them.

'And what if Frederick Delamere ain't really dead? What if he's back here – determined to get revenge?'

The hairs stood up on the back of Lavender's neck. Then his common sense returned. Susanna and Quinn had been standing beneath the battlements for some time; one of them was the intended victim.

But Woods hadn't finished. 'You see, I'm thinkin' this way: no matter how much Miranda dismisses the past, there's no gettin' away from the fact that by goin' after their precious son and heir, you ripped this family apart. There was consequences for all of them.'

'Supposing for one minute that Frederick Delamere still lived,' Lavender said slowly, 'why on earth would he try to harm his daughter?' He paused to let his words sink in.

'This creepy place gives me the willies.'

'Don't let superstitious fancies distract you, Ned,' Lavender said sharply. 'I need you focused.'

'Don't you feel it too?'

'What?'

'The misery in the bones of this old manor, stuck out here in this godforsaken wilderness.' Woods shivered when he spoke. 'This crumblin' house with its blasted secrets and half-lies. These walls are steeped in villainy – even the battlements are murderous.'

Fat drops of rain speckled the pile of mortar dust at their feet and darkened the newly exposed scar on the battlements where the merlon once stood.

Lavender swallowed hard and took a deep breath. Half of him wanted to laugh at Ned's fanciful thoughts; the other half of him wanted to unhear them. 'The only thing seeping into these old walls is damp from the fens,' he said firmly. 'And as for being murderous – all walls are dangerous when pushed.'

Woods shrugged. His eyes were blank and fixed on the horizon. 'If you say so.'

The rain had plastered Lavender's dark hair to the side of his head. Woods seemed oblivious to the trickles of water running down his broad face.

'I do say so,' Lavender said firmly. 'And as for your other suggestion – that the cove up here tried to kill *me* – well, I doubt it. I'd only just joined Susanna and Quinn when the accident happened. The villain wanted to kill one – or both – of them. I was never his intended victim.'

'Are you sure about that, sir?'

'Oh, for God's sake, Ned, what's got into you?'

Woods stared into his eyes without blinking. His next sentence almost took Lavender's breath away. 'I know you planted Delamere's snuff box down that damned well where we found the body of Irish Nell.'

'What! You knew all along I was lying?'

'Yes. I examined that well the previous day, remember? I knew there were nothin' down there. But it were impressive how you came up the ladder with that box in your hand. I thought you were a sly dog and I were fascinated to see how you'd pull it off.'

'So, you humoured me and let me have my deception?' Lavender paused for a moment and Woods nodded. 'I know it was wrong,' Lavender continued. 'I've suffered guilt over it ever since. But I didn't feel... I didn't have any choice.'

'I know you didn't,' Woods said smoothly. 'Those villains would have sailed to the continent the next day and got clean away with the murder if you hadn't intervened.'

'I swear to you, Ned, it's the only time in my life, in my career, I ever did anything like that.'

Woods gave a short laugh. 'Well, I know that – I've been watchin' you ever since in case you tried to repeat the trick. But my point is, sir – if *I* worked out you were lyin' about the snuff box, maybe Delamere and some others did too.' He lowered his voice and added: 'The more I've thought about it, sir, the more this case and these events seem like revenge to me.'

Lavender sighed. Maybe Ned was right. Maybe he wasn't as clever as he thought he was. Perhaps Delamere and other family members had rumbled his secret a long time ago. Maybe they'd just been quietly biding their time and waiting to wreak vengeance on the corrupt detective who'd ruined their lives.

'What I don't get though, sir,' Ned continued, 'is how you came across Delamere's snuff box in the first place?'

Lavender turned away abruptly. 'Later, Ned, later. We need to go down now. We've got the murder of Mabberley and the attempted murder of Susanna to solve. I want you to guard that girl from now on. I'll not leave her alone again.'

166

Chapter Twenty-One

The Delamere family were seated round the fireplace in the banqueting hall, awaiting their return. Miranda was in her wicker wheelchair, her face tense with strain. Lucy Pammenter fluttered behind her. Susanna sat on one of the settles, a tiny, tragic figure with scared, moist eyes, flanked by Adrian and his sister. Tobias and his fat wife were spread out over the settle opposite. Hal Pammenter and Quinn stood to one side, talking.

'Lavender!' Tobias bellowed. 'What the devil is going on? My son has just told us some ruffian has murdered the steward and tried to kill my great-niece. Is this true?'

'I'm afraid it is. Mr Mabberley was killed down at the old wind pump and Constable Woods just saw a man up in the battlements push down part of the parapet above where Miss Susanna was standing.'

Everyone exclaimed at once. Several seconds passed before Lavender could make himself heard again. 'We've been up there but the attacker has escaped. We need to know where everyone was at the time of the incident.'

'What? Are we suspects now in our own family home?'

'Well, who else do you think it was, Mr Delamere?' Lavender asked icily. 'We're cut off by the swollen river. This latest attack was perpetrated by someone here – on this estate. Everyone, apart from those who were outside with us, needs to account for their movements.'

'This is preposterous!' Tobias snarled.

'Yes, it is.' Lavender snapped. 'There's already one man dead this morning and if it hadn't been for the quick intervention of Constable Woods, the body count would have been higher!'

Miranda leaned forward in her wheelchair. 'Is this attack on Susanna connected with what's happened to poor Mabberley, do you think?'

'I don't know yet.'

'What happened to Mabberley?' Tobias asked.

The room fell silent while Lavender quickly explained how he and Adrian had discovered Mabberley's body, but he held back the details of his other discoveries at the wind pump, apart from the fact he suspected the killers had escaped by boat. Everyone, even Tobias and the stranger, Quinn, looked chastened by the time he'd finished his grim account.

'Who would do such a dreadful thing?' Miranda's hands gripped the arms of her chair so tightly her knuckles were white.

'Did he have any enemies?' Woods asked.

Miranda shook her head. 'Mabberley was respected and admired hereabouts. I believe most of our tenants considered him a fair and just steward.'

'Constable Woods and I have a theory,' Lavender said, 'but—'

'What's that, Lavender?' Adrian asked sharply. 'What do you suspect?'

'I'll explain later when I possess more information. In the meantime, we need – or rather, I need – to go straight to Ely and ask the magistrate to set up an inquest.'

'But what about Susanna?' Miranda exclaimed. 'I've charged you with her protection – and from what you've just told us, she was nearly killed outside not twenty minutes ago!'

'I'll leave Constable Woods with Miss Susanna while I'm gone.'

'I'll stick to your side, Miss,' Woods promised the young woman. 'There ain't no one who'll hurt you while I'm there.' With a theatrical flourish, Woods half slid his pistol out of his coat pocket and didn't replace it until he was satisfied everyone in the room had seen it.

168

'Thank you, Constable,' Susanna murmured.

'Are you both armed?' Miranda asked Lavender.

'Yes, ma'am.'

'I'm afraid I must return to Ely for business, Susanna,' Adrian said. 'Otherwise I would also have remained by your side.'

She lowered her eyes demurely. 'You're very kind, Adrian. But please don't concern yourself. I'm sure I'll be fine with Constable Woods.'

'Well, I'm more than happy to stay here and keep Cousin Susanna company.' Ursula patted Susanna's hand. 'You can spare me, can't you, Mama?'

Susanna gently withdrew her hand. 'Please don't trouble yourself, Cousin.'

Lavender was in no doubt Ursula's offer was prompted by her obsession with Hal rather than any concern for Susanna. He noted with interest that Hal hadn't offered to protect his cousin.

'Nonsense! It's no trouble at all,' Ursula persisted. 'I'm sure Mama can spare me for a few days until the mystery is solved.'

'Certainly, my dear, if it'll help,' Birgitta said. 'Family must help each other out in difficult times.'

Unless someone in the family is responsible for the difficulties...

Lavender wondered what Ursula was capable of. If her father inherited Willow Marsh Manor then the wealthy local heiress would be her, not Susanna – and Hal wouldn't be able to resist her.

'Right now,' Lavender persisted, 'I need to know where you all were at the time of the attack on Miss Susanna.'

Tobias looked like he would explode again but his wife held up her hand to silence him.

'That is easily explained as far as my family is concerned, Detective,' Birgitta said. 'My husband, daughter and I were in the parlour with Miranda and her lawyer. We'd been there for half an hour, waiting for Adrian so we could return to Ely. Our boatman has arrived.'

'Did any of you see or hear anyone come out of this hall into the entrance of the south tower, in the moments before you heard myself and Constable Woods dash through?'

They shook their heads.

'Tobias and I were arguing about my father's will again,' Miranda said, sighing. 'I doubt we'd have heard the four horsemen of the apocalypse traipse through the hallway.'

Lavender braced himself and turned to Hal Pammenter. 'And you, sir. Where were you?'

'You know damned well where I was, Lavender – and with whom.' Hal's voice was cold and controlled. 'We were deep in conversation.'

'It sounded more like an argument to me,' Woods interrupted.

Hal ignored him and glanced at Lucy for confirmation. 'We never heard anyone climb up or down that concealed staircase to the battlements. Nor did we hear the parapet topple over. The walls of the tower are incredibly thick.'

Behind Miranda's wheelchair, Lucy Pammenter nodded her head in agreement with every word he said. Lavender's eyes narrowed and his gaze shifted between the pair of them. The tension in the lofty hall ratchetted up as the other family members realised the significance of this line of questioning.

'I know what this looks like, Lavender,' Hal repeated firmly. 'But I'm a man of the law. I'd advise you to be careful before you make any outlandish accusations against me. I've an alibi for the time of the attack,' He pointed at Lucy. 'She can vouch for me.'

All traces of boyish softness had left Hal's face and voice. His eyes glittered with anger. He'd assumed that unemotional, confident, hands-on-hips stance Lavender knew so well from the fiery courtroom barristers in the Old Bailey.

'This is very convenient.'

'Convenient, yes, but it's true.'

'Is it, Lucy?' Miranda asked her companion.

'Yes, it's true.' The words of affirmation tumbled out of Lucy's mouth. Her throat sounded dry. This was the first time Lavender had heard her speak.

Unused to being the centre of attention, Lucy blushed painfully when she added: 'Hal and I talked for about twenty minutes. He didn't go up to the battlements.'

'What did you discuss?' Lavender asked, but her eyes lowered under the harsh scrutiny of Lavender's gaze and she refused to speak out further.

'Why would Hal want to hurt me anyway?' Susanna's tone was incredulous. 'He's never been anything but affectionate and kind to me throughout my life and he has nothing to gain.' She gave Hal a sweet smile, which he returned.

Her words eased some of the tension in the room, but Miranda's shoulders remained rigid. She stared coldly at Hal, as if assessing the level of his potential threat towards Susanna. 'I don't know why anyone wants to hurt you, my darling,' she said quietly, 'but unfortunately, someone does.'

Two large tears trickled down Susanna's pale cheeks. She fumbled for her handkerchief. 'Oh, I'm so sorry! Please excuse me, everyone! I can't stop thinking about poor Mr Mabberley.'

'I'm not surprised you're upset, but you'll be safe in the care of Constable Woods, Miss Susanna,' Lavender said. 'Now, if you'll excuse me, Miss Delamere, I'll set off to Ely immediately to seek out the magistrate. Speed is of the essence here.' He turned towards Tobias. 'I need to take your boat, Mr Delamere. Our own won't arrive until noon. You can return to Ely in that.'

Tobias started to protest at Lavender's 'damned cheek', but Lavender ignored him. He gestured to Woods and walked a short way down the hall, out of earshot of the family.

'Just stay close to the girl, Ned – and keep her inside. I'll be back as soon as I can, probably later this afternoon.'

'What about him?' Woods jerked his thumb in the direction of Hal Pammenter. 'I didn't believe a word of his denial, did you? That man's hidin' somethin'.'

'There's nothing we can do while Lucy is providing him with an alibi. Keep a sharp eye on him – and his Yankee mate. Pammenter is here to enact some scheme and I suspect Quinn is part of it.'

'I will do, sir.'

Lavender nodded. 'Keep questioning them all. If you manage to get Susanna alone, she might be a good source of information and she'll be more forthcoming than Miranda ever will be. I want to know how Hal Pammenter fits in here – and what his relationship is with that Lucy woman. I know she's their first cousin, but what's he?'

'He's treated like an adopted son,' Woods said.

'Yes – and maybe he has the aspirations of a real son and heir.'

Woods glanced over at the bowed, greying head of Lucy Pammenter. 'She's a funny one, too. I think she might be sixpence short of a full shillin'.'

Lavender followed his gaze towards the servant. 'Don't trust any of them. There's a lack of morality, a degeneracy about this household. Their respectability is a thin veneer and remember – this family has already bred one murderer.'

'It's like the shadow of that cove, Frederick, still hangs over this house,' Woods said grimly.

It was an irrational suggestion, of course, but one that left Lavender with a faint sense of unease. 'I haven't dismissed the notion that Tobias has hired an assassin who's hiding out somewhere on the estate,' he murmured.

Woods nodded. 'Yes, sir. And *I* haven't dismissed the notion that someone here means you harm. Take care.'

Lavender left the house and tramped across the wet gravel to find the boatman down by the river.

It was drizzling now and visibility was poor. But the soft caress of the rain on his skin and the scent of damp vegetation was a welcome relief from the tension and the cloying stench of deception in the Delamere family home.

Within a few minutes, the boatman had rowed them round the bend into the centre of the Great Ouse river.

For the first time, Lavender saw the area in daylight, albeit weak daylight. The banks of the swollen river were lined with a thick fringe of green reeds crested with the purple-headed froth of flowers, but further back the marshes turned to grey as the sky seeped down into them. Only the distant pale towers of Ely Cathedral broke up the monotony of grey.

The boatman had barely leaned into his rhythm when the air was rent with the powerful crack of a pistol shot.

Splinters leapt into the air a few inches from his face. Dozens of waterfowl rose, screeching in panic. Lavender fell back into the bottom of the boat, cursed and scrambled for his own weapon. 'Get down!' he yelled at the boatman. 'Get your bloody head down!'

The boatman laughed and continued his steady stroke. 'Tha's a rum 'un, maister. Wassup?'

'Someone's shooting at us. For the love of God, get down!' Lavender cocked his pistol and aimed it over the side towards where the sniper hid behind a curtain of swaying reeds.

The boatman chuckled. 'Git up, lad,' the boatman chuckled. 'It'll be nowt but a splodger huntin' fer ducks and other fowl.'

Lavender tensed and remained where he was. His sharp eyes scoured the bank for any sign of movement, a sudden glint of metal or the telltale puff of gunpowder. It wasn't his problem if the idiot boatman didn't heed his warning and continued to pull them towards Ely.

When they'd covered another hundred yards, Lavender sat up. At the other end of the vessel, the boatman still chortled with amusement and muttered about 'daft southerners'.

Lavender ignored him and examined the small, fresh nick on the tar-blackened edge of the prow of the boat. He had no doubt what had caused this scar on the wood and sent the splinters flying. The shot had skimmed the front of the boat, inches from his body.

Something prickled in the nape of his neck. The shooter was still watching them.

Ned had been right. Someone out here was determined to kill him.

Chapter Twenty-Two

Once Lavender left, Woods turned back to the family. Susanna complained of a headache and expressed her desire to return to her room.

'Shall I come upstairs with you, Cousin?' Ursula asked.

Susanna shook her head. 'No, thank you. I need to rest for a while.' Her family made sympathetic noises and she rose gracefully and left the hall with Woods by her side. 'I'll escort you to your room and wait outside, Miss.'

'There's no need to wait, Constable. There's a lock on my chamber door.'

'Good, but I want to examine your room first before I leave you.' He felt sorry for the gal. Any pleasure she may have felt this morning about her inheritance had now vanished. Money was a poisoned chalice sometimes, he reminded himself. It brought out jealousy, resentment – and sometimes murder, assuming money was the motive here.

As he accompanied her to the winding staircase, his eyes lingered on the panelled wall and the cupboard beneath the stairs. Didn't Lavender say something about a priest hole down there? He'd come back and examine it while Susanna rested. It was time this damned manor house gave up the rest of its secrets.

Even in the gloom of an overcast autumn day, Susanna's chamber was delightfully feminine. The soft scent of perfume lingered in the air. Frilled drapes hung at the window, a white counterpane embroidered with a soft green and yellow honeysuckle pattern covered the bed, and crocheted doilies adorned the polished wooden surfaces. On the dresser was an expensive array of tortoiseshell and gilt trinket boxes, along with silver hairbrushes, a musical box and a hand mirror.

Woods ignored these glittering and silky distractions and examined the bolt on the back of the door. He fingered the strong metal with satisfaction; no sly creepers would get past that.

Susanna sat on the edge of the bed and watched while Woods dropped down to peer beneath the iron bedframe and then flung open the closet door to check its contents. 'Sorry, Miss, I'm just doin' my job.'

She gave him a wan smile. 'I think I'll rest a while.'

'You do that, Miss – but make sure you bolt the door after I've gone. I'll be downstairs in the hallway. I intend to find the old priest hole and examine it.'

Another faint smile. 'You think the villain who tried to kill me is hiding in there?'

'I don't know, treacle, but it's worth a look.'

He turned to leave but her next words stopped him in his tracks. 'If you want to explore all the secret places, you'd better examine the old smugglers' tunnel down at the boathouse too.'

Woods started. 'A smugglers' tunnel?' No one had mentioned one of those.

'Yes, I think it was used for smuggling the Catholic priests in and out of the house unseen.'

'Along with a barrel or three of brandy?'

Susanna smiled ruefully. 'Probably. I'll show you later, after I've rested. Hal and I found the boathouse entrance years ago, but it's blocked and it's a mystery where the tunnel leads to. It's supposed to be the north tower. My cousins and I spent one rainy summer tearing the library apart trying to find it – but to no avail.'

'I'll look forward to that, Miss Susanna. Now please get some rest.'

But she didn't seem to want to let him go just yet. 'You make me feel safe with your care, Constable. Do you have children at home in London?'

'Yes, miss. Two small daughters – Rachel and little Tabby – and a pair of strappin' big lads, Dan and Eddie. My Eddie's nearly a full-grown man now. He works with me at Bow Street Police Office,' he added with pride.

'I've often thought how wonderful it must be to have brothers and sisters,' she said wistfully. 'I've plenty of cousins, as you've seen, but my dolls were my main playmates. Like Mr Quinn, I had a very quiet childhood.'

Woods gave her his broadest grin. 'That can be an advantage, miss, if you don't mind me sayin'. My nippers often scrap among themselves. It comes to blows sometimes.'

A small smile flitted around her lips, but it quickly vanished. Fear stole once more into her eyes. 'Do you think one of my family is trying to murder me, Constable?'

'I don't know, treacle, but I do know this: Detective Lavender will find out what's goin' on. He'll discover the fiend who pushed you into the water and tried to drop those stones on your head. He's the best detective in England and never fails to get his man. Or his woman. Sometimes the villains have been women.'

'Thank you, Constable. That's… that's comforting to know.'

'Do you worry about any of them in particular?' he asked cautiously. 'Have any of them ever made you fearful?'

'Heavens, no! But… but I suppose everything has changed since Grandfather left me Willow Marsh Manor. The relationships in my family have always—' She hesitated for a moment. '—always been complicated. More complicated than in most families, I suspect.'

Woods itched to question her further, but a dark shadow passed across her face. She touched her temple with her fingertips and tried to blink away the aching weariness.

'I'll only be in the hallway downstairs if you need me, Miss. Just shout out.' He left the room and once he heard her shoot home the bolt, he descended the stairs.

Adrian hovered at the bottom of the staircase. 'Is Miss Susanna all right, Constable?'

Woods bit back his smile. It was a while since he'd come across anyone as besotted as Adrian Delamere. 'Yes. She's restin' now.'

'Good, good. Constable Woods, I want to ask you—'

'All in good time, sir, I'm sure. But before you do, first things first. Where's this bloomin' priest hole? I understand it's here somewhere, below these stairs.'

Adrian blinked in surprise. 'Yes, yes, of course.' He dragged the large wooden chest beside the staircase to one side, raised the heel of his right palm and pressed it against the corner of one of the panels. With barely a creak, a low doorway suddenly appeared. It moved backwards under the stairs and, with further pressure from Adrian, slid silently to one side. Woods observed the gap thoughtfully. Only short, thin priests were welcome here, he decided.

'We loved to play hide-and-seek in here when we were children,' Adrian explained.

Woods ducked his head and peered inside the gloomy compartment. It contained a small, three-legged wooden stool and an ancient candle holder. A tiny ray of light with floating dust motes filtered down to the floor from a spyhole in the far wall.

Woods turned sideways, squeezed into the narrow space and lowered himself down on the stool. 'It's a good job we constables of the law don't need hidey-holes,' he muttered. 'You stay there, young fella. You may need to be a hero again and pull me out if I get stuck.'

178

He leaned forward and peered through the spyhole between the priest hole and the banqueting hall. He reckoned the hole had been discreetly drilled behind the armpit of a suit of armour mounted on a plinth on the other side of the wall.

He saw Miranda in her wheelchair and Tobias and Birgitta still sprawled across the ancient settles by the fireplace at the far end of the room. They were arguing again. Lucy Pammenter hovered beside Miranda but there was no sign of Ursula, Hal or his American friend. The youngsters must have left the room when he went upstairs with Miss Susanna.

'So, I'm a hero, am I?' Adrian was saying. 'Is that what Susanna called me?'

Woods started to inch his way out of the priest hole. 'I understand you saved her from drownin', sir. I'm sure she thinks of you as a hero.'

Adrian was still blushing when Woods finally emerged. 'I didn't know – I don't know – how she feels about me. I just wondered if the "hero" comment was something Lavender said – or Susanna.'

'All Lavender has said about you, sir, is you weren't suspected of shovin' those stones off the battlements.'

Confusion and disappointment flitted across the young man's face in equal measure. 'As I was also in the direct line of fire, it's hardly surprising he doesn't suspect me of that despicable act. Tell me, Constable,' he added quickly, 'who does he think killed poor Matthew Mabberley and why? I find this murder very disturbing.'

'It isn't Lavender's way to reveal his hand about anythin' before he's absolutely sure of the facts.' Woods shut the door to the priest hole. It slid back into place with a gentle click.

Adrian opened his mouth to question him further, but Woods cut him off. 'When he's sure of his facts, he'll tell us what we need to know. Is that the last one, sir? The last of the secret passageways and hidey-holes in this here manor house?'

'As far as I know. The secret staircase in the north tower and this priest hole provided plenty of storage space for priests and smuggled goods.'

'Your family was involved in the trade in the old days, was it?'

Adrian shrugged. 'Probably. I'm sure a significant part of the Delamere fortune came from their involvement in smuggling. My family have never been angels.'

You're right there, Woods thought. This twisted family would give half the villains in the rookery of St Giles down in London a real run for their money. 'You've been very helpful, Mr Delamere, thank you, sir.'

Adrian returned to his family in the banqueting hall and Woods sat down on a hard-backed chair in the hallway to wait.

Soon after, the manservant, Hawkes, came in to tell the Ely branch of the family the boat had arrived to take them back to the city. The next few minutes were a bustle of activity as Tobias, Birgitta, Adrian and Doctor Bendall donned their outdoor attire. Ursula reappeared from nowhere to kiss her parents and brother goodbye and Lucy Pammenter wheeled Miranda out of the great hall to say farewell to her relatives. Her parting with Tobias was frosty but polite.

Woods sighed with relief when the great wooden doors finally closed and the remaining family dispersed – Ursula disappeared upstairs to her own chamber and Lucy pushed Miranda into the parlour to join Symonds, who was still sifting through the estate papers.

But Woods' peace was short-lived.

Hawkes returned to the house and entered the parlour. A few moments later, Woods heard raised voices from within – Lucy Pammenter was yelling at Miranda. Woods suddenly made a connection: hers was the raised voice that had woken him that morning.

The parlour door flew open and Lucy stormed into the hallway. Hawkes followed and tried to restrain her. She shook off his hand and gave Woods a withering glance of disgust. 'You!' she screeched. 'This is all your fault, damn you!' She marched across and gave him a sharp kick in his shin.

It didn't hurt but he was so startled he cursed and leapt to his feet.

'Lucy! Behave!' Miranda yelled from inside the room.

'Easy now, ma'am.' Hawkes tried to grab her again and steer her away from Woods.

She shrugged him off once more, strode to the door and yanked it open. Hawkes hurried after her.

'Get off me!' she yelled as they crunched across the gravel towards the servants' quarters.

Woods watched from the door and chortled when the infuriated woman aimed another kick at the backside of a small piglet and a couple of hens. The animals squealed, squawked and scurried out of her way. Hawkes made no attempt to manhandle the woman again, but he followed her closely up the stone steps of the gatehouse.

Shrugging, Woods closed the door and returned to his post on the chair, shaking his head. This family loved their ruddy arguments.

Miranda was sat in her wheelchair in the doorway to the parlour. Her unexpected appearance made him start. She gave an apologetic smile, which came nowhere near touching those watchful eyes. 'I'm sorry for the disturbance, Constable. The events of the last two days have been too much for Lucy – she becomes overexcited.'

'Don't worry about it, ma'am.'

181

She backed her wheelchair into the room and closed the door behind her.

The front door soon opened again and Hal and Robert Quinn entered the house with a blast of cold wind and a flurry of dried leaves. They paused in the hallway to remove their wet outer garments.

'Where've you fellas been?' Woods asked abruptly. Hal was their main suspect and if he had his way, the young lawyer would be clapped in handcuffs and sitting in the damp cellar right now.

'For a long walk,' Hal replied sharply. 'We needed a break from my bickering family.'

The American was carrying a small bunch of yellow and purple marsh flowers and had one muddy boot on the bottom step of the staircase before Woods stopped him.

'No, you don't, young fella. If you're plannin' on takin' those up to Miss Susanna and disturbin' her, you can think again.'

Hal burst out laughing as he peeled off his gloves and dropped them into his hat on the hall table. 'Good God! It's worse than having a chaperone in the house.'

Woods rose to his feet. 'I'm serious, lads. We'll leave the poor gal alone for the time bein'. She's had a devil of a shock and has a splittin' headache.'

Quinn hesitated, glanced at Hal for support then changed his mind. 'Very well, sir, I'll give these to a maid to put in water.' He disappeared into the kitchen.

'I know you constables aren't famous for your intelligence,' Hal said languidly, 'but has it crossed your mind over the last hour or so that sweet little Susanna may not have been the killer's intended victim?'

Woods bristled at the insult. 'What do you mean?'

'Oh, I think you know what I mean.' Hal paused and when Woods didn't reply he lowered his voice and added: 'It could have been Quinn the murderer intended to kill.'

'And why would anyone want to kill Mr Quinn, sir?'

Hal laughed. 'Why indeed?'

'If you know somethin', sir…'

'Oh, I *do* know something, Constable – and it's a lot more than some folks want me to know. For a start, I suspect Quinn has more right to inherit this damned estate than the rest of us put together.'

Woods was surprised by the vehemence of his tone. 'You need to take a claim like that to the court of chancery.'

'Yes, I do, don't I?' Hal gave him a brilliant white smile. 'But knowing the truth is one thing, Constable – proving it is quite another. Never mind, they might throw him a crumb – provided they don't kill him first.'

'Who's *they*, sir?'

'Who indeed, Constable, who indeed.' Quinn reappeared and, ignoring Woods, Hal gestured for him to follow him into the banqueting hall. 'Come on. I need a drink. With any luck, there's some brandy left from last night – unless Cousin Ursula finished off the bottle.'

Quinn laughed. 'She sure is a feisty dame.'

The two men left Woods with his question unanswered. He stared after Hal with narrowed eyes, trying to work out how seriously he was supposed to take the young fella's flippant comments. He was a joker, Woods decided, a prankster.

Yet why was he left with the uneasy suspicion that Hal had tried to warn him about something?

Chapter Twenty-Three

Lavender was relieved to find Magistrate John Kester, a youngish man in his early forties, at home in his smart terraced house overlooking the Palace Green. Kester was stretched out in his chair by the fireside of his study, reading a book, when the maid showed Lavender into the room. He rose to greet him.

'Your reputation precedes you, Detective.' Kester spoke slowly with the soft burr of the local accent, but his slow, measured speech was deceptive. Intelligence gleamed in the magistrate's hooded brown eyes. 'Please take a seat. I can't wait to find out what brings an officer of your calibre to Ely.'

Lavender sat down and explained how he'd been invited to Willow Marsh Manor by Miranda Delamere, who was concerned for the safety of her niece. Kester looked shocked when he heard about the two attempts to kill the young woman and his broad face flushed with anger when Lavender told him about the death of the Willow Marsh steward. 'Poor Mabberley! He was well respected and much liked in these parts. Where did you say it happened?'

Lavender told him about the sabotaged wind pump and his suspicion that Mabberley may have disturbed a smuggling ring.

'What's the matter with these people?' Kester exclaimed. 'To kill a decent man like that and make a widow of his wife for the sake of a few casks of brandy and tobacco! Where's the sense in it?

'Are your local smugglers usually this vicious?'

The magistrate nodded grimly. 'They can be. Thirty years ago, a gang murdered an excise man and an officer from the Light Dragoons at Old Hunstanton, near King's Lynn on the coast.'

'We need to speak to Lieutenant Isiah Waterbeach, our customs supervisor – he'll know more about this generation of thieving bastards,' Kester continued. 'I'll take you to meet him now.'

Lavender struggled to keep up with the fast pace set by the tall magistrate as they strode down the cobbled streets towards the river, retracing the route he and Woods had taken through the poorer part of town the previous evening. The street narrowed and darkened as the weathered upper eaves of the medieval buildings leaned overhead towards the mouldy thatch of sagging cottages.

'How soon can you organise the inquest?' Lavender asked.

'As it happens, I've already assembled a jury for tomorrow morning – a local farmer accidentally shot himself last week with his own blunderbuss. We're holding his inquest at nine in The Lamb. It'll just be a formality, shouldn't take long. If Miss Delamere can arrange for Mabberley's body to be brought to the tavern by ten o'clock, we can hold both inquests one after the other. The body will be released to the family for burial immediately afterwards.'

'I'm sure that will be possible. Adrian Delamere and I found the body. Do you need us both to attend the inquest? He's returning home to Ely today.'

'Yes. I'll send a note to Delamere at his father's house,' Kester said. 'Lavender, are you and your constable quite happy to undertake this investigation into the attack on Miss Susanna on behalf of the city? And do you need any assistance from the local constabulary? I can spare you a man if you think he might be helpful.'

After a moment's thought, Lavender nodded. 'Yes, please. It would be useful to have an extra officer to help protect Susanna Delamere. This will free up Woods to assist me.'

They stepped aside to let a brewer's dray, piled with barrels and hauled by the rippling muscles of a broad-shouldered shire horse, squeeze past.

Kester led him another fifty yards down the street then paused on the narrow steps of The Angel Inn, a plain utilitarian building with peeling paintwork by the edge of the wharf. 'The customs men use a back room in here to conduct their business. Do you think these two incidents are connected? Did the same cove who killed Mabberley try to murder Miss Susanna?'

'I don't know,' Lavender admitted, 'but I doubt it. I suspect we're dealing with two distinct sets of criminals.'

Kester nodded. 'Waterbeach may be our best man to deal with the vermin who killed Mabberley. He can take over that case and leave you to focus on the threat to Miss Susanna.'

The thin-faced, bearded chief of the excise men was a former naval officer. He had a booming voice more suited to hollering out instructions amid a thundery squall on the high seas than the low-ceilinged back room of an old tavern. His restless energy would have left most men half his age standing. He glowered and shuffled angrily while Lavender told him how he and Woods had examined the scene of the crime and had come to suspect smugglers had murdered Matthew Mabberley.

Waterbeach barely waited for Lavender to finish before he reached up to a shelf behind his desk and pulled down a large map. 'These scoundrels get more imaginative with every load of contraband they bring ashore.' He smoothed out the map and, frowning, traced his finger down the Willow Marsh lode until it drained into the Great Ouse. 'There's a thousand of them old wind pumps in the fens. They make the ideal hiding place to stash their brandy and baccy until it's safe to move it further inland.'

'I don't think they're smuggling brandy or tobacco,' Lavender said, rubbing the flea bite on his wrist.

Two pairs of narrowed brown eyes turned sharply in his direction. 'What?'

'I know this sounds fantastical but I think it might be hides, animal hides or furs. The wind pump smelled of wet dog and was crawling with animal fleas.'

'Fleas!' Waterbeach snorted with laughter but the amusement didn't reach his eyes. 'Perhaps an old dog fox climbed inside and used the pump for a den.'

'No,' Lavender persisted, 'I think this gang are importing expensive animal furs into the country and trying to avoid the duty payable on them. The price of sable is phenomenally high – and the import tax on it likewise. Sable, ermine and Arctic fox all command a huge price in the fashion houses of London.'

A smile twitched at the side of Waterbeach's mouth. 'You seem very well informed about ladies' fashions, Lavender. Has Mrs Lavender been pestering you for a new fur cape?'

'It can take months for fleas to die once an animal has been skinned,' Kester said thoughtfully. Lavender welcomed his intervention. Waterbeach's cynicism had started to annoy him.

'These animals are hunted in the Siberian wilderness of Russia and shipped out through the Baltic,' Lavender continued. 'London's only a day's ride from here. It's an ideal location to sneak high-value merchandise into the country and avoid a tariff. With the right contacts in London, smuggling furs must be extremely profitable.'

Kester turned to face the still-sceptical excise man and spoke quietly in his low, measured manner. 'According to *The Times*, Detective Lavender has one of the finest minds in England. His knowledge and experience of the criminal fraternity is unsurpassed.'

Waterbeach chewed his upper lip. 'It's an unusual suggestion, Lavender.'

'But based on the evidence he found – and smelled – at the scene of the crime, it seems plausible to me,' Kester added.

Waterbeach stroked his beard thoughtfully. 'We've had word that there's a vicious new gang operating in this area. I wonder if there's a connection? They're tight-lipped and keep themselves to themselves and they don't share the profits with the locals.'

'I imagine this has ruffled some feathers in Ely,' Kester said.

Waterbeach nodded. 'We're hoping one of the locals will turn informer soon and lead us to them. Our homegrown villains don't appreciate strangers on their patch.'

That made sense, Lavender thought. The best organised and most carefully orchestrated smuggling runs usually involved teams of up to sixty local men and a whole herd of horses and mules to haul the contraband inland from the shore. There was hardly a hamlet or town along Britain's vast shoreline where the residents didn't collude with the local smugglers to avoid the heavy import duties on French brandy, Dutch gin and tobacco. And they didn't take kindly to anyone else stealing their profits.

'If what you've said about the tension between your local rogues and this new gang is true,' Lavender suggested, 'they may have murdered Mabberley as a warning. The gangs in the Seven Dials of London frequently do that. Do you have a map showing the location of the other water pumps in the area?'

'I don't – but Arthur Pennington over at the office of the local drainage board may have one. Why do you ask?'

'Because it's possible this gang may use other wind pumps in the area for the same purpose.'

'What?' Kester and Waterbeach exclaimed together.

189

'This is speculation, of course, but these wind pumps are dry and are ideal places to store goods like fur and hides that get heavy when wet.'

'Surely animal fur is waterproof?' Kester said.

'It is, but water doesn't just run off fur like it does a brandy keg. It becomes waterlogged and heavy. For ease of transport, it's important to store it somewhere dry.'

'So you think there might be more smuggled furs in the wind pumps out in the marshes?' Waterbeach said.

'Yes, especially in those that drain into the lodes that connect with the river.'

Waterbeach shook his greying head and laughed. 'Well, it's a shame we'll never get to find out if this theory is correct, Lavender.'

'Why not?'

'Because as I said earlier, there's over a thousand of these damned wind pumps in the fens!' said the excise man. 'I just don't have the men to investigate them all.'

'Can you narrow down the search to just the broken wind pumps?' Lavender suggested. 'That's why Mabberley was out there – investigating a damaged wind pump. The villains had jammed the machinery to still the piston and make more space for their contraband. And you only need to examine the pumps close to the Great Ouse. The river is the key to this operation. The smugglers must have sailed downriver via King's Lynn and used small boats to offload their goods into the wind pumps.'

Kester turned to Waterbeach. 'What do you think, Isiah?'

'I think,' the excise man said, tapping the map, 'your detective may be a very clever man after all. It's worth exploring this further. The local landowners pay the drainage company to keep the pumps in good order. My friend Arthur Pennington is in charge. He may be able to help us with that.'

'Will you introduce me?' Kester asked.

190

'Certainly. I'll take you to see him now.'

Kester leaned forward and rolled up the map, his mouth set in a determined line. 'Leave this investigation into Mabberley's death with me and Waterbeach, Lavender – and thank you for your help. This may be the best lead we ever get in our fight against these smugglers.'

Chapter Twenty-Four

As Lavender and the two men walked through the smoky tap room at the front of the tavern, Waterbeach promised to keep Lavender informed of developments. He seemed competent and dedicated; he and his men would be more familiar with this unforgiving watery terrain. This left him and Woods free to search for the heartless cove who'd tried to maim or kill young Susanna.

Before they reached the door, he heard a familiar, warbling old voice. 'Well! If it in't Detective Lavender!'

Jack Abbot's crinkled, watery eyes peered at him through a haze of tobacco smoke. He had an empty tankard in his hand and his clay pipe clamped between his toothless gums. 'An' if I recall roight,' Abbot continued, 'ye swore to stand me a tankard of ale in The Lamb last time we met.'

Lavender was about to make an excuse to leave, then changed his mind. 'I did make that promise, Mr Abbot. Please allow me to honour it.' Another half an hour and a quick bite to eat wouldn't hurt and Abbot may have some information that would throw light on the Delamere family mysteries that still perplexed him.

He said goodbye to Kester and Waterbeach, ordered a jug of ale and led the elderly man to a small rickety table beneath the bay window. 'How is Mrs Abbot? Does her rheumatism plague her in this damp weather?'

The old man's eyes widened with delight that Lavender had remembered him, and he rewarded him with a grin. 'No, my Martha be in fine fettle today, so I brought myself out for a while,' he said. 'So, have ye solved yer murder, Detective?' he added. 'And who were it that were killed? Yer didn't say yesterday.'

No, I didn't say, and yesterday no one was actually dead. Lavender's brain raced, and he decided to merge the events of the past two days. 'Alas, no – we don't know the killer – at least, not yet. The victim was Matthew Mabberley, the steward at Willow Marsh. He was stabbed in cold blood beside the Willow Marsh lode.'

'Mabberley!' The old fellow's pipe dropped from his mouth and there was a moment of panic as both men reached to extinguish the burning tobacco that fell onto his stained waistcoat.

'Did you know him?' Lavender asked.

'Yes, I knew him well – we all did round 'ere. My Martha is kin to the Hawkes who live at Willow Marsh. That ent roight. 'E were a decent fella and will be sorely missed.'

'I'm sorry for your loss.' Lavender let him grieve for a moment. He gestured to the barmaid to top up their tankards and fetch him a platter of bread and cheese.

''Tis a shockin' state of affairs,' said Abbot, shaking his head sadly, 'when decent men like Mabberley are slain in cold blood.' He sought solace in his pipe and had soon surrounded them both in voluminous clouds of smoke.

Eventually he sniffed, wiped his mouth and nose with the back of his coat sleeve and sat up a bit straighter. 'Is there anything I can do to help ye, Detective?'

'I would like you to tell me everything you know about the family and servants at Willow Marsh Manor.'

Abbot glanced at him sharply. 'Do yer think someone from the estate were the killer?'

'No,' Lavender said cautiously. 'It just helps me to understand the lie of things, the overall picture.'

Lavender's food arrived. He ate quickly while Abbot sucked on his pipe and stared at a spot over Lavender's shoulder with sad, glazed eyes. 'If that son of theirs, Mr Frederick, were still alive,' the old man eventually said, ''e'd be the first person fer ye to turn to fer a killer.'

'Did you know him?'

'I knew of him, aye.' Abbot's tone took on an uncharacteristic anger. 'Most folks in Ely knew of Frederick Delamere – especially after 'e were 'anged in London fer rapin' and murderin' a young gal.'

Lavender didn't put him right about Delamere's death.

''E were a nasty piece even in 'is youth,' Abbot continued. ''E couldn't leave the gals alone. 'E left several of the local wenches wi' a by-blow – includin' 'is own cousin.'

'His own cousin?' Lavender choked slightly on a piece of dry bread.

'Aye, that Pammenter woman who still lives with them,' Abbot confirmed.

'Is Lucy Pammenter the *mother* of Mr Hal Pammenter then?'

Abbot nodded, inhaled deeply and exhaled another billowing cloud of smoke. Lavender's mind whirled, frantically trying to make sense of this latest revelation.

According to the family Bible, Frederick Delamere and Lucy Pammenter were the same age; they would both have been fifteen years old when she fell pregnant. For a moment, Lavender was reminded of the great Shakespearean tragedy about star-crossed young lovers. But Lucy bore no resemblance to the vibrant Juliet Capulet and that fiend Delamere was no Romeo. Lavender winced at the thought of what the simple young girl may have suffered at his hands.

'She were sent away for a while in disgrace,' Abbot continued, 'but the family knew 'e were the devil incarnate and were mostly to blame. She were brought back after Frederick 'ad been sent fer a soldier. Maggie Hawkes told my Martha that Lawrence were glad to see the back of 'is son after 'e'd bought 'im 'is commission for the army. They reckon 'e didn't mourn 'im much when 'e were 'anged. Everyone knew Mr Frederick would meet a bad end one day.'

'So, Hal Pammenter is the son of Frederick Delamere,' Lavender said thoughtfully. That explained his strange comment to Ursula Delamere that there was a good reason why he couldn't marry his wealthy 'cousin' Susanna. He couldn't marry her because the girl was his half-sister.

But this closer relationship between Hal and Susanna only made the young man more of a suspect in Lavender's eyes. Hal would have been Lawrence Delamere's heir if he hadn't been hampered by his illegitimacy. Instead of inheriting the family estate, he had to settle for a mere five hundred a year while his young half-sister inherited the rest. That must be galling. It gave Hal a strong motive for murder.

Abbot took the comment for a question. 'Aye. 'E's a generous fella with his chinks is young Hal, easy-natured – but they say bad blood will out. Do ye think 'e may be a killer like 'is da? Did 'e murder poor Mabberley?'

Lavender hastily raised his hand. 'It's too early to come to any conclusions yet.' Several other men in the tavern were casting curious glances in their direction.

Abbot shrugged and sipped his ale. 'I'm sure you know yer business better than me, Detective.'

'Why was Pammenter raised at Willow Marsh Manor? Lawrence Delamere must have known folk would speculate that he himself might be the child's father.'

Abbot shrugged again. 'Maggie Hawkes said Miss Lucy pined badly for 'er child. So, Lawrence reunited mother and son. 'E claimed the babe were an orphaned cousin whom 'e planned to raise. But Miss Lucy is a bit sorft and only 'alf sharp. She couldn't 'ide 'er love for the boy. Folks round 'ere soon worked it out.'

Lavender felt new respect for the deceased owner of Willow Marsh Manor. Lawrence had done his best to right the wrongs caused by his vile son. This contrasted sharply with his brother and sister-in-law. When Lavender thought of the snide remarks and spitefulness of Tobias and Birgitta the night before, he frowned. No doubt Tobias knew the truth about Hal Pammenter's parentage but still preferred to slander his dead brother in front of strangers.

'Did Maggie Hawkes ever tell your Martha about how Miss Susanna came to live at Willow Marsh?' he asked Abbot. 'She's a few years younger than Hal Pammenter, isn't she?'

Abbot nodded and sipped his ale. 'Aye, she did – mind you, everyone knows the tale of that poor little mite.'

'They do?'

'Aye, that demon Major Frederick were away in India fightin' the black 'eathens when 'e met and married Miss Susanna's ma. The poor woman took ill on the return journey to England and she 'ad her babe on the ship but she didn't survive. The poor mite had already lost her ma when she first breathed English air.'

Died during the voyage? But Ginny Atkins met Delamere and his heavily pregnant wife in London. And Delamere later denied he'd ever been married. Something didn't add up.

'Miss Delamere took a coach straight down to London and brought the babe back to Willow Marsh.'

The door to the tavern opened suddenly and Magistrate Kester ducked his head below the lintel. His eyes scanned the room for Lavender and beckoned to him. Lavender downed the last of his ale and politely took his leave of Abbot.

Fastening his coat against the drizzle, he followed Kester out into the street. A man with a black hat pulled low over his dark hair waited for them there. Slightly disfigured with pockmarks, his nose had once been broken and hadn't set straight. But his eyes were clear and shone with intelligence.

Kester led them both down a quiet alley between the tavern and a thatched peat-drying shed, where no one would overhear them. 'I'm glad you were still in The Angel, Lavender. I've news for you. But firstly, I've made good on my promise to find you a good man to assist you with your inquiries. This is Constable Cudworth, one of Ely's finest. Cudworth, meet Detective Lavender, one of Bow Street's finest.'

The two men shook hands. There was strength in Cudworth's handshake and Lavender sensed the man was reliable and sharp-witted, if a bit nervous about meeting him.

'Secondly, there's been a development with your theory about the wind pumps.'

'Oh, yes?'

'Arthur Pennington from the drainage company has told us another wind pump has been recently reported as broken.'

A wave of excitement pulsed through Lavender. 'Where?'

'Brandon lode. It's further upriver from Willow Marsh lode, closer to the coast, but not far.'

'We must go there immediately. We need to see if this wind pump has also been rigged to store contraband.'

Kester laughed. 'Waterbeach and his excise men left ten minutes ago. I'm sure they would welcome an extra pair of hands – or two – if you and Cudworth wanted to join them.'

Lavender thanked the magistrate and turned towards the wharf with Cudworth by his side. 'Did Magistrate Kester tell you what's happened over at Willow Marsh Manor?'

His new constable nodded, frowning. 'Aye, it's very worryin', I'm sure. Is the attack on young Miss Susanna connected with Matt Mabberley's murder?'

Lavender shook his head. 'I don't think so – but I'm not prepared to rule out a connection just yet. There's something else you need to know, Cudworth,' Lavender added, as the two men clambered into a rowing boat down at the jetty. 'On the way here, some cove took a shot at me from the bank near Willow Marsh Manor. He kept himself hidden in the reeds but a pistol was definitely discharged.'

Apart from one raised eyebrow, the experienced constable's expression barely altered. 'I'll remember to keep me 'ead down when we go around the bend.'

Chapter Twenty-Five

When their boatman pulled on the oars and they glided out into the centre of the river, Lavender realised that this dull afternoon had become even darker. The grey clouds drooped lower over the flat landscape and wisps of fog drifted over the dark surface of the water. Lavender turned up his collar against the chilly damp and his eyes strained against the encroaching gloom for other traffic.

They travelled in tense silence. Only the cries of invisible waterfowl and the slap of the heaving water against the side of their boat ruptured the eerie quiet. When they approached Willow Marsh, both officers removed their pistols from their coat pockets and cocked the trigger. But they weren't needed. If Lavender's would-be assassin still lurked with his pistol in the riverbank reeds, the bastard would struggle to pick him out in such poor visibility.

A little further on, the boatman rowed into a narrow lode, identical to the channel that ran beside Willow Marsh Manor. Tall swishing reeds towered up on both sides, pulsating like waves on the sea, their small flowers a purple-headed froth.

'The wind pump is round the next bend,' Cudworth told Lavender.

'Pull over,' Lavender instructed the boatman. 'We'll walk from here. You can return to Ely.'

The fellow's weather-beaten face showed no emotion as he steered them to the muddy bank and held the boat steady while the two officers climbed out. It was impossible to know who to trust in this community and Lavender didn't want the boatman to witness whatever waited for them at the Brandon lode wind pump. The fewer people who knew his suspicions about the modus operandi of this smuggling gang the better. With luck, they'd be able to get a lift back with Waterbeach and his men.

Lavender and Cudworth walked in single file down the narrow towpath. In the misty distance, Lavender could just see the battlements of the north tower of Willow Marsh Manor.

The second they rounded the bend in the lode, he walked straight into the barrel of a loaded pistol.

'Whoa, there, fella,' The man behind the weapon was a large, whiskery brute with lank greasy hair. There was a distinctive click and the dry rustle of reeds and a second fellow in mud-splattered boots stepped out, his pistol aimed at Cudworth's head.

Lavender raised his hands and sent up a silent prayer that these were Waterbeach's excise men and not the smugglers. 'Is Lieutenant Waterbeach here?' he asked.

'Who the devil are you?' the big fellow growled, his face half hidden beneath the brim of his hat.

'Detective Lavender. Bow Street Police Office. This is Constable Cudworth from Ely. We're looking for Lieutenant Isiah Waterbeach.'

The gauger grunted and lowered his weapon. 'You'd best come this way. The lieutenant didn't say we were expectin' company like.'

He turned and led them towards the towering black pump, beside which four large rowing boats were moored. Just like at Willow Marsh, the pump's large white sails were immobile and the ground around it had flooded. Waterbeach and a dozen powerfully built excise men stood beside this large puddle on drier ground, examining the contents of two large barrels.

'Lavender!' Waterbeach boomed. The skin stretched taut over his sharp-featured face as he grinned. 'Come and take a look at this.'

Lavender splashed through the sodden ground and peered inside the open barrel. A wave of satisfaction flooded through him. The barrel was packed with glistening animal pelts.

Mesmerised by the luxury, he took off his glove and reached down to run his hands through the furs. He felt the weightless, silky satin texture of the sables and the denser ermine and fox. Even in the poor light of that foggy afternoon, the animal skins glimmered in luminous shades of beige, brown, gold, silver and shimmering black. The last time he'd touched something this soft was the down on his baby girl's head.

'These are definitely Russian furs,' Waterbeach told him. 'There's everything here from Siberian fox to sea otter, with a few Persian lamb skins thrown in for good measure. It's a valuable hoard, and no doubt their current owners will soon return to retrieve them.'

Lavender left the barrel and took a few steps to peer through the open hatch of the wind pump. Just as at Willow Marsh, the internal mechanism of the pump had been jammed with wooden staves.

'What do you plan to do?' Lavender asked, although he suspected he already knew the answer.

'Lie in wait for them, of course. After poor Mabberley stumbled across their other cache, I don't expect they'll leave these here long. They'll be back as soon as darkness falls.'

'They may not even wait until nightfall,' Lavender said thoughtfully. 'They seem quite happy to operate in broad daylight.'

'Which is why I need to hide my men as soon as possible.'

Lavender nodded. 'We'll get out of your way. Do you need any extra help? I've matters to deal with back at Willow Marsh, but I can come back with my constable tonight if you want?'

Waterbeach shook his head. 'Thank you – but no. You've helped us more than enough already. My men and I know what to do here. You concentrate on finding the villain who wants to harm that young girl. Besides which, they've been spotted. We've got a partial description of one of the bastards.'

Lavender turned towards him in surprise.

'We came across one of the local fen men and his donkey. He'd been collecting sedge for thatching and saw four men in two boats on Willow Marsh lode headed for the river. He was reluctant to talk but we *persuaded* him to tell us a bit. He said they wore hats and were hard-faced bastards – and one had a terrible scar – 'ere.' He ran a finger down his left cheek.

'Is he a reliable witness?' Lavender asked.

'I don't know. He also said the scar-faced cove yelled out to one of the fellows in the other boat in a posh voice but claimed they replied in a foreign language.'

A foreign language, Lavender wondered, or just some strong regional accent the fen man had never heard before? In a remote area like this, a 'foreigner' could be someone from Sheffield or Bristol. But by the sound of it, the scar-faced smuggler had an educated accent, which fitted in with Lavender's deduction that one of the men by the wind pump had worn expensive, smooth-soled boots.

'What about their cargo? What were they carrying?'

'Two large barrels – and a huge heap of something at the bottom of the boat, covered with oilskins.'

Furs, Lavender thought with satisfaction. He glanced over his shoulder at the faint outline of the towers of Willow Marsh Manor in the distance. 'Is there a way for us to return to Willow Marsh over the marshes?'

'Oh, there's always a way if you know it.' Waterbeach turned to one of his officers and beckoned him across. 'This is George Howard. He knows this area like the back of his hand. He'll lead you safely back to the Willow Marsh boathouse.'

'Thank you,' Lavender said, then added with surprise: 'There's a boathouse?'

'Yes, it's at the start of their lode,' Waterbeach replied.

'Take care, Lieutenant,' Lavender said when they parted. 'These men will be armed and dangerous. This is a valuable cargo and they'll fight hard to retrieve it.'

Chapter Twenty-Six

Woods shuffled uncomfortably on his hard, wooden seat in the draughty hallway. There was still no sign of Miss Susanna and after the unexpected drama of the morning it had been a dull few hours. Occasionally, he heard a burst of male laughter and the clink of glasses drifting out of the banqueting hall, or indistinct chatter and the clatter of pans in the kitchen, where Mrs Hawkes and her daughter had replaced the two Mabberley women today. But the only sounds that disturbed his solitude otherwise were the wind whistling through the porch roof outside the front door and the steady ticking of the large carriage case clock at the far, gloomy end of the hall.

He was therefore quite startled when the door to the small parlour suddenly opened and Mr Symonds appeared. The wiry little man squinted up at Woods through his pince-nez, inclined his head in a short bow, then disappeared in the direction of the privy.

Through the open door he saw Miranda Delamere sitting at the round table in the centre of the room with a pile of papers spread out before her. Lavender had told him to ask more questions about the family and this might be his only opportunity to get Miranda alone. If he left the door ajar, he'd be able to see and hear Miss Susanna if she descended the stairs.

'How can I help you, Constable?' Miranda said, without looking up.

'There's a couple of things botherin' me, ma'am. I've a few questions I'd like to ask, if you don't mind.'

'And I've a few questions for you, too, Constable,' she said, her head still bowed over her work. When he hesitated, she glanced up and gave him a pained smile. 'Please come in. We may be able to help each other.'

Woods nodded and approached her. She didn't ask him to sit down and he didn't suggest it. He didn't have Lavender's confidence and skill when it came to questioning the gentry and he knew he'd think better if he stayed on his feet. 'You first, ma'am. What do you want to know?'

'Lavender dashed off to Ely before I had chance to question him properly regarding his thoughts about poor Mabberley's death.'

Woods had expected this. Generally, Lavender didn't like to reveal his line of inquiry until he had enough evidence to support his suspicions, but Miranda Delamere was paying their bill and had a right to know.

'He thinks Mr Mabberley disturbed a gang of smugglers, ma'am.' Quietly, he explained about the sabotaged wind pump and the numerous muddy boot prints on the bank of the lode.

Miranda nodded thoughtfully but her lined face creased into a frown. 'That's a plausible theory up to a point. Running contraband has been a way of life for many generations of the fen men and women and a huge swathe of the population are involved in the illicit practice. Poverty is extreme in this area and even those who don't profit from it look the other way if they suspect something.'

'Was Steward Mabberley the kind of man to look the other way?'

'I honestly don't know.' She shook her head sadly. 'It probably would have depended how hard they pleaded with him to forget what he saw. But I do know he was well liked in this community. I still find it hard to believe someone from round here would stab him to death, even one of our local smugglers.'

Woods' bushy grey eyebrows met across the bridge of his broad nose as another possibility struck him. 'Perhaps these coves weren't local,' he said thoughtfully.

'Anyway, Constable, how can I help *you*?'

Woods stood up straighter and checked over his shoulder that no one was in the hallway, eavesdropping. 'Detective Lavender asked me to try and find out more about Mr Henry Pammenter, ma'am. I don't think he trusts him.'

'I see.' Miranda laid down her quill. 'I don't think he's capable of murdering Susanna, but since his arrival with Robert Quinn, like Lavender, I've found him sly and evasive. You do realise, don't you, that my cousin, Lucy, is his mother?'

Woods gasped. 'But when he arrived last night, he barely acknowledged her – nor she him!'

'Yes, I can see how strange that looks to someone not familiar with our family. To be honest, constable, Hal has been distant with his mother for many years now, especially in public. He's a bright and vivacious young man but he's sensitive about his illegitimacy and his mother's, erm, limitations – especially when there are strangers present.'

'Her limitations?'

'Yes. You may have noticed how volatile my dear Lucy can be. One moment she's withdrawn and timid – the next she becomes overexcited. I've sent her to lie down for the rest of the afternoon. She has trouble understanding things sometimes.'

Woods nodded and let her continue.

'Lucy had a terrible experience when she was young and was badly affected by it,' Miranda continued. 'She barely survived the tragic coach accident that killed her parents and although my family and I took her in and gave her all the love and care we could, she never really recovered.'

'And then she found herself with child?'

A flush of colour crept up Miranda's neck and she too glanced at the partially open door to the hall.

'Yes. My parents were scandalised, of course – she was fifteen at the time. They'd hoped to marry her off to a local clergyman or some other gentle neighbour who would make allowances for her limitations, but now that would never happen. The only course open to them was to send Lucy and her child to an institution that catered for disgraced young women from genteel families.'

'But they didn't send her away?'

'No, they were too fond of her – and eventually they grew to love her child too. We all did. I tell you this in confidence, Constable. I hope you can respect this?'

'Of course, ma'am. Miss Pammenter's disgrace has no bearin' on the case.'

She nodded, satisfied. 'Hal was a delightful child. I'm a few years younger than Lucy and was barely more than a child myself when this happened, but I grew up loving Lucy's boy like my own. Hal is – and always was – a most loveable young man.'

'This arrangement sounds very compassionate, ma'am, although I'm sure it scandalised your neighbours.'

'Of course, it did – you must have heard my Uncle Tobias last night. Most of the local gentry were shocked my parents continued to let their disgraced niece live under their roof. They had to weather a lot of disapproval, but they were determined.'

Woods shuffled uncomfortably. Tobias Delamere had made several pointed comments suggesting his brother, Lawrence, was Hal's father. But Miranda's constant references to her mother's involvement in this charitable treatment of Lucy Pammenter made Woods doubt that nasty notion. As a rule, women weren't kind to their husband's by-blow and mistresses. He decided to let the matter of Hal Pammenter's paternity drop. If Lavender was still desperate to find out who'd fathered the fella, he could ask her himself.

210

'May I ask you for your advice on another matter, Constable?'

'Certainly, ma'am. How can I help?'

Just at that moment, the lawyer returned.

'Oh, good,' Miranda said. 'You're back, Mr Symonds. I was just about to explain our predicament to the constable. I thought he may be able to help.'

Symonds looked doubtful about that but silently resumed his seat at the table.

Miranda waved towards a pile of documents on the table. 'As you may have gathered, Constable, Hal caught us by surprise when he appeared last night with Mr Quinn. He insists he's my sister's child and seems to think he has a valid claim against the estate of my late father, although on what grounds, I can't imagine. Mr Quinn has given us a selection of papers, which he claims prove his identity. I wondered if you'd ever come across a similar situation to ours in your line of work?'

Fraud, Woods thought. *For all her fine words about Hal Pammenter, she thinks he and Quinn are a pair of sharp swindlers who want to diddle Miss Susanna out of her inheritance.*

'Do his papers seem genuine, sir?' Woods asked Symonds.

The lawyer cleared his throat and adjusted his pince-nez. 'There's a letter from a church minister among his papers. But it's impossible to tell if it's genuine, Constable. It may be forged.'

'How Hal can't see that, I don't know,' Miranda murmured softly. 'I suspect he's somewhat blinded by young Quinn.'

'May I make a suggestion, Miss Delamere?'

'Please do.'

'I remember a case where a wealthy lady asked Lavender for advice about how to track down her cheatin' husband. He'd skipped over to Portugal with most of the family fortune.'

'Oh, my goodness!' Miranda looked intrigued. 'Did she want her husband back – or the money?'

'The money mostly, I think.'

'What did Lavender advise the lady to do?'

'He suggested she made independent enquiries through a British-speakin' lawyer in Lisbon. If I was you, ma'am – I'd ask Mr Symonds here to do the same and get a lawyer in Carolina to investigate the Quinn family. I've heard Charleston is a small town and Quinn is an unusual name on this side of the Atlantic, never mind over there. I'm sure a fellow lawyer in the Americas would be happy to oblige for a small fee. No offence, sir, but I've never heard yet of one of your ilk turnin' down a chance to make money.'

Miranda Delamere regarded him with frank admiration, although Symonds didn't look quite so impressed, especially with Woods' last comment.

'That's an excellent suggestion, Constable!' Miranda said. 'My only concern is it'll take quite a long time to do what you suggest. Several months, I imagine. Mr Quinn – and Hal – seem in a hurry to resolve the matter.'

'Ma'am, I'm sure that any woman who stood up to Mr Tobias – as you did last night – will have no trouble makin' Mr Robert Quinn wait for a few months before you grant him admission into the bosom of your family. You need to make your enquiries and thoroughly investigate his claim to kinship. The youngsters these days are all rush, rush, rush, but you don't owe this stranger nothin'. Don't let him – or that Hal – rush you.'

Miranda smiled and handed the papers in her lap back to Symonds. 'Thank you for your advice, Constable. Sometimes it helps to see the situation through the objective eyes of someone who's not involved.'

'My pleasure, ma'am. If there's nothin' else, I'll return to my post and wait for Miss Susanna.'

'One last thing.' Miranda picked up her quill again and dipped it into the inkpot. She'd stopped smiling now. 'I understand you were with Detective Lavender when he found the body of that poor girl my dreadful brother seduced and murdered.'

Woods hesitated, surprised at this sudden turn in the conversation. 'Yes, ma'am, although strictly speakin', it were me who found the dead gal. I called Lavender into the investigation.'

'Were you there when Lavender found the incriminating snuff box at the scene of the crime?'

Woods knew his neck and cheeks had started to burn. 'Yes, ma'am.'

She paused with her quill dangling mid-air. Her dark, heavily browed eyes stared at him without blinking. 'You saw Lavender find it in a pond?'

'Yes, ma'am – and no. I saw him find it, but the snuff box and the dead gal were both stuffed down a well.'

Symonds winced but Miranda never flinched.

'There was no pond,' he added.

An awkward pause followed.

'Is there some problem?'

'Yes, Constable – there's a bit of a mystery.' Miranda shuffled in her wheelchair and pulled herself up straighter. 'You see, my brother, Frederick, claimed he'd lost that snuff box many, many years before the incident at The George in Hampstead.'

Incident? This was rape, sodomy and murder, not a mere *incident.*

'The snuff box was stolen from my brother by a young serving girl,' Miranda continued. 'From a boarding house in Southwark where he lodged. He wasn't carrying it that night when he met the barmaid at The George in Hampstead and was startled when Lavender claimed he'd found it with the corpse.'

That wasn't a corpse. It was Irish Nell, a twenty-year-old gal from County Cork.

'Did you ask Detective Lavender about this earlier?' he said.

She didn't reply. Woods braced himself and met her unflinching gaze with a steely glare of his own. 'I were there, ma'am, and I watched him find it.'

She lowered her eyes back to the pile of papers on the table. 'Such a mystery,' she murmured. 'My brother was sure it had been stolen by that London serving wench. I believe she was called Jeanette – or Ginny – Atkins?'

Chapter Twenty-Seven

The roof of the Willow Marsh boathouse was a dark grey triangle of ancient thatch, which merged with the shadows of a small, overgrown copse of trees and shrubs on the edge of the orchard.

A simple, low-slung structure raised on vertical wooden beams above the oblong of water that formed the start of the lode, it was open to the elements on all four sides. Inside, two rowing boats rocked idly on the still water, secured with a fraying rope to rusty iron rings embedded in the wooden pillars. A pair of swans glided peacefully around the piles of the warped black jetty. At the far end of the structure, sheltered by the thatched roof, stood a small pile of chopped logs with a rusty axe beside them.

Fifty yards further down the lode, the channel turned sharply to the left and skirted the lower edge of the orchard where Lavender, along with Adrian Delamere, had joined the path earlier that day and followed its course out to the wind pump.

The fortified towers loomed up like a fortress out of the thinning fog. Lavender thanked their guide and sent him back to the excise men. He and Cudworth would easily find their way back to the house from here.

No sooner had Howard turned on his heel and disappeared than Lavender saw the stocky figure of Woods striding towards them out of the fog. The tiny cloaked figure of Susanna Delamere scurried by his side. She had colour in her cheeks again and laughed at something Woods said. When Woods glanced up and saw them, Lavender was surprised to see anger flash across his face. But it was only a fleeting impression. Was he mistaken?

'Ned! Miss Susanna!' he called. 'Well met! This is Constable Cudworth, whom the Ely magistrates have sent to assist us.' Woods and Cudworth shook hands. Susanna nodded shyly towards Cudworth and watched them curiously out of her large brown eyes.

'Constable Cudworth is here to protect you, Miss Susanna, while Constable Woods assists me. How are you now?'

'Much better, thank you, Detective. I managed to rest and recover from the shock and Constable Woods is an entertaining companion.'

Lavender smiled wryly. 'Yes, he's famous for his charm with young ladies. Have there been any further problems, Ned?'

Woods ignored Lavender and turned to Cudworth. 'The biggest problem in watchin' over Miss Susanna is keepin' the young men at bay,' he said with a wink. 'She's several suitors who dog her steps and watch her every move.'

Lavender started at the way Woods had ignored him, but the young woman and their fellow officer didn't seem to notice anything amiss. Susanna's gloved hand fluttered to her mouth to hide her giggle and she blushed prettily.

'So, no young men within ten yards, eh?' Cudworth asked, winking back.

'Make it twenty,' Woods suggested.

'Where were you two going?' Lavender asked.

Woods finally turned towards him. His eyes were wary. 'Miss Susanna has kindly told me about more secret passageways and hidey-holes. I've uncovered the priest hole beneath the main staircase in the south tower – and she's brought me here to show me the smugglers' tunnel that runs from the boathouse up to the house.'

'Another secret tunnel?' Lavender snapped. 'Strewth, this estate is riddled with them. It's like a rabbit warren.'

216

Susanna smiled. 'Yes, it is, isn't it? I found the boathouse entrance several years ago. But there's been a rockfall and it's impossible to walk through it the whole way. It doesn't go far, only about ten feet into the rock. Neither I nor my cousins ever managed to find the entrance in the house. It's rumoured to be in the north tower.'

'You risked climbing down there yourself?' Lavender asked, impressed. She nodded in reply.

'I told Hal about it when I found it. He fetched a lantern and we explored it together. Let me show you.'

She took them towards the rear of the boathouse, where several overgrown rhododendron shrubs twisted and curled in front of the jutting boulders of a small rise in the terrain. They were at the bottom edge of the shallow rocky outcrop on which Willow Marsh Manor was built. This made sense, Lavender thought. Any tunnel blasted out of this landscape needed to pass through dry rock. The sodden, peaty ground of the marshes would soon flood.

Heedless of the damage to her clothes and hair from the trailing briars that wove their way through the tangled undergrowth, Susanna forced her way into the wild heart of the shrub.

Ducking below the thick woody stems, the three men squeezed into the narrow tunnel she'd created and followed her. There was more space at the centre of the shrub, although the men still had to bend low. She pointed to a rusty metal ring lying among the mouldy leaf litter.

'Wait!' Lavender said sharply, when she stooped to lift it. 'When were you last here, Miss Susanna?'

'Not for several years. Hal and I lost interest in it once we realised it was blocked.'

'Someone else has been here since.' Lavender dropped to his haunches and ran his gloved hand over the fine film of soil that was the only residue on the surface of the wooden rectangle. 'It's been opened recently and the debris, the leaves, twigs and dust, have fallen off to one side.'

'Maybe the steward or those other estate workers have been here,' Woods suggested.

'Maybe.'

'Perhaps my cousin Hal showed his new American friend the tunnel,' Susanna suggested.

Or perhaps it was the murderous coves who roam these marshes. Would the smugglers have dared to come this close to the house? Lavender wondered.

He looked for boot prints and other evidence, but nothing was obvious among the crushed leaves, bracken and the gloom of the interior of this shrub.

'Step back, please.' He hauled open the trap door. A shower of fine soil and dust fell like soft rain on the leaf litter. A crude staircase of rough-cut stone led down into the darkness. 'Cudworth? Please stay up here with Miss Susanna. Ned – come with me.'

They descended slowly into the musty darkness, checking each stone as they went. The steps ended about ten feet down in a large puddle of water. He fumbled for his tinderbox and pocket lantern. His mind started to play tricks on him in the dark. The memory of his vivid nightmare of the previous night swept through him. For a moment, he was swaying on that coarse rope ladder again with his child wailing behind him. He breathed the foul air and tried to suppress his anxiety. As his eyes adjusted to the weak, flickering light from his tin lantern, his jaw dropped in surprise at the shapes emerging out of the gloom.

Woods jumped off the last step, landed with a splash in the water behind him and peered over his shoulder. 'Gawd's teeth!' he exclaimed, his bad temper forgotten. 'What the devil are they?'

Ahead of them the passage was blocked, not with the rockfall mentioned by Susanna, but with three large, sturdy barrels.

Conscious their conversation may echo in this confined space and drift upwards, Lavender lowered his voice and whispered, 'Unless I'm mistaken, those barrels are full of smuggled Siberian sable.'

'They're full of what?'

Ducking their heads below the uneven roof, they moved forward. Lavender pulled out his pocket knife and with Woods' help managed to prise open the lid of one of the barrels.

Woods gave a low whistle when the light caught the lustrous sheen of the fur inside. He sank his large hand into the barrel, lifted out a pelt and they both watched, fascinated, as it slithered back down to its fellows with the light smoothness of satin. 'This is what it's all about, is it? These little beauties.'

'Yes,' Lavender said quietly. 'They're worth a fortune and have been smuggled into the country to avoid custom duty. We were right about the smugglers. This is why Mabberley lost his life – he must have disturbed them. The excise men found more of these animal pelts at a second wind pump on the Brandon lode.'

'And they're here too,' Woods said thoughtfully. 'We need to let the gaugers know about this.'

Lavender shook his head. 'There's no point. Lieutenant Waterbeach and his men are at the Brandon lode, waiting for the smugglers to return there. They can't be in two places at the same time.'

'What if the coves come here first to retrieve these?'

Lavender took a deep breath. 'Then it's down to you, me and Cudworth to stop them.' He couldn't see Woods' face but he heard him give a low chuckle of delight. Woods missed the more active life of the horse patrol, the excitement and the sheer physical exertion of chasing and grappling with criminals.

'That'll surprise the bastards.' Woods grinned, and his teeth glinted in the flickering light. His bad mood had vanished.

'We can't tell anyone – apart from Cudworth – what's down here,' Lavender said.

'What about Miss Susanna?'

Lavender hesitated. 'Can we trust her?'

'I think so.'

'Very well, but she'll need to stay locked in her chamber for her own safety while we're out here. We'll conceal ourselves in the undergrowth at dusk and wait to see if the smugglers return. If they don't appear, we'll send word to Waterbeach tomorrow and let the excise men take over the surveillance.'

Woods ran his large calloused hand through the silky furs once more, savouring their softness against his skin. 'Why are you so wary? Do you think someone from the house is involved in this?'

'Someone has to be. Otherwise, how else did the smugglers know about this tunnel? I doubt its location is common knowledge outside the family and the estate workers. In fact, Ned, we need to consider the fact it might be more than one of them.'

'You think they all might be colludin'?'

Lavender nodded. 'Even Miranda may be complicit in this business. Smuggling is a notorious leveller. Men – and women – from every walk of life condone and take part in *the trade*. We must explore all options.'

Behind and above them, a shadow passed over the entrance to the tunnel. 'Are you all right down there, sir?' Cudworth's voice sounded distant.

'We're fine – we'll be on our way out soon,' Woods called back.

But Lavender was distracted. He raised the lantern and peered over the barrel to the tunnel behind, frowning. 'Good God.'

'What is it?'

'Look, Ned. That rockfall – the one Miss Susanna said had blocked the passage.'

Woods moved closer and peered over his shoulder, past the barrels into the gloom. 'Heaven and hell! It's been cleared!'

Before them, a black tunnel about three-foot wide and five-foot high gaped over a small pile of dust and rubble, beckoning them to enter and explore.

Chapter Twenty-Eight

'How is this happenin'?' Woods squinted through the gloom, his eyes fixed on the black hole before them. 'How did those coves manage to excavate tunnels, store stolen goods and roam over this estate without detection?'

Lavender shrugged. 'Someone may have known about it and turned a blind eye, especially if the rogues operated at night. Up until last week, there's only been a few servants, a frail old man, his disabled daughter and a shy young girl in this house. I doubt even Susanna wandered around the marshes at night. The smugglers will have had the run of the place.'

'Until Mabberley got too close.'

'Yes. Until Mabberley got too close.'

'We need to explore this tunnel.' Lavender heard the excitement in Woods' voice. 'Miss Susanna claimed it led to the north tower of the house.'

Lavender grimaced. He didn't relish the prospect of stumbling through the semi-darkness into the dripping bowels of the earth but he knew they should find out where it went.

'We need proper light. Let's go back to the house and get some lanterns. But don't tell Miss Susanna about this or she'll want to come with us and I don't want to risk her safety.'

Back up in the weak daylight, Woods thanked Susanna for showing them the tunnel and led her away while Lavender carefully replaced the trap door and kicked leaf litter over it.

They followed the lode back to the shadowy orchard.

Woods plucked a ripe pear from a heavily laden bough and munched it happily. He fell back into step with Lavender, who brought up the rear. Whatever had been bothering Woods when they first met up at the boathouse had now been forgotten in the excitement of their discovery, the prospect of exploring the tunnel and the promise of some action later that night.

'I've asked Miss Susanna to be discreet about our trip to the boathouse tunnel,' Woods said with his mouth full.

A twig snapped in the shadows between the trees. Lavender turned his head and frowned. The fog had cleared but the daylight was fading. Did something move behind one of the trees?

'I've told her we think smugglers use it,' Woods continued, 'and we'll come back tonight to catch them. She's promised not to mention it to anyone and is excited to be sharing secrets with us.'

'Ned…'

'What?'

A fat pig waddled out of the shadows, grunting. It lowered its head and snuffled through the fruit windfalls with its muddied snout.

'What's wrong?'

'Nothing. That pig startled me. Sorry, Ned. What were you saying?'

'I think she's a plucky young woman.'

'Yes, she is,' Lavender agreed. 'Thank you for your work with her, Ned. You've done well. Between us we're steadily uncovering the secrets of this house, although I still can't work out how the attacker escaped off those battlements.'

'Maybe they disappeared down the other end of this damned tunnel we've just discovered.'

'Maybe. We'll know if that's possible, later. I've found out about Hal Pammenter's parentage, by the way.' He told Woods what he'd learned from old Jack Abbot.

Woods sighed. 'I'm not surprised to learn that devil Frederick was Pammenter's father. Miranda told me Miss Lucy were his mother. If any man was likely to despoil his young cousin, it were Major Frederick. Mind you,' he added. 'She's a strange one, that Lucy. I find it hard to warm to her – or feel any pity for her sufferin' at the hands of that rogue.'

'Maybe we're assuming too much,' Lavender said thoughtfully.

'What do you mean?'

Lavender shrugged. 'Maybe she wasn't raped like Delamere's other women.'

Woods glanced at him quickly. 'She were very young.'

'Yes, I know – fifteen. But maybe she was a willing participant in the love-making. Perhaps she had strong feelings for Delamere.'

Woods gave him an incredulous look. 'Feelin's? What? For that monster?'

'Maybe he had more charm and kindness about him in his youth.' Woods didn't look convinced. 'Don't forget,' Lavender continued, 'Delamere charmed a woman to the marriage altar – once.'

'What? Sorry, sir, I don't know what fanciful sentimentality is affectin' you today,' Woods continued, 'but I'm not softenin' in my attitude towards that foul villain.'

They fell silent when they left the orchard and entered the lowest tier of the terraced garden. The intoxicating scent of the late roses and lavender drifted towards them.

'Did anyone leave the house immediately after me, when I set off to Ely?' Lavender asked.

'I don't know. I went upstairs with Miss Susanna – but the youngsters had all disappeared by the time I came back down. Hal Pammenter and Quinn definitely went outside. Why do you want to know?'

'Someone took a shot at me from the riverbank while the boatman rowed me back to Ely.'

'Gawd's teeth!' Woods exclaimed. 'I said you were in danger!'

Ahead of them, Susanna and Cudworth heard his raised voice and glanced back. Lavender nodded for them to continue, but stopped with Woods at the bottom of the shallow stone steps that wound up through the crumbling terraces.

'The boatman assured me it was a stray shot from a hunter after waterfowl, but I'm sure it was aimed at me.'

'We need to catch this murderin' cove – and soon,' Woods continued darkly. 'Perhaps I should lock you in the chamber with Miss Susanna for safety and track down the bastard myself?'

A small smile twitched at the corner of Lavender's mouth. 'We're better working together. You don't live a charmed life, Ned – and that shoulder injury you carry is proof of this.'

Woods scowled and rubbed his left shoulder and the top of his arm. 'Don't remind me. I only hope that when Doña Magdalena fired at that cove Nidar, she hit her mark and injured the bastard. It were a pity it were too dark to tell.'

'After we've explored the tunnel – rather than locking me in my chamber – I'd prefer it if you helped me search for a pistol and shot in the bedchamber shared by Hal and Quinn.'

'You think it may be Hal who took a shot at you?'

'He's still our main suspect for the attack on Miss Susanna, so yes, we need to eliminate him from our enquiries. From what you've just said, he and Quinn were the only two people unaccounted for at the time of the attack on me. If it was Hal, he must have moved quickly – it would take some time to get down to that spot in the reeds by the riverbank. But he grew up here and must know his way around these grounds better than anyone.'

'He might also be behind this smugglin' racket,' Woods said thoughtfully.

'Why do you think that?'

'From what Miss Susanna said, he knew about the old tunnel and it strikes me he's well placed to deal with the London end of this scam – to find buyers for them furs.'

'That's true.'

'And you overheard him say to that floozy, Ursula, he had a money-makin' scheme in hand at the moment.'

'Again, this is all true, Ned.'

'It's time you had a talk with him. He's up to somethin' – and he were arguin' with his mother this mornin'. By the way, Miranda asked my advice about how to investigate if Robert Quinn really is her nephew. I told her to hire a Yankee lawyer to do it for her.'

Lavender nodded. He watched Susanna and Cudworth reach the top of the terraces. Instinctively, he glanced up at the battlements to make sure there was no sinister figure lurking menacingly above the young girl's head. But there was nothing there except a large gap, like a missing tooth, where the fallen merlon used to stand in the parapet.

'That Hal is a tricky lawyer type,' Woods said. 'He could talk the birds out of the damned trees if he wanted to.'

Lavender smiled. 'You forget I once trained to be a tricky lawyer type.'

Woods didn't look convinced. 'Well, do you think you have his measure and can exert some pressure with him?'

'I do and I can. We'll interview him later.'

Woods took a huge breath and his countenance became serious. 'By the way, sir, Miss Delamere said somethin' a bit strange about that ruddy snuff box—'

'Detective! Constable!'

227

They glanced up to the top of the terrace. Susanna and Cudworth had rounded the corner of the building and disappeared. The manservant, Hawkes, strode down the path towards them. 'Miss Delamere wants to see yer, Detective.'

'Thank you, I'll come straight away.' Lavender turned back to Woods as Hawkes went back to the house. 'They must have been watching out for my return. Ned, I'm sorry to have to ask you to do this alone, but would you get a lantern and explore the tunnel while I report back to our employer?'

'Of course, sir. I'll get one from the stables.'

'I'll join you down there as soon as I can.'

Chapter Twenty-Nine

A small fire burned in the hearth of the cream marble fireplace in the parlour. Miranda sat beside it in her wheelchair. There was ro sign of Lucy Pammenter.

'I gather you've had a useful trip to Ely, Detective.'

'Yes, ma'am. I've returned with Constable Cudworth. Magistrate Kester sent him to assist myself and Woods in our investigation. At the moment, he's with Miss Susanna.'

'Yes,' Miranda said, 'Susanna came in here briefly to introduce him. Where's Constable Woods?'

'He's busy on a task I set him.'

'Take a seat, Lavender.' She pointed towards one of the chairs beside the fireplace. He sank gratefully into the plump upholstery. It had been a long day and it would be an even longer night, staking out the boathouse. Not that he intended to tell her about this.

For a moment, they observed each other coolly across the hearth rug. It would be easier to read her features and look into her eyes at this level, he realised, but this worked both ways. Had she sensed his distrust?

'Magistrate Kester requests that your servants take Matthew Mabberley's body to the inquest by ten o'clock tomorrow. Some of the jurors may wish to examine his injuries.'

Miranda winced.

'He'll be released for burial immediately afterwards.'

'Yes, yes, Thank you. Poor Mabberley – and poor Mrs Mabberley.'

'How is she?' Lavender asked.

Miranda sighed and pain flitted across her lined face. 'Very distressed. I've just spent some time with her. Thrup has already fetched us the undertaker and a coffin from Ely. Let's hope the floodwater subsides sufficiently for us to transport him by road tomorrow – it's not easy rowing a small boat with a coffin. But what of these murdering villains, Lavender? Susanna and Woods tell me you believe it was a gang of smugglers who killed Mabberley.'

'Waterbeach has increased his efforts to catch them,' he said vaguely. 'Meanwhile, Woods and I will continue to search for the rogue who tried to kill Miss Susanna this morning.'

She nodded in approval. 'Do you think Mabberley's murderers are the same gang who pushed poor Susanna into the lode?'

'It's possible. She was close to the wind pump where I suspect the smuggled items were hidden. But the attack on her today had nothing to do with the smugglers.'

'Ah, yes. About that – now Constable Cudworth is here, perhaps he can take over the investigation while you and Woods return to London?'

Lavender was stunned. Was she really dismissing them? And why? What had changed since this morning except that the murderer had shown his hand again? 'But there's another murderer on the loose at Willow Marsh Manor,' he said slowly, pausing to see what effect his chilling words had on the woman. Her dark eyes showed no emotion.

'I'm sure Constable Cudworth can manage from now on,' she persisted. 'Obviously, I'll reimburse you and Woods for any time and expenses incurred so far. There's an evening coach back to London, I believe.'

Yes, she was dismissing them. 'I can't go anywhere until after Mabberley's inquest,' he told her firmly. 'I found his body and I'm required there as a witness.'

'Yes, but Adrian was with you. Couldn't he…?'

230

'No, ma'am, that's not how the law works. We can't pick and choose whether we turn up for inquests, or not. In addition to this,' he added, 'there's been a new development. This case has become personal. Someone shot at *me* from the riverbank while I was on my way to Ely.'

She jerked in shock. 'I'm sorry to hear this, Lavender. Are you unharmed?'

'Yes, ma'am.'

'But why?'

'Either someone doesn't like me investigating these attacks on Miss Susanna – or someone still holds a grudge over my involvement in the arrest and conviction of your brother.'

She gave a short, frustrated laugh, but it wasn't a laugh of amusement. 'Are we back to that nonsense with the snuff box this morning?' she asked.

'I think we are, ma'am. I now wonder if it was a warning.'

'It's nonsense, surely? A daft prank.'

'Was it? The ghost of your late brother has dogged our steps ever since we arrived at Willow Marsh – and I've now learned Hal Pammenter is his son. Are you absolutely sure you can trust that man?'

A weak shaft of sunlight fought through the latticed windows. It illuminated the glossy patina of the furniture, the glittering silver candelabra on the sideboard and the dark recesses of Miranda's eyes. They contained the same golden flecks as those of her nephew.

She gave a laugh. 'I assure you, Hal bears no residual filial love for his father. He barely saw him as a child and he was away at school when Frederick was... disgraced.'

'Resentment is a strong motive, ma'am. It can eat away at the soul for years,' Lavender said cautiously.

231

'To learn his half-sister is to inherit everything while he's left with a paltry allowance – and to have to share his home with the officers who brought about his father's downfall – both might easily drive a man to violence,' he continued strongly. 'It wouldn't be the first time a bitter man has resorted to murder to ease his churning resentment.'

She held up her hand to stop him. 'No, Lavender. I won't have it. Hal's not bitter and he would never harm Susanna.'

'He left the house soon after I did and may be responsible for the attempt on my life.'

She smoothed down the black silk of her gown in her lap with her long, thin fingers. 'But Quinn was with him! No. Question Hal further, by all means, if you're not satisfied—'

'I will.'

'—but I won't accept he had anything to do with either incident.'

Lavender shrugged. 'Perhaps it wasn't Hal – but there's someone in this house who bitterly resents the part Woods and I played in the downfall of your brother.'

'Oh, that,' she said. She paused for a moment, then her face flushed with anger. 'Good God, Lavender, you don't think I placed that snuff box in your room, do you? How on earth do you think I climbed up there?'

He ignored her question. 'I do wonder if you ever truly accepted the jury's decision about your brother's guilt or if you still harbour a belief in his innocence. Exactly how close were you to Major Frederick?'

Her eyes flashed. 'You forget your place, Detective.'

'Then it's probably just as well we'll shortly be on our way back to London.'

For a moment, he thought she would rise to his goading, but she swallowed hard and lowered her glaring eyes to the rug.

232

'Family relationships are always... *complicated*, Lavender. When I heard Lieutenant Clarke give his evidence at Frederick's trial, I realised that this time my brother's violent proclivities had gone too far.'

This time?

'Frederick's conviction was... sound,' she continued. 'The jury was right to condemn him.'

She was holding something back. She knew more about her brother's violent sexual history with women than she was prepared to admit. In fact, she probably knew about Delamere's attack on Ginny Atkins. The thought sent a sickening jolt through his stomach.

'I suppose now someone has tried to kill you,' she added, sighing, 'you're determined to stay and get to the bottom of this case?'

'Woods and I don't walk away from a job half done.'

'I suppose I should be grateful to have such experienced officers determined to care for my niece. Her safety is always my priority. On reflection, I can see it's probably a good idea if you and Woods stay a while longer – at least until tomorrow after the inquest.'

'Thank you, ma'am.'

'I've not been thinking straight today,' she admitted. 'I still grieve for my father and I'm horrified at the thought that we've murderers wandering around this estate unchecked. My niece, Susanna, is... is very precious to me.'

As is Susanna's half-brother, Lavender thought. *Only you could care so much for the children of a monster like Frederick Delamere.*

He rose to his feet, bowed stiffly and left.

Woods would still be in the tunnel. It was time to track down Hal Pammenter.

Chapter Thirty

Hal lounged with his brandy glass on one of the settles in front of the fireplace in the banqueting hall. He'd discarded his coat and opened the buttons of his silk waistcoat. His long, booted legs stretched out before him towards the flames in the grate. Although he wasn't in his cups, his eyes shone and his cheeks glowed with drink. *Good,* Lavender thought, this might loosen his tongue.

Ursula was curled up on the settle beside Hal, once more smiling up at him with adoration. She'd kicked off her tiny shoes and tucked her legs beneath her. The hem of her black muslin gown was damp and muddy. Hal's arm lay across the back of the settle behind her slender shoulders. His fingers drummed the hard wooden surface as if they itched to lower themselves down onto the young woman's body. Their smiles belied the sombre effect of their mourning clothes; neither was grief-stricken for their Uncle Lawrence.

Quinn and Susanna sat in a more respectable manner on the opposite settle. She was still perched primly on the edge of the seat; he sat upright beside her, properly attired for the company of ladies in his grey coat and buttoned-up waistcoat.

Constable Cudworth lurked self-consciously halfway down the room, inspecting a suit of armour.

A scowl flitted across Ursula's face when she saw Lavender approach. 'And here's *another* police officer, determined to spoil our fun!' she complained.

Hal nodded and sighed. 'Aunt Miranda has become overzealous in her protection of you, Little Susie,' he announced. 'This place is crawling with more police officers than the streets of Paris under the tyrannical rule of Joseph Fouché.'

Lavender grimaced at the comparison while Susanna blushed, embarrassed and confused, and Ursula laughed in delight. 'We can never be overzealous when we're in pursuit of a murderer. Pammenter, I would like a word with you – in private.'

'Ooh, Detective!' Ursula pretended to be affronted. 'I don't like your tone.'

Hal just laughed. 'Damn it, Lavender! The ladies have only just joined us. Quinn and I hoped to enjoy a spell of their fair company. You're one devil of a killjoy.'

Susanna stood up hastily. 'I intended to take another stroll around the grounds anyway, before sunset.'

Quinn was on his feet in an instant. 'I'll escort you, ma'am,' he drawled. 'It'll be an honour to see some more of your home.'

Susanna flushed, delighted.

'Be careful, Cousin dearest,' Ursula teased. 'Take care he doesn't push you into a lode and claim the estate for himself.'

Hal laughed but something flickered across Quinn's face. What was it? Frustration? Embarrassment?

'Constable Cudworth will escort you both,' Lavender said.

'Of course, Detective,' Susanna said meekly. 'We'll see you later at supper,' she added to her cousin and her half-brother.

Quinn took her arm and led her with great gallantry towards the great double doors at the far end of the hall. Constable Cudworth trailed in their wake.

'And what am *I* supposed to do now?' Ursula whined. 'I hate walking outside when it's damp underfoot. I've already ruined one pair of shoes today. God, I'm so *weary* of the countryside. How I'd *love* to live in London.'

'We should retire to the library and leave Miss Ursula here in peace,' Lavender said.

But Hal had no intention of vacating his comfortable seat by the fireside. 'You could sit for a while with Aunt Miranda in the parlour,' he suggested with a twinkle in his eye. 'She'll be lonely now she's had that spat with my mother. Alternatively, you can retire to your room and try a little embroidery, like a proper lady.'

She gave him a playful slap and the sudden jerk made his hair fall over his forehead into his eyes.

'Don't tease, Hal. You know I'd rather burn myself with a branding iron than do embroidery. Very well, I'll amuse myself for a while in my room.' She slipped her stockinged feet back into her shoes and left them in peace.

Lavender took a seat on the opposite settle and waited until Ursula had left before fixing the young man with a cold glare.

Hal responded by rolling his eyes to the rafters and sighed heavily. 'What is it you want from me, Detective?'

'You can tell me what happened up there in that tower, for a start. Either it was you out there on the roof trying to drop heavy stones on your half-sister's head – or you heard or saw the man responsible.'

Hal's eyes narrowed. 'Half-sister? I see you've been snooping into my background, Lavender.'

'It's my job, Pammenter. And for the record, I also know that your mother is Lucy Pammenter.'

Hal shrugged. 'It's of little consequence what you know.'

'What happened in that damned tower?'

'I've already told you everything. I was talking to my mother and I saw and heard nothing. And – as I mentioned to your constable – whomever was responsible for that heinous attack also tried to kill Quinn. You need to broaden the scope of your investigation, Detective – and think more imaginatively.' His handsome features twisted into a smirk.

Lavender gave him another cold, hard glare. 'And there's your first lie, Pammenter. You weren't *talking* to your mother – you were *arguing* with her. I saw how flushed you both were when I entered your chamber – and I overheard you.'

Hal's mouth dropped open in surprise and he started to protest. But Lavender hadn't finished yet. 'In fact, it's not the first time you've had an argument with her today, is it? Constable Woods heard a man and a woman arguing this morning over in the servants' quarters. It was you and your mother, wasn't it?'

'Oh, for God's sake!' Hal grabbed the brandy decanter off a low table next to the settle and poured himself a generous measure. 'All right! We've had a small disagreement. What of it?'

'What did you argue about? And why has she quarrelled with Miranda Delamere?'

'Who says they've quarrelled?'

'You did, just now.'

Hal took a generous gulp of his drink and sat back, distracted. 'Look, Lavender, my mother is a simple woman – who's prone to emotional outbursts.' He spoke slowly and the admission seemed to cause him pain. 'Sometimes she gets strange fancies in her head. When this happens, Aunt Miranda and I have to talk her down from her high horse.'

'What strange fancies?'

'If you must know, she's taken a strong dislike to you and your constable. It's totally unreasonable, of course, but she's a passionate woman and we're concerned she may do, or say, something embarrassing or inhospitable.'

Lavender almost smiled. 'I don't know whether to thank you for your efforts to protect our feelings – or laugh at your lies.'

'You mock me, sir.'

'Yes, I mock you!' Lavender snapped. 'Stop patronising me, Pammenter, and tell me the truth about what's really going on around here.'

Hal took another drink. 'I don't know what you think you suspect, Lavender.'

'I suspect your mother has stronger feelings than *dislike*. I believe she holds a vicious grudge against myself and Woods because – as I'm sure you know – we successfully charged and convicted *your* father of the rape and murder of Irish Nell.'

Hal dropped his glass. He caught it before it smashed on the flagstone floor but some of the amber liquid sloshed out. 'Damn it, Lavender! That's preposterous!'

'In addition to this,' Lavender continued, 'I suspect she's now voicing her opinion that as the son of Frederick Delamere, *you* are the rightful heir of the Willow Marsh Estate – not your half-sister, Susanna. No wonder you and Miranda have tried to silence her.'

'My conversations with my mother are private,' Hal blustered. He poured himself another drink and downed it in one gulp. 'And do I need to remind you,' he added, lowering his voice to a seething hiss, 'that I'm illegitimate? Even Adrian has a better claim on this damned estate than I do!'

'And your American friend, Quinn? What's his true claim on this property? Does he have one?'

'Of course he does! I told you all last night – he's the son of my Aunt Olivia and her husband, Peter Quinn.'

'Or some passing American stranger you found on the streets of London whom you've schooled to play the part of your long-lost cousin?'

'That's a scurrilous allegation, sir!'

'What's the nature of your scam?' Lavender persisted. 'Because I know you have one. Do you and Quinn intend to share out the wealth equally once you've pushed Susanna out of the way?'

Hal slapped the arm of the settle with a balled fist. 'Of course not! As I've already said, Susanna is the rightful heir to this estate – but I genuinely think we owe Quinn some compensation. He's not responsible for his parents' wild behaviour. None of us are. No one should be punished for the sins of their parents.'

'Says the bastard son of a murdering rapist.'

Hal rose to his feet angrily. 'Damn you, Lavender!'

Lavender didn't flinch. 'Do your law chambers in London know your family background?'

Fear rapidly replaced the fury in Hal's face. He crumpled back down into his seat and stared at Lavender in horror.

'They don't know the truth, do they?'

Hal's tone was measured and surprisingly sober when he finally replied: 'You know as well as I do, it would be the death of my career if the truth about my father became common knowledge in London.'

'Yes, I imagine it would.'

'I've done nothing wrong, for God's sake!' His gold-flecked amber eyes cast an imploring glance at Lavender. 'I've spent my life living in the shadow of that fiend. You've no idea what it was like growing up with neighbours and school friends whispering about his atrocities every time you turned around.'

Lavender nodded. 'I imagine both you – and Miss Susanna – have suffered.'

'London is a fresh start for me. Surely you don't begrudge me that? I'm only trying to make a living for myself, like every other young fellow in this world. I mean it when I say *no one* should be punished for the sins of their parents.'

'Especially you?'

'Especially me – and Little Susie,' he added as an afterthought.

'Very well, I'll be discreet when I return to London. However, my silence comes at a price. Tell me about the scam you're operating with Quinn.'

For a moment, Lavender thought he'd refuse to answer, then Hal sighed, lowered his voice and leaned forward. 'It isn't a scam. He *is* Aunt Olivia's son. I tracked him down exactly as I said last night. It took me over a year to get him here to Cambridgeshire. Unfortunately, I was too late to reconcile him with Uncle Lawrence. I wouldn't dream of lying to Miranda about that – she's a lot shrewder and more connected than you'd think for a crippled woman locked away in a rural backwater.'

Lavender frowned. 'How so?'

'She has a network of spies and informants all over the place – even in London – and she's never thought twice in the past about hiring thief-takers or mercenaries to do her dirty work for her or undertake enquiries about people who interest her. A servant once robbed us – he took some of the silverware from the parlour. He was boarding a packet schooner in Bristol on his way to a new life in the colonies when her people caught him and hauled him off to the local magistrate. He was sentenced to transportation to New South Wales. She's a vengeful woman and doesn't trust *anyone* since Peter Quinn abandoned her.'

The hairs prickled on the back of Lavender's neck.

'As Uncle Lawrence grew weaker and handed over more of his money and power to her, she became worse,' Hal continued. 'There's nothing random or innocent in any of that woman's actions. She hired people to watch *me* while I was at Cambridge and when I first took the bar in London,' Hal continued. 'Her surveillance of my movements is obsessive. But what can I do or say? At the time, I was dependent on her goodwill for my allowance.'

241

Miranda's earlier request to Woods for advice must have been a ploy, Lavender realised. She didn't need his help.

Her people must have watched him and Woods in London and informed her about their planned trip to the Cambridge assizes. It had been nothing to do with Lawyer Symonds. How long had she plotted to lure them to Willow Marsh Manor, he wondered. But why? And now she'd used such an elaborate ploy to lure them here, why was she suddenly so keen to see them depart?

'We eventually scraped together enough cash for Quinn's passage to England,' Hal continued. 'He's almost as impecunious as I am – both of us are down to our last few shillings.'

Lavender struggled to concentrate. Lucy Pammenter was obviously Miranda's instrument; her legs. It was Lucy who'd crept into his bedchamber last night and left him the incriminating snuff box – but it was the twisted cripple, Miranda, who pulled the strings in Willow Marsh Manor. She was toying with him and Woods – and had been from the start.

'The plan is to push for a modest settlement out of the estate from Aunt Miranda,' Hal confessed. 'She won't want Quinn's parentage to become common knowledge around Ely. It'll raise too many awkward questions for her and reignite the gossip about the most embarrassing period of her life, when she was jilted.'

'That's blackmail, emotional blackmail – against a woman who's given you a home and an education and shown you nothing but kindness.'

'Oh fie, Lavender! I can't afford qualms. I'm broke and I've just explained to you the sort of woman Miranda really is. Don't waste sympathy on her. I expect her to offer to buy Quinn a passage back to the Carolinas very shortly and send him away with a fat, jangling purse.'

'And once Robert Quinn is compensated, he'll share the spoils with you?'

242

'Of course – I've gone to considerable expense and trouble to find him. Although the game changed somewhat once we arrived last night.'

'How so?'

Hal laughed, gave Lavender a quizzical glance and leaned forward to flick a small speck of dirt from his buckskin breeches. 'You're not a very perceptive man in some ways, are you Detective? I imagine women often leave you confused.'

Lavender bristled. It was one thing to hear this criticism from Woods, his friend and companion for the past thirteen years, but he didn't want to hear it from this fellow who toyed with the affections of his cousin while plotting to rob his half-sister of her inheritance. Woods had earned the right to mock him. Pammenter hadn't. 'What's your point?'

'Haven't you noticed the effect Quinn has on sweet Little Susie? She's the point, Lavender. Since meeting her last night, they're smitten with each other. He decided there's no point walking away with only part of the prize; he's resolved to have it all. The full estate, all the money – and the gal.'

Lavender's voice caught in his throat with shock. 'He wants to marry her?'

'Of course. He told me about an hour ago. According to the terms of Grandfather's will, Aunt Miranda still controls the purse strings until Little Susie reaches her majority, but after that, it'll be all his.'

'That's very cynical.'

'Well, that's how it works with heiresses, isn't it? Don't look so glum, Lavender. If it wasn't Quinn, it'd be someone else – and at least he genuinely likes her. I say good luck to them both!'

Chapter Thirty-One

When Lavender caught up with Woods at the boathouse, his constable had just emerged from the trap-door entrance to the secret tunnel with a rusty axe in one hand and a lantern in the other. Covered in dust and cobwebs, Woods grinned from ear to ear.

'Miss Susanna were right,' he said as he clambered up into the low clearing in the middle of the shrub. 'This tunnel goes right up to the house – but not to the north tower like she thought. It comes out into the hallway of the *south* tower, next to the noisy carriage clock. It chimed the hour while I was in there and I heard the damned thing boomin' from two hundred yards away.'

'Is it safe down there?'

'It's a steep climb in some parts and slow-goin', with patches of stale air, but it seems solid enough.'

Lavender slammed the trap door back down and kicked dead leaves and soil over it. The less evidence they left of their visit the better. 'Have you left anything down there? We don't want to scare off the smugglers tonight.'

Woods raised his lantern and the axe and shook his head. 'I took this axe with me in case I needed to smash my way out at the other end. But the door's well greased. I opened it a crack and peeped through to make sure.'

They crouched down, squeezed their way out of the shrub and walked back to the boathouse where the two boats still bobbed idly at their moorings. Woods swung the axe and embedded it in the top log of the small pile of firewood at the end of the jetty.

'You say it goes into the hallway of the south tower? Isn't that where you said the priest hole was located?'

'Yes, the priest hole and the entrance to this tunnel are both behind the wood panelling in the hallway. Handy, I suppose. Mr Adrian said the family used the tunnel to smuggle Catholic priests into the house. I supposed they'd just take them up to the house through the tunnel, and then two steps later shove them into the priest hole for safe keepin' and all is well.'

Lavender bit back a smile. 'I'm not sure that's how it worked, Ned. The priest hole was only used in an emergency, when the Protestant authorities conducted a search of the premises. The priests didn't have to stay in there all the time. Anyway, let's hope we've uncovered the last of the manor's secrets.'

'Maybe not. There's somethin' else down there. My lantern were weak and I couldn't tell if it were just a large alcove, a passin' place or another secret tunnel leadin' off.'

Lavender swore. 'Another bloody tunnel?'

'I were runnin' short of oil in my lantern so I didn't stop to explore it on my way back. That's somethin' for Miss Susanna and her cousins to do when we've gone.' He paused for a moment and watched Lavender's face. 'Do you think this is how that villain escaped from the top of the battlements this mornin'? Did they leg it down, race across the main hall and escape this way?'

Lavender sighed and thought back to the accusations he'd just levelled against Hal Pammenter. 'Perhaps. The family were arguing in the parlour and wouldn't have noticed someone dash into the hallway of the south tower and hide in the tunnel. They would have had to move fast, though, to get down from the battlements and across the banqueting hall before we arrived. We must have missed them by seconds.'

Woods shrugged. 'Maybe a second is all it took.'

Lavender stared back at the large shrub covering the trap door, frowning. Was it possible one of the smugglers had tried again to murder Susanna? But why? This morning she'd been nowhere near their precious contraband. Did they have another motive to kill her? His brain ached when he tried to make sense of it all.

'That's not safe. It needs blockin' up and securin'. Anyone could sneak in and out of the house – and them smugglers know it's there.'

Lavender hesitated; Woods was right. The inhabitants of Willow Marsh were vulnerable with such easy access into their home. 'We'll tell Hawkes when we've finished tonight. He may be able to secure the entrance.'

'It's a good job them smugglers don't know we've discovered it.'

'Yes, Scar-face and his murderous band have been very clever – but not as clever as us.'

Woods looked at him, aghast. '*Scar-face?*'

'Waterbeach found a witness who caught a glimpse of the coves fleeing the scene after Mabberley's murder. He said their leader sounded like a gentleman and had a bad scar on the left side of his face.'

Woods' eyes were round with excitement and shock. '*Scar-face!*'

'What the devil is the matter, Ned? You look like you've seen a ghost.'

'I have! Don't you remember? *Scar-face*. That's what the barmaid at The George called that cove Frederick Delamere.'

'What?'

'It's him!' Woods was shouting with excitement. 'It's Delamere come back from the dead! He didn't die on a ruddy convict ship. He escaped and turned to piracy and smugglin' to survive!'

'But—'

'No buts. It's true! And the bastard has been creepin' round Willow Marsh ever since we arrived, tryin' to kill you out of revenge. Woods puffed out his chest with pride. 'I've solved the case.'

'Frederick Delamere is dead, Ned.'

'Are you so sure? Was his death recorded in that family bible you read?'

'No, but…'

Woods waved a dismissive hand. 'In that case, he might still be alive. Look at the facts, sir. We've got a known felon with a scarred face creatin' havoc in the area who matches Delamere's description.'

'He doesn't necessarily match Delamere's description. The witness only said it was a scar on the left side of his face.' He hesitated. He hated deflating Woods when he was so excited.

'It seems too much of a coincidence for me,' said Woods stubbornly.

'Is it, though, Ned? Think about it. We've been at war with the French for ten years. Half the men in England have scars, thanks to the bayonets and artillery of Bonaparte's military forces.'

'You're just bein' picky now.'

'Well, if so, answer me this question: If Frederick Delamere *was* alive, why on earth would he want to kill his own daughter?'

This took the wind out of Woods' sails. He visibly deflated before Lavender's eyes.

'Delamere's dead,' Lavender continued cautiously, 'and no one comes back from the dead. It was a good theory, Ned, but I'd rather try and solve this damned case with hard facts and logic.'

Woods shook his head and started to stamp back up to the house. 'I've got a bad feelin' about this,' he snapped. 'I've had a bad feelin' about this place ever since we arrived.'

248

Lavender fell into step beside him and silently agreed. He heard the bitter disappointment in Woods' voice. 'Apart from Miss Susanna, I don't trust any of them,' his constable continued. 'And that Miranda's the worst of the lot.'

Lavender's head turned sharply. 'Why? What's happened now?'

Woods scowled and stopped in his tracks. 'She's been spreadin' lies.'

'About what?'

'About my family, that's what—' Lavender's breath caught in this throat. '—and about that damned snuff box you pulled out of the well to use as evidence against her brother.'

'How so?'

'Her brother told her he weren't carryin' a snuff box on the day he killed Irish Nell. He said it were stolen several years before.'

Lavender froze and silently cursed Miranda Delamere. He wished her a painful early death and a long, agonising stint in the fiery torture chambers of hell. Why had she challenged Woods and not him about the snuff box?

'She said he claimed it were stolen by a servin' wench at a Southwark lodgin' house.'

'Did he remember by whom—'

'Oh, yes,' Woods snapped. 'He told Miranda it were some thievin' wench called Jeanette or Ginny Atkins. Odd that, isn't it? Seein' as my sister-in-law is called Ginny Atkins and she were a maid at Ma Forster's lodgin' house on Tooley Street in Southwark.'

'Yes, it's odd – and I think it's odd that he remembered the name of a mere maid. I think Miranda must have found out about your family.'

'That's what I were thinkin'. Our Ginny ain't a thief.'

'No, of course she's not.'

'But I don't see why she'd blame her.' They stopped beneath the partial shade of a gnarled apple tree. Lavender saw pain and fear in Woods' angry, narrowed eyes. 'What does this woman want with us? Why did she entice us up here?'

A heavy silence fell between them. Woods waited for his reaction, watching him closely. He desperately wanted Lavender to exonerate Ginny from any involvement.

Lavender swallowed hard and his Adam's apple lurched dryly in his throat. 'You're right, Ned. Ginny isn't a thief. But Miranda's also right – Ginny had the snuff box.'

Woods cursed. 'Gawd's teeth! How did that happen?"

Lavender braced himself and kept his voice calm and measured. 'Delamere *was* a guest at the Tooley Street lodging house where Ginny worked twenty years ago. He attacked her. She hit him over the head with the snuff box and cut him. Then she fled. She was still clutching it when she ran home.'

Woods recoiled in horror. 'That bastard – that bastard attacked my little Ginny?' He turned away and stomped a few yards back towards the boathouse; his curses rent the air like the scream of an injured animal. Then he turned back. The pain in his voice was raw, like the shock in his eyes. 'You say Delamere *attacked* her? Did he… did he *rape* her?'

Lavender couldn't speak. He just nodded his head.

'You knew about this? You knew about this – but you never said anythin' to me!'

'I was sworn to secrecy, Ned. I only found out about it ten years ago when we investigated the murder of Irish Nell.'

'Sworn to secrecy!'

A vein throbbed in Woods' thick neck above his necktie and he curled his fist into a ball. 'So, Ginny, a woman I've always loved as a sister – and the man I think of as my brother – have colluded between them for the past twenty years to make a damned fool out of me? This is *my* family. *My* responsibility!'

Lavender braced himself, half expecting Woods to lash out. 'It wasn't like that, Ned. You need to let me explain. It wasn't my choice – and I still believe we made the right decision.'

Woods grabbed his arm. Cold anger blazed in his eyes but was replaced by raging fury when he comprehended the full situation. '*We?* Heaven and hell! Don't tell me my wife knew about this too?'

Lavender ignored the pain from Woods' vice-like grip and tried to stay calm. The last thing he wanted to do right now was compound Woods' misery and admit Betsy's part in the deception. But it was time for the truth.

'Of course Betsy knew, Ned,' he said quietly. 'Betsy knows *everything* that goes on in your family. She always has. It was she who suggested I used the snuff box to frame Delamere.'

Woods gave a strangled, heartbroken sob, 'You *all* lied to me! You, my Betsy – *my wife* – and her sister!' He turned on his heel and stormed off through the orchard towards the house.

'Ned! Wait!'

But Woods didn't slow down or look back. By the time Lavender reached the kitchen entrance at the side of the house, he'd disappeared.

Chapter Thirty-Two

Lavender had no wish to see Miranda Delamere again that evening, or any of her damned family if he could help it. He ate an early supper with the servants in the kitchen and relieved Cudworth for half an hour while he had his own meal. Then Lavender grabbed an old blanket from the stables and made his way down through the terraced gardens and the orchard towards the old boathouse.

Woods had vanished and Lavender was worried sick. They'd never argued like this before and for all he knew Woods was halfway back to London by now.

The great, golden-red ball of the sun dipped below the horizon and shot arrows of fire and blood-red streaks across the mirrored surface of the lode. Somewhere in the distance a dog fox barked and a curlew gave a mournful cry.

Lavender chose a small copse of gnarled elders for his vantage point. Provided the sky remained cloudless, he would have an unimpeded view of both the boathouse and the large rhododendron shrub that concealed the entrance to the secret tunnel. He forced his way between a few low-slung boughs, dropped his blanket onto the wet earth and lowered himself to the ground.

Pocketing his white cravat, he darkened his face with mud and pulled his black coat collar up around his chin. Next, he pulled out his pistol, loaded it and checked his powder was dry. He had no idea how he would ambush and capture these smugglers alone, but one thing he did realise as the damp seeped through his blanket – it was going to be a long, lonely night.

The first of many.

The dark-timbered and black-thatched boathouse slowly merged into the dusky shadows of the night. Glancing over his shoulder, he saw the outline of the battlements of the north tower silhouetted against the black velvet sky.

He heard the snap of a twig as a nocturnal animal moved in the undergrowth, and smelled the coal smoke drifting down from the chimneys of the manor. A tawny owl screeched in the distance. His eyes and ears strained against the night.

While he waited, he cursed himself for not telling Woods sooner about his and Betsy's deception. Deflated and already sulking after Lavender had quashed his theory about Frederick Delamere, his constable had been in no mood to take such a revelation.

His anger switched to Miranda and he cursed her for her slyness. Damn the woman. If she already knew about Ginny Atkins, why didn't she mention it this morning when he told her the snuff box had suddenly materialised in his chamber? Was this all part of her revenge for his role in the downfall of her brother? Did she always intend to cause irreparable damage to his relationship and partnership with Ned?

Grief welled up inside him.

Ned would never trust him again after this. He'd head back to Bow Street and demand to be reinstated to the horse patrol.

Sighing, he shifted uncomfortably as cramp twinged in his leg.

Thirty, maybe forty minutes later, he heard the soft dip of oars in water and the gentle creak of metal oarlocks.

A boat bumped against the jetty in the boathouse and two heavy-booted men clambered out onto the creaking wooden planks.

Muffled up to their eyeballs in scarves, with their hats pulled low over their faces, they hesitated for a moment while their eyes adjusted to the greater darkness of the boathouse and the copse.

Lavender couldn't see any metal weapons glinting in the moonlight, but this didn't mean they weren't carrying pistols or knives. In order to overpower them both, he must wait until at least one of them was down in the tunnel with the contraband. Then he might be able to slam the trap door shut while he arrested the other one above ground.

One of the smugglers pulled out a small pocket lantern, similar to his own. He led the way towards the concealed entrance of the tunnel. 'This way,' he muttered to his companion. He had a nasally twang to his accent. Was he from Birmingham, perhaps? Or Liverpool?

'I know the damn way, Goldsmith,' his companion replied. 'I brought you here and showed you the tunnel, remember?'

Lavender exhaled sharply as he recognised the voice of this second smuggler. Adrian Delamere. Was there no end to the extent of this family's depravity?

The sound of his gasp made Adrian turn his head in Lavender's direction. Lavender sank back into the shadows.

'Shut yer gob and keep quiet!' Goldsmith snapped.

Adrian's claim to be an importer of timber from the Baltic was a lie. Lavender's mind whirled as he wondered what else the young man may have lied about. Was his rescue of Susanna as straightforward as he'd claimed? Or had he been there all along, talking with his murderous colleagues when one of them had shoved her into the lode?

Lavender pushed speculation aside and tried to decide what to do next. The two men had now reached the straggly shrub covering the trap door. Adrian wasn't aggressive and probably wouldn't put up much of a fight, but Goldsmith was a big man and he seemed to have a sharp temper.

The trap door creaked as they forced it open.

Lavender tightened his grip on his weapon and rose to his feet, cringing at the stiffness in his calves.

255

But before he could move forward, Goldsmith gave a foul curse and swore. 'It's the warnin' – damn it! See thee – there – the warnin' light!'

Adrian spun round and Lavender followed his glance. Behind him, up in the battlements of the north tower of Willow Marsh Manor, someone was frantically swinging a lantern backwards and forwards. Lavender cursed beneath his breath.

The sound of muffled musket fire suddenly broke the silence of the still night. Over at the wind pump at Brandon lode. Lieutenant Waterbeach and his men had opened fire.

'Gaugers! We must go back!' Goldsmith shrieked. The trap door fell back down to earth with a loud crash.

'No!' Adrian replied sharply. 'Open it up again – get the furs! He'll be furious if we return empty-handed.'

'You get 'em then!' Goldsmith yelled. 'I'm damned if I'll risk bein' taken by gaugers!'

He turned and ran back towards the boathouse.

Lavender raised his pistol and stepped out into his path. 'Halt! In the name of the King I say, halt!'

Goldsmith hurled his pocket lantern at Lavender's head. Lavender ducked just in time but Goldsmith barrelled into him and he was knocked off his feet. The pistol flew from his hand and disappeared into a clump of willow weed.

Adrian Delamere followed his accomplice, nimbly leaping over Lavender's prostrate and winded form. But he wasn't fast enough. Gasping for breath, Lavender reached up and grabbed Adrian's boot as it sailed over him.

The young man fell heavily to the ground, swearing.

Lavender forced himself up and rolled on top of him. Adrian had the speed and strength of youth, but Lavender had thirteen years' experience of grappling with criminals. In one smooth move, he yanked one of Adrian's arms behind his back and snapped his hands into the cold embrace of his metal handcuffs. Now immobile, Adrian lay face down on the moonlit path, yelling.

Ahead, there was a furious roar, a crash and an enormous splash. Something or someone had gone into the lode. Over Adrian's squeals he heard Goldsmith yell: 'I can't swim! Get me outta 'ere, you bastard!'

Lavender stood up, brushed down his coat and hauled the whining young man to his feet. He'd lost his pistol and didn't know what the devil had caused the commotion ahead, but Adrian would make a useful shield.

'In the name of King George – show yourself!' he yelled into the darkness. 'I'm armed!'

'Oh yeah? What with?' growled back a voice. 'I saw your pistol fly off into a bush. Are you fightin' these devils with an ink quill?'

Never had Lavender been so pleased to hear that voice.

The furious and soaking wet body of Goldsmith was suddenly propelled forward out of the darkness. The smuggler stumbled and landed with a curse at Lavender's feet. His arms were also secured behind his back with regulation Bow Street iron handcuffs.

Woods strode out of the gloom, wringing water out of his right coat sleeve. 'Armed, my foot,' he sneered. 'It's a good job you've got me to watch your back.'

The emotional surge that pulsed through Lavender at that moment was as powerful as the one he'd felt when little Alice was first placed in his arms. He couldn't tell whether it was relief, joy or even a flush of love that overwhelmed him. Probably all three. 'I'm fortunate in my friends,' he said quietly, 'especially in you, Ned. Well met.'

'Well, don't think you're forgiven.' Woods wagged a large finger in Lavender's face. 'Don't think it's over yet.'

'I won't make that mistake,' Lavender said solemnly – but he couldn't help a grin of triumph. Woods' gruff tone belied the excitement in his eyes, brought on by the chase. 'You look a bit damp. Did you fall in the lode?'

Woods grunted and jerked his thumb in Goldsmith's direction. 'No, I didn't. I pushed him in when he ran past. How were I to know the daft sod couldn't swim? I had to lean down to haul him out and my sleeve got wet.'

'You've done well, Ned.'

'Yes, I know – but stop smirkin', will you? Your teeth shine like a cat's in the dark and if there's any armed smugglers still out there, they mark you out as a perfect target.'

Lavender lowered his face to hide his grin. 'Look who I've just caught.'

Woods glanced at Adrian and gave a low whistle. 'Heaven and hell, son! You? Your da's not goin' to be happy about this.'

'It's a mistake!' Adrian whined. 'A terrible mistake!' He'd lost his hat in his tussle with Lavender and his dark hair flopped across his distressed features.

'How's that work then?' Woods asked. 'You thought you'd pop out for an evenin' stroll, and accidentally fell into step with a bunch of smugglers who'd found a secret tunnel full of contraband?'

'Release me and I'll explain,' Adrian persisted. 'They forced me to do it.'

'Yes, and my aunt's the Queen of Sheba.' Woods turned to Lavender. 'Did you know he were involved?'

'No, I'm as surprised as you to find him here. We need to get them to Lieutenant Waterbeach.'

258

'No! Take me to Aunt Miranda now! I insist! She'll want to avoid the scandal. She'll make it worth your while. She'll pay you to let me go…'

'Ooh, now he wants to palm us a dawb or two,' Woods mocked.

'Aunt Miranda – or my father – either one of them will make you rich men. Get me to my family. I'll tell you things – many things – give evidence…'

'Shut up with your whinin'!' Goldsmith snapped. 'You tell any tales and you're a dead man!'

'Shut up, the both of you,' Woods intervened. 'I can't hear myself think.' He turned to Lavender. 'If we can get them to the house and locked up,' he continued, 'I'll stay with them while you fetch Waterbeach. I need to change my coat.'

Lavender shook his head. 'No. They've got an accomplice in the house. Didn't you see the warning lights just before the musket fire started?'

'No! I didn't see anythin'. An accomplice?' Woods rounded on Adrian. 'Who the devil is it? Who's workin' with you up at the house?'

Adrian tightened his lips and lowered his eyes sulkily. Woods gave him an infuriated cuff on the side of his head.

'I know you're soaked, Ned,' Lavender said, 'but the house isn't safe. Let's get these coves to Brandon lode and leave them with Waterbeach so we can come back here and root out the accomplice ourselves.'

'They'll have scarpered by then,' Woods said.

'It's a risk we'll have to take – I think I know who it is.'

'You do?'

'Yes – they won't go far.'

'Come on then,' Woods said cheerfully. 'Let's get these devils to the gaugers.'

Adrian groaned.

'I can't hear the gunfire any more.' Lavender walked over to the clump of willow weeds, parted them and searched for his lost weapon. 'They must have caught the rest of the gang. Is your pistol loaded in case we run into any trouble on the way?' He finally found his pistol and straightened up.

Woods winked and raised his gleaming weapon in response.

'You're making a huge mistake, Lavender,' Adrian wailed as they prodded their two captives forward through the marshes. 'I'm an innocent man! I was forced to do this!'

'Spoken like a true Delamere,' Woods replied sarcastically. '*It's not my fault.* You forget, son, we're the officers who arrested your cousin Frederick. He squealed about his innocence too.'

The mention of Frederick had a sobering effect on Adrian. 'What... what will happen to me?'

'Smugglin's an 'angin' offence,' Woods replied cheerfully, 'they'll line you up for the mornin' drop.'

'You were caught red-handed,' Lavender added. 'But they may commute your sentence to transportation.'

'*Transportation!*' Adrian sounded close to tears.

'If you're headin' Bayside, young Adrian – they might put you on the same ship they used to transport your cousin Frederick down under. The one where he caught gaol fever and died. Now, won't that be somethin'?'

'I'll not survive that long.' Adrian's face was already whitewashed by the pale moonlight, but fear had turned it totally bloodless. 'You don't understand – he'll kill me for this mistake.'

'Who will?'

'You 'old yer tongue, yer sneakin' cur!' Goldsmith snarled.

Delamere ignored him. 'He will – their leader. He's a merciless bastard – deranged.'

'What? This gentlemanly chap with smooth boots and a scarred face we've been hearin' about?' Woods asked.

'He's no gentleman!' Adrian's voice rose in distress. 'It doesn't matter whether I'm in Newgate or halfway round the globe on a ship – he'll find me!'

'His name?' Lavender demanded.

But Adrian just lowered his head and said in a voice choked with emotion: 'You may as well sign my death warrant here and now, Lavender.'

'Gawd's teeth!' Woods gave Adrian another hearty shove in the direction of the Brandon lode wind pump. 'You're makin' my old heart bleed, son.'

Chapter Thirty-Three

It wasn't an easy journey, stumbling along the narrow path in the dark through the treacherous marshes, but it wasn't far and the weather was on their side. Once they left the small copse of trees around the boathouse, they were bathed in silver moonlight. Nocturnal creatures rustled in the reeds beside them and they startled a pair of swans off the bank. The birds slithered down into the water, squawking loudly.

Lavender sighed with relief when they finally saw the light from the gaugers' flickering lanterns ahead. Woods hailed the excise men and they were intercepted by the man called Howard who'd acted as Lavender's guide earlier that day. He led them towards the wind pump.

Waterbeach's men were loading the barrels of furs into boats. A pair of wretched and manacled prisoners sat with their backs to the wind pump, their greasy heads bowed in defeat. Woods forced Adrian and Goldsmith down on to the ground beside them while Lavender explained to a surprised – but delighted – Lieutenant Waterbeach what had occurred over at Willow Marsh Manor.

'The rest of the contraband is still in the secret tunnel. I assume it'll be safe there for tonight, now we've captured these villains. Woods and I can show one of your men its location in the morning.'

Waterbeach shook his head. 'I daren't risk it, Lavender. That damned warning light from Willow Marsh Manor forced our hand. We had to show ourselves sooner than we intended and only caught two of the bastards. The rest escaped – apart from the fellow whom we shot.' He gestured towards a dark shape lying prone on the path about twenty yards away. 'We need to retrieve the rest of those furs from your tunnel tonight, before the gang return for them. Who gave them that bloody warning?'

'I'm not sure,' Lavender said, 'but I have my suspicions. The smugglers have an accomplice in the manor house. Woods and I intend to return to flush them out.' He pointed to Adrian. 'He knows who it is, but he won't talk. That's Adrian Delamere; he's one of the gang.'

Waterbeach gave a low laugh of surprise. 'Tobias Delamere's son? He'll find Ely gaol a tad uncomfortable after the lifestyle he's been used to.'

'He'll be a useful mine of information, but he needs a night in a cell with the town's drunken scum to help loosen his tongue,' Lavender said. 'Look, there's several rowing boats in the boathouse – including the one used by Delamere and Goldsmith. Send a couple of your men back with us. We'll show them where the furs are hidden and they can take them back to Ely in the smugglers' own boat.'

'Thank you, Detective,' Waterbeach said. 'We'll do that. Once more we find ourselves indebted to you. You've been a tremendous help.'

Accompanied by two of Waterbeach's heavily armed gaugers, Lavender and Woods retraced their steps to the tunnel entrance by the boathouse.

'So where were you hiding yourself for the last few hours?' Lavender asked, as they tramped through the dry, whispering marshes. He knew Woods would never admit he'd stormed off sulking.

'I hid myself in the secret staircase in the north tower just outside the entrance to Pammenter and Quinn's bedchamber.'

'Why?'

'I were followin' your instructions.'

And sulking, Lavender thought.

'I waited until the coast were clear then I went through their possessions, lookin' for pistols.'

'Quinn's as well?' Lavender was impressed.

'It seemed rude not to, seein' as his trunk were sat next to Pammenter's and were unlocked.'

'Did you find anything?'

'Yes, sir. Pammenter has a fine pair of duellin' pistols in his trunk and Quinn has some dark, evil-lookin' piece the devil himself must have forged over in the Americas. It were impossible to tell if any of them had been fired today.'

So, both these young men owned weapons. It might mean nothing, of course. America was a lawless place full of wild animals and hostile natives; Quinn probably never left home unless he was armed. As for Pammenter, it was quite normal for an elegant gentleman about town to own duelling pistols and the roads between here and London were still plagued with highwaymen.

Once they reached the Willow Marsh Estate, they opened up the trap-door entrance to the secret tunnel and helped the excise men to load the barrel of furs into the rowing boat left by Adrian and Goldsmith. The excise men pushed away from the jetty and disappeared into the night. All that remained of their presence were the gently swelling concentric circles of ripples caused by the gentle dip of their oars.

Lavender was just able to make out the time on his pocket watch by the starlight. It was nearly midnight.

Woods frowned. 'Wasn't there another boat moored in here this afternoon?'

'What?'

Lavender frowned and followed his gaze. Woods was right. This afternoon, two boats had bobbed in the water by the jetty. The smugglers had brought a third, which the excise men had just taken back to Ely. But only one remained now. 'Strewth, yes. Was it here when you hauled Goldsmith out of the lode?'

Woods scratched his stubble and frowned. 'I can't remember. I weren't countin' boats. Do you think another one of the smugglers took it?'

Lavender's sigh came out as a hiss. This desolate landscape was crawling with bloody thieves. 'Come on,' he snapped. 'Let's round up Adrian's accomplice.'

When they strode through the orchard, a large animal snorted and crashed off to their left, startling them both.

'Damned pigs.' Woods pointed ahead to the manor house, where the great arched windows of the medieval hall gleamed with soft, creamy candlelight. 'Someone's still awake. Do you think the family heard the muskets firin' from the house?' he added.

'I don't know. The walls are very thick.'

'Who do you think sent that signal?'

'I think it's Adrian's sister, Ursula,' Lavender said quietly.

Woods whistled between his teeth. ''Heaven and hell! That young slip of a lass with the sour face?'

'Yes. She makes the most sense. Someone was out here listening to us when we walked back to the house after finding the smugglers' cache. We were talking about returning tonight. I wasn't sure then – but I am now – I think it was Ursula. She later claimed to hate walking outside in the damp, but her shoes and gown were splattered with mud.'

'Do you think the minx were followin' us?'

'I think that's been her plan all along – ever since she remained behind when her family returned to Ely. She's been spying for the smugglers.'

'But why? Why have either of those youngsters got mixed up with these murderin' rogues?'

'Money and greed. Their branch of the family is poor compared to the Willow Marsh Delameres. I think brother and sister are in this smuggling lark together. Adrian told me earlier today he was in the import-export business,' Lavender added, 'but I didn't realise the cheeky cove meant illegal imports.'

'Seems a strange thing for a young gal to get herself involved with.'

'Women often play an important role in smuggling gangs Like their cousin, Susanna, the siblings will have known about the secret tunnel entrance since childhood. In exchange for a slice of the profits, they probably offered the tunnel – and maybe the Willow Marsh wind pump – as a hiding place for the contraband, and Ursula promised to send a warning if any law men got too close.'

'And there were me thinkin' she were still here because she were sweet on Hal Pammenter,' Woods chortled to himself.

'I don't think there's anything sweet about Ursula Delamere,' Lavender said grimly. 'There was something false about her affection for Pammenter this morning – she threatened to find herself another beau if he didn't propose marriage soon. Be on your guard, Ned,' he added. 'She may be armed.'

They left the orchard and started to mount the steps up through the terraced garden.

Above them, the treacherous north tower loomed up into a blue-black velvet sky sprinkled with glittering diamonds. But Lavender wasn't in the mood to appreciate the beauty of the night sky. The battlements were shrouded in shadow and if someone was waiting up there to drop rocks on their heads, they'd never see him. The hairs on the back of Lavender's neck prickled again at the thought of an unknown malevolence peering down at them through the darkness.

'Ursula doesn't like her cousin Susanna much,' Woods commented. 'Maybe she were the one who pushed her into the lode?'

'Maybe.'

'Perhaps it were her who tried to kill her and Quinn this afternoon?'

'I don't know,' Lavender replied. 'Birgitta Delamere said Ursula was with them at the time of the attack, waiting for Adrian's return.'

'It strikes me the woman doesn't pay much attention to her daughter.'

Lavender nodded. 'She certainly managed to slip away from the watchful eye of her parents for an intimate tryst with Hal Pammenter this morning. If I'm right, this wretched girl has run rings around everyone.'

'What will you do now? Hammer on her bedroom door and arrest her?'

'Yes.'

'That Miranda won't like it.'

'Miranda Delamere can keep her opinion to herself. This is a customs and excise matter now. They're the law round here – not her.'

'They're full of surprises, these ruddy Delameres, aren't they?'

'Yes,' Lavender replied, 'and we still don't know the full extent of what these people are capable of.'

Chapter Thirty-Four

The kitchen door was locked when they tried to gain entry back into the manor house. Lavender hammered on it and called out. Eventually, the manservant, Hawkes, opened it a crack and pushed the barrel of an ancient flintlock musket towards them.

Woods threw his hands in the air and called out hastily, 'Steady on, fella! It's us – Lavender and Woods.'

Hawkes squinted at them cautiously. 'You two alone?'

'Yes, for God's sake, let us in, man!'

Hawkes stepped back and they entered the building. His ancient musket looked like it had first seen action in the English Civil War. 'We 'eard the gunfire and figured the smugglers and gaugers were abroad,' he explained. 'Miss Delamere is waitin' fer you in the big hall.'

Miranda sat in her wheelchair, a woollen shawl pulled tight over her thin shoulders, with Susanna by her side. The two women looked nervous and held hands.

Robert Quinn and Hal Pammenter sat together on the fireside settle. They looked tense and spoke in lowered voices.

Constable Cudworth lurked in the shadow of one of the huge arched windows, halfway down the cavernous room. He sat uncomfortably on a faded tapestry window seat with his pistol in his lap but leapt to his feet when Lavender and Woods approached.

'Where's Miss Ursula?' Lavender asked.

'She took herself off to her bedchamber soon after supper, sir,' Cudworth replied. 'The family retired to the parlour after their meal and she left them soon after that.'

'Was this just before the shooting started?' Lavender asked.

Cudworth thought for a moment, then nodded. 'Yes, it were. The servants heard the muskets firin'. They came and told the family and locked up the house. Everyone scurried in here, but they decided to leave her sleeping. Everyone's been waitin' for you to return. Miss Delamere ain't pleased you weren't here when the trouble started up.'

Lavender nodded and bit back a cynical smile. The ire of Miranda Delamere was the last thing he cared about tonight. 'When the girl, Ursula, left the room, did you see her go upstairs to her room in the south tower?'

Cudworth hesitated. 'No, I didn't, sir. You'd told me to watch out for Miss Susanna, I weren't watchin' out for Miss Ursula.'

'No, none of us were,' Lavender admitted thoughtfully, 'and because of her youth and her gender, we've overlooked her. Go to Miss Ursula's chamber in the south tower and fetch her down – at gunpoint if necessary. And be careful – she may have a pistol herself.' Cudworth nodded and left the hall.

'Lavender!' Miranda called out angrily from the fireplace. 'If you've finished with your constable, perhaps you'll come here and tell me what's happening out there on my property.'

Miss Susanna's property, Lavender thought.

An elaborately engraved duelling pistol lay on the small table beside Hal Pammenter, its hammer drawn back ready for firing, and an intriguing black caplock pistol of foreign design sat in Quinn's lap.

Hal saw Lavender's glance. 'We weren't taking any chances once we heard the gunfire,' he explained. 'We had to protect the women.'

'You were right to be cautious, Mr Pammenter,' Lavender replied. 'Tonight, the marshes were crawling with dangerous smugglers – but fortunately the excise men, under the command of Lieutenant Waterbeach, were waiting for them. Why isn't Miss Ursula with you?'

'Ursula went to bed hours ago. Why were you outside with the excise men, Lavender?' Miranda snapped. 'I pay you to protect my niece – not to assist Waterbeach.'

'Actually, no, ma'am, you're paying us to catch the villains who tried to drown Miss Susanna in the lode – and I suspect we're a step closer to solving this mystery tonight.'

'You dare to contradict me?' Miranda's tone was deadly.

'Damn it, Lavender,' Hal intervened hastily, 'what the deuce happened out there?' There was a slight flush along the line of his sculptured cheekbones, but he sounded sober.

Lavender took a deep breath and told them how he and Woods, along with the excise men, had set traps for the smugglers at both the Willow Marsh boathouse and the Brandon lode water pump and how they'd caught them in the act of trying to recover the smuggled furs.

'Furs?' Hal exclaimed. 'That's a surprise. It's normally brandy and tobacco they smuggle round here.'

'I can't believe they dared to come so close to the house!' Susanna said breathlessly. She shivered.

Miranda patted her hand. 'How on earth did they know about the secret tunnel next to the boathouse? Even *I've* never seen it. I thought it was merely a legend.'

'Hal and I found it years ago,' Susanna said, 'but there's been a rockfall and it's blocked.'

Lavender braced himself. 'Your cousin, Adrian, must have also found it and showed it to the smugglers. He was working with them.'

'You're mistaken, surely?' Miranda exclaimed.

'No, ma'am, Woods and I captured him with another member of the gang by the boathouse.'

Susanna's hand flew to cover her mouth. '*Adrian* is a smuggler?'

'Strewth!' Hal stuttered. 'Who'd have thought he'd have such roguery in him!'

'Uncle Toby and Aunt Birgitta will be devastated!' Susanna looked close to tears.

Miranda slammed her clenched fists down on the arms of her wheelchair. 'The stupid young fool! This will reflect badly on *all* of us. All of us.'

The others turned in surprise at her outburst.

'I'm not worried for myself,' Susanna murmured.

'Well, you should be,' Miranda snapped. 'This family doesn't need another scandal. Dear God! We've had to suffer enough over the last twenty years.'

'Yes.' Hal nodded. 'Your generation and Uncle Lawrence's provided enough gossip to keep the tattling tongues of Ely wagging for at least another decade.' Miranda was too angry with Adrian to react to Hal's barbed comment.

'Poor Ursula will be devastated to hear about this,' Susanna said. 'Oh, my – Adrian! What have you done?'

'That's not the end of it,' Lavender said hastily. 'Someone in this house climbed to the top of the north tower and sent a warning signal out to the smugglers. Adrian had an accomplice in Willow Marsh Manor.'

Shock flashed across Hal's face. 'The deuce he did!'

'I've reason to believe it's Miss Ursula.'

'*Ursula?*' Susanna gasped.

'I think she's in league with her brother and the smugglers. When she realised Woods and I were gone from the house, she decided to warn them that armed officers of the law were abroad and went up to the tower.'

'That's ridiculous, Detective.' Hal angrily brushed his hair out of his frowning eyes. 'Ursula wouldn't do that. You must be mistaken.'

272

Was this family pride, or was the young man genuinely fond of the little minx?

'Ursula isn't a criminal,' Hal persisted. 'Her brother, yes – Adrian is silly enough to let himself be drawn into criminal activities – but a well-bred young woman like Ursula? No, no, that's a preposterous notion, Lavender.'

'Your trust in her is commendable, Mr Pammenter,' Lavender said, 'but I suspect it's misguided. I've sent Constable Cudworth to fetch her, so we'll know soon enough. In the meantime—' He pointed towards the library. '—please excuse us for a moment while we look for clues in the battlements of this wretched tower once again.'

Without another word, he picked up a lamp from a side table and headed into the library. Woods followed him and they squeezed into the hidden entrance to the staircase behind the panel and cautiously started to climb.

Lavender didn't think for one moment the smugglers' accomplice would still be up there but for the second time that day, he hesitated just below the trap door, reluctant to raise his head above the parapet.

The battlements were deserted. The ancient stonework emitted an eerie glow in the silver moonlight. Down in the orchard an owl hooted softly. Whoever had been up there earlier had left no trace.

'What now?' Woods asked.

'Now we talk to Ursula.'

As they clambered back down, Lavender paused by the entrance to his own bedchamber. 'Wait a minute,' he said, 'there's something I forgot to check this afternoon.'

He pushed his way through the swinging coats in the cupboard into the chamber and turned around to examine the garments. Woods lit the candle beside the bed and brought it across.

273

It didn't take Woods long to identify one of the coats as similar to the outer garment worn by the mysterious man who'd tried to kill Susanna and Quinn earlier. Woods reached up towards a dark shape that lurked at the back of the shelf above the coats. It was a man's hat, tall and slightly conical in shape. 'I swear that's the same hat the murderin' cove wore. I recognise it.'

Lavender examined it closely. Something fine and delicate gleamed in the semi-darkness of the felt interior.

He pulled off his glove with his teeth, reached inside and pulled out a long fair hair. 'Our murdering cove may have been a woman.' He held up the delicate item for his constable's inspection.

'Heaven and hell!' Woods squinted against the poor light. 'Is it blonde? Is it Miss Ursula's?'

Lavender held it as close to the flickering flame of the lamp as he dared and frowned with frustration. 'I can't tell in this light. It could be either blonde or silvery grey. We need to look at it again tomorrow.'

'She's got a good reason to murder both Miss Susanna and Quinn,' Woods said.

'Who has?'

'Miss Ursula, of course.' Woods gave him a queer sideways glance. 'If Quinn and Miss Susanna were both dead then Willow Marsh would pass to Mr Tobias's branch of the Delameres. She'd benefit from this, the same as the rest of her family would. Maybe Tobias put her up to it.'

'Let's not get ahead of ourselves.' Lavender twirled the long hair round his finger, pulled out his pocketbook and slid it carefully into a small leather compartment. 'If it's a hair from the head of Miss Ursula – there might be several excellent reasons to explain why she's suddenly taken to wearing men's hats.'

Woods gave him that lip-curling, quizzical look he reserved for when Lavender was being a bit dim. 'I think you may be overthinkin' this, sir. Miss Delamere suspected Tobias were behind the attack on Miss Susanna all along. Maybe she were right?'

'Maybe,' Lavender said vaguely, 'although the credibility of Miranda Delamere isn't what it was earlier in the day – I know she's holding something back about these violent events at Willow Marsh. Anyway, let's go and ask the young woman herself. And by the way, Ned—'

'Yes?'

'Did you say there was a second bed in your chamber over in the gatehouse?'

'Yes. Why?'

Lavender glanced round his room with distaste. 'Someone in this godforsaken place wants me dead and last night someone entered my room while I slept.'

Woods nodded sagely, with no hint of cynicism curling his lips. 'Yes, you've managed to make yourself very unpopular, sir. In fact, I'd say you're the most unpopular person here right now – which is quite an accomplishment, considerin' how much this family detest each other.'

Lavender ignored his goading. 'I'll come and sleep with you tonight in the gatehouse.'

'You do that, sir. No nasty creepers will find you in there.'

Rather than squash themselves back down the narrow stone passageway, they used the exterior wooden staircase to descend to the great hall.

Cudworth had returned but there was no sign of Ursula.

'Where's Miss Ursula?' Lavender asked, when they finally reached the flagstone floor of the hall.

'I'm sorry, sir,' Cudworth stammered. 'The young lady – ain't there. Her bed hasn't been slept in and her chamber's empty. She's gone.'

'Gone? Gone where?' Lavender snapped.

'Gawd's teeth!' said Woods. 'Well, that explains the missin' boat in the boathouse.'

Chapter Thirty-Five

No one wanted to believe Ursula Delamere was now out in the deadly, black marshes, either rowing or running towards the smugglers.

Hal Pammenter and Miranda insisted Lavender and Woods were mistaken. They called for the two manservants and, leaving Cudworth to guard the women, Hal and Quinn organised a thorough search for Ursula in the manor house, outbuildings and grounds.

Sighing, Lavender and Woods agreed to help.

'This is a waste of time,' Woods growled, as they poked around the back of the stables. 'She's sailed off into the night with a ship full of smugglers.'

'I suppose we need to be sure she's not still here,' Lavender snapped. The excitement he'd felt earlier in the evening after the capture of the smugglers had been replaced with exhaustion, irritation and alarm. He didn't like the missing girl but that didn't stop him worrying about her fate among a vengeful and brutal gang of rough men.

In addition to this, the weather turned against them. The moon and stars disappeared behind a high bank of clouds and it started to drizzle. The drizzle soon turned to heavy rain as they searched the orchard.

'Do you think she might have gone home to her parents?'

Lavender ran his hand through his damp and tangled hair and let his tired eyes strain against the gloom. 'I doubt it, but I guess we need to check.'

He didn't relish the prospect of telling a furious Tobias Delamere that his son was clapped in irons and his daughter had eloped with a ship full of murdering thugs, but someone would have to do it eventually.

He decided that he and Woods would go to Ely with the very deaf Thrup as their boatman and he sent Hal, Quinn and Hawkes back to the house with instructions to tell the family to retire for the night. There was nothing else anyone at Willow Marsh could do.

The reeds bent and swayed like a tunnel over their heads as Thrup eased the boat down the lode. The tide was with them when they pulled out into the river. The strong current picked them up and hurled them along towards the small city, whose lights glimmered faintly in the distance.

When they reached the spot where someone had shot at Lavender from the riverbank earlier that day, he tensed, half expecting to hear the crack of a pistol again.

Woods must have been sharing the same thought and glanced at him in concern. 'I'll correct anyone who ever says these bloody marshlands are lonely and isolated. The ruddy place is swarmin' with gangs, coves and villains of every description, age and sex.'

Lavender gave a half smile but shivered when the cold wind bit into his face. Despite his hat and raised coat collar, rain seeped down the back of his neck. Was it Ursula who'd fired at him, he wondered? Had the smugglers furnished her with a weapon and taught her how to use it? She'd had the opportunity to slip out of the manor house and hide herself in the reeds when Woods went upstairs with Susanna.

His tired brain whirled with possibilities, each one more outlandish than the last. Was it Ursula who'd donned the men's clothing and hurled masonry down onto Susanna's head? He knew there was no love lost between the two young women. But did Ursula hate and envy her cousin so much she might try to murder her? In fact, was it Ursula, rather than Adrian, who was meeting with the smugglers at the wind pump when Susanna innocently walked their way? Was it Ursula who'd crept up behind her and shoved her into the lode?

278

Lavender's eyes and ears strained against the night. He heard the hiss of rain hitting the water as another sudden squall moved swiftly upriver towards them.

'Do you think they forced her to work for them?' Woods raised his coat collar against the wet.

'I don't know. But I don't think we should underestimate her. It wouldn't surprise me to learn it was her idea to hide the smuggled goods on Delamere property. Maybe she set it up with the gang and recruited Adrian to help. But she's in great danger right now – those smugglers will be furious about losing their goods.'

Woods nodded, his mouth a tight line of concern and repressed anger. 'Adrian needs to work out where his loyalties lie. If he has any care for his little sister at all, he needs to start talkin'.'

'Maybe we should speak to him again, once we've told his parents Ursula is missing,' Lavender said thoughtfully. 'If she's not at home, pressure must be put on Adrian to talk. Ursula's disappearance has changed everything. Whatever happens, we might as well stay the rest of the night in Ely. The coroner is opening the inquest into Mabberley's death tomorrow morning and I need to be there. We'll get a room at The Lamb.'

'I can't believe we spent the day suspectin' Hal Pammenter, while all the time it were his cousins who were the real criminals.'

'Pammenter's no angel – and Quinn's just as ruthless.' Lavender told Woods about the young man's scheme to extort money from Miranda Delamere and how Quinn was courting Susanna for her fortune.

'Gawd's teeth! All the young fellas around seem to fall for her. That Adrian were besotted as well.'

'I think her fortune may be a huge part of the attraction – but I'm no expert on the fairer sex,' Lavender said.

'That's an understatement if ever there was one,' Woods retorted. 'I think you should just stick with the detectin', sir, and leave speculatin' about the womenfolk to me.'

Lavender's mouth opened as if to dispute something, then he thought better of it and decided to change the subject. 'Hal told me a few other things this afternoon, too. Some unpleasant things about his Aunt Miranda.'

'Oh yes?'

Lavender glanced again at Thrup, hauling on the oars at the other end of the boat. He hoped Woods was right and the manservant was deaf as a post. He quietly told Woods about Miranda's spy network. 'She's a clever woman. She's manipulated us from the start, although oddly enough, she tried to dismiss us this afternoon and send us back to London.'

'So why are we still here?' Woods sounded incredulous.

Lavender didn't reply.

'Gawd's teeth! And to think I could have been halfway home to my little nippers by now!'

'I told her we were staying until I'd discovered who wanted to hurt Susanna,' Lavender said firmly. 'But initially, she dismissed this as unimportant. I think she's worked out who threw that stone off the battlements and has decided to protect them.'

'What? Did she suspect Ursula?'

'I've no idea. I'll confront her again after the inquest tomorrow. By then, everything should be clearer. I think she's obsessed with what happened to her brother and she's lured us up here to find out the truth about the snuff box.'

Woods shuffled uncomfortably beside him. 'All this fuss about that blasted snuff box.'

'From what Hal told me,' Lavender continued, 'I suspect she had someone watching us down in London and probably paid for information about our trip to Cambridge.'

He paused for a moment before adding: 'I'm sorry to tel. you this, Ned—' He lowered his voice still further. '—but she also seems to know what happened between her bastard brother and poor Ginny – although she doesn't seem to care a damn about Ginny.'

But how did she know about Ginny in the first place? he wondered. Frederick Delamere hadn't struck him as the kind of man who'd remember the name of a maidservant.

There was a long silence. Lavender couldn't see Ned's face in the dark. The swaying black hulls and the lanterns of moored vessels loomed out of the river as they drew closer to Ely. When his constable finally spoke, the sound resembled the growl of a wild animal: 'Oh, I'm quite sure the likes of her don't care about the likes of our Ginny.'

'If her web of spies is as widespread as Pammenter suspects, she may even know of your family connection with Ginny,' Lavender suggested tentatively. 'She lured you into a false sense of security this morning by asking for your opinion about Quinn. Her plan all along was to interrogate you about the snuff box.'

Woods remained silent.

'I think she wanted to cause a rift between us,' Lavender added. 'It's part of her revenge.'

Still Woods didn't reply. The moon came out from behind the clouds and the towers of the cathedral were silhouetted against it. Laughter and drunken singing drifted across the water from the quayside taverns. A few more minutes and they'd be at the wharf.

'Do you think that's why she never married?' Woods finally said.

'What? Miranda Delamere?'

'No. Our little Ginny. Did that violent bastard put her off men for life?'

Lavender felt wretched. He rose unsteadily to his feet and reached out to grab the slimy black timbered leg of the jetty to steady the boat. The action calmed him. 'I don't know, Ned. You need to ask Betsy. Betsy will know.'

'Aye,' Woods growled from his seat in the stern. 'My wife – the woman who kept family secrets from me for over twenty years!'

Lavender dipped his head to Woods' ear to hide his next words from anyone on the wharf. 'Yes, Betsy – your wife. A brave woman who sought – and found – a means to get justice for Ginny, Irish Nell and the rest of Delamere's victims, while you and I struggled to convict him. Think about that, Ned. Think about it.'

Chapter Thirty-Six

The home of Tobias Delamere on St Mary's Street was shrouded in darkness as Lavender and Woods trudged up the hill towards it This part of town was quiet and dimly lit but the rain clouds had cleared away above and the moon illuminated their path once more.

Set back from the cobbled road behind a creaking gate and a small garden, the Delamere home was a modest, double-fronted dwelling whose low, narrow doorway didn't seem wide enough to accommodate the girth of its rotund owners.

Lavender hammered on the door several times before a sash window jerked open on the floor above.

Tobias Delamere poked out his head. 'Who the devil is that? What do you want at this time of night?' His bald, domed pate gleamed in the moonlight.

'It's Detective Lavender and Constable Woods. We've come from Willow Marsh with disturbing news about your son and daughter. You need to let us in immediately.'

'What are you talking about, man? Is this some new trick of Miranda's? Damn the woman.'

'Let us in, for God's sake,' Lavender snapped. He owed this family nothing, but he didn't want to discuss Adrian and Ursula's criminal activities at the top of his voice in the street.

Birgitta's voice drifted down from above. 'Let them in, Toby. I'll go and wake Adrian.' The window slammed shut, rattling the glass.

'She's in for a shock,' Woods murmured beside him.

Several minutes later, Tobias Delamere yanked back the bolts, opened the door and scowled. 'What's going on, Lavender? My wife tells me Adrian's not in his bed.'

'It would be better if we talked inside.'

Reluctantly, Tobias stepped back to let them enter the hallway. He wore a billowing green banyan over his voluminous nightshirt and carried a lamp in his fat hand. His hospitality didn't extend to a seat in the parlour.

Behind him, Birgitta, also in her nightwear, with her white hair tightly bound in rags, unsteadily descended the staircase.

'Adrian's safe for the moment,' Lavender said as he took off his hat and shook the rainwater off it. The dark oak beams above seemed particularly oppressive in the gloom. 'It's Ursula we're more concerned about.'

'Why?' Birgitta joined her husband at the bottom of the stairs. 'What's the matter?' she asked. 'Is she ill?'

Lavender cleared his throat and braced himself for their shock. 'Tonight, we – along with Lieutenant Waterbeach and his excise men – surprised a large group of smugglers out at Willow Marsh and Brandon lode. We captured several of the gang. Adrian was among them.'

Birgitta gave a strangled sob and Tobias began to bluster. 'No! No, that's not possible. This is a mistake! Damn you, Lavender. Someone's made a mistake!'

'This is Miranda's doing!' Birgitta snapped. 'She's out to ruin us. First there was that nonsense with the will – and now this, this preposterous lie! Toby! You must do something!'

One side of Tobias's jowly face twitched. 'Yes, that's it! This is one of Miranda's tricks – damn her eyes! The woman has set her lackeys on our son.'

'No,' Lavender said firmly. 'Your son was caught red-handed working with a gang of smugglers.'

'To think she'd turn on us like this!' Birgitta said, her face contorted with spite. 'Her only family!'

284

'Doesn't Miss Delamere have some relatives on her mother's side of the family?' Lavender asked suddenly. Woods gave him a quizzical sideways glance.

'No! Of course she doesn't,' Birgitta snapped. 'Her mother was a friendless orphan – all alone in the world.'

Any mention of Tobias's first love, the dead Gertrude, clearly still annoyed Birgitta. But Lavender gave a half smile and forgave the woman; she'd just helped him solve the mystery at the heart of this case.

'What the hell does this have to do with my son and daughter?' Tobias asked.

'It doesn't,' Lavender replied cheerfully.

'We've news of your daughter, too,' Woods said hastily, casting Lavender another concerned glance.

'Yes, where's Ursula?'

Lavender took over again. 'Just before we arrested your son and the other smugglers, someone flashed a warning light to the gang from the top of the north tower at Willow Marsh. By the time Woods and I got back, this accomplice had disappeared. And so had your daughter, Ursula.'

'What?'

'You mean they took Ursula with them?'

'No, she *was* the accomplice in the tower. It looks like both your son *and* your daughter were part of the gang.'

'Nonsense!'

'This is calumny!'

'It's preposterous nonsense, Lavender!' Tobias said. 'Clearly Ursula has been kidnapped by one of the gang!'

'No, there was no one else in the house except the family. She left of her own accord.'

Lavender had become weary of their enraged denial. He felt Tobias's hot breath on his face every time the man shouted. His breath stank of onions.

'Miranda will have let it happen deliberately to get at us!' Birgitta added. 'She's out to defame us. I've always said...'

Lavender interrupted her sharply. 'I take it Miss Ursula isn't here? In this house? She hasn't returned home?'

For a moment, the Delameres hesitated.

'No, of course she's not,' Tobias said. 'I locked up just after ten o'clock and there's only us and our maid here.' He hesitated. 'We thought Adrian...'

'Your son's in Ely gaol,' Woods said. 'We're goin' there now to see him.'

Birgitta's wail could have woken the dead. Tears streamed down her fat cheeks.

'That's all I needed to know,' Lavender said, hastily backing away towards the door. 'That Ursula isn't here. We must continue with our enquiries. Lieutenant Waterbeach will have raised a hue and cry for the capture of the smuggling gang. I'll tell them to look out for Miss Ursula as well.' He turned and marched out of the house with Woods at his heels.

'Where do you think you're going?' Tobias yelled after them. 'Come back here and explain yourself, Lavender!'

Lavender and Woods continued to stride up the road towards Ely gaol.

'That went well,' Woods said sarcastically, once Tobias's curses had faded away behind them.

'Well, at least we know she's not there,' Lavender said.

Woods nodded. 'It looks like the silly chit of a gal has thrown her lot in with the smugglers after all.'

Lavender frowned. 'Finding her at home with her parents was my last hope of finding her safe.'

'She may have drowned in the river.'

Lavender nodded and said grimly, 'That may be a far preferable fate to the one waiting for her at the hands of that gang.'

Ely gaol was a large, squat building at the top of the small city, near the cathedral. The lower windows were barred with iron rods and the entrance could only be reached through a gated archway surrounding a cobbled yard. The iron gate was padlocked and guarded by a pair of nervous gaolers with lanterns.

'I'm Detective Lavender from Bow Street. We need to speak with one of your prisoners, Adrian Delamere.'

But Lavender's fame and the news of the part they'd played in thwarting the smugglers with Waterbeach's men clearly hadn't reached the ears of the gaolers.

One of them pulled out a pistol and aimed it at Lavender's head through the bars of the gate. 'I don't care if you're the Prince Regent himself – no one's to come in 'ere tonight. These cells are packed with prisoners.'

'Yes, we know about the smugglers—'

'Lieutenant Waterbeach says there's still more of the coves abroad and 'e thinks they may try to break into the gaol and free their mates. We ain't lettin' no one inside these gates.'

'We must speak urgently with Adrian Delamere about his missing sister.'

'I've told you – there's only smugglers in 'ere.'

'Adrian Delamere—'

The guard cocked the pistol and lifted it slightly higher. 'The Delameres live out at Willow Marsh. Now, cut orf home afore I shoot you.'

Lavender opened his mouth to protest but Woods took hold of his arm and pulled him back. 'They're frightened – and probably with good cause.'

Despite his frustration, Lavender knew Woods was right. Gaol-breaking was rare in England these days but it still happened – especially when the gaols were poorly maintained and guarded. Furious mobs, made up of the friends and family of the prisoners, had been known to storm the buildings, chase off the gaolers and release prisoners. The Ely guards would be no match for a ship full of angry smugglers.

'They're not goin' to let us inside tonight,' Woods continued. 'Let's go to The Lamb, put our heads down for a few hours and try again in the mornin'.'

Lavender rubbed his hand across his tired eyes. Somewhere in the town, a muffled clock struck a single note. It was one o'clock. 'We've got the inquest tomorrow,' Lavender said.

'We can see Delamere afterwards. He'll be all the more talkative for havin' spent a full night in there with the other rogues.'

Lavender sighed. He was drooping with exhaustion. 'You're right, Ned, but my heart sinks every time I imagine the danger surrounding this foolish young woman.'

With a polite nod at the gaolers, Woods pulled him away from the gate. 'We've done everything we could, sir. They're not goin' to let us speak to Adrian.'

With a heavy heart, Lavender turned and headed towards The Lamb.

Chapter Thirty-Seven

The servants at The Lamb were startled and wary when Lavender and Woods arrived seeking a bed for the night. Lavender had to show them his bronze-tipped badge of office from Bow Street, to calm their nerves.

'You'll have to excuse my caution, sir,' the landlord said, 'we've heard there's some bad villains abroad tonight in the marshes.' He led them to a clean and pleasant room on the first floor.

Lavender fell into bed, exhausted, and slept a deep and dreamless sleep until Woods roused him the next morning.

'I left you as long as I could,' he said. 'The coroner and the jury are already here and they've just started the inquiry into the death of that farmer who accidentally shot himself. I reckon you've still got time to clean yourself up a bit' – he pointed to a jug of warm water on the washstand – 'and grab a bowl of porridge before they begin Mabberley's inquest. I can recommend the porridge.'

'Thanks, Ned. I'm surprised I slept so long.'

'I'm not. You spent our first night here chasin' your phantom visitor round Willow Marsh – and things were a bit hectic yesterday.'

'That's an understatement if ever I heard one.' Lavender poured the water into the bowl, washed his face and rubbed his hand over his stubbly chin, frowning.

He took pride in his appearance, especially at formal events like inquests and court hearings. Normally, he shaved carefully and wore a clean shirt. But these weren't normal times; he'd spent half the night chasing smugglers and the rest hunting for a missing girl, and his shaving brushes and razor were back at Willow Marsh. 'Is there any news about Ursula Delamere?'

'Not as I've heard. There's no message for us and all the talk is about how Lieutenant Waterbeach foiled a smugglin' gang. Oh, and Tobias Delamere. Everyone's talkin' about him.'

'Why? What's he done?'

'It turns out the old fool followed us to the gaol and got the same reception from the guards when he asked to see his son. He kicked up a right rumpus and woke up half the town with his shoutin'. He were nearly tossed beneath the hatches with young Adrian. Now everyone knows his lad is in the gaol.'

Lavender shook his head at Tobias's foolishness. He dressed and reached for his coat.

Pulling out his pocketbook, he carefully removed the long, fair hair coiled inside and held it up to the light.

Smiling, he replaced it.

The spacious, if slightly dusty, back room of the tavern where inquests were held was crowded with people. Magistrate Kester stood a full head above the other men milling around the room.

Lavender led Woods across and introduced them.

'You've done well – both of you,' Kester said. 'Waterbeach is already here. He told me about the assistance you gave him last night and how you uncovered another cache of stolen furs in the Willow Marsh boathouse. It's just a pity so many of the smugglers escaped but I've raised the hue and cry for the rest of the gang.'

'There's another issue I need to share with you, sir.' Lavender told him how Ursula Delamere had worked with the gang as an accomplice and fled.

'The foolish girl!' Kester looked horrified. 'No doubt she'll turn up floating in the Great Ouse. Let's try to get her back before we decide if she's to face criminal charges. If she doesn't slink back to her parents or to Willow Marsh House by tonight, I'll treat this as a missing person's situation and issue her description to the news-sheets. Tobias Delamere can pay for some notices to be printed.'

'Thank you, sir,' Lavender said. 'I'm sure the Delameres will be grateful for this. Offering a reward for her safe return may help too. The smugglers might risk returning her if they get paid for it.'

Kester nodded. 'Yes, I'll speak to Delamere. If he wants his daughter back in one piece, I'm sure he'll offer a reward for her safe return. Now, if you'll excuse me, Lavender, I think Sir Nicholas Barat would like a word with me. He's the coroner.' He gestured towards a thin, grey-haired man with a broad, pale face, who wore wire spectacles.

Lavender thanked him and led Woods over to a vacant bench. The seating set aside for the public was almost full.

A voluminous cloud of tobacco smoke indicated the location of Jack Abbot among them. He caught Lavender's eye, gave a toothless grin and raised his clay pipe in salute.

Curious eyes followed Lavender and Woods around the room. Lavender heard his name whispered among the crowd along with the words: ''E were there too.'

Woods was right. Mabberley's murder and the capture of the smugglers had created a real frisson of excitement in this quiet little city.

At the far end of the room, Mrs Mabberley, her tearful daughter, Annie, and two tall young men, whom Lavender assumed were her sons, were gathered around the open coffin.

Hal Pammenter was standing with them, wearing a fashionably cut black coat and a lavender silk waistcoat. He held his high-crowned beaver hat in his gloved hands when he bowed his tawny head respectfully at the dead man, his chin dropping into the rakish knot of his cravat. Even in mourning clothes, Hal cut a striking figure. He saw Lavender and Woods and came across to join them. 'Aunt Miranda asked me to accompany Mrs Mabberley and to represent the Delamere family,' he said.

Lavender nodded. Miranda's disability would make travel difficult and, as a trained lawyer, it was more suitable for Hal to attend an occasion like this.

'Is there any news about Ursula?'

Lavender shook his head and quickly told him about their unsuccessful attempts to find the girl the previous evening and the plan he'd hatched with Kester to offer a reward for her safe return.

A shadow flitted across Hal's face and he swallowed hard. 'Let's pray she's safe,' he murmured.

Sir Nicholas Barat cleared his throat, called for order and explained to the jurors and the audience that the purpose of today's inquest was to open an investigation into the lamentable and unexpected death of Matthew Mabberley, steward of Willow Marsh Manor, and to try to establish how, when and where his death had occurred. Mrs Mabberley sobbed quietly into her handkerchief, attracting pitying glances.

A makeshift area had been set up behind a table to represent a witness stand. The first witness called was one of Mabberley's sons, who confirmed the identity of his father. Next, Doctor Bendall related how he'd been called out to the water pump by Willow Marsh lode, where he'd found Matthew Mabberley already dead. 'It's my belief Mr Mabberley was deliberately stabbed by a person or persons unknown and judging by the amount of blood at the scene, soaking into the ground, I believe the attack took place at the same spot where his body was found.'

'Who alerted you to this incident?' Sir Nicholas asked.

'I was called to the scene of the crime by Mr Adrian Delamere, who, along with Detective Lavender, found the body.'

'Thank you, Doctor, you may sit down. I call Mr Adrian Delamere to the stand.'

There was a hushed silence, then someone tittered.

Lieutenant Waterbeach stood up. 'If I may approach you, Sir Nicholas?'

The titter had now become a ripple of giggles. Sir Nicholas's lined face creased with annoyance as Waterbeach whispered something in his ear.

'It would seem Mr Delamere has been unavoidably detained—'

'—*at His Majesty's pleasure*,' whispered some wag behind Lavender. There was more laughter around the room.

'—so, I'll call Detective Stephen Lavender to the stand instead. And I will – I repeat – I will have silence and respect at this inquest or else I'll clear the public from the room. This is a serious affair. Do I make myself clear?'

The laughter subsided and Lavender went across to the makeshift witness stand.

He gave a short statement about how he and Adrian Delamere had found Mabberley's body beside the wind pump. Without prompting, he told them how he'd examined the muddy ground on the bank of the lode, where he'd found multiple sets of footprints, and how he'd discovered that the wind pump had been deliberately disabled.

'I suspected it had been used to conceal illicit items. I wondered if Mr Mabberley, while carrying out his duties as steward of Willow Marsh Manor, had stumbled across a group of smugglers removing contraband from the wind pump.'

'When I later reported the news of Mr Mabberley's death to Magistrate Kester,' he continued, 'we shared this theory about the smugglers with Lieutenant Waterbeach.'

Sir Nicholas made a note on the paper in front of him and frowned at Lavender over the top of his wire spectacles. 'Is this the same Adrian Delamere who's currently in Ely gaol under suspicion of assisting the smugglers?'

'Yes, sir.'

'And yesterday morning, you found him already outside in the grounds of the estate, less than half a mile away from the murdered man?'

'Yes, sir.' Lavender's jaw tightened as he realised with a jolt of dismay where this line of questioning was leading.

'With hindsight, do you not think this is quite a coincidence? As you surmised, it looks like Matthew Mabberley was probably murdered by smugglers. And Adrian Delamere, whom we now know to be one of the same gang, was loitering nearby at the time?'

A murmur of consternation swept round the room. Someone went: 'Ooh!' The audience whispered; they liked this theory.

Lavender cleared his throat. 'Adrian Delamere was relaxed and helpful when he led me out to the wind pump. At no time did he give me the impression he'd just stabbed a man to death and was leading me back to the scene of the crime. There was no blood splattered on his clothing either. I suspect – perhaps Doctor Bendall can confirm this – the murderer would have been heavily splattered with Mr Mabberley's blood.'

Barat nodded and referred to the doctor, who confirmed Lavender's comment about the blood splatter.

'I notice Lieutenant Waterbeach is present,' said the coroner. 'Perhaps he can take the stand next to talk to us more about the unwelcome presence of these rogues in the area around Willow Marsh. Thank you, Detective.'

Hal Pammenter leaned over and whispered in Lavender's ear when he sat down again. 'For a moment there, I thought poor Adrian was for the long drop.'

'His future is far from safe,' Lavender replied grimly.

Waterbeach's testimony was the highlight of the morning's proceedings for everyone in the public seats. There were several journalists present among the crowd, their pencils and quills poised expectantly above their notebooks.

Everyone listened with rapt attention as the excise man with the booming voice told them how, following Detective Lavender's suggestion, they'd examined other 'broken' wind pumps in the area and discovered the cache of stolen furs at Brandon lode. He explained how they'd hidden themselves around the wind pump and waited for the smugglers to come back and how Lavender and Woods had stumbled across another stash of illicit furs down at the Willow Marsh boathouse and had waited there to ambush the smugglers. Finally, he explained how they'd surprised the gang, killed one of them and caught four others. All of whom now languished in Ely gaol, awaiting trial.

Despite the height of the raftered, cobweb-strewn ceiling, the crowded room had become hot and smelled strongly of body odour. But no one noticed the discomfort. All eyes were riveted on Waterbeach as he spoke.

When he finished, Lavender sensed they wanted to break out in spontaneous applause. But no one dared put their hands together and risk Sir Nicholas's displeasure.

Sir Nicholas leaned over and exchanged a brief word with Magistrate Kester and the chairman of the jury before turning back to Waterbeach. He thanked him and his men for their bravery and professionalism and dismissed him from the witness stand.

'It seems the city of Ely owes Detective Lavender and his constable many thanks for their help in this matter. Not only did his clever deduction help our excise men understand how these smugglers operated, which led them to the contraband at Brandon lode, but if I understand correctly, they also risked their own lives to assist Lieutenant Waterbeach last night. Thank you for that, Detective. This city is in your debt.'

Lavender nodded his head in response.

'In addition to this,' the coroner continued, 'you've also helped us to establish, without a doubt, what happened to Mr Matthew Mabberley.'

'The jury agrees with me that Mr Mabberley's death is suspicious and having examined the evidence, we believe he was feloniously murdered by a person or persons unknown who are associated with the smuggling gang disrupted by our brave excise men last night.

'As several of the villains are behind bars already, I don't feel any need to adjourn this inquest pending further enquiries. We shall move straight to trial at the next assizes. In addition to the charges those men in custody face for smuggling, they shall now all be charged with the murder of Matthew Mabberley – including the prisoner Adrian Delamere. Let him account to a jury of his peers for his actions.'

Chapter Thirty-Eight

The room exploded into a cacophony of excited voices as Sir Nicholas closed the inquest. No one had expected such drama. *Another* one of the Delamere family on trial for murder?

Hal turned deathly white. 'Good God – poor Adrian!'

'That'll shake up your Uncle Toby,' Woods murmured as they rose to leave. He turned to Lavender while they waited for the crowd to disperse. 'Can they make a murder charge stick if they don't know who wielded the blade? Won't it be commuted to manslaughter?'

'I suspect they hope the shock of this charge will loosen some tongues and Mabberley's real murderer will be identified,' Lavender replied. 'Either way, Adrian will need a damned good lawyer.'

'Don't look at me!' Hal replied. 'Uncle Tobias would never allow it. I'm too close to Aunt Miranda, remember? I'm the last person Tobias will trust to save his son from the gallows. Have you asked Adrian if he knows where Ursula might be?'

'We're on our way there now. We couldn't get access before.'

'In that case, I'll come with you. I've some money for him. Aunt Miranda sent it. It might buy him a blanket and a few meals.'

Lavender nodded and wondered if this family crisis would bring Tobias and Miranda closer together. They'd had their differences in the past, but faced with this latest threat to their family honour and reputation, the wealthy Delameres might work together to save Adrian's neck.

The ground floor of Ely gaol was divided up into metal cages, strewn with rotting straw and crammed with filthy, stinking and vocal men. A terrible stench emanated from their unwashed bodies and the open buckets of faeces in the corner of each cell.

Some prisoners begged for money or food with bony hands outstretched through the bars, while others whistled, cursed and yelled insults at the three men. Hal, in his smart coat and expensive hat, with his handkerchief held over his nose, attracted the most attention from the inmates. One pointed at him yelling: 'Lookee ye at that dandy bor!'

Adrian cowered at the back of his cell, his fine lawn shirt in tatters, hugging his knees as if he were chilled to the bone, which he may well have been. The smuggler known as Barnabus Goldsmith now wore Adrian's smart coat. Filthy, dishevelled and with a cut lip and swollen eye, Adrian had clearly spent a rough night among these brutal men.

'Lavender! Hal!' Adrian's leg irons clanked as he staggered to his feet.

Two of his cell mates sat wrapped in luxurious wool blankets. One of them, a toothless fellow with long greasy hair, gnawed on a chicken leg. ''Ave ye come from his ma?' he yelled, ''ave ye brought us some more bread and pullit?'

The other prisoners burst out laughing.

The gaoler hauled Adrian out of the cage and pushed him towards a flight of stone steps. He'd lost his expensive leather boots as well as his coat and he limped as he gingerly picked his way over the uneven flagstones. 'They took everything, Hal!' he whined. 'My coat, the food and blankets mother sent – everything.'

'Now, now, Adrian. Have courage, man,' his cousin soothed, 'we're moving you into a private cell. Little Susie and Aunt Miranda have sent money.'

'Just get me out of here!' Adrian snapped.

'That won't be possible, cousin,' Hal replied smoothly. 'You're in a lot of trouble – more than I think you realise.'

The gaoler took them upstairs to a corridor lined with sturdy wooden doors, each with a metal grille. The stench wafted upstairs with them, but it was quieter up here away from the raucous yelling in the main part of the gaol.

'These are fer the debtors,' the gaoler explained as he let them into a small cell.

A narrow truckle bed with a stained mattress was pushed up against the dripping stone wall. It reeked of damp but there was a fireplace with an empty grate and a small desk and chair.

'Kindling, coal, ink and paper are extras,' the gaoler said. Then he left.

Adrian slumped down into the rickety wooden chair, plonked his elbows on the desk and buried his head in his hands. 'This is a nightmare! I can't live like this.'

'Have courage.' Hal glanced away, embarrassed. His eyes fixed on the small barred window.

Woods stepped forward and shook Adrian's shoulders until he lifted his tear-stained face from his arms. 'Look, son, there ain't time for you to be feelin' sorry for yourself. If you think this is bad for you – try to imagine what your sister is sufferin' right now at the hands of those rogues.'

'Suffering? Ursula? How so?'

'Didn't your parents tell you when they brought you food?' Lavender asked. 'She ran away last night after she sent that warning signal out to your smugglers. We believe she's with them. You must tell us who they are and where they are. We can't get her back unless you help us.'

Adrian dashed away the tears from his eyes. 'But she won't be *suffering*, Lavender – and she won't thank you for searching for her. She's with her lover. *I'm* the one suffering – she got me into this mess!'

'Lover!' Hal exclaimed. 'The deuce she is!'

'How so?' Lavender asked. 'How did she get you involved?'

'Ursula and him set the whole thing up together. The smugglers have used the old boathouse tunnel and the wind pumps for storage for their goods for months. You know nothing about her, Hal – nor you, Lavender.'

Hal stared at his cousin in disbelief. 'How the devil did Ursula end up as the mistress of a criminal?'

'She's not the woman you think she is,' Adrian snapped. 'My little sister is a ruthless minx. I don't know how she met that cove. He's a charming bastard – but deadly. He'd been educated as a gentleman and soon had her under his spell, although I suspect they're well matched. He drew her into *the trade* with him. She loved the excitement.'

'And you, too?' Lavender asked. 'What happened to your import business?'

Adrian squirmed beneath his steady gaze. 'I made some bad investments and lost a lot of money when a ship went down in the Baltic.'

'So, you thought you'd recoup your losses by cheating the revenue men?'

'Is this leader of theirs the fella with the scar on his face?' Woods asked.

'Yes, it's a bad scar, more of a burn really. A pistol shot grazed his cheek and took off part of his ear a few years ago.'

Lavender started. A burn from a pistol shot? A voice from the past, the voice of a dead gypsy girl called Laurel Faa Geddes whispered gently from her Northumbrian grave: '*Watch out fer the man with the burnt face – he'll threaten yer happiness…*'

'What, no ear?' Hal sneered. 'He sounds like a handsome fellow.'

Adrian shrugged. 'Ursula says his scar is attractive. He's got unusual green eyes.'

'What happened with Matthew Mabberley?' Lavender asked.

'They were concerned when I told them two Bow Street runners had arrived unexpectedly at the manor.'

'You told them?'

Adrian dropped his gaze and shuffled uncomfortably on his hard-backed chair, his chains rattling. 'Yes, just after you'd arrived I left the dining room and walked out to the Brandon lode wind pump. I knew they were unloading a new consignment there. I thought they ought to know there were police officers in the house.'

Lavender thought back to that first evening and remembered hearing the gentle crunch of gravel beneath a booted foot outside in the terraced gardens of the estate while he and Woods talked about Frederick Delamere.

Frederick Delamere! Lavender almost laughed at his own naivety – and would have done so if the situation hadn't been so tragic. While he and Woods had been distracted by the ghost of the dead man, a far more menacing threat lurked in the marshes.

'He was furious,' Adrian continued. 'He said they'd have to get those furs out of the wind pump at Willow Marsh as soon as possible.'

'And that's what they were doing when Mabberley stumbled across them the next morning,' Lavender said, nodding.

'I was appalled at his murder,' Adrian assured them. 'They'd gone too far.'

'But you *are* partly to blame,' Woods said.

Woods' accusation hung heavily in the air and there was a short, tense silence while the three other men digested his words. The colour drained from Adrian's face.

Lavender intervened hastily; Adrian was talking freely and he didn't want him distracted with self-pity. 'Do you know the names of the men responsible for Mabberley's murder?'

'No, but they definitely did it. They told me to go with Goldsmith last night and remove the furs from the tunnel and they were bragging about the murder. I said this was the last time I'd work with them. I don't consort with murderers. I want to turn King's evidence now in exchange for my freedom.'

Lavender, Woods and Hal exchanged a swift glance. Unless Adrian had some new information about Mabberley's killers to pass on to Magistrate Kester, the chances were his offer to turn King's evidence would be refused and he'd still end up in the dock with the rest of the smugglers, standing trial for the steward's murder.

'The bastard also offered a guinea to any man who'd shoot Lavender dead.'

'What?'

'Yes, Ursula's fellah – their leader. He started raging when he found out you were in Ely, Lavender. I've never seen him so bad – so incoherent. He wanted me to take a pistol, go straight back to the manor and shoot you dead on the spot.'

'Did you?' Woods asked angrily. 'Did you try to shoot Detective Lavender?'

Adrian's face creased in indignation. 'No, of course not! I've already told you – I'm not a murderer!'

'Well, some bugger did,' Woods snapped. 'Try to shoot him, that is.'

'When?'

'Yesterday afternoon, when he returned to Ely.'

'Does your sister have a pistol?' Lavender asked.

'Yes, he gave her one some time ago – for her own protection. He taught her how to use it.'

This was one revelation too many for Hal. His face contorted with shock and he walked across to the barred window and stood with his back to the others.

'Did you tell your sister her lover had offered a guinea reward to the person who kills Detective Lavender?' Woods asked.

'Well, yes. I never thought for one minute… No, this isn't possible – surely you're not suggesting Ursula tried to shoot him? Ursula's no more a murderer than I am!'

'Tell that to your jury,' Hal said quietly. He turned around and eyed his cousin with distaste. Any sympathy he'd had for Adrian when he'd entered the gaol had vanished. 'Ursula slipped out of the room for a while immediately after you'd left for Ely, Lavender,' Hal added. 'Constable Woods had taken Little Susie up to her room. Ursula claimed she needed some air.'

'I bet she did,' Woods growled.

'Oh, come on, Hal!' Adrian pleaded. 'You can't think Ursula tried to kill Lavender?'

'Why not?' Hal asked. 'She's an evil, two-faced jilt.'

'You've already told us she's been happy to break the law and work with a murderous smugglin' gang who killed Mabberley,' Woods said. 'Of course she's capable of killin' Lavender! It seems to me, son, it's you who's bein' the fool here.'

Adrian sat back. He looked even more wretched beneath the dark stubble, filth and bruises. 'I think I've told you enough. I want to turn King's evidence. I need a lawyer and a guarantee of my freedom before I say any more.'

'You haven't told us enough,' Woods contradicted him angrily. 'We need the name of this murderous ringleader.'

'I want to turn King's evidence,' Adrian blustered. 'I want guarantees.'

'The name,' Woods insisted. 'What's the name of this bloody cove?'

'I think we already know him,' Lavender said quietly. 'He calls himself Nidar, doesn't he?'

Chapter Thirty-Nine

Lavender, Woods and Hal left Adrian as soon as he'd nodded and confirmed Lavender's suspicion that Nidar was the leader of the smuggling gang. Subdued and thoughtful, the three men paused on the cobbled street outside the gaol while their squinting eyes adjusted to the weak sunlight. The air was fresh, with the familiar tang of coal smoke. Lavender breathed deeply to rid himself of the stench of the gaol and the unpleasant taste of treachery. Their conversation had left him with little sympathy for the unprincipled, cowardly young man and he was deeply disturbed to hear that his old nemesis Nidar was behind Mabberley's murder.

'Who is this Nidar fellow?' Hal asked.

'Nidar's one of the worst rogues in the country.' Woods' voice was tinged with anger. 'We've bad history with that cove. He's wanted for murder back in London.'

'He runs an extensive criminal network – especially in the north of England,' Lavender explained. 'He's involved in every kind of nefarious activity, from robbing immigrants on the docks in Liverpool to political assassination, highway robbery and the slave trade.'

'We ran him out of London a few years ago,' Woods added, 'but not before he'd shot a lump out of my shoulder and nearly drowned Lavender in the cellar of a ruined church.'

'So, this Nidar fellow doesn't have much respect for consecrated ground?' Despite his sarcasm, Hal's good-looking face was ravaged with alarm. 'Maybe my sweet cousin has met her match – Ursula has little respect for anything.'

There speaks a man who's prepared to apply emotional blackmail to his aunt in order to extract money from her, Lavender thought grimly.

'She's in great danger,' he said sharply. 'Nidar's unstable, a madman. He can be very charming with women when he wants something from them.' His stomach lurched at the memory of how Magdalena and their friend, Lady Caroline Clare, were initially enthralled by the rogue. 'But he's a deadly manipulator with no conscience or empathy. He'll dispose of Ursula when she's no longer any use to him. We need to warn Magistrate Kester and Lieutenant Waterbeach about him immediately.'

They pressed themselves closer to the prison wall while a coal wagon, hauled by two great shire horses, trundled down the street. Gleaming lumps of coal slithered off the pile and fell into the road. A thin woman in a threadbare dress scurried to collect them in her basket.

Hal waited until the rumbling vehicle had moved away before he spoke again. 'Maybe now his smuggling operation has been thwarted, he'll just vanish?'

'Not if he knows Detective Lavender is somewhere in Ely,' Woods said grimly. 'He'll stay. He's got a score to settle.'

'He's vengeful, really vengeful,' Lavender added. 'Once we'd got his measure and spoiled his slaving racket in London, he set a trap for me. Frustrating him merely inflames his madness.'

'Good heavens,' Hal said, alarmed. 'I think I'd better return to Willow Marsh and my family immediately. Will you come with me? The river has subsided now and the road is clear.'

'No, we're on our way back to London,' Woods said cheerfully. 'Your aunt has dismissed us.'

Hal's leonine eyes widened in horror. 'She's done what?'

'Once she knew it were smugglers who'd pushed Miss Susanna into the lode, she told Detective Lavender she doesn't need our services any more and we were to return home after the inquest.'

'I think she's worked out who tried to drop that masonry on your cousin's head.' Lavender spoke slowly, watching Hal's reaction carefully. 'She's decided to protect the culprit.'

The young man flushed with shock and embarrassment. 'The deuce she did! What a mess! But everything's changed now. I'm begging you, sir, please return with me to Willow Marsh and give my family your protection until we know for sure this Nidar has left the area. I'll explain to my aunt she's been too hasty.'

Lavender glanced uneasily at Woods but then nodded. 'We'll have to come back to collect up our belongings anyway. But first I must warn Magistrate Kester about Nidar. We'll follow you back to Willow Marsh.'

Disappointment flashed across Woods' face but before he could protest Lavender said: 'I'm sure you'd welcome an opportunity to catch the man responsible for your injured shoulder, Ned, wouldn't you? Besides which, I now know who attacked Miss Susanna yesterday morning – and why.'

'You do?' Woods and Hal spoke in unison.

'Yes – and I've quite a story to tell when we get back to Willow Marsh. Miss Delamere has kept secrets from you all – including you, Mr Pammenter.'

'That doesn't surprise me,' Hal said.

A small boy, dressed in rags and with a thin, impish face, suddenly appeared by Hal's side. He clutched a piece of folded paper in his grubby hand. 'Are you Mairster Pammenter?'

'Yes.'

'There's a geezer given me this fer you.' He held up the note in one hand and held out the other for a coin. ''E said you were visitin' the gaol and I'd find you 'ere.''

'What geezer?'

Hal reached for the note but the child drew it back and raised his open palm higher. Sighing, Hal fished out a penny from his pocket.

The child wiped his snotty nose with his filthy sleeve and bit the coin. 'Ta. He were a big, ugly fella – down at the wharf.'

Before they could question him further, he turned on his heel and darted across the road, narrowly escaping death beneath the hooves of the swift-moving mail coach. He vanished down a side alley.

'If Thrup or Hawkes have brought a message from Willow Marsh,' Woods said, 'why didn't they just bring it here themselves?'

Hal read the note and frowned. 'It's from Susanna.'

'What's wrong?'

'She wants me to return to Willow Marsh immediately. She says they have a visitor who wants to meet with me.'

'Are you expecting a visitor?'

'No, not at all.' The young man continued to frown down at the paper in his hand. He started to chew his bottom lip.

'What's wrong?' Lavender asked.

'Maybe – it's just that… no, this is silly.'

'What?'

'She's signed it *Susanna Maud*.'

Lavender frowned. 'How is that significant? It's her name, isn't it?' He remembered the entry announcing her birth in the Delamere family Bible.

'She hates her middle name,' Hal explained. 'Maud is an old family name on the female side and she loathes it. She never uses it in correspondence. When we were younger and she was a naughty little girl, I used to tease her by calling her *Susanna Maud*. I'd always use her full name whenever she was in trouble and it would make her cry. As she grew older, it became a joke between us.'

'We do that at home,' Woods said, 'when my nippers are in trouble – especially our Dan. Betsy calls him *Daniel Aaron*.'

'I hope to God I'm not reading too much into this,' Hal said, 'but I think she's trying to tell me she's in trouble.'

'Heaven and hell!' Woods exclaimed. 'It'll be them damned smugglers! Maybe they returned to the house. Maybe Nidar forced her to write the note.'

A cold chill swept through Lavender. Fear compounded with alarm when he remembered the tunnel running from the boathouse to the manor house. He'd intend to tell the servants to block it off last night, but he'd been distracted by the search for Ursula and forgotten all about it. 'We must return immediately.'

'We'll take a boat from the wharf,' Hal said. 'It's quicker than by road.'

He started to walk away but Woods grabbed his arm.

'Wait a minute, Mr Pammenter. We'll all go together but let's think this through first. A man on a fast-movin' horse is a harder target to hit than a man in an open boat.'

'Woods is right,' Lavender said. 'He's probably already got his men lined up in the reeds on the riverbank with pistols, waiting to pick us off.'

'What I don't understand, though,' Woods said, 'is why is he urgin' Mr Pammenter to return when it'll be Lavender he wants in his grasp? He's the one who thwarted their criminal activities.'

There was a short silence while the three men considered this.

'If he's in control of Willow Marsh, he'll know Woods and I need to return to collect our luggage,' Lavender said, 'so he wouldn't send a message to me.'

'He's definitely after Mr Pammenter too, for some reason,' Woods said. 'What were your plans for the rest of the day, sir?'

'I'd told Aunt Miranda I intended to spend some time with an old friend after the inquest before I returned home.'

'He wants to distract you from this,' Lavender said. 'Does The Lamb have a livery stable? Woods is right, it'll be safer to ride out there.'

Hal nodded and the three men set off in the direction of the tavern.

'Have you brought your pistol, Mr Pammenter?'

Hal patted his coat pocket. 'Yes, sir – and I'll happily use it if I have to.'

'Gawd's teeth, I hope we're wrong,' Woods said grimly.

'Me too,' Lavender said. 'But it's better to be safe than sorry.'

'Should we ask Magistrate Kester for more constables?' Hal asked.

Lavender hesitated for a second before he realised they couldn't afford the delay. 'No, let's try and deal with it ourselves. Nidar's crew will be a few men short – we captured three of them last night and killed another. Let's find out what's going on before we involve Kester.'

'What I don't understand,' Hal said as they marched down the street, 'is if those bastards are there – how did they get into the house? Quinn and the servants are armed – and it's a fortified manor house, for God's sake. It held off the Roundheads in the Civil War.'

'Do you remember that old tunnel that runs from the boathouse?' Lavender asked.

'The one where you found the furs? Yes, Susanna and I discovered it years ago. It's blocked.'

'Not any more, it isn't, son,' Woods said.

Chapter Forty

The three men galloped along the road beside the swollen river, splashing through the shallow puddles of stagnant water that still remained after the flood. The exertion of the ride and weak sun above in the clear sky warmed them. Sweat trickled down Lavender's spine. The flat, waterlogged countryside flashed past in a haze of green and brown reeds and sedge. The only sound was the steady drumming of the hoofbeats.

Lavender's thoughts shifted to Miranda and he wondered how the middle-aged, disabled woman would cope with an invasion of her home and the threat posed by Nidar and his gang. Adrian and Ursula's reckless involvement with the smugglers had put everyone's lives at risk. But this wasn't the first time Miranda had been let down by her family. Her brother had turned into a monster who'd preyed on vulnerable women and her sister had stolen her lover from under her nose.

He felt a flash of sympathy for Miranda, which surprised him, considering the damage she'd tried to inflict on his relationship with Woods. But one glance at the firm set of his constable's jaw and the grim determination in his eyes reassured him her vengeful ploy had failed; he and Woods would weather this crisis of trust. The betrayal of her family made her a sorry figure and her compassion and love for Susanna, the true extent of which he'd only just realised, redeemed her.

The towers of Willow Marsh soon came into view and Lavender reined in his wide-eyed and sweat-flecked horse beneath him. Nidar may have posted a lookout in the battlements. It would be better to walk stealthily through the reeds from here.

'You grew up in these marshes, Mr Pammenter,' Lavender said. 'If we leave the horses here, do you think you can lead us through the reeds to the boathouse?'

Hal pushed aside a strand of damp tawny hair and his eyes swept across the dry, rustling landscape. The reeds were taller than them, each clump identical. Would it be impossible for Pammenter to do what he asked?

But the young man nodded confidently and grinned. 'Yes, I spent enough time out here dodging my tutor. I should be able to get you there safely. What's the plan, Lavender?'

Lavender swung himself out of the saddle and tied the reins of his horse to a low-slung bough. The others did the same.

'There's only one way to get into the house without being seen and that's through the old tunnel. Like I said back in Ely, it's probably the way the smugglers entered the building. We'll follow them in.'

'Perhaps they came back to the boathouse this mornin' to see if their second lot of furs were still there,' Woods said. 'When Adrian and Goldsmith didn't turn up with the cache, maybe they decided to investigate.'

'Of course! Damn it!' Lavender chided himself. 'We should have thought about this. They'd no way of knowing we'd arrested Adrian and Goldsmith last night and marched them over to Brandon lode – even Ursula, their spy, didn't know this.'

'Before she stole that rowin' boat and escaped, she may have checked the tunnel and seen the barrels of furs were still there,' Woods said. 'She probably told the gang this when she joined them.'

'Of course!' Lavender cursed himself again. 'I should have thought this through. I intended to ask Hawkes to secure the tunnel last night but forgot.'

Hal shook his head. 'Don't berate yourself, Lavender. You had other priorities last night – we all did. My sweet cousin caused chaos with her treachery and deceived everyone.'

'When Nidar returned this morning and found his last lot of goods taken, he'll have been furious,' Lavender said. 'He probably ordered his men into the tunnel to come after us – but all they found was Quinn, Cudworth and two terrified women when they burst out of the tunnel into the hallway of the manor.'

'If it's the way they went in, it's their escape route too,' Woods warned. 'They'll have left men to guard it.'

'Yes – we'll have to pick them off quietly – one at a time.'

In grim-faced silence, they loaded and primed their weapons then set off through the marshland towards the house, beneath the melancholy call of the wheeling birds. Hal soon found them an old overgrown path but it was difficult, soggy terrain. Every now and then the reeds would part to reveal a treacherous expanse of silver barely feet away. Lavender saw a small water snake curled up on a lily pad, basking in the warm sun. It slithered off into the water as they trudged by.

They followed Hal in silence, apart from one occasion when Woods lost his footing and slithered sideways down to his knees with one leg in the water. He scrambled back to his feet covered in mud. Growling a curse, he brushed himself down and continued. With every step, the twin towers of Willow Marsh grew larger above the sea of billowing reeds.

Hal brought them out of the marsh at the edge of the copse by the boathouse. They moved stealthily into the shadow of the trees. Ahead, they could just make out the timber-framed building with its thatched roof. Several boats rocked at the moorings.

A broad, heavily tattooed man, roughly clad with silver rings glinting in his ears, sat beside the boats with his back to them. A pistol lay in his lap.

Lavender sucked in his breath in a tight gasp. Their worst suspicions were confirmed. He glanced around, looking for other smugglers.

Woods was already on the move. For a big man, Woods could move quietly but the creaking planks of the jetty gave him away. The smuggler spun round but he wasn't fast enough. Woods had the muzzle of his pistol in the man's face before the fellow raised his own.

'Drop that weapon – now!'

The pistol clattered to the wooden decking. Woods spun the cursing smuggler round, forced him face down onto the jetty and kneeled down on his back.

'For God's sake, Ned!' Lavender hissed. 'It's a good job he was alone!'

Woods just grinned and pulled his metal handcuffs out of his pocket. He pointed towards the shrub that concealed the entrance to the tunnel. 'They lost five of their crew last night; they'll be thinly stretched. You two go ahead – I'll catch up with you.' He pressed harder with his left knee and the smuggler swore. While he was distracted with pain, Woods slid the cuffs round one of his captive's hands and yanked his other arm back.

Lavender and Hal moved cautiously towards the tunnel entrance and descended the steps with their pistols raised, half expecting to find more of the gang lurking in the dank interior. No one was there.

'They didn't expect us to follow them in this way, did they?' Hal said smugly.

'They don't know we've been warned. Your Cousin Susanna's warning worked well – she's a clever girl.'

'Cousin? She's my half-sister, Detective – not my cousin.'

Lavender didn't correct him.

'Come on. It won't be pleasant. We'll have to feel our way through in the dark. A light might alert someone at the other end.'

It was a slow and arduous journey into nothing and quite a steep climb in parts. Lavender gritted his teeth to fight back the claustrophobic panic that threatened to overwhelm him. He swung his booted foot cautiously before each step to locate fallen rubble. A stumble and a sprained ankle down here would be fatal. He soon pocketed his pistol and used both his hands to feel where the slimy walls beside them narrowed and to locate jutting and jagged rocks. Despite his whispered warnings, Hal, who was slightly taller, twice banged his head on the low roof.

Only the steady, ominous drip of water punctured the silence. He sent up a silent prayer that they wouldn't meet any smugglers down here. His ears strained for sound.

Finally, he saw a pinprick of light ahead and felt the gentle waft of fresh air on his cheek. The door to the hallway was open. 'We're nearly there,' he whispered.

Suddenly, his left hand fell away into nothing. Confused, he reached out for the wall, but his groping fingers flailed through the air. Then he remembered Woods had mentioned some sort of alcove, or second tunnel entrance.

The pinprick of light grew into an oblong. He wondered with a gnawing sense of unease what Nidar had done with Constable Cudworth and Robert Quinn. His nemesis had scant regard for human life.

The hallway came into view through the open doorway. He paused and pulled out his pistol. Hal bumped into him. The hallway was empty and silent apart from the ticking longcase clock. Ahead, one of the double doors into the banqueting hall stood slightly ajar. He thought he heard the low murmur of voices.

Should they wait for Woods? The coast seemed to be clear.

Cautiously, he stepped forward into the light. A quick glance assured him the hallway was empty. He strode silently across the flagged floor towards the open door to the medieval hall. Hal followed.

315

Suddenly, there was a click. Before either man could react, a wood panel slid open beside them and the cold steel of a pistol barrel jabbed into Hal's neck.

'Drop your weapons, you scum,' growled a voice in a strong Liverpudlian accent.

Lavender froze and cursed. He'd forgotten about the priest hole next to the tunnel entrance. But Ursula hadn't. Nidar had put one of his men in there to wait. Once more he'd walked straight into one of the lunatic's traps.

A well-built, swarthy seaman emerged from the priest hole to stand beside them. His weapon knocked viciously against Hal's jawbone. Hal winced.

'Drop your weapons, I said!'

Their weapons, their last hope of survival, clattered down onto the flagged flooring. Their captor stooped down to retrieve them, never taking his eyes or the barrel of his pistol off Hal.

No, this wasn't their last hope. Woods. Woods was still at liberty. He must keep this man distracted and away from the tunnel.

As if reading his thoughts, the black-haired smuggler glanced at the entrance and growled. 'Where's the other one?'

'Ely. He's arranging our coach travel back to London. I've just returned for our luggage.'

The smuggler grunted. 'Ye've chosen a funny way to enter. Arms up.' He jabbed at Hal again.

They both raised their arms.

The smuggler turned back to the tunnel entrance and peered down into the gloom, frowning.

Lavender deliberately took a large and noisy step in the direction of the front door.

'Oi! Stand still, will youse!' Distracted, the man jabbed them towards the door of the banqueting hall and ushered them through. 'Look who's turned up,' he announced proudly.

Slowly, Lavender walked into the cavernous room.

Brilliant sunlight poured through the vast mullioned windows.

It illuminated a scene of pure terror.

Chapter Forty-One

All the servants, apart from Lucy Pammenter, cowered at the far end of the room, where another one of the gang towered menacingly over them with a pistol. Meanwhile, poor Cudworth lay unconscious and unattended on the flagstone floor with a large pool of blood encircling his head.

Miranda and Susanna huddled together at the nearest end of the great banqueting table. Both were ashen-faced with terror. Susanna whimpered when she saw them forced into the room at the end of a gun barrel.

Opposite sat Nidar, with Ursula perched on his knee, a pistol on the table before him. Nidar was toying with the weapon on the table, smiling down at it.

A wave of fear swept through Lavender but he forced it down and glanced around, trying to assess the level of danger.

Two more burly seamen lounged on the cushioned window seats. Both carried knives. Including their captor and Nidar, there were five gang members in the room in total, each of them hard-faced and powerfully built. But only three of them were armed with pistols.

Quinn? Where the hell was Robert Quinn?

Ursula grinned in delight at the sight of Hal, but her smile didn't reach her eyes. 'Ooh, look! How lovely of you to join us, Hal. I'm so glad you got Susanna's message. We've a score to settle, my darling.'

'I can't wait to find out what it is,' Hal said sarcastically. 'Are you going to introduce me to your charming new friend?'

'He's Captain Nidar, my dearest, and he's promised me revenge for your broken promises.'

Lavender ignored her threatening tone and watched his nemesis, who so far had not looked up at him. Handsome, wind-burned from his life at sea and smartly dressed, from this angle Nidar hardly seemed to have changed over the past eighteen months.

But when the fiend turned his head towards him, the illusion of fresh-faced cultured innocence was shattered.

A jagged burn disfigured the left-hand side of his face and a large chunk was missing from his ear, around which much of his hair had gone. His mutilated exterior now reflected the horror within and he was a creature of nightmares – Lavender's nightmares.

'Watch out fer the man with the burnt face – he'll threaten yer happiness…'

'Well, if it ain't our old shipmate, Detective Lavender.' The grin that spread over Nidar's maimed face caught at the scar tissue on one side and twisted into a hideous grimace. 'How good of you to join Nidar.' Referring to himself in the third person again, the sure sign of a maniac. His brilliant green eyes observed Lavender coldly. *How had he ever failed to see the evil madness shining there?*

'Nidar and Lavender have unfinished business. But first, where's your fat constable?'

''E says, 'e's back in Ely,' said the smuggler behind Lavender. 'I checked the tunnel and there were no one there.'

'He's back in Ely organising our return journey to London.'

Nidar narrowed his vivid green eyes suspiciously. 'There's a lot of folks in Ely today. That gal—' – he pointed towards the trembling Susanna – '—tells me the American went with you to town.'

'Yes, that's right,' Hal intervened hastily. 'I've left Quinn in The Lamb with friends.'

Hal's quick thinking gave Lavender strength. Wherever Quinn was hiding, Lavender hoped he was armed. But he still needed to distract Nidar from Ned. The villain might organise a second search for his constable. 'What have you done to Constable Cudworth?' Lavender said sharply. *Keep him talking.*

Nidar waved a hand casually in the direction of the unconscious bloodied man on the floor. 'What, him? Oh, that's nothing – Nidar just gave him a tap.'

Their captor still lingered curiously beside them. Any minute now, Nidar would send him back to look for Woods. *Give Ned a chance.* 'So, what happened, Jim? Who spoiled your good looks? Where do I send my congratulations?'

Nidar didn't flinch at the goading or at Lavender's use of his real name. 'We believe we have your delightful wife to thank for this embellishment, Lavender. 'Tis a souvenir of our last encounter.'

Lavender winced.

How the devil did this vengeful madman know it was Magdalena who'd shot him?

The news-sheets only reported that Ned had rescued Lavender from a watery death in the flooded bowels of the church. *How—?*

Then he saw Ursula's grin spreading across her narrow face.

Damn it.

He and Woods had been talking about this incident yesterday while she was spying on them in the orchard. She must have told him. There was no point in denying it. He took a deep breath and plunged in. 'Yes, you were disfigured by a woman.'

One of the gang sniggered. Nidar shot him a poisonous glance and the man fell silent.

'It's good to see that my wife marked you for life,' Lavender continued as brazenly as he could. 'It'll be easy for us to catch you now we know what an ugly cove you are. Perhaps you didn't hear her shout of joy when she took off your ear that night? Perhaps you're just a deaf bastard now?'

Hate burned in those glassy eyes. 'Methinks Nidar will have to pay your interfering wench a visit on our next trip to London.'

Lavender's heart sank. 'You're still wanted for murder in London. Our officers are always on the lookout for you.'

Nidar ignored him, turned to his men and winked. 'What do you think about that, lads, eh? A voluptuous Spanish beauty with plenty of soft flesh to squeeze? You can take it in turns to dock with her.'

His men laughed and growled salaciously. 'After bein' wed to this fool, she'll be gaggin' for it,' one of them said.

'Oh, he'll be dead soon anyway,' Nidar said casually. 'Very soon.' He lifted his pistol and pointed it at Lavender's head. 'We'll make sure she dies too, Lavender – but not until my entire crew have drubbed her.'

Forgive me, my darling, querida...

Nidar's men laughed again and made more coarse comments, making the women blush. Miranda squeezed Susanna's hand tighter.

'You don't fancy her yourself, Nidar?' Lavender said, his voice catching slightly. *Keep him talking.* 'Not up to the job any more? Now you're only half a man with half a face?'

Nidar gave a snarl and squeezed Ursula's thigh through the thin muslin of her gown. The girl smiled with pleasure. 'As you can see, Lavender, I've got fresh meat now.'

Ursula gave a shrill laugh of delight.

'What the devil are you doing with this monster, Ursula?' Hal demanded.

322

The little she-devil slipped off Nidar's knee, walked provocatively over to her cousin and chucked him under his chin with her tiny hand. He stepped back in revulsion.

'Dear Hal,' she purred. 'So stupid – and always so selfish. I warned you I would find myself another man – a real man.' She threw a sweet smile over her shoulder towards Nidar. 'But you still left me dangling with false promises, didn't you?' Bitterness turned her voice shrill. 'False promises – and that was only when you could be bothered to write me a short note!'

'What a shockin' way to treat a lady,' Nidar drawled.

'So, I found myself a real man. One who loves me—'

'He's a murdering rogue!' Hal yelled. 'He'll drop you when you cease to be useful to him. He killed poor Mabberley, Cudworth – and God knows how many other people! They're murdering scum, Ursula – all of them.'

Vile laughter and a low growl emanated from the gang.

Steady, Hal.

Instinctively, Lavender reached out an arm to stop him provoking them further. But their guard raised his pistol and indicated that Lavender should edge away from the couple and move closer to Nidar. The smugglers were enjoying the spectacle.

Ursula gave another shrill laugh and slapped Hal hard across his face. The sharp sound echoed round the hall. Her eyes blazed as she leaned into his face and pointed back to the grinning, leering fiend at the table. 'Yes – but he's the man who's promised to marry me – *and* give me my revenge. In my book, that's a *real* man.'

Lavender's stomach lurched at the thought of what Ursula and Nidar had planned for Hal. The madman at the table had no argument with the young lawyer but he wouldn't baulk at torture. He would enjoy every last agonising moment of Hal's life.

Hal stared calmly at the spitting she-cat before him, her handprint burning on his cheek. 'Do you know the real reason I wouldn't marry you, Ursula?'

Everyone in the room held their breath.

'Because you're a two-faced, greedy, shallow little whore. It wouldn't surprise me if you weren't the one who pushed Little Susie into the lode out of sheer spite.'

Ursula screamed and flew at him. Hal stepped back and held up his arms to defend himself, but not before she'd punched him in the right eye with her balled fist. He blinked in pain.

Nidar slammed his own fist down on the table. 'Enough!' he roared. 'That's enough of the lovers' tiff, my gal.' He pushed his pistol towards her. 'Get on with it. Nidar promised you could deal with the feckless bastard. So, shoot him. Nidar must deal with Lavender.'

Ursula walked back to the table and picked up the pistol, grinning.

'No, Ursula – no!' Susanna murmured.

Ursula ignored her and turned back to Hal.

The young man brushed back a fallen lock of hair out of his eyes, pushed back his shoulders and faced her squarely. His fearless tawny eyes watched her approach with a strange mixture of regret and sadness.

Beneath the calmness of his unblinking gaze, she hesitated. The enormity of what she was about to do suddenly hit her. The hand holding the weapon began to shake.

Lavender froze. Every instinct wanted him to leap to the young man's defence, but his guard still watched him closely, with his pistol aimed at his head. One movement, one twitch and his captor would fire.

'Get on with it, gal!' Nidar snarled. 'If you can't kill him – just shoot him in the nutmegs. That'll teach the bastard a lesson and stop him fathering any of his own.'

Ursula gripped harder, raised the pistol a fraction higher, her finger tightening on the trigger.

Then Robert Quinn suddenly burst though the library door at the far end of the hall brandishing a pistol in both hands – and fired.

Chapter Forty-Two

Once his prisoner was cuffed, Woods stood up and brushed down his coat. Still soaked and caked with mud from his slip into the lode, the action had more to do with brushing away any contaminating evil filth from the cove he'd just arrested than a genuine desire to clean himself. He retrieved the smuggler's pistol from the wooden deck and checked it was primed and loaded.

He pocketed it and turned towards the tunnel entrance, but stopped as his eyes rested on the gently rocking boats tied to the jetty.

It was one of his deepest regrets from last year that Nidar had managed to escape arrest. The villain had rowed off across the Thames to his ship and fled London.

'Not this time.' He strode over to the small woodpile in the sheltered corner of the boathouse and yanked the rusty axe out of a log. The blade looked sharp enough but sheer brute force might be needed. He had plenty of that.

It took only a few massive swipes of the axe to shatter the planks at the bottom of each boat. Water surged through the splintered holes he'd created and the vessels started to sink.

He grunted with satisfaction. It'd take a while for them to fill with water but they were scuttled. The coves wouldn't sail merrily off into the sunset this time.

Bracing himself for an unpleasant squeeze through the dank tunnel in the pitch black, he followed Lavender and Hal. But this was his second trip and despite the dark he moved swiftly. He soon saw the faint pinprick of light up ahead and heard the steady ticking of the large carriage clock in the hallway.

He also heard voices. Several voices. Including one he didn't recognise, with a northern accent. He'd reached the recess where the side tunnel led off to the left. He slid inside it in the nick of time. The light dimmed ahead as a figure came to the tunnel entrance in the hallway and peered down into the blackness.

Woods held his breath and waited. A weak shaft of light illuminated the rocky tunnel again and the voices faded away. They'd gone.

Frowning, he took out one of his pistols and inched his way towards the exit.

The wood-panelled hallway was empty and the door to the priest hole gaped open. He paused, blinking, while his eyes adjusted to the light. His nose caught the faint smell of food left unattended burning in the kitchen and he sent up a quick prayer that it wasn't his supper.

He squeezed into the small cavity of the priest hole and shut it quietly behind him.

The sound of Lavender's raised voice berating Nidar in the banqueting hall about him being *half a man* distracted him as he sank down onto the small stool to peer through the peephole.

Good goin', sir, he thought grimly as Lavender taunted Nidar about his face. *When unarmed and faced with a murderer, why not provoke him to anger?* He grimaced as Nidar taunted Lavender back and threatened Doña Magdalena.

The peephole was large enough to fire through, he noted. His vision was partially obscured by the suit of armour on the other side of the wall but he could clearly see the guard with the servants – and poor Cudsworth unconscious on the stone floor in a pool of blood.

Another cove had a pistol aimed at Lavender's head. Meanwhile, an ugly bastard with a damaged face and vivid green eyes sat in front of him at the table, with Ursula dangling on his knee.

Nidar.

Woods gave a quiet groan when he saw the third weapon on the table. He was outgunned three to two. It would take time to reload but hopefully the confusion he would cause by firing from his concealed position would give the servants, Hal and Lavender a chance to overpower the rest. It all depended on the accuracy of his two shots.

He left one pistol in his lap – that was for Nidar – and aimed the other at the armed man holding Lavender prisoner.

Ursula was now on her feet, screaming at Hal, who was just out of his line of vision to the left. He heard her slap his face but didn't see it. He watched in dismay when Ursula returned to the table to pick up the pistol.

His heart sank and he held his breath. The damned gal intended to kill the young fella in cold blood. He saw the hesitation in her plain, pinched face, but he knew that if she didn't pull the trigger, Nidar would take the weapon from her and do it himself.

Woods hesitated in dismay, torn with indecision. She was right in front of him – he could shoot her now. But he had to save his shots for Nidar and the cove pointing his weapon at Lavender. Sweat rolled down his back. His hand twitched to turn his pistol towards Ursula.

The next second was magical.

Never in his life had Woods been so pleased to see a foreigner.

The young American burst out of the library door, firing off two pistols simultaneously with a deafening bang. His loose grey coat flew out like batwings behind him as he hurled himself through the air and landed, rolling, on the ground. The smuggler guarding the servants crumpled to the floor and dropped his weapon. Quinn continued his roll towards it and grabbed the pistol from beside the dead man. He then turned it on the two smugglers armed with knives. They added their curses and yells to the screaming mayhem and charged for the door.

Quinn's second shot had also hit its mark. A large red stain suddenly bloomed like a rose across the white bodice of Ursula's high-waisted gown. An expression of utter surprise flitted across her small face as she watched her lifeblood drain away down her dress. Then she closed her eyes and floated gracefully to the floor like a poppy petal.

Nidar leapt across to grab Ursula's loaded pistol. But he was too late. Her finger twitched in its death throes and finally found the trigger. The pistol discharged its shot as she collapsed and Hal Pammenter let out an agonised scream.

Woods hesitated no longer. He fired. A neat black hole appeared in the forehead of the man with the gun trained on Lavender. It gushed like a bloody geyser as he fell.

Woods grunted with satisfaction and reached for his second pistol. His grunt turned to a splutter as the acrid smoke from his gun barrel swirling in that confined space bit into his throat.

Lavender grabbed the unused weapon out of his captor's hands. 'Halt! Put your hands up!'

But the smugglers were already at the door. Woods caught a fleeting glimpse of Nidar's departing form. He fired.

The bastard yelped but he didn't fall. Then he'd gone.

The gang clattered out into the hallway and exclaimed viciously when they found no one there. He braced himself for discovery. But instead of looking for the mysterious shooter from this end of the hall, the smugglers scrambled for the tunnel, with Lavender and Quinn in pursuit.

'Gawd's teeth! Slow down, sir! Wait for me!' Woods eyes streamed from the intensity of the smoke as he struggled to reload.

Outside, Lavender and Quinn discharged their weapons simultaneously down the tunnel after the fleeing smugglers. It was a terrific bang.

Then a deep, ominous rumble and terrific crash filled the house. The whole building shook as if the mighty gods themselves had joined in the fray and were hurling rocks. Woods stumbled to his feet on the shaking floor. His stool fell over as he burst out of the priest hole with his reloaded pistol into a scene of chaos.

Lavender and Quinn were retreating from the entrance to the tunnel, shielding their faces from a hailstorm of grit and pebbles. A billowing cloud of dust and rubble swirled around them, covering everything with its filth.

The sharp retort of their parting shots had brought down the tunnel roof on the smugglers' heads.

Chapter Forty-Three

Leaving Woods and Quinn to guard the tunnel entrance in case any of the smugglers tried to return, Lavender took control of the carnage in the medieval hall.

Deathly pale, Miranda was in shock, barely able to speak. The female servants were hysterical – until Susanna rallied and chivvied them to help her tend to the wounded. Miranda silently wheeled herself across the rubble-strewn hallway into her parlour and closed the door behind her.

Lavender reloaded Woods' second pistol and gave it to Thrup. He told him to climb up to the battlements on the north tower and report back if he saw anyone he didn't recognise heading towards the house. He grabbed the spent pistol from beside Ursula's dead body, reloaded it and gave it to Hawkes with instructions to gallop to Ely and fetch help.

Standing back, he wiped the hair from his face with a grimy hand and took stock of the slaughter before him.

Susanna and the women servants had fetched sheets to cover the two dead smugglers and Ursula, who still lay where they'd fallen.

Hal Pammenter had been shot in the thigh when Ursula's pistol discharged. He leaned back, groaning, against the wall. He'd used his cravat to make a tourniquet round his leg and bore the pain bravely while Susanna pressed on the wound with a cloth to stem the bleeding.

Two other women crouched beside Constable Cudworth. One bathed his bloodied head with warm water while the other ripped up a clean cloth for a bandage. Cudworth was still breathing but only just. He had a deep wound on the back of his head where Nidar had 'tapped' him.

They needed the doctor here – and fast.

Everyone else was occupied and bravely trying to ignore the lifeless forms beneath the sheets and the spreading pools of blood. Apart from offering a few words of encouragement to Hal, there wasn't much else to do here.

He returned to Woods and Quinn. The smell of burnt food hung heavily in the hallway, mingled with the smell of dust and wet stone from the tunnel.

Quinn's brown eyes still gleamed with excitement out of his grimy face. The lad was filthy. Lavender rubbed his palm over his own gritty cheek. He must look just as bad. They'd tried to shoot the smugglers in the back. The tunnel collapse had caught him by surprise. Had the smugglers survived down there?

Woods was reading his thoughts. 'If they escaped, they'll have to swim back to their ship. I smashed up their boats,' he added with a wink.

'Good work, Ned. Climbing into the priest hole was an act of sheer genius. You winged Nidar, by the way. He clutched his shoulder as he fled. There was a lot of blood.'

Woods humphed with satisfaction. 'Serves the bastard right. That's sweet revenge for what he did to *my* ruddy shoulder last year. Pity I didn't kill him, though. Was he first out of the room and down the tunnel – or last?'

'First.'

'Pity. I hoped he was last and one of your shots picked him off.'

'Perhaps it's time to find out,' Lavender said. 'Have there been any more disturbances down there since I left you?'

'None. It's gone quiet.'

They fetched lanterns and, leaving Quinn at the entrance, Lavender and Woods cautiously entered the tunnel.

The narrow passageway was treacherous underfoot. Debris from the rockfall lay everywhere. Lavender glanced nervously up at the unstable roof and more dust drifted down over his face. Another wave of claustrophobia swept through him and he hesitated. There were more lethal dangers down here than a group of unarmed and injured smugglers.

Bracing himself, he moved gingerly forward, carefully picking his way over the rubble.

They soon reached the rockfall, an impenetrable pile of wet earth, loose stone and tons of jagged rock. Pebbles still slithered down the slope.

There were no obvious signs of any men trapped beneath it and he couldn't tell how much of the roof had collapsed or how far back the obstruction went.

Woods let out a low whistle, which brought down another shower of dust on to their heads. 'There won't be much left of them if they're beneath that lot.'

'We need to examine the tunnel from the other side,' Lavender whispered, 'but we can't do that until Waterbeach or Kester arrive with reinforcements. Don't talk – it's still dangerous. Let's get out of here.'

They retraced their steps and clambered gratefully back out into the light and fresher air of the house.

Quinn grinned with relief when he saw them reappear, his white teeth contrasting brightly with his grimy face. 'I've great news, sir. Miss Susanna has informed me Constable Cudworth is stirring. Thank the Lord! He's got a mighty headache but has regained consciousness.'

A wave of relief swept through Lavender's tense frame. 'That is good news. There's nothing down the tunnel except rubble. It's blocked – no one's coming back through it. We can relax our guard now. Tell us what happened when the smugglers attacked.'

Quinn put away his pistol in the pocket of his shapeless coat and wiped the back of his palm over his face. 'I'm not exactly sure, sir. I was in my room reading when I heard a mighty furore down in the main hall. I thought it was a family argument at first. The Delameres seem to be a family who like to argue.'

'Yes, we've noticed that,' Woods said.

'I didn't like to intrude. So, I just peeped out of my door and watched the smugglers swarm into the banqueting hall. The ladies were already down there and were quickly surrounded. Some more of the devils dragged poor Cudworth's body in there from the hallway and dumped it on the floor.'

'He must have been in the hallway on that chair when they burst out of this tunnel,' Woods suggested. 'Poor fella probably didn't know what hit him.'

'Their captain sent off two of his men to round up the servants and they herded them into the banqueting hall. They couldn't fight back because the villains already had Miss Delamere and Miss Susanna as hostages. I was mighty scared for the ladies at the hands of such rough men. Then I heard Miss Susanna tell Miss Ursula I'd gone to Ely with Hal.'

'She's quick-thinkin' and courageous, that gal,' Woods said.

'I didn't know what to do but I knew I must hide. I grabbed my pistol and Hal's second duelling pistol and hid in the secret staircase that winds up the tower. Hal showed the staircase to me yesterday – and thank the Lord he did! It wasn't long before I heard them searching the rooms in the north tower – but fortunately Miss Ursula didn't think to tell them about this secret passageway. They never looked for me.'

'They'd have found my bag and shaving gear in my chamber,' Lavender said quietly. 'Nidar would have known I was on my way back here. He only had to wait.'

'I have to confess, sir, I was in turmoil,' the young man drawled in his soft accent. 'It was uncomfortable in that narrow staircase – and dark. Sometimes I went up to the battlements to look out for you. Eventually, I came back down to the library, crept to the door and watched. I was heavily armed but alone. Apart from the attack on Constable Cudworth, they didn't harm anyone else. But my blood ran cold when I heard Miss Ursula dictate that letter to Hal. I knew she was drawing him back from Ely for a reason. And when I saw her aim that pistol at his head, I knew I had to act to save my friend.'

'I'm glad you did, son.' Woods said.

'We're *all* glad you did,' Lavender insisted. 'You were outnumbered and had no idea Woods was there to support you. That was courageous – and your marksmanship is excellent.'

Quinn's filthy face lit up with delight at the compliment.

'I doubt I could shoot dead two men while flying across a room,' Lavender continued.

Woods chuckled. 'No, but your wife could.'

Lavender ignored him. 'Where did you learn to shoot so well?'

'My father used to take me hunting in the woods near our home. He taught me everything I know.'

Susanna suddenly appeared beside them in a bloodied apron, with more blood smeared up her arms. Her angelic face was pale and strained.

'Can you help us carry the two wounded men into the parlour, please? We think they might be more comfortable in there, away from, away from…' She glanced over her shoulder towards the dead bodies in the banqueting hall.

Quinn was already on the move. 'Yes, of course, ma'am. Anything we can do to help.'

Cudworth had a large bandage wrapped round his head. He staggered to his feet, but it took the support of both Lavender and Woods to walk him across the hallway. He winced with every step. 'I'm so sorry, sir,' he muttered quietly. 'They came at me like demons out of nowhere.'

'You don't have anything to apologise for, Constable,' Lavender reassured him as they gently lowered him into a chair.

Miranda watched silently from her wicker wheelchair. Her thin shoulders seemed more stooped than ever.

'Are you all right, ma'am?' Lavender asked.

'I'm fine, Detective,' she replied. 'In far better shape than our injured men. I'm just shocked, that's all.'

'Do you want me to fetch Miss Pammenter to tend to you?'

She shook her head and gave a small smile. 'No, thank you, Detective. I've had to restrain Lucy in her chamber. Leave her where she is. Even Ursula and her... her *associates* decided it was better Lucy remained in her room. Mrs Hawkes will see to my needs.'

Lavender nodded. He'd suspected something like this since Lucy Pammenter had disappeared from sight the previous day. 'Why? Why have you restrained her?'

Miranda gave a weak smile. 'We'll discuss this tomorrow if you don't mind, Detective.'

Lavender gave a short bow and turned back to the door.

'By the way, Detective,' she called after him. 'Thank you for your help today. God knows what the outcome would have been if it hadn't been for the courage of you and Woods.'

'And your nephew, Robert Quinn,' he reminded her. 'He's a brave young man.'

The faint ghost of a smile flickered across her thin lips again. 'Yes, of course. My *nephew*, Robert.'

Hal Pammenter's handsome face was pale from the loss of blood but he forced a weak smile when Lavender appeared. 'Lavender! We soon sent the villains running, eh? That was good work, yes?'

Lavender smiled as he stooped to help Woods and Quinn lift him. 'Yes, thanks to help from these two.'

'Yes, yes, we had to keep them talking until Woods arrived and rescued us. I realised that.' His face contorted with pain when he was raised. 'Ursula's damned bullet's still in my thigh,' he gabbled. 'The vicious little wench.'

'You're lucky you still have your nutmegs,' Woods said. 'When you've recovered a bit, son, we need to have a good talk about the foolishness of provokin' an armed woman.'

Hal's face puckered in protest but Lavender intervened. 'You did well, Pammenter, very well. Especially when you confirmed Susanna's claim that Quinn was still in Ely. That made his dramatic appearance more effective. The smugglers didn't know what the devil hit them. The distraction you provided was also... helpful.'

Hal chuckled, despite his pain. 'It gave me great pleasure to tell that madam what I thought of her. I hope she died with my words still ringing in her ears.'

They settled him on a sofa and Susanna immediately fussed around him with cushions and blankets. Lavender left the room, crossed the hallway and shut the double doors on the dead bodies in the banqueting hall.

Let the dead rest in peace.

Chapter Forty-Four

The doctor, Kester and Waterbeach arrived a few moments later, along with a dozen heavily armed men. They'd brought carts for the dead and injured.

Waterbeach instructed most of his men to come down to the boathouse entrance to the tunnel with himself, Lavender, Woods, Kester and Quinn. The sun was softly sinking below the flat line of the horizon in the west.

The only person they found at the boathouse was the handcuffed smuggler whom Woods had left face down on the jetty. Lavender glanced at the clear water of the lode and raised an approving eyebrow when he caught sight of the scuttled boats lying on the bottom.

They hauled the prisoner to his feet and Waterbeach's voice boomed menacingly across the marshes as he asked him if he'd seen or heard his fellow gang members leave the tunnel.

The smuggler just cursed and spat in his face.

Frustrated, Waterbeach cuffed him around the head and ordered his men to drag him back up to the house.

'Adrian Delamere has a lawyer provided by his father and has turned King's evidence.' Kester told Lavender as they watched the excise men drag the smuggler away. 'He's told us the name of Nidar's ship and its location.'

'Have you captured the ship?'

'Not yet. We've sent men after it.'

'Let's pray they're in time.'

'He's also told us it was Nidar himself who killed Mabberley.'

'That doesn't surprise me.'

'Another corpse to add to his tally,' Woods snapped. 'It's a pity we can't hang a man several times – one long drop on the gallows for each victim.'

'In that case, it would take several days to hang Nidar,' Lavender replied grimly.

'Will turning King's evidence be enough to save Adrian Delamere from hangin'?' Woods asked.

The magistrate shrugged. 'I don't know. I think that'll depend on the circuit judge.'

They cautiously approached the open trap door in the shrub. The tall magistrate stooped low to avoid the boughs.

'You'll have to stay above ground,' Lavender commented. 'You're too tall to go down there. And you too, Waterbeach. Woods and I will go down alone.' He didn't want to add that he was worried by the volume in Waterbeach's voice and feared it might bring down more of the roof on their heads.

They paused around the trap-door entrance to the tunnel. Their ears strained for the sound of movement and falling rocks below. But the only sounds were the breeze rustling the branches of the trees above and the cries of the waterfowl out in the marshes.

Cautiously, they lowered their lanterns. The small entrance chamber was empty.

'Remember – they had knives,' Lavender said, as he descended the short flight of steps with Woods behind him.

The black entrance to the tunnel gaped before them. Lavender braced himself for another long and cramped trudge up the steep incline through the bowels of the earth. But he didn't have to suffer long. They soon came across an impenetrable wall of fallen rocks.

'They must be dead,' Woods whispered. 'No one could have survived that.'

342

'What about that side tunnel? The recess we found halfway up?'

'I don't know... we never had time to explore it. But it were big enough for me to hide in earlier.'

'They might be trapped in there.'

'That'll be a slow, lingerin' death,' Woods said with satisfaction.

'Or it might be another tunnel – an escape route that brought them out somewhere else in the marshes or the grounds.' *And they've had plenty of time over the last few months to explore it.* 'If anyone knew the true nature of that gaping recess, it was them.'

Woods grunted. 'If it was another tunnel, the roof in there may have caved in too.'

'True.'

They retraced their steps to the entrance chamber and Lavender straightened up gratefully. He'd had enough of being bent underground. Exhaustion and relief swept through him. 'At least we know now that if Nidar and his men have escaped, they'll never be able to return this way and threaten the occupants of the house again.'

'Yes, they're safe from that.' Woods looked thoughtful but disappointed beneath the stubble and grime.

'Even if Nidar lives, Ned, we've struck a huge blow against him. We caught or killed Adrian and four other members of his crew last night. Ursula and another three men have been captured or killed today. He'll be seriously weakened.'

'I suppose so.'

'Last year we foiled his attempt to form a criminal network in the capital and, thanks to Magdalena, he's now disfigured and easily recognisable. He can't blend in with the gentry and set up his fraudulent and lucrative scams. He's destined to spend the rest of his life working from the shadows with whatever he's got left of his ragged crew.'

'So, behind them fancy words you think we've clipped the wings of this devil?'

'Definitely. He's irreparably damaged.'

Woods paused and his large moon of a face relaxed into a broad grin. 'So, we've done well, have we, sir?'

'Yes, Ned. We've done well.'

Susanna was waiting nervously for them at the entrance to the south tower when they arrived back at the house. Her tearful eyes watched the last of the wagons rumble out of the courtyard, carrying away the bodies.

Quinn was beside her in an instant. 'Is everything all right, ma'am?'

'Yes, yes.' But she reached out and clutched his arm for support. 'I've waited here to tell you that Mrs Hawkes has managed to prepare a bit of supper for everyone. It's waiting in the kitchen.'

Woods made an appreciative noise and bounded up the steps into the house.

'Constable Cudworth has been taken home to his wife,' the young woman added, 'the doctor said it was safe for him to travel.'

Lavender nodded, pleased and relieved. 'I'm sure he'll recover quicker in the comfort of his own home. You'll be pleased to know, ma'am, the tunnel is blocked at both ends. You'll never be bothered again by those smugglers – or anyone else creeping into your home.'

'Thank you, Detective,' she whispered. 'That's welcome news – although I can't say I'm comfortable with the thought that there may be unburied bodies lying below the house.' Her haunted eyes never left the arched gateway where the tailgate of the last wagon was just visible. A small lantern swung merrily at its rear as it vanished. Her face crumpled with distress.

'Miss Susanna,' Quinn said, 'what's the matter?'

'It's Ursula.' She gave a strangled sob. 'God forgive me – I didn't always like her – but…'

'You grew up with her,' Lavender said softly. 'She was a friend to you as well as family.'

'They've taken her body home to her parents. I can't comprehend how they'll react to this news…or the extent of their grief.' She broke down and Quinn gathered the sobbing young woman into his arms.

Lavender sighed heavily and followed her gaze to the empty archway. The strain of the day had taken a heavy toll on everyone. It would take the Delamere family years to come to terms with the traumatic events of today. Tobias and Birgitta may never recover. Even the impassive and controlling chatelaine of Willow Marsh sitting quietly inside in her wheelchair wouldn't escape these events with her confidence and poise untouched.

He felt a sudden yearning for the peace of his own fireside, Magdalena's warm embrace and the smiles and innocence of his children.

He turned and entered the house. But as he did so he was struck again by the similarity in appearance of these two dark-haired youngsters. Susanna had inherited more than her fair share of the family good looks while Quinn was marred by that prominent nose, but their resemblance was uncanny.

Once again, he was reassured in his conviction that they shared more than a birth month.

Chapter Forty-Five

After a good wash and a hearty supper, Lavender went up to sleep in Woods' room. Despite the loud snoring emanating from the other bed and his own troubled mind, he managed to get a good night's sleep.

He rose early, enjoyed a leisurely shave, and put on a clean set of clothes. He was ready for the world now.

Or rather, ready for his confrontation with Miranda Delamere.

After breakfast, he went to the cavernous banqueting hall and walked slowly down the room, thinking about the previous day's terrifying ordeal.

Above him, the rows of antique swords and pikes glittered in the sunlight pouring in from the huge windows. This ancient armoury may have protected the Delameres in the past, but it had proved useless in the defence of the current family. The servants had tried to restore order to the medieval hall but even their vigorous mopping hadn't removed the bloodstains. Several new, dark patches stained the flagstone floor.

He paused where Ursula had fallen. What a waste of a vibrant young life. He still couldn't envisage what had motivated a genteel young woman to turn on her family like that. The excitement of the smuggler's way of life, perhaps? Nidar's charm? A burning desire to be revenged on Hal for spurning her? Or had she simply been overwhelmed with greed and envy for her wealthier cousins and their lifestyle?

He wondered how many other Delameres had been slain in this room over the centuries, especially during that bloody confrontation, the Civil War. As Catholics, the Delameres would have been on the losing side. Had Ursula's blood seeped down through the cracks in the flagstones to mingle with that of her ancestors?

Shaking off his morbid thoughts, he walked down towards the library, his footsteps echoing in the silence.

An inkpot and a new quill sat on the small table beside the family Bible. Someone else had opened it since he'd last been here. He saw a surprising new entry:

September 8th, 1813, death of Ursula Delamere of Ely, aged twenty-three

The writing was shaky and the ink had been smudged with tears but he recognised it from the note she'd sent Hal the day before. Susanna had forgiven her treacherous cousin and faithfully recorded her death in the Delamere family history.

Her compassion was humbling. Miranda and Hal might object when they found out, but the young girl had grown into a woman over the past twenty-four hours. The future of this ancient manor would be safe in her hands.

He closed the tattered old Bible thoughtfully and decided to take a turn around the grounds while he waited for Woods to finish his second helping of breakfast.

A gentle sun sailed low across the shimmering silver and green landscape, where dragonflies dodged and weaved among the reeds and bulrushes. A pair of golden marsh harriers circled above. The pale-blue sky stretched from one edge of his vision to the other.

He doubted he would ever return to Ely – and he never wanted to bump into any members of the Delamere family again. Twice in one lifetime was more than enough. But this didn't stop him appreciating the unique beauty of this part of the world.

Behind him, the mellow stone walls of Willow Marsh House gleamed like honey in the soft light and the tall arched windows of the medieval hall sparkled. The building spoke of peace and permanence. Already, its thick walls had forgotten the violence and bloodshed of yesterday and consigned them to history. For a house that had survived three centuries of war and pestilence, they were just another small ripple in its timeline.

When he returned, the servants told him the family had just finished their breakfast in the parlour. He beckoned Woods away from the kitchen table and the two of them walked towards the parlour.

'So, what's goin' to happen now?' Woods asked as he wiped his greasy chin with the back of his coat sleeve.

'I have a surprise for Miranda Delamere. I need you to stay calm and not react to anything I say.'

'I'm your man.'

Unable to walk, Hal Pammenter had slept the night in his shirt on Miranda's sofa beneath the latticed window. Before he'd left the previous evening, the doctor had removed the pistol shot from his thigh – a painful operation Hal had borne bravely and with minimum fuss. He was propped up with cushions today and he'd regained some colour below the stubble on his unshaven cheeks. He hailed them cheerfully.

Miranda, Susanna and Robert Quinn were seated at the inlaid teak table in the centre of the room, surrounded by fine bone china crockery. Susanna and Quinn also greeted them warmly and even Miranda managed a wan smile. The women were still dressed in mourning and both had dark circles beneath their eyes, but the atmosphere was genial.

'Are you leaving us now, Detective?' Miranda asked. 'We're just enjoying a second cup of tea. Would you like to join us?'

'No, ma'am. Thank you – but no. We've come to say goodbye, although I do have a report to make before I leave.'

349

'Do you want us to leave so you can speak to Aunt Miranda alone?' Susanna asked.

'Well, I'm not going anywhere,' Hal said cheerfully.

'No, ma'am. I'd prefer you to stay – and Mr Quinn and Mr Pammenter. The content of my report is pertinent to everyone. You need to hear it.'

A slight frown passed over Miranda's face, but she pushed a small cloth purse across the table towards Lavender. 'Please take this. It's the fee required by Bow Street Police Office for your services. I've added an extra guinea each for you and Woods in recognition of your bravery.'

'Thank you, ma'am.'

'The help you gave my family yesterday went far beyond the call of duty. We can't thank you enough for your brave and fearless assistance. I dread to think what would have happened to us if you'd followed my foolish instructions and returned to London straight after the inquest.'

Hal snorted from his bed on the sofa and laughed. 'Well, I'd have been a eunuch, for a start.'

'How are you today, sir?' Woods asked him.

'Bearing up remarkably well, thanks to the tender ministrations of Little Susie and the laudanum provided by Doctor Bendall.' Hal winced when he spoke. 'It still hurts like hell when the powder wears off, but the doctor assures me I'll walk and ride again.'

Lavender picked up the purse from the table and pocketed it. 'Thank you for this, ma'am, although I trust you appreciate that Woods and I couldn't have overcome those villains without the bravery and assistance of your family.'

'Yes, I was very proud of them all.'

'So you should be.' Lavender turned to Susanna. 'That clue you inserted in the note to Mr Pammenter to warn him you were in trouble was cleverly thought out. And your quick thinking when you told them Mr Quinn had also gone to Ely should be commended.'

The young woman blushed prettily at his praise.

'As for you, Mr Pammenter, you were strong and steadfast.'

'If slightly foolish,' Woods muttered.

'I was proud to have you by my side, sir,' Lavender continued. 'I thought we were facing death together. Your assistance in distracting the smugglers probably saved Woods' life and postponed my own death. Nidar would have dealt with Woods as callously as he'd treated Constable Cudworth if they'd found him.'

Finally, Lavender turned to the quiet young American. 'Your actions, sir, were those of a true hero.' Quinn turned as red as Susanna and his eyes shone with delight.

'In fact,' Lavender concluded, 'the late Mr Lawrence Delamere would have been proud of *all* of his grandchildren yesterday if he'd lived.'

'All of his grandchildren?' Hal exclaimed. 'Are you including Quinn in this?'

'Yes, sir, I am. It's my firm belief Mr Quinn is who he claims to be and his parents were the late Peter Quinn and his wife, Olivia Delamere.'

Hal whooped with delight. 'Well said, Lavender! Do you hear that, Aunt Miranda? I must say this is a fine turnaround from two days ago – when you accused me of scooping a random American off the streets of London and schooling him to play the part.'

'I would like to know how Detective Lavender came to this conclusion,' Miranda said cagily.

Lavender drew himself up to his full height, glanced at Susanna and Quinn and compared their strong likeness to the gilt-framed family portraits hung on the wood-panelled walls.

'Apart from the obvious physical resemblance between Mr Quinn and Miss Susanna, he also told her he was born the day after her in New York. It was an innocent comment in itself – but rather a coincidence. In my opinion, a fraudster who'd been carefully tutored to play the part wouldn't have said that – he'd have declared himself to be slightly younger.'

'Why?'

'Because if we look back at the events of 1793, it's quite an embarrassing admission.'

'How so?' Susanna asked.

Quinn had started to blush again – but not with pleasure this time.

Lavender looked hard at Miranda. 'If I remember rightly, from what I've been told – and from what I've seen in your family Bible – your sister and Peter Quinn eloped to the Americas in the summer of 1793. Your mother died shortly afterwards. Following this, you left Willow Marsh for a few months to care for a dying relative. Is that correct?'

Beneath her thick eyebrows, Miranda's eyes were veiled again. 'Yes, that's so. It was the worst period of my life and I'd appreciate it if you didn't dwell on it.'

'Unfortunately, I must. Because in that summer the seeds of a lie were sown, which has had repercussions for this family for two decades – and still threatens to distort the future happiness of everyone in this room.'

'That sounds dire,' Miranda snapped. 'What on earth do you mean?'

Hal chuckled. 'What he means, Aunt, is that Peter Quinn had already bedded Aunt Olivia before they fled that summer. They didn't wait until the wedding to consummate the marriage, or evens the banns. I say, Quinn, you never mentioned this to me before. You nearly joined me in bastardy!'

'It's not something I like to talk about,' the blushing young man replied. 'Yes, my father was a rake and a bit of a rogue in his youth, but he was steadfast in his love for my mother and my parents were happy together.'

Miranda winced but Susanna reached across and squeezed Quinn's hand. 'No one will judge you for this.'

'Don't worry about it, Quinn,' Hal said. 'Considering the scandal the rest of this family has caused, being born four or five months after your parents wed is small meat. But what do you think, Aunt Miranda, eh? Do you accept Lavender's opinion that Quinn is your nephew?'

'I would still recommend you follow my constable's suggestion and seek evidence and reassurance from a lawyer in the Carolinas,' Lavender said.

There was silence for a moment while everyone looked at Miranda.

'I already know Robert is my true nephew,' she confessed. 'I've already done what you suggested and I've been aware of his existence for some years.' Hal and Susanna gasped. 'I've followed his progress through life with interest,' Miranda continued. 'I also knew my sister and her husband had died.'

'Good grief, Miranda!' Hal's face flushed with shock. 'Why didn't you say something before? I knew your spy network was extensive, but I didn't realise you had contacts across the Atlantic!'

'I needed to find out what he wanted from us.'

Susanna squealed in joy and squeezed Quinn's hand harder. 'So, you really are our cousin? How wonderful! Now you've a family again!'

Ah, but he wants more than a family, Lavender thought. He wondered how the grinning young man would react when he revealed the rest of his discoveries.

'We'll talk about this more when Lavender and Woods have left,' Miranda said firmly, 'it's a family matter. Right now, I want to know what else he suspects happened in the summer of the year 1793 beside my wanton sister's brazen seduction of my fiancé.' The bitterness lingering in her voice betrayed her; it would take Miranda a long time before she fully accepted Robert Quinn.

'If you would bear with me for a moment, Miss Delamere, I'd like to discuss another mystery first.' He didn't wait for her permission. 'Let me return to the reasons why Woods and I were called here. Initially, as you know, Miss Delamere used a false name – her sister's – to lure us here to find out who had attacked Miss Susanna down at the lode.'

'Yes, I've wondered about that,' Hal said. 'Why did you deceive two of the most famous law officers in the country?'

'Because she feared Woods and I wouldn't come if she used her real name,' Lavender explained. 'Don't forget, we were the officers who arrested your father ten years ago and amassed the evidence that ensured his conviction for rape and murder.'

Hal looked less excited now. Susanna and Quinn shuffled uncomfortably in their seats. 'Yes, I gathered that you knew my dear papa. What was he like?'

'Nothing like you,' Lavender replied.

'Let's just say that murderin' poor Irish Nell weren't his only crime,' Woods interjected.

Hal winced.

Lavender reached out and steadied Woods' arm. This wasn't the time or place to mention Frederick Delamere's attack on Ginny.

He turned back to Hal. 'Your aunt had some unanswered questions regarding her brother's trial. She asked us here because she wanted answers, and again she thought we would decline if we knew this was the former home of Major Frederick Delamere.'

Hal recovered his equanimity quickly. 'Hah! Lured here under false pretences, eh, Lavender? How come such a brilliant detective didn't foresee this?'

Lavender ignored the jibe. 'I've since given Miss Delamere the answers she desired, which I hope were satisfactory.'

'For now, Detective,' Miranda said calmly. She picked up her china cup and sipped her tea.

Lavender cleared his throat. 'It soon became apparent that someone in the smuggling gang attacked Miss Susanna down at the lode and later killed Mabberley. With hindsight, I suspect it was more than a coincidence that Mr Adrian was in the vicinity when they pushed Miss Susanna into the lode. I think he'd met the smugglers there.'

'Did Ursula push her?' Hal asked.

'Maybe. Solving the mystery of that first attack on Miss Susanna and Mabberley's subsequent murder wasn't difficult. However, as you know, catching the villains proved harder.'

'You can say that again, sir!' Quinn grinned.

'However, the second attack on Miss Susanna was more perplexing.'

Susanna leaned forward, concentrating hard. Miranda and Hal froze.

'Constable Woods saw the figure of a man up there in a coat and a conical hat,' Lavender continued, 'but we've since discovered those items were taken from the closets in the north tower. The hat contained an unusual piece of evidence: a long fair hair from the head of a woman.'

'Was it Ursula again?' Susanna whispered in shock.

'No, ma'am. As two of the people in this room already know, the hair belonged to Miss Lucy Pammenter, your aunt's maid. She's the one who tried to kill you.'

Chapter Forty-Six

'Lucy!'

Susanna sat back in shock. Her cup clattered down into its saucer. 'Lucy tried to kill me?'

'Yes, ma'am.'

'Lucy's not a killer!'

'The woman's hair I found inside the hat is light grey in colour, rather than a blonde strand from Miss Ursula's head. It definitely belonged to Miss Pammenter. When Woods and I raced into the tower, the garments had been replaced in the closets and she was there, involved in a heated argument with her son.'

Hal fell back against his cushions and groaned.

'But *Lucy*!' Susanna said. 'She's kind. She's looked after me all my life! I can't believe she'd do such a thing!'

'Mr Pammenter quickly worked out what his mother had just done,' Lavender continued. 'He was berating her when we arrived. He lied to me to protect her and let us suspect him of being the culprit. But he quickly informed Miss Delamere what had occurred.'

'That's speculation, Lavender!' Hal warned.

'Miss Pammenter has been restrained in her room for the last three days,' Lavender continued, 'and Miss Delamere tried to send us back to London. Those are facts. I think it's time we knew the truth, ma'am.'

Everyone turned to look at Miranda.

Miranda swallowed hard. 'Lucy has become quite unstable since your arrival, Detective,' she said slowly. 'It was a mistake on my part to invite you here. I should never have asked you to come.'

'In which case, most of you would be dead by now.'

Lavender paused for a moment to let the reality of his words sink in. 'And Mabberley's killers would have got away with murder.'

Miranda smoothed down the material of her black gown in her lap to calm herself. She wasn't used to interrogations. 'It's my intention to send Lucy to a sanitorium for some much-needed rest. We'll deal with this matter from now on. I don't need your help with her, Lavender.'

'You mean an asylum, don't you?' Woods asked.

'Mr Symonds knows of a suitable place. He went back to Ely to organise it. I expect to hear from him soon.'

Hal groaned. 'Poor mother.'

'Obviously, Lucy can't be allowed to roam freely about the estate and attack people,' Miranda said sharply. She turned to Susanna and her voice softened. 'I intended to explain this to you after the officers had left, my dear.'

'Had she threatened to harm us too?' Woods asked. 'I got the impression she hated us for some reason.'

'Yes, she threatened to poison you both.'

Woods stiffened and made a curious sound in his throat. Lavender wondered if he was remembering all the second helpings he'd devoured in the kitchen.

'Susanna will be quite safe from Lucy in future, I'll make sure of that. There was no further need of your services, Lavender. I have the matter in hand.'

'My mother is a strange and deluded woman, Lavender.' Hal spoke slowly. 'She's fine when she performs simple tasks like caring for a child or attending to Aunt Miranda. She's never needed or wanted anything more out of life than she's had here at Willow Marsh. But she's long held the conviction my father married her – and I'm the rightful heir to the Willow Marsh estate.'

'Which he didn't?'

'No, of course he didn't.' Hal narrowed his eyes and his tone turned sarcastic. 'She's a very confused woman. You talk of my father's atrocities in London, Lavender, but you've no idea of the mayhem he created here in this family – and in this district. He was a notorious womaniser.'

'Was Major Frederick also estranged from his father?'

'Yes. Uncle Lawrence couldn't stand him after he violated my mother. He packed him off to the army and Father never returned to Cambridgeshire. I didn't know the man, and I never wanted to, once I'd learned what he'd done to my mother – and other women in the district.'

'But didn't he return here in January 1794 to bring his motherless child to be raised by your family?' Lavender asked.

'No. Aunt Miranda went down to Kent to fetch Little Susie.' He paused and his manner softened. Turning to Susanna, he smiled. 'I still remember the day Aunt Miranda and the nurse brought you home from Kent. I was so excited to get a little playmate. I was about seven and I was dreadfully bored rattling around this place on my own. Adrian and Ursula weren't allowed to visit because Lawrence and Toby were still feuding.'

Susanna smiled back, her face radiant with affection. 'Wasn't I a bit young to be a playmate?'

'God, yes! I was so disappointed. You were so little, Little Susie. That's when I gave you your name. It took years for you to grow.'

She laughed. 'And by the time I was old enough to play with you, you weren't interested in a little girl any more. I'd just become a nuisance toddling along behind you and your friends.'

'You never were a nuisance.'

Still smiling, Susanna turned back to her aunt. 'But I still don't understand why Lucy turned so violently against me. Or against poor Constable Woods and Detective Lavender. It just doesn't make sense.'

'I've already told you, Susie,' Hal said patiently. 'My mother is deluded. She still thinks my father married her and I am the rightful heir to Willow Marsh. I think the will reading triggered anger and panic in her confused mind. I had trouble with her the next morning; she raged about the injustice of it all.'

Woods nodded. 'I overheard your argument.'

'But this doesn't explain why she made death threats against these officers.'

Lavender shook his head. It was time to take over. 'If I may be allowed to explain, sir?' he said to Hal. 'There's a lot you don't know.'

Hal shrugged and sat back thankfully against his cushions. The strain of their conversation showed in his face.

'There was more to the events of that first night than just the will reading.' He glanced at Miranda, who stared back coldly. 'As I said earlier, your aunt had some unresolved issues about her brother's trial and she involved Miss Pammenter in this initial round of enquiries.'

He stopped there. He didn't intend to tell them Miranda had sent the deranged woman into his chamber with a snuff box in the middle of the night. 'I'm not an expert on matters of lunacy,' he continued, 'but I've read about the subject. I know that sometimes under extreme stress, when several things conspire at once, it can trigger a violent episode of insanity in a sufferer. I think involving Miss Pammenter in this way was a huge mistake. Reminding her about her lover's conviction, imprisonment and death – on the day her son was effectively disinherited – provoked a great rage in her deluded mind. A rage levelled at Miss Susanna and us.'

A short silence ensued, then Miranda held up her hands in resignation. 'I accept your greater knowledge in these matters, Detective. Yes, I can see now it was probably an error on my part to involve Lucy in my, er, *enquiries.*'

Lavender cleared his throat. 'In addition to this, there was a third thing troubling her. Miss Pammenter has been the keeper of a great secret for twenty years, one she was sworn – or perhaps bullied – into keeping. I suspect this secret has always tortured her and on the night of the will reading, the injustice of it tore her apart.'

'What secret?' Hal asked.

'Lucy Pammenter was one of only two people alive who knew the truth about Miss Susanna's birth. She knew Miss Susanna is *not* the legitimate daughter of Major Frederick Delamere.'

Hal sat upright, his face suffused with anger. 'What the devil are you talking about, Lavender?'

Miranda never flinched. She glared at Lavender through her ice-cold, inscrutable eyes.

'Miss Susanna is the illegitimate daughter of your aunt, Miranda Delamere, and her fiancé, Peter Quinn.'

Chapter Forty-Seven

For a moment, there was uproar. Hal shouted out in indignation and Quinn joined him in protest. Susanna gave a scream of surprise and covered her mouth with her hands.

Even Woods exclaimed in shock, 'Gawd's teeth!'

Outside, the sun had gone behind a cloud and Miranda's face fell into shade, but he saw the fire in her eyes blazing out of the shadows. 'How dare you! That's ridiculous!'

'Is it?' Lavender asked calmly.

'But my mother was called Susan, Susan Pendar,' Susanna protested.

'She never existed,' Lavender replied gently. 'Miss Delamere invented her.'

'That is a scurrilous allegation, Lavender!' Hal yelled. 'Vile calumny! Aunt Miranda is a woman of great strength and virtue.'

Lavender waited until they fell quiet. 'Is this so hard to believe? Especially now we know Peter Quinn had already seduced one of the Delamere sisters out of wedlock. Miss Olivia Delamere wasn't even his fiancée; he was betrothed to Miss Miranda. What's to stop a dissolute man seducing *both* women? He obviously had considerable charm and played a dangerous game with their affections.'

Before Hal and Quinn could protest further, Lavender turned to face Miranda directly. 'Please be reassured, ma'am, that if what I suspect did occur, I won't judge you – and neither I, nor my constable, will ever breathe a word of this beyond these four walls.'

She said nothing, but the glittering hate in her eyes didn't diminish. Her thin frame quivered with anger.

Lavender spoke gently as he continued. '1793 must have been a horrendous year for you, ma'am. It started off so well, didn't it? You and Quinn were betrothed. You loved him and thought you had a wonderful future ahead. But by that summer, you were cruelly betrayed by the two people you loved most in the world – your fiancé and your sister. Soon after that, your mother died and you and your father were consumed with a second wave of grief. I've no idea if you already knew your sister carried Quinn's child before they left—'

'No. I didn't know.'

'—but you must have been horrified when you discovered you were also carrying Quinn's baby. Not only had he caused you intense embarrassment and distress when he fled with Olivia, virtually jilting you at the altar, but now he'd ruined your reputation and spoilt any future you had left. You found yourself in the same perilous position your cousin Lucy Pammenter had endured a few years before. You knew only too well how unmarried, pregnant gentlewomen were spurned by society.'

He paused, but she said nothing.

'In desperation, you turned for help to the one person who didn't care about immorality and wouldn't give a fig about your pregnancy – your brother. Although your father and Major Frederick were estranged, I know you still kept in touch with him. I believe Major Frederick had recently returned from India and was staying in London. Immoral and debauched, he didn't give a damn about your condition, provided you didn't interfere with his life. He gave you sanctuary at a time when you needed it most.

'I don't know how you managed to deceive your father. Perhaps he was too grief-stricken after the loss of your mother to notice what was happening? But as a result, you and Lucy Pammenter were able to depart quietly for London. You stayed with Major Frederick, masquerading as his wife, Mrs Delamere, until the child was born.'

Hal snorted. 'This is nothing but speculation, Lavender.'

'Please bear with me, Mr Pammenter. Once the child, a little girl, was born in December, you left her with a nurse and returned home for a short while. You explained your absence with some tale that you'd spent time with a sickly maternal aunt.'

'I did look after my aunt.'

'No, you didn't. Your Uncle Toby – who was once intimately acquainted with your mother – has confirmed she had no living relatives.'

Hal shuffled uncomfortably on his cushions. 'Is this true, Aunt Miranda? I must say, I've often thought your love for Susanna transcended that of a mere aunt.'

Miranda didn't respond.

'What follows is breathtakingly clever. News reached Willow Marsh that your brother had just returned from India and his wife, the mysterious Susan Pender, had died in a Kentish port giving birth to a girl. This was all fabricated. Mr Pammenter has just told us how you went south to retrieve the baby and bring her to be raised at Willow Marsh. Somehow, with guile and cunning, you'd managed to deceive everyone – even your own father – and ensured the future of your child. Not only was she safely growing up with you in the family home, but – as Major Frederick's daughter – she was also the only legitimate heir to a vast estate. Did the Major even know about this final twist in your plan, I wonder? Did he know you'd supplanted your own child in the family home and were raising her as his heir? Or if he did know, did he care?'

Susanna turned to Miranda, her face lit up with smiles. It's true, isn't it? It all makes sense now, the way you've loved me all these years. You're not my aunt – you're my mother!'

Miranda flinched, then smiled, as the young woman reached for her hand. Susanna's affectionate gesture and excitement were weakening her implacable resolve.

She must be in torment, Lavender decided. Miranda desperately wanted to maintain the tissue of lies she'd spun for two decades but her heart must have ached to pull Susanna into her arms and claim her for her own.

'Hold on a minute, Susie,' Hal growled. 'Lavender hasn't provided a shred of evidence for any of this.'

Lavender turned towards the young lawyer. 'Ten years later, when Woods and I questioned Major Frederick at the time of his arrest, he announced he was a bachelor. Not a widower, as you'd expect – but a bachelor. There was no mention of a dead wife and a motherless child.'

Hal snorted. 'That means nothing. You knew the kind of man my father was. His words meant nothing.'

'But it did set us wonderin' once we arrived here and met Miss Susanna,' Woods said. His comment silenced Hal.

'I have evidence,' Lavender said quietly. 'I've a witness.'

Miranda turned sharply. 'A witness?'

'Yes. While you were in London, you lodged at a house in Tooley Street, Southwark. A young serving girl who worked there remembers a heavily pregnant woman called *Mrs Delamere* and her maid. I know this woman personally.'

Beside him, Woods stiffened. *Hold fast, my friend. Hold fast.*

'Although I'm sure both you and Lucy Pammenter have changed considerably over the last two decades,' Lavender continued, 'I'm sure – if pushed – she'd be able to identify you both and support my theory.'

A small smile crept to the lined corners of Miranda's mouth. 'So, you do know her after all?'

'Yes, ma'am.'

'Who?' Quinn asked suddenly. 'What's the name of this witness?'

Lavender and Miranda ignored him.

'But you said if you were *pushed* to reveal your discoveries, Detective,' she said. 'Do I take it you don't intend to *push* ahead with this identification – or make this information common knowledge?'

'I've already given you my promise of discretion, ma'am. As far as I'm concerned, the information I've revealed today is only of concern to the people in this room – they had a right to know.' He glanced at Quinn. 'However, if you make my witness's identity common knowledge – there will be repercussions.'

Miranda gave a low laugh and shook her head. 'You threaten me.'

Hal suddenly grabbed his head with both hands and pushed his fingers through his thick mane of tawny hair. 'Oh, my God, it's true, isn't it? Susanna and I aren't brother and sister – we're cousins! And she's half-sister to *Quinn*!' He roared with laughter. 'That'll scupper your plans to marry Little Susie for her inheritance, my friend!'

Quinn looked furious. *Was it the loss of the girl that bothered him most, or the loss of the money?*

'Good grief!' Hal continued. 'I can marry her myself now! What do you say about that, Little Susie? Will you take a one-legged man for a husband?'

Susanna blushed furiously, uncomfortable with his comments.

Lavender and Miranda ignored them and continued to weigh each other up.

'I firmly believe the past should remain dead and buried in this case, ma'am,' Lavender said.

'Like my dead brother? A man convicted on the evidence you – and *your witness* – provided?'

Lavender stared back at her coldly. 'It would profit no one to rake up the events of that time. There's nothing to gain but misery. We've all made mistakes in the past.'

'Including *you,* Detective?'

'Yes, including me. I made a mistake in pursuit of justice for a dead woman.'

She laughed. 'Well, at least you've the integrity to admit it. So, you're offering me a bargain, are you Lavender? My silence for yours?'

'Yes, ma'am.'

'What the devil are you both talking about?' Quinn asked. 'Who is this mysterious witness?"

Lavender held his breath and waited for Miranda's next move. Everything: his reputation, his future, Ginny's happiness – and his friendship with Ned – everything depended on her decision.

She shook her head and laughed. 'I badly underestimated you, Detective. I knew you had an excellent reputation but never for one moment did I think you'd wheedle out so many of our secrets in such a short space of time.'

'Do we have an understanding, ma'am?'

'Yes,' she said slowly. 'We do. Now, if you'll please leave us, I need to talk to my family. You've done enough damage for one day.'

She picked up Susanna's hand, squeezed it again and gave the young woman an affectionate smile. 'Yes, I'm your mother, my darling – but you must still call me *Aunt Miranda*. We don't want the servants to know.'

Susanna burst into tears, leapt up and threw herself into Miranda's arms.

Lavender bowed and backed away towards the door. 'I wish you and your family nothing but good luck and good fortune in the future.'

'I think we'll need it!' Hal laughed as he waved farewell.

'Is this true?' they heard Quinn demand as they left the room. 'Am I the only legitimate grandson of Mr Lawrence Delamere?'

'It looks that way, Quinn,' Hal replied cheerfully.

'I need a good lawyer,' said the nonplussed young American.

Hal laughed again. 'Well, lucky for you, there's one in this room.'

Chapter Forty-Eight

Lavender and Woods borrowed horses from the Willow Marsh stables to return to Ely. For a while they rode in companionable silence. It wasn't until they'd left the tall shadow of Willow Marsh Manor and its towers and reached the slow-moving river that Woods finally spoke. 'That gypsy girl, Laurel Faa Geddes, were right all along – you *did* need to beware the man with the burnt face.'

Lavender smiled. Of all the things they had to discuss now the case was over – Ned had chosen to start with this foolish poppycock. 'The gypsy girl's prophesy was superstitious nonsense, Ned.'

'Nonsense? It didn't look like nonsense to me when Nidar were aimin' a pistol at your head. And is *nonsense* what you'd call this?' Woods grabbed his injured shoulder. 'That gal told me to watch out for a hairy beast with a ring through its nose – and I were shot by a man called *Captain Bull!*'

'Well, yes – maybe.'

'Maybe?' Woods' tone was incredulous. 'There's no *maybe* about this damned injury!'

'That cove Nidar was with Captain Bull, Ned. We never found out which one of them actually fired at you.'

'Well, it's too much of a coincidence for me,' Woods declared hotly.

Lavender let him sulk for a minute or two, then said: 'I'll grant you this, Ned – Laurel Faa Geddes did seem to have an uncanny knack when it came to predicting the future.'

Woods grunted and they rode along in silence for a few moments more.

A pair of swans glided gracefully on the river beside them with a brood of large, almost full-grown, grey cygnets trailing in their wake. In the marshes, the waterfowl called to each other and a hawk circled above. They were totally alone for the first time in days. The smugglers had gone and Ursula no longer lurked just out of sight, eavesdropping.

'Do you think that woman will honour her promise to keep quiet about how you framed her brother with that damned snuff box? She could cause us a lot of trouble.'

'Who? Miranda? Yes, she'll keep quiet – she's got too much to lose. The family reputation is important to her and she doesn't want us to reveal the truth about Susanna's birth. That would bring social disgrace to both women.'

'I'm baffled to see how this family will unravel the mess you've left them.'

Lavender smiled. 'Oh, I'm sure Miranda – and Hal – will find a way.'

'Is that American the rightful heir to the place?'

'Not necessarily. A good lawyer will argue Lawrence Delamere knew all along about Susanna's true parentage but left her the estate anyway. And without Ginny's name and evidence, no one can prove Susanna's illegitimacy.'

Woods scowled. 'I doubt Ginny will want the past rakin' up.'

'Don't worry, Miranda won't tell anyone her name.'

'You took a huge risk there, sir – admittin' you knew Ginny.'

'I know, Ned, and I'm sorry I had to bring her into it. Really sorry. But it was the only way to prove my theory that Miranda was Susanna's mother.'

'You and Betsy have a lot to answer for with your meddlin'. You're both lucky you're not up on a charge of pervertin' the course of justice.'

'Yes, we are – but come on, Ned! You told me yourself you've always known there was something fishy with how I found that snuff box. You never challenged me and both of us knew that without it, we'd never convict Delamere. And the more I've learned about the man since we arrived here, the more I'm convinced Betsy and I did the right thing.'

Woods snorted and the corners of his mouth twitched. 'Maybe,' he said. 'That were a good idea of hers to use it to frame Delamere. Mind you, I shall still have strong words with Mrs Woods when I get home about her habit of keepin' secrets from her husband. From now on, she leaves the police work to me.'

Lavender hid his smile. He knew how this would turn out.

Betsy would regard Ned quizzically from beneath her greying eyebrows as if she were dealing with one of their stroppy sons. Then she'd plonk a huge steak pie with a golden crust down on the table in front of him and Woods' indignation would melt away like pastry in his mouth.

'Besides which,' Lavender added mischievously, 'you have to forgive me. I'm your brother.'

'My what?'

'Your brother. Two days ago, you said you thought of me as your brother.'

Woods humphed loudly. 'Well, that's no compliment, is it? I know you don't have one of your own, but you've met our Alby – and seen what a great hulkin' gormless lump he is. Why, if he didn't run a tavern and enjoy fishin' – I don't suppose I'd like him at all! Brothers? Humph.'

Lavender smiled again and didn't respond. The sun's rays turned the glittering surface of the river into a ballet of dancing diamonds.

'So, what'll happen now back at Willow Marsh?' Woods asked eventually.

373

'I think everything will carry on as before. Susanna will remain mistress of the manor and Miranda and Hal will buy Quinn's silence with a lot of money and the promise of inclusion within the family. I think the young man may be swayed by this – he seems lonely.'

'I think he thought to have both the gal and the house,' Woods said. 'It'll take a lot of golden boys to compensate him for that.'

'Yes, it will. But obviously he can't marry his half-sister.'

'If you hadn't intervened and he'd continued to woo her, do you think Miranda would have told them the truth?'

'No. I think she would have simply found some way to separate them.'

'It seems a shame. After his heroics yesterday, that young American deserved to win the gal. Well, one thing's for sure, Hal can't wed her – everyone thinks they're still brother and sister.'

'True,' Lavender said. 'And despite his sudden proposal – which I sincerely hope was in jest – I don't think Susanna will have him. Loving someone like a brother isn't the same as loving someone like a husband.'

'Thank goodness for that,' Woods said with a sideways glance at Lavender. 'Otherwise, folks would be talkin' about us.'

Lavender smiled. 'Besides which, she's a remarkable young woman – surprisingly competent and strong for one so young and tiny. I saw this last night, the way she rallied the servants to help her take care of the injured. If she goes out into society, no doubt she'll soon attract other suitors.'

'Hal won't like that.'

'Oh, I doubt he'll be too upset. I'm sure he will also come out of this morning's revelations a much richer young man and quickly return to his life in London. Miranda needs to buy his silence too, remember.'

Woods raised an incredulous eyebrow. 'It never ceases to amaze me, the confusin' way rich folks live their lives.' He sighed. 'But it ain't our business any more. It's back to London and Bow Street for us.' Grinning at the thought, he urged his horse forward into a trot.

Lavender caught up with him. 'Wait a minute, Ned, there's something I need to tell you.'

Woods hauled on the reins and turned in the saddle. 'What's amiss?'

'Nothing. But you need to know, when I return to London – I plan to take a trip away with Magdalena and the children.'

Disappointment flashed across Woods' face. 'You feel you need a rest?'

'No, not quite. I think it's time I honoured my promise to her and Sebastián to take them to their estates in Spain. I've thought about it a lot over the last few days, while I've been helping to secure the future of the Willow Marsh Estate. It's not right that I was so busy restoring law and order for the Delameres and their estate while Magdalena's family estates rot through neglect after the retreat of the French. The irony has bothered me.'

'I'm sure there's a quack who'll have a powder to cure that,' Woods said. 'But isn't it dangerous? The war isn't over yet – and Spain is full of foreigners who jabber in a strange tongue like Doña Magdalena and her maid.'

'It'll be quite safe – and don't forget, I speak Spanish too.'

'How long will you be gone?'

'It may take a few months to put their affairs straight.'

Woods gasped. 'A few months! But what'll happen if you get into trouble? Look what happened yesterday! You'd be dead if I hadn't come to your rescue – *again*.'

Lavender smiled. 'I know that, Ned – and I'm grateful, eternally grateful. You're always there and have my back covered. I'm also touched you worry about me so much – it's just like a brother would.'

'Oh, we're back to that brother thing again, are we? One loose comment and a man is harangued for the rest of his life.'

Lavender grinned. 'It's something I have to do, Ned – you know it is. And I think Spain might have too many foreigners for your liking.'

'Well, I don't know,' Woods grumbled. 'Seems like a poor plan to me. You'll get involved in somethin' mysterious and find yourself in trouble again.'

The sun came out from behind a cloud and illuminated the gentle beauty of the landscape around them, including an abandoned reed-warbler nest. Spun from spider silk, it dangled precariously halfway up the stalk of reed.

'Look! Even the sun's shining on us now. There's nothing to worry about, Ned. I'll be back before you know it. The French have retreated to their own country. It's only a matter of time before Wellington forces Napoleon to surrender.'

He turned and gave Woods a beaming smile, as he urged his horse forward.

'What could possibly go wrong?'

Author's Note
and
Acknowledgements

Many years ago, I developed an urge to write a traditional closed-house mystery, where a murder takes place when the characters are confined to one bleak and unnerving location, thus limiting the pool of suspects and heightening the tension. Originally, I imagined an ancient tavern full of coach passengers cut off either by a ferocious snowstorm or a flood. My mother, who'd found a Kentish smuggler called Barnabus Goldsmith in her family history, also begged me to write a book about smuggling. But my ideas are as fluid as mercury and take on the ever-changing shape of inkblots before they finally settle into a substantial form.

As you can see from this novel, my closed-house mystery eventually ended up in an ancient, fictional estate in the watery fenland of Cambridgeshire.

This eerie location with its Gothic overtones had tugged at my imagination ever since I'd first read Susan Hill's terrifying novel, *The Woman in Black*. Although Hill doesn't tell us the exact location of her fictional town Crythin Gifford and the bleak Eel Marsh House, I'd often felt they were set in a landscape like the Cambridgeshire fens.

Willow Marsh Manor is entirely my own invention.

I decided I needed an old house with a violent history and plenty of secrets of its own. I can still remember the thrill I used to get as a child when the characters in books stumbled across secret passageways and tunnels. I decided to make them an important feature of this book.

I went to Ely in the early autumn of 2017 on a research trip and soon fell in love with the quaint streets of this tiny cathedral city. I took a chilly cruise on the Great Ouse to check out the lie of the land and I haunted the riverfront, trying to imagine the warehouses and breweries that would have dominated the wharves two hundred years ago. I also visited the city's museums and the wonderful nature reserve at Wicken Fen. Here, I sailed down a Roman lode with a boat full of tourists, learning about the flora and fauna of the marshes and listening to our guide bring the people and the traditions of this watery world to life.

Everyone I met in Ely was friendly and helpful. I amassed a whole folder of texts, maps, books, ideas and information about the unusual area and its history.

I also spent several valuable hours with Ely historian Nora Gardner, on a private walking tour of the city. Nora has since kept in touch and fed me extra information about the local customs and excise men and the riverside taverns of Ely. I owe her thanks for this.

After my return from Ely, I became distracted with the story of *The Park Lane Murder*. I wasn't able to return to writing my 'Ely book' until October 2018. At this point I named it *The Willow Marsh Murder*.

But I don't think this novel suffered through the delay. In fact, I rather fancy the characters in my head, and the complicated mystery I'd devised, mellowed like a good barrel of smuggled brandy. Not that there's any brandy-smuggling in this book. When someone in Ely mentioned the illicit fur trade that swamped the eastern ports of nineteenth-century England, I was inspired to use fur instead of brandy and tobacco. Government import duty was high on all luxury goods and the nineteenth-century coastal inhabitants of Britain would have smuggled anything, even their own grandmothers, if they'd had any value.

Many years ago, while researching the real-life Stephen Lavender's many appearances in Regency newspapers, I came across the disturbing story of some poor woman whose evil lover murdered her then dropped her head-first down a well. Unfortunately, I can't remember the names, date or town of this grisly event, but I do know she was killed by her common-law husband during a heated argument. Her killer quickly vanished from the scene of the crime, but the real-life Stephen Lavender soon tracked him down and provided sufficient evidence to convict him. This unpleasant tale lingered in my mind for years and I resolved to use it in my fiction.

The idea to include Lavender's deliberate perversion of justice grew from a comment made by my former editor, Sophie Missing. Sophie worked on the first four Lavender mysteries and apart from being a brilliant editor, she was also a keen fan of the series. In *The Sans Pareil Mystery*, I wrote: '*Betsy knew more about him [Lavender] than he cared to admit...*' At the time, I was simply referring to the fact that Vivienne, Lavender's dead fiancée, had been carrying their child when she died just before their marriage. But Sophie was convinced Betsy knew another dark secret about our enigmatic detective. When the next two books passed through her hands for editing, she encouraged me to develop this idea.

I thought about it for years. How could Betsy possibly know something about Lavender that Woods didn't? And how would Woods react if he found out his wife and best friend had colluded to keep secrets from him? It was a situation potentially fraught with conflict. The result, as you've just seen, was the story of the incriminating snuff box.

As the readers of my previous novels already know, Stephen Lavender and Magistrate Read from Bow Street are loosely based on real characters. The rest of the characters are fictional.

I'd just like to thank my wonderful editor Jenni Davis, my loyal proofreader and friend Sandra Mangan and my special gang of Alpha-readers and fellow authors, J.G. Harlond, Kristin Gleeson and B.A. Morton, for their brilliant and helpful insights into structural, historical and editorial issues with this novel.

Finally, to you, the reader, thank you for reading my book and following this series. If you enjoyed it, please leave a review on Amazon. And please visit my website to sign up to my occasional newsletter for advance notice about forthcoming releases, book news and competitions.

Karen Charlton
16 September 2019
Marske, North Yorkshire
www.karencharlton.com

ABOUT THE AUTHOR

Karen Charlton is the best-selling author of The Detective Lavender Mystery series, which is set in Regency London and features Bow Street's Principal Officer, Stephen Lavender, and his humorous sidekick, Constable Ned Woods.

A former English teacher, with two grown-up children and a small grandson, Karen lives in a remote North Yorkshire fishing village and writes full-time. She's a stalwart of the village pub quiz team.

Karen always enjoys a good mystery and loves historical fiction and TV. She's an avid reader herself and loves to hear from her own readers. You can easily contact her via her website. For the latest news about her fiction, her public appearances and some special offers, sign up for her occasional newsletter on the home page:

www.karencharlton.com

Made in the USA
San Bernardino, CA
23 June 2020